Portland, OR, April 2004—In a strange but true twist on family love and loss, regarding those twins separated at birth who were featured last month, Adam Bartlett and Lissa Carwright, an even more shocking revelation has recently come to light. It seems a construction foreman bearing an uncanny resemblance to Adam came forward claiming to be related to the twins. Blood tests revealed that not only was Sam Lowery a sibling…he was their triplet! Sources tell the *Press* that the arrival of Sam proved once and for all for Adam and Lissa that miracles really do happen! As Lissa's husband, Sullivan Grayson, was quoted as saying, "The hugging, the laughing, the excitement on their faces…it was incredible." It was after seeing the recent television specials featuring the twins that Sam knew, without question, that he was related to them. Initially hesitant after a lifetime of heartache, Sam took some convincing by his daughter's pretty nanny to take the leap. But now that he has, he feels as if he's finally come home. This reporter can only wonder what other surprises are in store for this reacquainted family.…

Dear Reader,

It's spring, love is in the air…and what better way to celebrate than by taking a break with Silhouette Special Edition? We begin the month with *Treasured,* the conclusion to Sherryl Woods's MILLION DOLLAR DESTINIES series. Though his two brothers have been successfully paired off, Ben Carlton is convinced he's "destined" to go it alone. But the brooding, talented young man is about to meet his match in a beautiful gallery owner—courtesy of fate…plus a little help from his matchmaking aunt.

And Pamela Toth concludes the MERLYN COUNTY MIDWIVES series with *In the Enemy's Arms,* in which a detective trying to get to the bottom of a hospital black-market drug investigation finds himself in close contact with his old high school flame, now a beautiful M.D.—she's his prime suspect! And exciting new author Lynda Sandoval (look for her Special Edition novel *One Perfect Man,* coming in June) makes her debut and wraps up the LOGAN'S LEGACY Special Edition prequels, all in one book—*And Then There Were Three.* Next, Christine Flynn begins her new miniseries, THE KENDRICKS OF CAMELOT, with *The Housekeeper's Daughter,* in which a son of Camelot—Virginia, that is—finds himself inexplicably drawn to the one woman he can never have. Marie Ferrarella moves her popular CAVANAUGH JUSTICE series into Special Edition with *The Strong Silent Type,* in which a female detective finds her handsome male partner somewhat less than chatty. But her determination to get him to talk quickly morphs into a determination to…get him. And in Ellen Tanner Marsh's *For His Son's Sake,* a single father trying to connect with the son whose existence he just recently discovered finds in the free-spirited Kenzie Daniels a woman they could *both* love.

So enjoy! And come back next month for six heartwarming books from Silhouette Special Edition.

Happy reading!

Gail Chasan
Senior Editor

Please address questions and book requests to:
Silhouette Reader Service
U.S.: 3010 Walden Ave., P.O. Box 1325, Buffalo, NY 14269
Canadian: P.O. Box 609, Fort Erie, Ont. L2A 5X3

And Then
There Were Three

LYNDA SANDOVAL

Silhouette®

SPECIAL EDITION®

Published by Silhouette Books

America's Publisher of Contemporary Romance

Special thanks and acknowledgment are given
to Lynda Sandoval for her contribution
to the LOGAN'S LEGACY series.

For Gail Chasan.
Thank you for believing in me.

 SILHOUETTE BOOKS

ISBN 0-373-24611-0

AND THEN THERE WERE THREE

LYNDA SANDOVAL

is a former police officer who exchanged the excitement of that career for blissfully isolated days creating stories she hopes readers will love. Though she's also worked as a youth mental health and runaway crisis counselor, a television extra, a trade-show art salesperson, a European tour guide and a bookkeeper for an exotic bird and reptile company—among other weird jobs—Lynda's favorite career, by far, is writing books. In addition to romance, Lynda writes women's fiction and young-adult novels, and in her spare time, she loves to travel, quilt, bid on eBay, hike, read and spend time with her dog. Lynda also works part-time as an emergency fire/medical dispatcher for the fire department. Readers are invited to visit Lynda on the Web at www.LyndaLynda.com, or to send mail with an SASE for a reply to P.O. Box 1018, Conifer, CO 80433-1018.

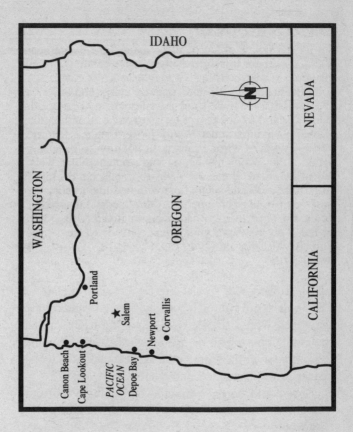

Chapter One

Sam Lowery sat, sprawl-legged and guilt-ridden, in the nondescript waiting room of Portland General. He glowered with disinterest at the talking heads on the pole-mounted television in the corner, all the while obsessing over the fact that he was officially the worst father in the history of parenthood.

How could he have thought for a single moment that the mobile home offices of a construction work-site would be a safe place for his two-year-old daughter to hang out while he worked? His rationalization seemed weak at this point: he hadn't wanted to put Jessica in daycare when she was so young and still so traumatized. But he had to wonder if his aversion to daycare said more about him than it did about her.

He shoved his fingers through his hair. The knowledge that he'd placed Jessica in the very type of danger he sought to avoid made his gut clench with pain. He never should've held on so tightly, never should've expected his secretary to watch his daughter. He never should've worked overtime that fateful night six months ago, but hey, that was a whole 'nuther guilt trip, now wasn't it? He had a plethora of them from which to choose.

The musical tones of his cell phone yanked him back to the present. Had to be the job; it wasn't like he had a pack of buddies who rang him up on a regular basis. He pulled the small phone off his belt clip and checked caller ID on the LED screen before answering. The number popped up: Mia, his secretary. Flipping open the face, he lifted it to his ear. "Hey, Mia."

"Oh, Sam." Mia, a married mother of four herself, had been more than amenable to watching Jessica in the offices while Sam was out on the site, but they both should've realized Mia had her own work to do. A curious two-year-old was more than a full-time job. "How is the poor little darling? Did she need stitches?"

Sam ran a hand slowly down his face, feeling sick and trying not to recall the disturbing picture of the deep cut in his baby girl's pudgy little hand. His heart squeezed. "Yeah, they're stitching her up right now."

"I'm so sorry."

"Don't be. It wasn't your fault."

"Well, listen. I just wanted to check in, but I'll let

you go comfort her while she goes through this ordeal.''

"No need," Sam said, wryly, lifting one ankle to rest it over the opposite knee. "To tell you the truth, Doc kicked me out of the suture room."

"What?" Mia's disbelief came across loud and clear. "How can he kick that darling girl's parent out of the room."

He shook his head. "Seems I was 'hovering,' and making it worse for Jessica. Agitating her, Doc said."

Mia laughed, sadly. "Well, hon, no offense intended, but I can certainly see that."

Sam straightened. "What's that supposed to mean?"

"You're not the typical father, is all."

Sam grew immediately defensive, all the while knowing he didn't need to be. Not with Mia. But, still. "I repeat, what's that supposed to mean?"

"Oh, don't get your back up. I meant it as a compliment. You do have a tendency to…well, to hover. Nothing wrong with that. Mothers do it all the time, believe me, and you care for that little girl like a mother would is all I'm saying." Mia's breath hitched, and for a moment, that old familiar tension hung between them. "I'm sorry. I shouldn't have said it that way."

Sam closed his eyes, shaking his head slowly. It had been six months since the fire, and people still walked on eggshells around him as though he could snap at any moment. He couldn't blame them, though. It wasn't like he shared his emotions freely, or let anyone know where he was coming from. To be honest, he preferred it that way. He didn't want anyone too close to him or his world. "Don't apologize. It's a fact, Mia. I have to be both father and mother to her now."

"Well…you don't *have* to." Mia's tone took on a subtle change. "I happen to know there are a lot of women out there who would jump at the chance to be Jessica's new mommy." Her voice took on a softer tone. "Not to mention your new love."

Sam stiffened. He chose to ignore the "new love" half of Mia's preposterous proposition. When he spoke, his words came out ultra-controlled, through a clenched jaw. "Mia, I've told you before, Jessica had a mother—"

"God rest her soul."

And fry his. "You can't just replace a parent." He knew that all too well, but held back a scoff of derision.

"Well, I know. But, Jessica was so young when her mama—" Mia sighed. "She could come to love another mother figure. I know you don't believe that, but it's true nonetheless." A beat passed, and in typical Mia form, she decided to push the other issue. "Plus, if you had someone for yourself—"

"Don't even go there." Love? Ha. He hadn't even managed to pull that farce off the first time, when he'd really wanted it to work out.

Mia's exasperated sigh carried over the line. Her desire to see Sam remarried—happily this time—was an ongoing point of contention, but it was an argument the woman would lose. In the stubbornness department, no one rivaled Sam Lowery. He had stuck his neck out once in the love arena and been sadly disappointed. Oh, he respected Jenny as the mother of his child and always would, but it had quickly become clear theirs wasn't the love match he'd dreamed about. Still, he'd said "I do," to the "for better or worse" part that day in the Justice of the Peace's offices, and he'd meant it, even if the worse outweighed the better—which it had, by a long shot. Real men didn't leave their families, no matter how dissatisfying the arrangement.

He certainly hadn't wanted Jenny dead and buried.

A shudder moved through him at the flashback image.

Jenny may not have been the perfect wife, but she'd given him one amazing gift for which he'd always be grateful: their daughter. With Jessica, he knew true connection, true abiding love, for the first time ever. Maybe parental love was the only type he was meant to have in this life. Who knew? If so, fine with him. In any case, he didn't plan to test the theory by traveling the rocky road of romance again. Ever.

"As I've told you a million times, no new women for me. End of topic," he said, in a tone that would brook no argument. He cleared his throat and switched direction. "I'll tell you what I am going to do, though."

"What's that?" Mia sounded resigned.

"I'm going to suck it up and hire a nanny." Sam slid down in the uncomfortable waiting room chair, stretching his legs out in front of him, feet balanced on their heels. "I can't bring Jess to the job site any longer. She's too much of a handful."

"It's probably a good idea, Sam," Mia said, with sadness threading through her tone. "Much as I loved having her here with me…"

"I know. I appreciate everything you've done, but you have your own work to do, and now that she's two—"

"Goodness knows what the Terrible Threes will bring."

"Exactly. It's a recipe for more disaster." He fished the dog-eared business card out of his pocket and studied the face of it. "Bruce Nolan gave me the name of an agency. Supposed to be a good one—"

"Nannysource?"

"That's the one."

"They are good. You can't go wrong there."

Her vote of confidence helped him relax slightly about the whole prospect of some stranger horning in on the raising of his daughter, but only *slightly.* "I know we're working overtime tomorrow morning, but the agency has Saturday morning hours. I guess I'll take the day off tomorrow and set up some interviews," he said, in a glum tone. "Find some sweet little grandmother who'll treat Jessie like her own grandchild."

Another parental guilt pang went through him when he realized Jessie didn't, and never would, have grandparents of her own. His late wife had grown up with a much older single mother who died just after

Jenny'd graduated from high school, and Sam, himself, had grown up—damn quickly—in the foster care system. When he really analyzed it, their mutual lack of familial connections had been most of what brought Jenny and him together in the first place, but time had proven that being orphaned wasn't enough of a glue to bond them forever.

Still, a nice surrogate grandma for Jessica…yes. That would be good. He actually started to look forward to calling Nannysource. "Yes, a nice, old Mary Poppins sort would do."

"I'm sure you'll find the perfect match. Don't you worry about a thing here. Just take care of that sweet baby. We won't even miss you."

A rueful half smile hiked up one side of Sam's mouth. "Gee, thanks. Just what the boss wants to hear."

"Oh, Sam," Mia scolded.

He checked the clock mounted on the wall of the waiting room. How long did it take to stitch up a tiny little hand anyway? He'd arrived at the hospital with Jessie just after 5:00 p.m., and it was a few minutes past seven. "I just hope—" He stopped, pressing his lips into a thin line.

"Hope what?"

He wrestled with the thought, then decided to share it. "That Jessie will tolerate someone new in her life."

"Jessie's more resilient than you give her credit for, hon. She's a people person in baby form."

Sam pursed his lips, not so sure he agreed. Since

the fire, his formerly giggly, sparkly baby had turned reticent and fearful of strangers and new situations. It ate him alive inside, witnessing the manifestation of her fears, especially since he was responsible for her trauma—a fact no one but he knew.

The apartment fire that night had broken out while he'd been working overtime on a job. *Voluntary.* He'd told Jenny it was mandatory OT, but it hadn't been, and he'd had to live with what he'd thought was a harmless white lie on his conscience for six months now. No one but he knew he'd worked so much overtime back then in order to avoid a less than perfect home life, but there it was. The ugly, unvarnished truth. Had he been home that night, like any decent husband and father, he might've been able to help Jenny escape the inferno.

Instead, she'd died protecting Jessica.

His biggest source of guilt, however, came from the fact that he'd actually felt a flash of gratitude that night when he'd learned it was his Jessica who'd survived rather than his young wife. Not that he'd wanted Jenny dead. Not that at all. But if he'd had to choose a survivor…

Sam stifled a groan. What kind of monster was he, anyway?

Sure, he and Jenny had moved from love to a kind of mutual and dissatisfying tolerance before her death, but that damn well didn't matter. He wouldn't wish a death like Jenny's on his worst enemy, much less the mother of his baby girl—a woman who'd sacrificed her own life in order to save her daughter's. He would respect her forever for that decision, and he'd feel guilty forever, too.

Guilt. So much guilt. Ah, well, at least he had one constant in his life.

"Oh, honey, I've got to go," Mia said, interrupting his brooding silence. She'd become so accustomed to his drawn-out silences during their conversations, they didn't even faze her. Sam Lowery was a loner, plain and simple, and Mia knew and accepted it. But, the excitement that had crept into Mia's voice made him curious.

"Why? What's going on?"

"They're about to air the segment about those reunited twins on my news show."

He frowned. "What twins?"

She clucked her tongue. "You're so out of the loop. I don't have time to explain. Call me in the morning to give me a Jessie update. Or anytime during the night if you need an ear to bend. You know I'm here."

"I do. And listen, this wasn't your fault."

"Thank you for saying that, but I still feel guilty."

"Yeah, well, join the club."

They rang off, and Sam hooked his phone back on his belt before glancing up at the television. It had to be tuned in to the same channel Mia had been watching, he realized, because the blonde announcer was in the midst of an intro about reunited adult twins. Might as well watch, he supposed, since he'd been banished from his daughter's bedside and Mia thought he was hopelessly "out of it" when it came to current events.

Sam glanced around and spied a remote on one of the unoccupied chairs. He pushed a few well-worn buttons on the control and increased the volume.

The story centered around a man and woman—coincidentally his age—who hadn't even known they were twins. After their young mother died in a car accident, they'd been relinquished to an adoption agency connected to Portland General and adopted separately. A subsequent fire destroyed their birth records, hence they never knew the other existed. But, lo and behold, their biological father saw fit to search for them recently, when his young son needed a bone marrow transplant.

Sam sat back, twisting his mouth to the side and bouncing the remote against his palm. Something about *that* little detail irked the hell out of him. What was it about the first children the man had created that made them unworthy of keeping? Clearly he hadn't had a problem holding on to the second wave of children he'd fathered, or seeking the first kids when he needed something from them. A muscle in Sam's jaw ticked, and he pushed away his distaste. This wasn't about him. Still, he had to admit, it was a sore point. He couldn't imagine ever living without Jessica, giving her up to strangers to raise.

He thought about turning the idiot box off, but the story intrigued him enough to be a distraction, so he refocused on it. Leaning forward, he rested his elbows on his spread knees, the cracked, vinyl chair squeaking beneath him. The announcer finished her lead and brought out the long lost siblings, Lissa Cartwright and Adam Bartlett. The camera panned to a wide shot, as they sat down across from the reporter, and then it closed in on the twins.

Sam's entire body tensed. The hair on his neck raised, and for a moment, he failed to move, to draw a breath, to blink. When his heart actually started beating again, it was a steady, hard drum against his rib cage. A death knell. He squeezed his eyes shut, shook his head, then peered cautiously at the television screen again.

No way. Couldn't be.

Inconceivable as it was, Sam himself could be Adam Bartlett's scruffier, blue-collar double. They were both about six-foot-one, with dark brown hair and green eyes. They were the exact same age. They had both been abandoned by their birth parents and adopted out of the same agency, the Children's Connection, around the same time. Could it possibly be…?

He sat back and crossed his arms over his chest, as if to protect himself from what he was seeing, and shrugged off the eerie sense of realization creeping up his spine. Ridiculous. A lot of men would fit his and Adam Bartlett's description.

But—he squinted at the screen—it was more than a simple height/weight/hair color/eye color connection. The way Bartlett talked, his mannerisms, the shape of his hands. Even the woman, Lissa Cartwright, resembled Sam in a lot of intangible ways.

And then there was the uncanny adoption timeline. Could this story have more layers than the news media realized? Could these reunited twins actually be two in a set of...triplets? Could Sam himself—

No. No. No. Ridiculous again.

The stress of Jessica's accident was getting to him, that was all. He scrubbed his palms over his face, trying to make it all go away. His whole train of thought made no sense.

Yes, it does.

"Yes, it does," he said, repeating the words that had whispered through his mind. And it did. It made a kind of sense Sam couldn't explain. Not even a little bit. He had always felt like something was missing, some deep and important connection he had never been able to fully understand. It was more than just having grown up orphaned, more than missing out on his parents while he fought his way through a foster care system that left a lot to be desired. He'd always felt some...stronger connection, more elusive and confusing. And what was it the scientists said about twins? Or triplets? If this wild theory had any merit, he'd been closer to these two strangers than he'd ever been to anyone since. He'd shared a womb with them, for God's sake, and then they'd been unceremoniously ripped apart. Could that account for his lifelong, inexplicable sense of loss? His lack of belonging? His illogical belief that someone, somewhere shared just a little bit of his soul?

He watched a little longer, enough to learn that Adam Bartlett was some bigwig CEO of a company called Novel Programs, Unlimited, and Lissa had lived an idyllic childhood on a vineyard a couple hours outside Portland.

Gosh, how nice for them. An unpleasant emotion welled up inside his gut. If he had to label the sour feeling, he'd reluctantly call it jealousy. Because, if these two truly were his siblings, he'd obviously drawn the short stick at the placement agency. While they were experiencing "Leave it to Beaver" childhoods, Sam had been shuffled from one foster home to the next, some better than others, some so intolerable he'd made it a life goal to block them from his memory. But, all of them had one thing in common: they'd been devoid of true connections.

A sneer lifted his lip. Fate was truly cruel.

Bitterness bubbled inside him, and he let it. He must've been the least attractive baby. But, of course, he wouldn't know. No one in his life had cared enough to record his babyhood on film. Surely Lissa Cartwright and Adam Bartlett had albums full of baby pictures of themselves.

Having seen more than enough and not liking the direction his thoughts were taking, he switched off the television and tossed the remote aside, settling in for some serious brooding. Even if Adam Bartlett and Lissa Cartwright were his siblings—and deep down in his darkest place, he knew they were—he made the decision right then and there, ironically in the hospital in which they'd been born, that no one would ever know it. Not Adam, nor Lissa, and least of all the supposed "father" who'd thrown him to the wolves twenty-seven years earlier. Sam hadn't had family in all those years. As far as he was concerned, he could live without them forever. He had Jessica, and she was all the family he would ever need.

He could only hope that Mia hadn't noticed his resemblance to Adam Bartlett, too. If that happened, he'd be in a world of hurt.

Chapter Two

The waning evening sun stretched long, low, golden fingers of light across the road as Sam drove Jessie home. She was groggy from her pain medicine, and every time Sam caught a glimpse of that tiny, bandaged hand, he wanted to jump off a cliff. He'd tilted his rearview mirror to allow him a view of his baby girl in her car seat as he drove.

"You okay, honeypot?"

She didn't answer, but her eyes—so much like Jenny's—met his in the mirror. Was it his imagination, or did they look accusatory?

Sam swallowed thickly, his heart thudding. "How do you feel about having a new Grandma, Jessica? Someone to bake cookies with you and play and read you stories."

Jessica just blinked. She didn't even have a frame of reference for the word "Grandma," so how would she know? Plus, she was only two.

"Daddy's going to find you a nice Grandma to come live with us. Okay? You'll love her. I promise."

No response, but he hadn't really expected one.

"I love you, Jessica," he said, his words husky.

"Yuv you," Jessica murmured, before settling her little head against the side of the carseat and closing her eyes. She looked so innocent, so out of it, the sting of unshed tears burned Sam's eyes. He refocused on the road, trying not to think about the fact that tomorrow would bring the second biggest change in Jessica's life, and all of it, thanks to him. He felt like he was parenting blindly, bound in steel cords and fighting his way out of a dark corridor he'd never been in before. If only he'd had a father to teach him how to be a father, perhaps he wouldn't be so lost.

His thoughts jumped back to Lissa and Adam, and their supposed father, Jared Cambry. Biology be damned, the man was no father, and two complete strangers would never be his family. Anger blossomed inside him. It was a good thing Adam Bartlett had been a bone marrow match for the little boy, because Sam would've closed the door in his face had Jared so much as dared to seek him out after all he'd gone through as an unwanted child. Just as quickly as the anger had come, a flash of remorse for his uncharitable thoughts followed. He glanced at Jessica in the rearview mirror. It wasn't true, and he knew it.

As a father, he'd do anything to save Jessica's life if it came to that. He couldn't blame Cambry for his desperation, but he also didn't have to forgive him for the abandonment. Lucky for all of them, the happy little reunited family had no idea Sam Lowery even existed, and he meant to keep it that way.

But, what *would* it be like to have siblings?

They seemed to care for each other. Would they have room in their hearts to care about another brother?

His hands gripped the wheel tighter, and he pushed the preposterous train of thought away. The stupid twin show on TV had him thinking crazy. The "if onlys" would kill him if he let them, and he refused to let them. Sam Lowery was an orphan. Period. He'd made his peace with that fact long ago.

And, as for his parenting skills, he might be a trial-and-error dad, but he'd make damn sure Jessica never felt slighted. He'd do everything in his power to be the best father he knew how to be…which clearly, given today's debacle, wasn't saying much.

Erin O'Grady loved the time she spent at her brothers' homes, especially Saturday mornings, when all the families got together for brunch. At twenty-three, she was the only unmarried O'Grady, and had no children of her own yet. *Yet* being the operative word, because she planned to produce a passel of them as soon as she fell in love with the right guy and got married. But, for now, doting on her nieces and neph-

ews was the second best option, and with five married, Irish Catholic brothers, she had a slew of them.

That Saturday, at her brother Mick's, Erin sprawled
happily on the living room floor, trying to catch her
breath while a pack of her nieces and nephews
climbed all over her. She was perpetually bruised and
had taken more than one sharp little elbow in her
tender parts over the years, but it was worth it. She
loved being the favorite aunt. She even loved being
the human jungle gym.

The muffled ring of her cell phone from inside her
purse brought her head up. She glanced toward it, but
her nephew, Jason, had her in a full nelson.

"Jase, buddy, I need to get that."

"No way!" He giggled. "Say Uncle!"

"Jase, really—"

"Want me to answer it, sis?" asked Mick, who was
the closest to her in age, at twenty-five.

"Please do. It might be the agency calling."

"The agency." Her second-to-the-oldest brother,
Patrick, rolled his eyes. "I'm still not sure about
that."

Erin scowled. "I'm not a child anymore, Pat, and
I want to be a nanny. It's not an issue of whether or
not you're 'sure' about it, okay?"

Patrick pointed a finger toward her. "You're not a
child, but you'll always be our little sister. You have
no idea what could happen."

Brothers Matthew and Miles nodded, and she rolled
her eyes in response. God save her from her overprotective brothers. Thank goodness Eamon, the eldest,

was out of town on a business trip. He was the worst of the bunch. She loved them, adored having a big, raucous family, but the short leash they kept her on could get tedious at times. The bane of being the only girl, she supposed, and the baby of the family, to boot.

When Mick retrieved the cell phone, her heart started to pound in anticipation. She'd only registered with Nannysource three days earlier, but the manager had been extremely enthusiastic about her credentials and said she hoped to place her soon. Erin said a silent prayer of thanks that she'd chosen her particular specialty. Helping kids who'd suffered some sort of trauma seemed to have put her on the A-list of available nannies at the agency.

"Hello?" Erin watched Mick listen, then nod. "No, you called the right number. This is her brother, Mick O'Grady. Hang on." Mick held the phone away from his ear and whistled. "Okay, kids. Let Aunt Erin up. This is business."

The kids grumbled, but they peeled themselves off her, one-by-one. Erin winked at them, then straightened her clothing and stood, reaching for the cell phone.

"This is Erin."

"Erin, I'm so glad I got you," said Karla, the placement coordinator for Nannysource.

Erin broke into a wide grin. "Hi, Karla. I was hoping it was you. Good news?"

"Well, keep your fingers crossed. I have an interview and I think you're perfect for the position."

"That's fabulous!" Erin listened intently while the

manager described the situation: working with a two-year-old girl who'd survived an apartment fire that had claimed her mother, a mere six months earlier. The father had been hesitant about bringing in outside help because the child seemed to suffer some PTSD, or post-traumatic stress disorder, from the incident. The whole scenario sounded perfect to Erin. Plus, it was a live-in assignment, which would work out great since she was having no luck finding an apartment she could afford, and she was tired of living under her parents' roof, God love them both. This was exactly the type of gig she'd hoped to land when she registered with Nannysource.

Erin's excitement grew to the bursting point. She spun around in a circle but fought to keep her voice businesslike. "It sounds more than ideal."

"Well…there's only one problem."

Erin stilled, tucking one wayward lock of hair behind her ear. She sank into the nearest available chair and braced herself. "Uh-oh. Okay, lay it on me."

"He requested…a grandmotherly type," Karla said, her voice turning a bit regretful.

"Oh no! I'm twenty-three!"

"I know. But in light of the circumstances, Erin, I couldn't think of anyone more equipped to handle the job than you. I'm sure you can win him over."

"Gosh, I hope so." Erin bit her lip and said a silent prayer, but her excitement cooled slightly. "Anyway, it sounds wonderful. I at least want to give it a shot." Erin fished in her handbag for a pen and paper to jot down all the information. She hated to think of a sad widower with an emotionally fragile child going it alone. "When would he like to meet? I'm more than ready."

"As soon as possible. This afternoon, if you can swing it."

"Of course. I take it he's not remarried?"

"Nope, single father."

"That makes sense considering he only lost his wife six months ago." Erin studiously ignored her eavesdropping brothers, but she could feel their protective radar kick into high gear. Testosterone snapped, crackled, and popped all around her.

When Erin had collected all the information she needed for the interview and hung up, the four available O'Grady brothers were staring at her intently, suspicion clear on their faces. "What was that all about?" Patrick asked. Well, growled.

"What?" She tucked away her notes, avoiding their glances.

"You're considering working for a single man? As a live-in nanny?" Mick asked, incredulously. He exchanged narrowed glances with Patrick and Matt.

Erin wouldn't be intimidated out of this interview. She raised her chin. "I'm going to be a nanny for a traumatized two-year-old named Jessica—" She crossed her fingers. "—if all goes well at the interview. That's the point."

"I'm not sure I like it," Mick said slowly, clearly chewing on the idea. "Working for a couple is one thing, but a single man? What if it's all a ploy to get a young, naive woman into his home?"

Erin groaned, then pantomimed feeling for walls all around and above her. "Oh, I'm sorry. I'd forgotten I lived in a glass box, Mick. And, newsflash, I'm not naive."

"Don't be flippant."

"Well?" She spread her arms wide. "It's a job, and a good one at that. It's absolutely ideal for me, and I'm a big girl, perfectly capable of making wise decisions."

"You're twenty-three!" Miles leaned forward to make his point. "And you're our baby sister."

"Maybe we should check him out first," Matthew said to the other men, ignoring Erin completely. "Make sure he's not using this nanny thing as a cover to lure young, naive—"

"I am not naive!" Erin shot to her feet and planted fists on her hips. She glared at each of her brothers in turn, then couldn't help but give them a grudging smile. She loved the big, annoying oafs. Can't live with 'em, can't kill 'em. "Gosh, you guys are so friggin' irritating."

"You don't need to swear," said Mick, reproachfully.

Erin ignored him. "I don't need you dogging my every footstep. Do you really have that little faith in my judgement?"

"It's not a matter of faith, Erin," Mick said. "It's a matter of family protection."

"Great, we're in the mob now."

"There she goes, being flippant again."

Erin knew they meant well, but she'd had enough.

She hiked her purse on her shoulder and tossed her auburn hair. "Look, I love you guys, but I don't need bodyguards. Please, just let me do this and trust my instincts. You make me feel like I'm in prison." Wary silence ensued. Erin sighed with exasperation. When it came to her brothers, smothering was an understatement. "I'll check in by phone the minute I get to the man's house and the moment I leave. Will that satisfy you?"

"Nope." Mick lifted his chin toward Matthew, the middle of the five boys and the burliest. "Follow her. Park down the street, and if anything seems out of the ordinary—"

Erin growled playfully. "You're all impossible."

Matthew rose and lumbered off behind her. At the door, she turned and aimed a finger up toward his face. Narrowing her gaze into her best threatening scowl, she said, "Stay out of sight, and don't you dare come barreling into my interview and ruin it. I swear, if you do, I'll go find some Hell's Angels and date every single one of them."

"Okay, okay, go easy. No need to make threats."

"It could take up to an hour," Erin said, still scowling. "I'll program your cell number into mine so I just have to press send if something goes wrong, which it won't."

"I said okay." Matthew turned her toward the door.

She wiggled back around and grabbed his thick arm. "I mean it! I need this job. Don't screw this up for me."

Matthew held two meaty hands up, palms forward. "Just go. Sheesh, sisters. You'd think a little gratitude wouldn't be so far out of the question."

Erin stared at him, dumbfounded, before uttering a sound of disbelief and flouncing out the door toward what she hoped was the most stellar interview of her life. Forget her brothers. Forget everything. She wanted this job.

The doorbell rang, and Sam checked his watch. Excellent start—the nanny was right on time. He appreciated promptness. He took one quick moment to straighten his hair in the hall mirror and smooth his clothing before facing who he hoped would be Jessica's new "grandma."

Fixing an enigmatic smile on his face—not too friendly, not too grumpy—he pulled open the door.

Sam's stomach contracted, and the smile faded. No, no, no. This wasn't right at all. He'd asked for a grandmotherly type, and the enticing young woman standing on his doorstep was anything but. From her stylishly messy mop of red hair to her charming crooked grin, she was the antithesis of what he'd hoped to find waiting on his stoop. Wait—maybe she wasn't the nanny at all. He cocked his head to the side. "Can I help you?"

She straightened her shoulders and stuck out her hand. Her nails, he noticed against his will, were short and neatly manicured. Bare of polish. He'd always found natural nails on a woman very sexy, and his chest tightened. "I'm Erin O'Grady, Mr. Lowery. Nannysource sent me over for the interview."

"Call me Sam. But there must be some mistake. I requested an older woman," he blurted. Then, as if just realizing how rude that sounded, he shook her hand, the very hand he'd found sexy mere moments earlier. Unacceptable.

"Yes, but Karla thought you might change your mind after we talked." She hiked one shoulder. "You see, I specialize in working with children who've faced some sort of trauma. She thought I'd be perfect for what you and Jessica need."

What he needed. Something disturbingly feral swirled inside Sam's body as Erin's smooth, warm palm slid from his. Miss Erin O'Grady might be perfect for a lot of things, but caring for his daughter wasn't one of them. And, no matter what Mia suggested, he wasn't looking for those *other* things. What he needed was a grandmother for his daughter, not a too-sexy-for-her-own-good nanny living under his roof, perfuming the air with her laughter and feminine scent. He was only human, after all.

Still, he supposed he should at least feign giving the interview before calling Nannysource later to reject Erin. "Well, come on in then. I have to warn you, Jessica has been reticent since…"

Erin laid a hand gently on his forearm. "I'm sorry to have heard about what happened to Jessica and her mother."

Another zing of attraction moved through Sam at the feel of that smooth palm against his skin. He glanced from Erin's face, to her hand on his arm, and back again. She quickly removed it. "Thank you. It's been…difficult. Mind you, Jessica's a wonderful little girl—"

"I'm certain of that." The unsuitable nanny's face turned all business. "One problem with a child facing trauma at eighteen months or thereabouts is she has enough memory to know and remember parts of what happened, but she doesn't have the vocabulary to talk about it like an adult might. But there are ways we can work with her, to bring her out of her shell."

"And you're familiar with these…ways?"

"Intimately."

Sam eyed Erin thoughtfully. Damn. She would be perfect if she weren't so…young? Attractive? Distracting? He couldn't decide which word described her best, or if all of them combined made her completely wrong for the job. She might be great for Jessica—that remained to be seen—but he couldn't imagine having someone like Erin underfoot 24/7. Yes, he'd sworn off love and he meant it, but he was a red-blooded, American male with needs and desires. A magnetic young redhead was just what he didn't need in his life right now—in any capacity.

"Make yourself comfortable," he said, taking no pains to hide his less than enthusiastic tone. "Let's meet Jessica."

"Can't wait!"

He waited until she was settled on the sofa, then headed down the hall to get his baby girl. He wasn't sure what he'd expected when the prospective nanny met his daughter. Polite conversation, maybe? A few thoughtful compliments—that slightly cheesy way people speak to children—all the while maintaining a businesslike air? Maybe not that, exactly. But he hadn't expected Erin to drop her purse and get right down on the floor with Jessica, speaking to her like she was a little person and not a baby. And he absolutely hadn't expected Jessica to open up to a complete stranger, even one so captivating as Erin O'Grady.

But she did.

"Well, hello, precious girl," Erin said, opening her arms.

Jessica broke into a grin and toddled right over. "See doggy?" She thrust her bedraggled, stuffed St. Bernard into Erin's face.

"He's beautiful. What's his name, Jessica?"

Jessica flashed a questioning smile at her father.

"His name is Doggy," Sam said, almost apologetically, sinking into an armchair to watch the interaction.

"Doggy's a perfectly beautiful name," Erin said, her focus never leaving Jessica's face.

Sam watched as her gaze dropped to Jessica's bandaged hand. Erin reached out and gently touched the bandage.

"What happened here?"

"Me owie," Jessica said, hugging the injured hand to her chest.

"She slammed her hand in a file drawer at my

worksite,'' Sam said, ashamed. ''She has twelve stitches.''

''Well, that's not good, is it, Jessica?''

''Not good.'' Jessie shook her head vigorously. Then, as though her brain switched gears instantaneously, Jessica ran from the room. ''Be back!''

Erin flashed Sam another crooked smile, and he averted his gaze, fighting to ignore the quick fireball of desire that rushed through him.

''She's adorable. She looks like you.''

Reluctantly, he dragged his gaze back to her face. ''Thank you.'' Before either of them could say more, Jessica bounded back into the room. Her arms were filled with treasures—a puzzle, her stuffed frog, and most surprising to Sam at least, a framed picture of Jenny. He'd framed it for her and placed it in her room just after the new house had been built, but Jessica had never acknowledged it until that moment.

She dropped everything at Erin's feet. ''Play.''

''I'd love to play.'' Erin picked up the framed photograph first. ''Is this your mama, sweetie?''

Sam momentarily ceased breathing, praying this wouldn't send Jessica deeper into her shell. They never talked about Jenny.

Jessica, true to recent form, kept her focus remaining solidly on the puzzle. ''Play puzzle.''

Sam watched as Erin carefully set the framed photograph up facing them, then reached for the frog. ''And is this Kermit?''

Jessica shook her head as she squatted down and dumped the puzzle pieces onto the rug.

Erin glanced toward Sam, one eyebrow raised.

"Froggy," he answered, one corner of his mouth lifting despite everything. "It's a pattern with her lately. Doggy, Froggy, Kitty. You get the idea."

Erin laughed, a light, effervescent sound, then set Froggy next to the photo of Jenny. Something in the way she gave all of Jessica's prized possessions equal attention without focusing on Jenny's picture, like a funeral director might, impressed him. He also liked that she hadn't pushed, prodded. That wouldn't help Jessica get over the fire.

"Okay, let's do this puzzle."

Sam watched his daughter and the unwanted nanny for a few more minutes, astounded by Jessica's reaction to Erin. His daughter acted like she'd known the young woman forever. Still, Erin wasn't right for the job, and the sooner he could get the formal interview part over, the sooner he could call the agency and ask for a grandmotherly sort. This time, he'd be a little more forceful with his request.

He cleared his throat. "So, Erin. Tell me about your professional background."

Erin caught the cue and moved to a nearby armchair. Jessica dragged her toys and her mother's photograph over to sit at Erin's feet, but kept on playing. "I have a degree in early childhood education with an emphasis on childhood trauma."

"And why that? If I may ask."

Erin nodded once. "I come from a large family. I'm one of six, actually. My oldest brother and his wife lost one of their sons to a swimming pool acci-

dent when little Bryce was two." As if both realizing
Jessica's age, they looked momentarily at her. Erin
absentmindedly threaded her fingers through Jessica's
soft hair. "I saw how it affected the other kids.
Bryce's siblings and cousins. And my brother and his
wife, too. I guess I just wanted to do something to
help."

"I'm sorry." Sam was totally taken aback by her
candid sharing. He couldn't imagine what her family
had gone through, losing a child. "That had to
be...horrible."

"Thank you. It was. But being able to make a difference took away some of the helplessness I'd felt."
She pressed her lips together for a moment, sadness
clouding her eyes. "Anyway, I started studying ways
to work through the grief with my niece and nephew
and found I had a knack for it." She shrugged, as if
it were nothing. "I spoke with my advisors and
worked it into my major." She cut her glance away,
then back, an air of determination and confidence on
her face that Sam found appealing and impressive. "I
will tell you I've never been a nanny before, but I
have 15 nieces and nephews and I take care of all of
them. I love children. More than anything."

He allowed one corner of his mouth to lift in a half
smile. It wasn't that he had anything against Erin
O'Grady. On the contrary, he was completely
charmed by her. He just didn't want her sharing his
home. But, he had to give credit where credit was
due, and the fact that she loved children was not in

question. He glanced from her to Jessica, pointedly. "It's obvious you love kids."

Erin smiled, and it truly lit up the room. "I know you wanted an older woman, but I really think I could make a difference with your daughter. If you'd let me."

"I'll think about it, Erin." He stood, hoping to give a polite enough clue that the interview was over. "Thank you for coming. I'll be in touch with the agency."

Erin studied him for a moment, then pulled in a deep breath and blew it out. It was as if she knew what his answer would be, too. He could see the disappointment like a shadow on her face, and for some reason, it made him feel like a heel.

She stood, glancing down regretfully at Jessica. "Well, you have a perfectly lovely daughter. I hope you find what you're looking for, Sam."

They shook hands, and Erin turned toward the door with Sam just behind her. Suddenly, from behind them came Jessica's anguished cry. "No!"

Both Erin and Sam whipped around to find little Jessica standing, her eyes round and moist, her hands clasped together. Sam rushed to her and knelt down on one knee, taking hold of her chubby little arms gently. "What's the matter, honeypot?"

Jessica pulled away and ran to Erin, wrapping her arms around Erin's legs. She pressed her face into Erin's thighs and sobbed. "No go. Play."

Erin seemed as startled as Sam himself was. She

blinked up at him pleadingly, then smoothed Jessica's hair back. "It's okay, angel. Don't cry."

"No go!"

It seemed like interminable minutes passed while Sam and Erin merely stared at one another. She looked torn. He felt torn. Finally, he scrubbed a palm down his face as resignation seeped through him. He had no choice in the matter. Jessica had chosen her own nanny. This was the worst set-up in the world for him, but clearly not for Jessica. He couldn't break his baby girl's heart. Not again.

"Well," he said, finally. "I'll be honest, you wouldn't be my first choice."

Erin flushed, but didn't seem to take offense. "I know. You wanted a grandmother. But keep in mind, the best grandmothers were mothers first, and before that, I'm sure they were young women who adored children." A beat passed. "A lot like me. You don't have to be an older lady to be compassionate and nurturing."

"I can see that." He offered her a sheepish smirk. "I guess there's only one thing left to do."

"What?" Erin's eyes widened, her expression an endearing mix of hopefulness and trepidation.

He shrugged. "Call the agency and tell them you're hired. That is, if you're still interested in the job."

Erin's face broke into the most beatific smile, it couldn't help but warm Sam's heart. He cut his glance away, focusing on Jessica. "Jess, baby, do you want Erin to come and live with us? Take care of you?"

"No go," Jessica said.

He cocked an eyebrow at Erin. "Well?"

"Oh, Sam. Of course I want the job."

She reached out a hand to shake on the deal, and when her warm palm slid against his, he felt another zing of recognition, a male-female awareness that left him disturbingly off-kilter. "Shall we talk about arrangements? I'd want you to move in as soon as possible. I can't afford to miss more work."

"Of course. I can move in tomorrow and be ready to take care of Jessica when you go back to work on Monday." She bent down and easily lifted Jessica into her arms.

Sam watched as his baby girl nestled her head in the crook of her new nanny's neck, and he wondered how that soft skin smelled. *Don't think that way.*

"You won't regret this. I promise," Erin said.

Yeah. Right. Sam nodded, but he wasn't so sure. If the short time she'd spent with Jessica was any indication, Erin could be just the miracle his daughter needed. No arguments there. Yes, she was beautiful, spirited, sexy, but she was also his daughter's nanny. That made her strictly off-limits. If he wasn't careful, this forced proximity with Erin O'Grady could end up being a colossal disaster for him.

Damn good thing he was a careful man.

Chapter Three

Erin didn't release her breath until she was actually locked safely in her Volkswagen Bug, seatbelt on, pulling away from the curb. But, when she finally drove off, she threw her head back and laughed in delight. She had a job! A perfect job! Jessica was a doll, and her daddy—holy moly.

Her heart had lodged firmly in her throat the moment Sam Lowery had opened the door. Not only was the assignment perfect, but the man himself was a fantasy come to life. Tall, dark, brooding. Ultra-yummy. Her brothers *so* wouldn't approve, and somehow that made it all the better.

She laughed again, cranking her radio up louder as Sheryl Crow crooned about wanting to have fun. She planned to have a whole lot of fun with this job.

Okay, get your brain straight, Erin. She was only *working for* the tall, dark, brooding, ultra-yummy guy, not truly *moving in* with him, but still. It felt like a scenario straight out of one of her beloved love stories, and she couldn't help but hope that Sam had felt some of those fireworks between them, too. She'd had to focus on Jessica fully during the interview, just to keep the attraction she'd felt from exploding out of her like a big, neon sign that read, "TAKE ME, I'M YOURS!" She never had been very good at keeping her emotions hidden. Of course, Jessica was an absolute angel herself, and Erin couldn't wait to work with her. But Sam had been an extra, very unexpected but very pleasant bonus.

Even at the beginning, when she could tell he didn't want her for the nanny position, she felt an immediate bond with him. And an instantaneous attraction. He didn't look to be much older than she was. From his slightly scruffy sexiness, the sinew and muscles in his arms, to his piercing eyes, he'd been the polar opposite of what she'd imagined. Why had she automatically assumed he'd be older? The word "widower" had thrown her, she supposed. She'd been expecting a nice, older gentleman who'd started a family late and then lost his wife tragically, and instead she was faced with Mr. Utterly Perfect.

And she was going to live in his house!

"Thank you, God," she whispered, a little shiver moving through her. With any luck, she'd get to know Sam better as she cared for his daughter. She wasn't going to act inappropriately or throw herself at him or anything. But the proximity, the inevitable intimacy they'd develop because of his daughter, the whole dang situation—well, it all spelled possibility to her, with a capital P. And, in time, maybe…just maybe—

Don't get ahead of yourself.

Hey, she was an unrepentant hopeless romantic, but she knew when to be reasonable. Sam Lowery epitomized the word "untouchable." But things could change quickly with luck, couldn't they? And she had the luck of the Irish firmly on her side. Just that morning, she'd been unemployed and living with her parents, and now look at her.

Giddy with excitement, she slowed as she drove past her brother, Matthew, who sat hunkered down stakeout-style in his truck a few houses away from Sam's. She laid on her horn, then stuck her tongue out at her brother when he looked over. Shaking his head, he kicked his engine over and whipped a quick U-turn to follow her home.

Hoo-boy, she couldn't wait to spread the news. She was going to be living in the same house with a certified single hunk, working at the job of her dreams, and nurturing her fantasies of happily forever after at the same time. Best of all, there wasn't a darn thing her brothers could do to stop her, because despite their collective and annoying—although, admittedly, endearing—overprotectiveness, she had her own mind, and she was perfectly capable of taking care of herself.

She could hardly wait to spill her news and see the

reactions on their faces. Newsflash, world: Erin O'Grady was more than ready to grow up.

Especially in the eyes of her brothers.

As it turned out, the only way Erin could appease her brothers was by agreeing to let them ''help her move in'' the following day. The whole idea was absurd. Her rooms at Sam's house were furnished, so all she had to bring was her personal effects, all of which fit into her bright yellow Volkswagen Bug. Her parents had been no help to her; they agreed with her brothers. Maybe it was a good idea for the boys to make sure this Sam Lowery was okay, they'd told her.

Argh!

She decided she owed it to Sam to warn him before the entire O'Grady clan infiltrated his home. Dialing his number on her cell phone, she glanced at the caravan of full-sized pick-up trucks in her rear view mirror and groaned. Humiliating, that's what it was. They were undermining her professionalism.

Sam picked up on the second ring. ''Hello?''

''Hi, Sam. It's Erin. I'm on my way over.''

''Good, I have your rooms all ready for you.''

''Great. There's…just one thing you should know.''

''And what's that?'' His voice had turned immediately apprehensive, which made Erin cringe. She didn't want to get off on bad footing with the man who hadn't wanted to hire her in the first place.

"My brothers—well, four of the five—are coming to help me move in."

"Oh. That's fine."

"Yeah, the thing is, I don't have enough stuff to warrant four men assisting me." She sighed. "I'll be honest. I'm the baby of the family, their only sister, and—"

"They want to make sure I'm not an ax murderer?"

Erin laughed nervously. "Something like that, yes. I'm so embarrassed and sorry. Brothers can be so overprotective. Do you have sisters?" He hesitated for a beat too long, which left Erin perplexed. "Sam?"

"No," he said, a bit stiffly. "No sisters or brothers."

"Well, some days I'd say you're lucky being an only child."

"In a lot of ways, I'm sure you're right."

Oops. She didn't want him to think she wasn't a fan of family. After all, she was going to be caring for his daughter. "Don't get me wrong, I love my family. But, they act like I'm Snow White, running through the forest in those stupid high heels, hapless and helpless."

Sam actually made a small sound that could've been mistaken for a laugh. That pleased her.

"Look, it's fine. If you were my sister, I'd do the same thing."

But I don't want to be your sister. "You're sure you don't mind?" She bit her lip.

"Of course not. As long as they don't feel the need to beat me up or anything."

Now it was Erin's turn to laugh. "Okay, well, we'll be there shortly. Thanks for understanding."

"No sweat."

Erin hit the end button, and her phone immediately rang again. She frowned, her tone quizzical as she answered. "Hello?" Had Sam forgotten something? Changed his mind?

"This is your big brother, Patrick, behind you."

"I know who you are and where you are, Pat. How could I forget? You've been tailgating me since Mom and Dad's house. What's up?"

"Don't talk on a cell phone when you drive, Erin Marie. It's not safe."

Incredulous, she pulled the phone away from her ear and stared at it a moment. Lifting it back to her ear, she rasped, "Are you insane? *You* called *me!*"

"Yes, but just to tell you that. You were on the phone before. I saw you."

"I was speaking to my new boss. Warning him about impending O'Grady infestation of his home."

"Hang up and watch the road."

Erin muttered as she hung up, then tossed her phone in the passenger's seat and gave a surly wave to Patrick behind her. For the love of Pete, she couldn't wait to get out from under her brothers' constant watch.

The moving-in process went quickly, thank goodness, because Erin had never been a packrat. Although each of her brothers had done the squeeze handshake/suspicious size-up routine with Sam, there hadn't been any overt grilling, and they'd been polite. Hey, when it came to Eamon, Patrick, Matt, Miles, and Mick, Erin had learned to be grateful for the little things.

She let her brothers preen and puff their chests and check out the place to their hearts' content. She didn't even interfere, just sat at the kitchen table, elbows propped, chin resting in her palm. But when all the O'Gradys had left, Erin finally relaxed. Strangely, she felt like she'd come home.

The silence fairly hummed in their absence, and Erin slipped into a very un-Erin-like shyness as she glanced up at her new boss. "Well, that was uncomfortable."

Sam smirked, but didn't say a word about her brothers. She didn't know what to make of that.

"Let me show you your quarters."

"Cool, I've never had quarters before." She grinned, smoothing her palms together and scrunching her shoulders up with excitement. "Except for the round, twenty-five-cent kind."

"Well, we've got the whole shebang here." He lifted an arm, indicating the hallway off the kitchen through which her brothers had carried her belongings. Erin bounced a little on her feet, then headed off, but Sam's warm, solid, silent presence behind her made her shiver.

He cleared his throat. "If you're cold, there are extra blankets and comforters in the linen closet outside your bathroom. Feel free to take whatever you need.''

''Oh.'' Whoops. She wished she were better at reining in her emotions. ''Thanks. I do tend to be on the chilled side. You know, that female thing.''

He had no reply to that.

At the door of the bedroom, they stopped and peered in. It was the first time Erin had viewed what was to be her new bedroom, and she sighed. ''Wow.''

''I want you to be comfortable here, so feel free to change the room however you'd like.''

She glanced over her shoulder at him, then leaned into the doorjamb and wrapped her arms around herself. The room was decorated in yellows and blues, with what looked like a handmade quilt, in some sort of intricate star pattern, draping the bed. Sunlight streamed in the large windows, which were covered by gauzy, white curtains. He'd taken the time to set a vase of daisies on her hickory dresser, which touched her. They matched the daisy motif of her Bug. ''But it's so beautiful. I can't imagine changing a thing.''

Sam shrugged. ''That's fine, too.''

Erin glanced around suddenly, realizing she'd been so worried about what egregious things her brothers might do or say, she hadn't seen or greeted her new little charge. ''Hey, where's Jessica? Napping?''

Sam aimed a thumb over his shoulder. ''I actually left her at my secretary's house for the afternoon. I didn't want her upset over the moving in process.''

Erin bit her lip. "You think she would be? But we got along so well."

"I wasn't sure. Didn't want to risk it." A line of worry bisected his browline. "Sometimes it's the oddest things that set her off. I just worry. Probably too much."

"Nonsense. A child can tell when she's well cared for. But there are things you can do to help her out of her shell." Sam said nothing, so she sucked in a breath and blew it out, offering a smile. Clearly, he didn't want to talk parenting techniques. "Well. I can't wait to see her."

Sam nodded once. "After I've shown you around, I'll leave you to unpack while I go pick her up. Maybe—" He raised a hand. "Now, normally, you'll have weekends off. But I thought, tonight, maybe we can have dinner together, the three of us. A get acquainted dinner. And you and I can talk about expectations and pay, that sort of thing. I'd like to hear about your plan to help Jess get over her residual…"

"Grief?"

"Do you think it's grief? At her age?"

"Absolutely. But she can overcome all of it."

"Well. You're the expert, and you sound confident. I like that. Dinner, then?"

Erin didn't want to seem too swoony and corny, but the thought of dining with Sam and Jessica made her heart pound. "I'd love that. What would you like me to make?"

Sam blinked, appearing taken aback. "You don't

have to cook. That's not one of your duties. We'll just order a pizza."

"Oh. Sounds fine." She dipped her chin. "But, you know, I will have to cook for Jessica."

He rubbed his chin thoughtfully with the side of his hand. "I suppose so, but not every meal."

Erin turned to fully face him. Did he have any concept whatsoever of what a nanny did? "What time do you leave for work in the morning?"

"As early as five."

"So she'll need breakfast and lunch."

He conceded the point with a nod.

"Do you generally get home from work the same time?"

Sam huffed. "I wish. My job can be unpredictable. I used to take her with me, so we ate on the fly a lot."

Erin smiled gently. She had a sense that it wouldn't be smart to point out any faults in Sam's parenting philosophies—not that there were true faults. Just…adjustments that may be needed. "One of the ways we can help Jessica readjust is to get her on a normal, set schedule of meals, naps, bedtimes, etc. so she can feel secure."

His eyes narrowed. "You think she doesn't feel secure?"

Erin's throat tightened. She still didn't quite know how to read Sam, and it made her nerves stand on edge. She didn't want to offend him, or take over too much and put him off. "No, I didn't mean it that way.

She's been through a lot, Sam. You both have. Not just the fire and losing her mother, but a move to a new house, new routines, all of it. Those schedule upheavals affect little ones.''

"I hadn't thought of it that way.''

"As long as you have me here, you might as well let me do everything I can to bring Jess around. Cooking's part of that. Besides, I love cooking.''

Sam swallowed warily. "Don't you want your evenings free? I mean, you're a young woman. Surely you have friends, boyfriends?''

"No boyfriends,'' she said quickly.

He raised one eyebrow, and Erin checked her tone, not wanting to sound like she was flirting. Or desperate. Or twenty-three-years-old and a hopeless romantic, completely crushing on her new boss. She bestowed a droll, playful look. "Hello, have you forgotten my brothers already?''

A half-smile lifted Sam's mouth. "Not hardly.''

"Yeah, well, they scare every guy in the Pacific Northwest away, believe me. Any potential boyfriends meet the Evil Five and turn tail immediately.''

"They just love you.''

"Yeah, straight into spinsterhood.''

"Oh, I think you're at least a year away from that.''

She laughed. "I do have friends, but I'm Jessica's nanny. I'm here for her, first and foremost. I can go out with friends and see family on the weekends.''

Sam pressed his lips into a flat line. "I don't want you to burn out, or feel like an indentured servant.''

Erin scoffed at the notion. "Are you kidding? Burn out? This is my dream job, Sam. I plan to have a brood of my own someday, but for now, working with Jessica is going to be my pleasure. I promise."

Sam studied her for a few moments, then gave a grudging smile. "You know, I think this is going to work out better than I imagined. I wanted a grand-mother who would treat Jessica as her own grand-daughter. But maybe having a…"

Erin waited, her pulse pounding in her neck. She wondered just how Sam Lowery viewed her. New mommy? Wouldn't *that* be a fantasy come true?

"Maybe having a…big sister figure is just as good."

Ugh. Just what she wanted—another flipping brother. Even figuratively speaking, it didn't appeal, especially considering her wholly inappropriate and yet very real attraction to Sam. Still, she managed a weak smile. "Jessica and I will have great fun, and with time and some solid grief work, she'll come out of her shell even more."

"I want that for her more than anything." He pulled a face. "As long as you think I passed muster with your formidable brothers, of course."

Erin winked at his seemingly out-of-character play-fulness. "I'm still here, aren't I? If you hadn't met with their approval, trust me, they'd have dragged me home by the scruff of my neck, job or no job."

The ice sufficiently broken by that absurd image, Erin and Sam walked down the hall toward a large bathroom. The tile was blue and white checkerboard, with the occasional yellow tile thrown in for punch. The shower curtain was blue and yellow stripes, and all the white porcelain gleamed. Erin absolutely loved it, but she bit her lip to keep her reaction composed. Instead of cheering and clapping, she said, "It's lovely."

"Glad you like it. I used to have your bedroom outfitted as a study, but I moved that upstairs to a smaller bedroom near mine. I wanted you to have your privacy."

"I'm sure my brothers approved," she said, in a wry tone.

"In fact, the dark-haired one—"

"Patrick."

"Patrick did ask me where my bedroom was."

Erin groaned and covered her face with both hands. "I'm so sorry. That was uncalled for."

"Not a problem. It's nice that you have people looking out for you."

"Yeah." She huffed. "Nice like a prison sentence."

He gave one of those almost-laughs again as he guided her toward a small sitting nook off her bedroom, and indicated a sliding glass door. "You have a small patio there. I'll be installing a Charlie Bar onto the door for safety. Your brother, Mick, suggested it."

Erin gave him an incredulous look, then squeezed her eyes shut. "Gosh, I'm really embarrassed. You must think I'm sixteen years old. God knows, they all do."

"No, it's a good idea, the Charlie Bar. If you'd like an alarm system, too—"

"No. God. No alarm system." Annoying O'Grady men. They'd ruin her entire life if given the chance. Needing space to cool down her humiliation, Erin reentered the bedroom and crossed to the closet, opening one of the mirrored glass doors.

"Is it big enough?"

"More than." She shrugged. "I'm not one of those women who collects clothes and shoes."

"That's unusual."

"There are some of us around. Growing up with all brothers, it was hard to become a girly-girl." She grinned, proudly. "I don't collect clothes and shoes like a girl, I don't squeal like a girl, I don't take hours to get ready like some girls. I don't even throw like a girl, but that's actually a bonus."

He smiled, this time for real—albeit enigmatically. Sam never dropped that wall of emotional safety completely. "I just want you to know, the bedroom, sitting room, patio, and bathroom are yours alone. Neither I nor Jessica will come into this section of the house unless there is an emergency."

Erin crossed her arms, hoping Sam would eventually find occasion to enter her rooms. Pipe dream. The guy was so professional about the whole thing, clearly he hadn't felt spark number one during their interview. Erin really did need to rein in her romantic fantasies, because they were just that—fanciful little daydreams that would never come true. "It's a lovely design, this wing. Did you plan it?"

He nodded. "With help from an architect friend of mine. I had…a lot of support and help from my company after the fire. My insurance didn't cover much, but they picked up the slack. This house is a real blessing for Jess and me."

"That's wonderful."

"I think a set-up like this is intended as a mother-in-law's suite. It's separate, but has access to the kitchen and living room. I didn't use it that way, of course." He cleared his throat. "Also, if you'd like me to put a deadbolt on the outside hallway door leading in to this part—"

"Sam," Erin said, gravely, holding up one hand. "Please tell me one of my brothers didn't suggest that?"

He paused, as though weighing the wisdom of his next words. Finally he nodded. "The big one. Sorry, I have a difficult time remembering names."

"Matthew," she said through clenched teeth. "I'll be sure to kill him later."

Sam looked amused. "Erin, it's no problem."

"Let me ask you something." She looked at him directly. "Do I *need* a deadbolt on my room?"

He looked vaguely affronted. "Of course not."

"Then I won't have you bother with the expense. It's ridiculous. I'm perfectly comfortable here with you." She crossed her arms protectively over her chest. "If I felt threatened in any way, I wouldn't have taken the job."

His eyes softened momentarily, then grew remote again almost as quickly. He cleared his throat, backing away. "Good. Well. I'll just go get Jessica and the pizza, give you a little time to settle in. Anything you don't like on your pizza?"

"The usual answer. Anchovies."

"Jess would probably have a meltdown of epic proportions if I fed her furry little fish of any kind, so you're safe. She loves pineapple and ham, though."

"Cool, that's my favorite, actually."

Sam watched her intently for a moment, and it almost looked like he had something to say. But, instead of giving voice to his thoughts, he simply nodded, turned, and left. Erin sank onto the edge her bed, releasing a sigh and smoothing her palms over the softly crinkled texture of the quilt. For certain, Sam Lowery wasn't going to be an easy man to get to know, but Erin planned to do her best to bring him out of his shell, just as she hoped to do the same for his daughter. She flopped backward on the bed and stared up at the ceiling.

Miracles *could* happen. She'd seen it before.

Chapter Four

World of hurt took on several new layers of meaning as Sam drove to Mia's house to pick up Jessica.

What in the hell had he gotten himself into?

Half of him pondered that question. The other half greedily soaked up Erin's sunny presence in his home, and he realized, with dismay, that he was inexplicably ravenous for the pure, platonic company of a woman like her. She was so guileless and enthusiastic, it made his heart squeeze. Her blue eyes always smiled, and she seemed genuinely happy and grateful for everything he showed her. Even her yellow Volkswagen Bug, with those silly daisy wheel covers, exuded a happy-go-lucky attitude.

Erin was so different from Jenny, who'd always been a bit of a dark soul, much like himself. Jenny had never been happy with his work schedule, never contented with their apartment, with their life, with herself. She'd never been quite happy, period, and on a lot of levels, he'd understood it. Both of them had come from difficult backgrounds. Of course, he had always hoped having each other, creating a family of their own, would help both of them heal and move on, but that hadn't happened for Jenny. Erin, on the other hand, felt like a balm to his soul in just the short time he'd known her.

Wait. Hold up. Why was he comparing Erin to Jenny?

With effort, Sam shook off the notion. Jenny had been his *wife*. Erin was his daughter's *nanny,* period, and he'd known her for exactly two days. Having met her brothers, he knew he'd be wise to remember the difference.

For a moment, knowing Erin and he couldn't get to know each other on a different level made him feel grim and bleak. Then again, hadn't he sworn off romance forever? He had, and it had been the right thing to do for his daughter's sake. He would have to settle for enjoying Erin's presence while she was around. Perhaps having a live-in nanny would be a safe, commitment-free way of enjoying the presence of a woman in his life. No ties, no lies, no complications of love and sex—no heartbreak.

And no Erin. Not really.

The thought bummed him out.

A man would have to be half-dead not to notice Erin's appeal, to be sure, and if he was picking up the cues correctly, she found him attractive as well. He'd have to watch his step. He knew damn well what her brothers feared: a guy who was out to take advantage of what their baby sister had to offer and then unceremoniously break her gentle heart.

Lucky for the O'Grady men, he wasn't interested in taking his relationship with the new nanny in that direction, because he *would* break her heart eventually. Erin needed and deserved a forever kind of guy, one who would give her that giant brood of smiling Irish babies she so wanted. He wasn't that guy and never would be. Not after Jenny, after everything that happened.

Sam groaned. Enough heavy thoughts. He just wanted to pick up his baby girl, buy a pizza, and get back home.

To Erin.

But, no. Not like that. Only, he reminded himself sternly, so that the three of them could get acquainted, and so Jessica could get used to the idea of having a stranger live with them. As the *nanny*. He'd take on the role of looking out for Erin just like her brothers did, and he'd protect her from himself.

Suddenly the thought of Lissa Cartwright intruded on his ruminations. She was *his* sister, like it or not. Did she have an adoptive brother to look out for her? To keep her away from the less than honorable men?

Then again, he didn't care, right?

He pushed the thought of Lissa out of his mind. Why was he thinking of *them* again? Lissa and Adam, Jared Cambry and his new little son, Mark, who'd reccived the, hopefully, life-saving bone marrow transplant from Adam. They had no place in his thoughts. It was just the O'Grady family closeness he'd witnessed making him think crazy about all the rest. It didn't help, of course, that the news show about the reunited twins had sparked a media frenzy of follow-up stories he couldn't seem to ignore. He felt as drawn to the story as half of America was, it seemed. More so because they were—no. He stopped himself, gripping tightly to the steering wheel and clenching his jaw.

They weren't and would never be his family. Not really.

He couldn't think that way, now or ever.

He had family, and her name was Jessica.

With determination, Sam sped up slightly. All of a sudden, the tumultuousness of the past few days pressed down on him and made him crave a touchstone of sanity. He needed to hold his daughter, breathe in the sweet baby scent of her hair, and remind himself of what mattered. Not a sister and brother he'd never known, nor a "father" who'd given him up. Not a nanny who was too enticing for her own good, and already too imbedded in his world for his peace of mind.

Just Jessica. His daughter.

She was all Sam needed in his life. End of story.

It didn't take long for Erin to unpack and settle in, and by the time she was done, Sam and Jessica still hadn't returned. Edgy and anxious to see them, she went into the kitchen, turned on the Bose under-cabinet radio to her favorite light rock station, and set about tossing a salad to go with the pizza. When she finished that, she whipped together a batch of no bake lemon bars from a mix she found in the cupboard. Sam and Jessica still hadn't returned, so Erin filled her time by unloading the clean dishes from the dishwasher, reloading it with the few dishes she'd used, and wiping down all the surfaces with kitchen cleanser. She found a simple, white emergency candle in a drawer and placed it into a taper holder on the table, lighting it. Might as well make their first dinner together festive.

She peered into the large laundry/mud room, which angled off the kitchen and led to the three-car garage, and noticed a hamper filled with toddler clothes that needed washing. Humming as she worked, she loaded the washer and got that task underway as well. She'd just as soon fill idle moments with productive work than sit around doing nothing. She'd learned that from her mother.

Smiling sadly, she realized she already missed her parents, despite the fact she'd been so eager to move out of the house. Hey, she was a young woman now. Yearning for independence wasn't a commentary on her parents or how much she loved them. It was a normal growing process. Crossing to a wall-mounted phone in the kitchen, she dialed the familiar number without even thinking. Mom answered on the first ring.

"Hi, Mom. It's me."

"Erin, honey! We're missing you already here."

"I was missing you, too. That's why I called."

"Oh, dear. Are things not going well? The boys called and said this Sam Lowery seemed like a decent enough fellow. I thought surely things would be okay."

"No, no. Things are going fine. My rooms are gorgeous, and Sam has been very polite and cordial." She twirled the cord around her finger, inexplicably charmed that Sam still used at least one phone with a cord. "It's just...he went to pick up Jessica, the baby, and I'm waiting for them to get home so we can eat dinner. I'm not used to having a quiet house."

Sarah O'Grady laughed softly. "No, I suppose you aren't. You know you can come home any time, if things don't work out."

"I know, Mom. But I'm determined to make it work." Suddenly, she heard the garage door lift. "Oh, they're here. I'll call you tomorrow, okay?"

"Be careful, sweetie. And bring that wee baby over to meet your family some time."

"I'll try, but it might be a while." She glanced toward the mud room door that led to the garage and lowered her tone. "Sam's pretty overprotective over Jessica. Of course, it's understandable, with the fire and all. But...I'll work on it."

"I'm sure you'll do a wonderful job."

"I love you, Mom."

"I love you, too."

Erin rang off just as Sam and Jessica entered through the mud room. Sam held a large, white pizza box in one hand, and Jessica toddled beside him. When she saw Erin, she broke into a wide, albeit shy, grin and hid her face in her father's leg.

Sam touched her head. "Honeypot, do you remember Erin?"

Erin squatted down and opened her arms for a hug. "There's the pretty little miss. Hello, Jessica!"

Jessica didn't speak, but went slowly into Erin's embrace and nestled her soft baby head into Erin's neck.

Erin smiled up at Sam, who was peering around the kitchen with a surprised look on his face. The washing machine hummed from just behind him, and the smell of lemon and crumbly, buttery crust permeated the air.

Finally his gaze settled on her. "Erin, you didn't need to clean up or start the laundry. And—" He glanced toward the countertop. "—did you make dessert?"

Erin nodded. "And a salad." She shrugged. "I had time. It's no trouble." She lifted Jessica, settling her onto one hip, moving further into the kitchen. "You're going to have to get used to me doing things around the house, Sam. I'm not one to sit around idly."

He set the pizza on the counter. "But, you were supposed to unpack. Get settled."

"Done."

He cocked his head to one side. "Where'd you learn to be so efficient?"

"From a mother who had to raise five slob brothers."

One corner of Sam's mouth quivered up. "Well. Okay. Thank you." He glanced at the dessert. "I say, let's eat the pizza so we can get to the lemon stuff."

"Why, Sam Lowery." She turned her head to the side and peered at him out of the corner of her eye, playfully. "Would it be fair to say you have a sweet tooth?"

He opened the pizza box, watching her over it thoughtfully. "I do like sweet things. Yes."

Erin's heart fluttered, and she focused on settling Jessica in her high chair, unable to maintain eye contact with Sam. She knew her Irish complexion all too well, and she was most likely crimson right then. "What would you like with dinner, little miss? Milk, juice, or water?"

"Milk," murmured Jessica, squirming to get down. "I pour."

Erin glanced at Sam for confirmation. He shook his head slightly. "Let her T-H-I-N-K she's pouring."

"Gotcha." She lifted Jessica back out of the high chair and set her on the floor. The little girl dashed toward the fridge, going on tippy-toe to pull the door open and wrestle the milk out of the door. Erin rescued the carton from Jessica, who was walking with it, half-tipped, toward the table.

He lifted a chin toward the cabinet closest to the fridge. "Sippy cups are in there. And, how about you? Care to join me in a beer or a glass of wine? I have a good Chianti. It goes great with pizza, and I sure could use it.''

"I'd love a glass, if it's okay." She glanced at Jessica.

"It's fine. I'm certainly not suggesting we get plowed. Just a nice, civilized glass of wine with dinner."

She inclined her head. "Sounds wonderful."

"How about you serve the pizza and I'll pour?"

"Deal."

For several quiet moments, save the radio music, they moved easily around one another in the kitchen, preparing dinner. The opening and shutting of cabinets, sounds of a cork being pulled and the subsequent glug, glug, glug of wine filling goblets, Jessica's quiet little chatter to her beloved Doggy—it all seemed so comfortable, so warm. Happiness filled Erin until she thought she might burst. She said a silent prayer that she, Sam, and Jessica would share a lot of intimate meals together in the days to come. She wouldn't say for sure that doing so would warm Sam up, but it certainly couldn't hurt.

Erin awoke the first morning in Sam's house while dawn was still hazy and blue. She listened to a sound she couldn't quite place, then realized someone was prowling the kitchen.

Sam.

Despite the early hour, she couldn't pass up this chance to speak with him alone. They hadn't really discussed much about her plans for Jessica's treatment at dinner the previous night, but she wanted to get started as soon as possible. Six months had already passed since the trauma. Time was of the essence. Tossing off the quilt, she wrapped herself in a blue, fleece robe, brushed her teeth and finger-combed her hair, then made her way down the hallway into the kitchen.

When she opened the door, Sam spun to face her, a butter knife in one hand and a jar of mayonnaise in the other. He looked momentarily stunned, but recovered in short order. "I'm sorry. Did I wake you?"

Erin crossed her arms and smiled. "No. I'm an early riser. I wanted to come out and chat with you before you left, if it doesn't disrupt your routine too much."

"Oh. Well." Sam seemed at a loss, then he indicated the coffeemaker with the butter knife. "Join me in a cup of coffee. If you'd like. Are you a coffee drinker?"

"Thank you. Yes," said Erin. "Don't mind if I do." She crossed to the cupboards, opening two before finding mugs inside the third. "What time does Jessica usually get up?" she asked, as she filled her mug with the aromatic brew.

"There's a question that should be easy to answer but isn't. I used to have to wake her and get her ready before I left for work, poor thing." He pulled a face. "She didn't like it one single bit. I don't think she's going to be a morning person."

"I can imagine, and I can't blame her, either." Erin took her mug and sat down at the table. "I'll wait until seven-thirty to wake her, I think."

Sam worked on his lunch in silence for a few moments, then sealed it all in a black lunch container. He poured himself a cup of coffee, then turned toward Erin. With his hip propped against the counter, he studied her but said nothing.

Erin tried not to squirm beneath his scrutiny as he eyed her over the brim of his mug while he drank. She swallowed thickly, curling her fingers around the warm comfort of her own mug. She had to say something. Anything. This silence was like a big elephant hunkered in the corner of the kitchen. "So...um, should I hold dinner for you tonight?"

"Never any need for that," Sam said, with a decisive huff. "I don't ever know when I'll be home, unfortunately."

She bit her lip and nodded, her gaze drifting slowly down toward the steaming dark brew in her coffee cup.

"But...I'll call if I'm going to be home at a reasonable hour. If you want."

"Yes, please. I'd like to feed Jessica dinner at six o'clock in the evenings. So, if it's not by then, I'll have to save you leftovers."

"Duly noted."

She dipped her chin slightly, but kept her tone light. "It would be good, too, if you maintained her meal schedule as much as possible on the weekends if I'm not here."

"Okay, you'll have to remind me..."

"Maybe I can type up some sort of schedule for the fridge."

"Great idea. You're welcome to use my computer. It's in the den, upstairs. Second door on the right."

Erin almost told him she had her own laptop and printer set up in her sitting room, but what was she—crazy? He was giving her free rein to enter his private area of the house. "Thanks. I appreciate it."

"So," Sam asked, "is that what you wanted to talk to me about? Dinner? Or…schedules?"

"No." Erin lifted her shoulders and let them drop. "I just have a few questions, so I can start working with Jess in the way that will help her best. I don't mean to be overeager, but—"

"Fire away. I'm eager, too."

Erin cleared her throat. "How does Jessica react when you share your feelings about what happened to your wife."

A muscle in his jaw ticked, and he looked away. "This isn't about me. It's about my daughter."

"Well…yes. But you're grieving, too. Right?"

He paused for an uncomfortably long time, then gave a grudging half-nod.

"At her age, Jessica is just learning how to deal with emotions, Sam. She's going to take all her cues from you."

"Meaning what?"

"If you want her to come out of her shell, you'll have to venture out of yours a bit."

"I don't have a shell," he said, sharply.

Erin softened her tone, but her heart started to pound. She hated confrontations. "I'm not trying to pry, Sam. But, we're going to have to work together on this. You're the closest person to that baby girl. I'm just here to help. I need to know how she…and you…handle the tragedy."

His face took on a pained mask. "I know. Okay, fine. What do you need from me?"

"Well, basic information so I know how to approach Jessica."

Sam spread his arms. "I'm right here listening."

Erin fought back the urge to roll her eyes, then adjusted in her chair and met his gaze directly and repeated her question in a slightly different way. "How does Jessica act when you talk about her mother?"

"I don't talk about her mother."

A frisson of shock spiraled through Erin, and she had to blink a couple times to keep it off her face. "Ever?"

Color rose up Sam's neck at her incredulous tone, and he cut his glance away. "I don't want to upset her. I'm trying to help her get over the whole… thing."

Thing. He was so deep into denying his own pain, he couldn't even say the words. Erin pressed her lips together, then bought a bit of time by taking a sip of coffee. Maybe she needed to come at this topic from another direction. "What about looking through her pictures? Family photos of good times, memorabilia, her mother's clothing, that stuff?"

"I actually put all the pictures of Jenny away, except for the one I framed for Jessica's bedroom. Same deal with her clothes, perfume, and any stuff that wasn't lost in the fire. I didn't want—"

"To upset her."

He muttered an exasperated sound. "I'm trying to be strong for her, Erin, after all she's been through."

"I understand. I'm not judging you. I'm simply trying to gather information about what's been done so far." Erin blew out a small breath. "Does she cry about the fire? Or about losing her mother? Any of it?"

He considered it. "No. I mean, sometimes she seems withdrawn and glum, but I just let her be. She might not even be thinking of Jenny. Who knows what her moods are about, really?"

Not you, if you don't ask.

"I don't want to interfere or pressure her if she's feeling...however a two-year-old would feel about such a thing." He looked puzzled suddenly. "How *would* a two-year-old feel about such a thing?"

Erin flipped her hand. "As many different ways as there are children. It depends on the child. All people handle loss differently, even tiny people." She sipped, gathering her courage to get back to the central issue again. "What do you do when you feel especially upset about what occurred?"

A muscle in his jaw jumped, and his gaze drifted to somewhere above her head. "I guess I...leave the room. Take some time alone to get my head straight."

"Just...leave?"

He hiked one shoulder, a tense jerky movement.

"No sense laying that rap on a tiny child. She doesn't need a weak father on top of everything else."

"Mmmmmm." Her non-answer visibly agitated him.

"We keep busy, you know? Try not to think about it."

Erin peered up at him from beneath her lashes.

"What? Am I doing everything wrong? Great. That would be about par for the course," he muttered, almost to himself.

She tilted her head side to side, slowly. "Not *wrong*. But I think there are things we can do...together...to make it better for Jessica. We need to start with you, though."

"This isn't *about* me," he said, voice slightly raised.

"It's very much about you, Sam. Your wife died."

"Jessica's *mother* died."

"Jessica's mother, who was also your wife."

"I don't understand where we're going with this."

The exasperation in his words was palpable, and Erin decided she'd pressured him enough for one morning. She eased back. He hadn't given her much information, but his reticence spoke volumes and gave her a place to start. He probably had no idea. Erin wrapped her fingers loosely around her mug and gave him a bland smile. "Someday soon, when you're ready, I want you to tell me the details about the fire. That'll help me."

"O-okay. But, I'd really like you to focus on my daughter. You're *her* nanny. I'm doing just fine."

"I understand."

He turned and gathered his lunchbox and Thermos, and Erin sucked in a deep, calming breath. She had her work cut out for her with this little family, especially starting with papa bear.

She centered her mind and squared her shoulders for confidence. So much of his attitude mirrored her brother, Eamon's coping method when little Bryce had died. Fathers often felt they had to be the pillar of strength for everyone else, without understanding what kind of an example that set for the very children they wanted to help, and without ever coming to terms with their own private pain.

"But, I want you to know, Sam, that I'm very focused on Jessica. Please don't ever doubt that. That's why I'm asking these uncomfortable questions. I apologize for having to do that, but we're going to have to work together, and I know I sound like a broken record. Unfortunately, it's true." She tilted her head apologetically. "I can't make big changes in Jessie's life without you. I'm a stranger, though hopefully not for long. Still, you're her parent. Your impact is greater."

Sam turned, appraising her through an inscrutable expression. "I hear you," he said, finally, in an oddly gentle gruff tone. "I'm not trying to be difficult."

"Comes naturally, huh?"

His momentary surprise was replaced with a sexy half-smile.

Erin stood, smiling back and hoping to leave the conversation on a light note. "I'm just kidding. Anyway, we can talk about it more later. I didn't intend to make you late for work.''

Sam swallowed thickly, seeming to accept her olive branch. "It's okay. What are your plans today?"

Erin shrugged, glancing around the pretty red and cream kitchen. "I thought Jessica and I would just hang out around the house, get used to each other."

Sam nodded. "I'd like to install a carseat in your Bug before you drive anywhere with her."

"Of course. I'd never take her out without proper child restraints." Her brow furrowed, and she tapped her bottom lip with the pad of her index finger. "We should do that soon, though, in case there is some emergency."

Sam got a distant, haunted look in his eyes for a moment, then nodded. He set down his Thermos and lunch container. "You're absolutely right. I'll do it now."

"Oh, but—" Surprised, Erin stood and pulled the lapels of her robe around her more tightly. "You'll be late."

"Doesn't matter."

"Yes, well, like I said, we're not going anywhere today."

"I know. But like you also said, you'll need that car seat in case of emergencies. You never know when something will crop up, which is why they're called emergencies. Believe me, I know that all too well."

Respecting his pain, Erin knew better than to argue the point. And, anyway, it was true. Who's to say she and Jessica wouldn't run into some sort of crisis on day one of the job, and she'd absolutely hate to be stranded. "Okay, well, let me just get dressed and get my keys, and I'll help you."

"I'll meet you outside. Incidentally, you're welcome to park your car in the garage. There's plenty of space."

She smiled. "Thank you, Sam. That's very considerate. Daisy Mae will love living inside."

He narrowed his gaze, studying her as if she were crazy. "You named your car?"

"Doesn't everyone?" Sam shook his head, and Erin headed off toward her wing, happiness and hopefulness making her footsteps light as air. First she moved in, and now her VW Bug, Daisy Mae, would be moving in, too. Other than pulling teeth when it came to getting any help or information out of Sam, Erin liked the way their relationship was progressing so far. Yes, indeed, she liked it a lot.

Chapter Five

Sam was in a full-blown brood by the time he reached the worksite, complete with dark thoughts, "buyer's remorse" in the nanny department, and a whole-face scowl that would bring small children and tender-hearted women to tears. He stomped his way into the trailer that held the site offices, slamming the door behind him and then setting down his metal lunch container harder and louder than necessary. He shouldn't *be* this angry, but he couldn't seem to shake it.

"Wow," Mia said, used to his mercurial moods and nonplussed by them, as always. Sam liked that about her. "Did you find a rock in your cereal bowl this morning, or what?"

Sam deepened his scowl, ignoring the question

while he hung his jacket on a hook by the door. He stalked over and warmed his coffee with fresh, hot brew from a pot Mia had just made, taking his time to formulate an answer. Other men might take a problem like this to family to discuss, but Sam had no one. He'd had Mia available as a friend and sounding board for several years now, although he still held her at arm's length—to the extreme. He'd always been a lone wolf, but Erin's questioning had him spooked, and right now he really did need to vent to someone. Mia was it.

After a fortifying sip of coffee, he turned toward Mia. Leaning his back against a four-drawer file cabinet, he hooked his legs at the ankle and studied his secretary from beneath his furrowed brows. He had so much to say and no skills for molding it all into logical conversation. Defeated, he settled for, ''I don't know about this nanny thing.''

''Second thoughts already?'' Mia sank into her desk chair, pulled out a file drawer, and propped her feet on it. She didn't look the least bit surprised by his comment. ''Well, I'm all ears. What did the poor girl do? Breathe in your air space?''

''Very funny.'' Sam filled her in on the grilling he'd received in the kitchen that morning.

To his surprise, Mia didn't look horrified. Baffled was more like it. ''And what exactly do you have a problem with, Sam? The fact that she asked the questions? The way she asked them?''

He bugged his eyes, unable to grasp that Mia couldn't see the wrongness of it all. ''I can't seem to make her understand that it's Jessica's pain and suffering I'm worried about, not mine. This has nothing whatsoever to do with me."

Mia fussed with the buttons on her blouse, avoiding eye contact and saying nothing. Her lips were pursed in that way that told Sam she had a lot to say but didn't plan on saying a word of it for fear of his wrath.

"What?" Sam spread his arms. "I know you have an opinion on this, so go ahead. God knows, the women I've been around lately aren't exactly holding back."

Mia peered up at him for several long, scrutinizing moments. "Everyone's pain and suffering deserves validation."

"Geez." He snorted. "Is that from some feel-good wall plaque down at the Hallmark store?"

Mia rolled her eyes. "Seriously. Have you ever talked with anyone about Jenny's death? About how *you* feel about Jenny's death, the fire, any of it?"

Sam hung his head back and stared at the ceiling, not liking the ninety-degree turn of this conversation any more than he'd enjoyed the discussion with Erin earlier that morning. He didn't need to be double-teamed right now. "Not you, too."

"There is absolutely nothing wrong with the question I just asked," Mia said, in a prickly tone. "It's a simple question about a complicated and emotional situation."

"Doesn't mean I want to talk about it."

She sighed and gentled her words. "Sam, I know

you're the strong, silent type, and I also respect that you're a private person. I'm not prying, nor am I asking you to talk to me. Unless you want to, in which case you know I'm always here.''

"I do know that.''

She dipped her chin and gave him a reproachful look. "But, maybe you should give this Erin a fair shot before you write her off. She's only been there a day, and although she's not the sweet, Gingersnap-scented Grandma you'd hoped for, she seems to have your best interests at heart—''

"I want her to have Jess's best interests at heart, that's the problem.''

"Your best interests *are* Jessica.''

She had a point. He rolled his shoulders uncomfortably. "Still. There is no sense in me discussing Jenny's death. I'm an adult. I can handle what happened better than Jessica can.''

"Says who?''

He spread his arms wide. "What's talking about it going to do—bring Jenny back?''

"Of course not, but that's not the issue.''

"I wish I knew the issue, then, because I don't see one.''

"Didn't you listen to what you just told me? All the questions Erin asked you were directly related to Jessica.''

He cocked his head to the side and narrowed his gaze. "How so? She seemed to be asking a whole lot about yours truly.''

"Yes. *Because* you're Jess's parent. And this Erin is also some sort of an expert with this kind of grief, right?"

"Right, but—"

"Humor me here." She held up a finger and moistened her lips. "Could it be that she knows a little something about the recovery process that you or I don't?"

His jaw ticked, but he nodded. Grudgingly.

"Well, then. Set limits with your sharing if you need to maintain your personal space. That's fine. But give Erin every advantage in working with Jessica the best way she knows how. Jessica deserves that much, Sam, and it's what you want." He started to protest or defend, he wasn't sure which, but she held up a hand. "Giving Erin total support in this might mean touching on uncomfortable topics for you. Buck up and accept it. You can take it. God knows, you've suffered through worse."

He chewed on that for a few. "I don't feel comfortable discussing my life with...the nanny."

"Ahhhh."

His gaze shot to her face and narrowed. "What's that supposed to mean?"

"Could it be—and I'm musing to myself, now— that you're simply looking for reasons to be dissatisfied with Erin because she's gotten under your skin a little bit?"

"Mia," Sam warned. His matchmaking secretary had been sniffing the romance trail since the moment he'd called and told her he hired a twenty-three-year-old, single, Irish beauty to care for Jess instead of the elderly woman he'd envisioned. "Don't even go—"

"Just food for thought, and the question was rhetorical anyway. I have my theories, you have your denials." She flicked her hand as though shooing away a fly. "Bottom line, though, is that Erin has a job to do and you shouldn't stand in her way."

"I'm not trying to."

"Then answer her questions."

Sam threw his arms up in the air. "Fine, fine. I'll try and be more…forthcoming if she corners me again."

"*Corners* you. Probably not the most effective way to frame the whole thing in your mind, but I've done all I can for one day." Mia flipped her feet off the file drawer and swiveled her legs under her desk. "Now, with that, kindly remove yourself from my office. I've got work to do, as do you, so put on a hard hat and get out there, will you? This place isn't going to run itself."

Sam shook his head and hid a half-admiring, half-exasperated smile as he donned his yellow hard hat and gathered his supplies for the workday. Fine, he'd talk to Erin a little bit. Clearly Mia saw it as a positive step toward helping Jessica, and he was all about Jessica. Plus, he trusted Mia's advice. She wouldn't lead him astray.

It wasn't until he was out on the site, contemplating Mia's words, Erin's questions, and his uncharacteristic capitulation in one big jumble, that he realized he'd been railroaded by females twice already that day, and it wasn't even 7:00 a.m.

After Sam had left, Erin took a quick shower and dressed in comfortable, staying-at-home clothes. Jessica was still sleeping, so Erin took the opportunity to walk through the house and acquaint herself with her surroundings.

The house was good sized and decorated in a comfortable, warm style neither too feminine or too masculine. The upholstered pieces sported a lovely plush, plum fabric and appeared big enough to sink into. The wood pieces were in a clean, Shaker style and stained a light cherry. From the lemon and pine scents, it was clear to Erin that everything had been freshly cleaned.

It should've seemed like a very inviting house.

But, something was missing.

Erin stopped in the doorway to the living room and rubbed her chin thoughtfully. She took in the oval shaped rag rug, the corner toy box. Studied the furniture and smiled at the angled sunbeams reaching through the south-facing windows.

Plants.

She peered around and spotted a healthy spider plant in one corner and a potted fern by the sofa. He didn't have a lot of plants, but he did have those two, and they didn't look beleaguered like so many plants in households without women. So, that wasn't the missing puzzle piece.

Erin moved further into the room and focused on the electronic equipment. A decent sized television, along with all the accompanying black boxes of modern entertainment, held court with a large stack of colorful children's videos in a sleek entertainment center. All very homey, very normal. So, what was it? What felt...off?

Turning her attention to the walls, it struck her like a blow. Sam had no family photos displayed. In her parents' house as well as each of her brothers' homes, framed family photos brought life to the walls and chronicled the passing years, the joy of family life. She was used to seeing that kind of thing, but in Sam's house...nothing.

Four framed photographs adorned the mantel, but they were all of Jessica. None of him, none of his late wife, and not a single photo of any cousins or uncles, grandparents, or other extended family. It struck Erin as rather sad.

Then again, not everyone liked to decorate with personal photographs, at least not in common areas. Surely Sam would have his study more personalized. Lucky for Erin, she had carte blanche to enter his private space and use the computer, and while she was there, if she happened to peek around for pictures, well, it wasn't really *snooping*. She was merely trying to get a handle on this very confusing, intriguing man.

She quickly refilled her coffee mug, then took the stairs two at a time. No staggered photos in the stairwell, she noted in passing. The upstairs hallway was similarly bare. She peered into Jessica's room, pleased to find the baby sleeping soundly, then moved on to the study.

A desk and credenza. Two bookshelves. Filing cabinets and a nice computer system.

No family photographs.

Intrigued, Erin sat in Sam's office chair and smoothed her palms over the hunter green leather desk blotter. One thing she could give Sam, the man was neat. But, some instinct deep inside her said there were more layers to Sam Lowery than met the eye. He might be a successful construction foreman with a strong work ethic, he was certainly a devoted father. But the Sam deep inside held secrets Erin couldn't begin to imagine.

She sat back, rocking in the office chair with her hands folded over her torso. He was a puzzle, and she was going to enjoy every moment of piecing him together. Another instinct, however, told her she'd be unwise to let him know he was as much her personal project as caring for Jessica was her job. Sam and Jessica had suffered a tragedy, losing Jenny, but Erin felt pretty sure that Sam had suffered loss long before the fire. What type, she didn't know, but she aimed to find out. Nonchalantly, of course. She didn't think the very private Sam Lowery would appreciate his nanny's scrutiny of his life, but hey, with five brothers, Erin was nothing if not stealthy. Sam Lowery would never know what hit him. And someday, if things went well, he might even thank her.

With a smile on her face, Erin booted up Sam's computer, hoping to knock out Jessica's schedule be-

fore the baby awoke and they started the day. She
was going to prove her worth to Sam no matter what
it took.

Sam arrived home that evening fully prepared to
buck up and replay the conversation with Erin, this
time answering at least the questions that didn't make
him feel sick to his stomach. He figured he could start
there; Jessica was worth it. He entered through the
mud room, like usual, removing his steel toed work
boots and shrugging out of his jacket. He paused, remembering suddenly that he'd forgotten to call Erin
about dinner, and a little knife of regret stabbed him.
He pressed his lips together and checked his watch.
It was past six anyway, but he could smell dinner
wafting on the air, and his mouth watered. It would've
been nice to share a meal with Jessica.

And with Erin.

The door into the kitchen was almost closed, and
the dryer tumbled and emitted the smell of fabric soft-
ener, which, combined with the enticing kitchen
smells, made coming home feel pleasurable for the
first time in a long time. He reached for the doorknob
and stopped short.

What was that sound?

He eased the door open slowly, cocked his head,
and listened. Laughter. Jessica's laughter mingling
with Erin's, and in the background, one of those
teeny-bopper singers playing on the stereo. Was it
Britney Spears? He smirked, shaking his head. Even
that music was preferable to entering a silent, dark
house night after night.

He walked on stocking feet through the kitchen and into the dining room. From there, he could see into the living room, where Erin and his sweet baby girl danced with wild abandon to the music. Both of their faces shone with happiness, and Jessica's cheeks were pink and chipmunk-chubby with her grin. A wild curl of poignant happiness twisted his middle. He didn't want the moment to end, and on the other hand he desperately wished he were a part of it. He crossed his arms and leaned one shoulder against the door jamb, hoping to watch them longer, but the hardwood floor beneath him creaked. Both Erin and Jessica spun toward the sound. Erin had a palm against her chest, eyes wide with alarm.

"Oh, you scared me."

"Daddy!" Jessica toddled toward him with her arms raised.

"Hi, honeypot." He bent and lifted her, planting big kisses on her face. He glanced up at Erin, twisting his lips to the side. "Sorry, I didn't mean to scare you."

"Me dance." She pointed toward Erin.

"Yes, I saw you. It looked like fun. Was it fun?"

Jessica nodded, then nestled her head on his shoulder. She smelled of baby powder, shampoo, and healthy exertion. His gaze lifted and locked with Erin's, and something raw and real clutched his insides. God, she was beautiful and vibrant and…so off limits. He swallowed hard. "Hi."

She ran her long, slim fingers through her hair and

laughed a bit self-consciously. "Hi. I didn't even know you were there. How embarrassing."

"Don't be embarrassed. You looked...free."

"Like someone who might drive a car named Daisy Mae?" She winked, then set about straightening the living room. There were toys, coloring books, puzzles, stuffed animals, and again, Jenny's framed photograph strewn everywhere.

"Definitely like that." He kissed Jessica and set her down and gave her a playful smack on the rear. "Help Erin clean up, honeypot." Jessic immediately squatted down and started picking up primary colored blocks. She was a good girl.

Erin glanced up from a stooped position. "There's meat loaf and mashed potatoes on a plate in the fridge. Vegetables, too." She crinkled her nose. "Are you a veggie eater?"

"I eat anything."

"I wish we could say that about the little miss, here."

"Yeah, vegetables are not her friends. She does like green beans, corn, and tomatoes."

"Okay. Good."

The living room was sufficiently neat, so Erin stood up and pressed two fists to her lower back. "Why don't you eat while I give the wee one a bath."

"Actually, if you don't mind, I'd like to tend to her bath and get her ready for bed. I feel like I haven't seen her for days."

"Of course. I'll just head off to my room, then, unless you want me to heat up your meal."

"No, Erin. You don't need to do that. Believe me, I've been taking care of myself for a long time." He scooped Jessica into his arms. "I'll eat after this one is down for the night."

"No!" Jessica protested, even though her little fists kept finding their way to her eyes to rub away the sleepiness.

"I've set bedtime for 7:45 p.m., if that's okay. She's a sleeper, this one."

"That's fine." He hitched her higher in his arms. "Did everything go well today?"

Erin nodded. "I've completed a schedule. It's posted on the fridge. We walked to the park, had a couple of naps, and got the laundry done."

Sam shook his head slowly, his approval for the nanny growing exponentially the more he was around her. He didn't want to feel these waves of affection and respect, but they just seemed to come without warning. "You're a pretty amazing person, Erin O'Grady."

Her face flamed immediately, and she cut her glance away. He could tell she was pleased by the compliment, though. "Thank you. It was easy. Jessica is a very amenable baby."

"She's my little honeypot."

Erin met his gaze directly. "I really think we're going to be able to work with her, Sam. It'll take time, but—"

"I'd actually like to talk to you about that. You caught me off guard this morning, but—"

"I'm sorry."

"No. It's okay. I'd like to talk to you more about it. Do you mind sitting with me while I eat dinner, so we can pick up where we left off?"

Erin's whole face lit up at this small concession, and darn if it didn't make Sam's heart lift. She had the knack of making a man feel like an absolute knight on a white horse. Danger.

"I'd love to. I'll meet you in the kitchen in about forty-five minutes?"

"Deal. See you there."

Erin was freshening up in her rooms when her private phone line rang. She checked the caller ID and smiled. It was Karla, from the agency. "Hello?"

"Erin! How are things going so far?"

She sank onto her bed and wrapped an arm around her torso. "Oh, I can't even tell you. Jessica is a great baby. We have so much fun together, and I can tell she's starved for female attention, poor doll."

"And what about Sam?"

Erin flopped back on the bed. "He's a tougher nut to crack, but I'm pretty determined."

Karla laughed. "I knew you'd be right for this job."

"Thank you for your faith in me."

"It's well-deserved, sweetie. Well, I just wanted to give you some moral support. I know it's hard taking a new assignment. And if you have any trouble at all—"

"Believe me, I'll call."

"Goodnight, Erin."

"Nighty-night."

After she'd hung up, Erin studied the texture on the ceiling and thought about Sam. Was there anything sexier than a man who did hard physical work all day long and slipped into daddy mode so easily the moment he entered the house? His well-worn jeans and fitted T-shirt molded to a body honed to perfection by hard work, not gym visits. His beard had started to come in, and his hair bore the telltale hard hat dent. But he'd cradled his baby daughter like she was made of spun sugar, and Erin didn't think anything in the world could be sexier.

How could she be crushing so hard on her boss this soon? She'd only just met the guy, but then again, she believed in love at first sight, kismet, soulmates— even faeries and sprites. She really was a hopeless, daydreaming romantic.

A light knock on the outer door to her wing startled her, and she shot up into a sitting position, heart lodged in her throat. "Yes?"

"Jess is out cold," Sam said, through the still closed doorway. "I didn't even get to read her a story. I know we said forty-five minutes, but if you're ready to talk, I'm ready to eat."

Erin fluffed her hair nervously. "I'll be right there." She waited until she heard him retreat, then stood, smoothing her moist palms along the legs of her jeans. Gosh, it felt like a freakin' first date. She needed to shake these schoolgirl jitters if she was going to be effective as Jessica's nanny—regardless of how sexy Jessica's daddy was.

As she brushed her teeth and slicked her lips with gloss, she decided the questioning method wouldn't work with Sam. Instead, she'd show him by example. She'd suffered a loss in her family, too, with little Bryce. If she opened up to Sam, maybe he'd reciprocate. Eventually.

Chapter Six

"This is really good," Sam told Erin almost sheepishly, after swallowing his first bite of meat loaf.

"Thank you." Erin flushed with pleasure at his words and fiddled with the cup of tea she hadn't really wanted, but had made for herself, anyway, so he wouldn't have to eat with an audience. She could see he was conflicted about "taking advantage" of her cooking skills. Clearly, Sam Lowery was a man unused to accepting help, and every step was going to be a struggle. She wondered if he knew how much information he telegraphed about himself just by *being* himself.

"No, thank *you*. You've managed to make a meal that Jessica and I can both enjoy. How'd you do that?"

"I told you, Sam, I have tons of nieces and nephews, and I'm the favorite sleepover aunt." She shrugged. "I know my way around a child's palate. They can be picky."

"Don't I know it."

Erin laughed softly. "I've learned ways to trick everyone. With a big Irish Catholic family like mine, it's almost inevitable that the adults and kids will eventually eat together, and the thought of making two separate meals is wholeheartedly unappealing, even to someone like me who likes to cook."

He inclined his head. "Well, my compliments to the chef."

Her pulse quickened, in part because Sam was so darn sexy without even trying. In part because she knew she had to bring up Jessica's treatment again, and doing so could snap the little thread of companionship that stretched tenuously between them. Now was her chance, though, and she had to take it. If she was going to broach this difficult topic, she'd have to do so with a believable and logical conversational segue. Sam might be a man who worked with his hands, but he was sharp of mind and wiser than his twenty-seven years might indicate. She wouldn't be able to railroad him, and didn't even want to. Games weren't her style.

She cleared her throat and tossed her hair. In as breezy a tone as she could manage, she asked, "What about you? Do you have nieces and nephews?" Her stomach plunged when Sam went very still, his eyes focused down on his plate rather than across the table toward her. She thought she saw his forearm tighten and wondered if she'd blundered again.

Finally, he glanced up. "Only child. Remember?"

"That's right. Well, bummer. I really enjoy my brothers' kids. I can rattle their cages, get them really riled up and then hand them over to mom and dad. It's awesome." She winked. "I consider it paybacks for the hell my brothers put me through on a yearly basis."

To her relief, Sam's muscles seemed to relax.

"Being an aunt is really cool." She was rambling and she knew it, but she needed to forge ahead into more dangerous territory before she lost his attention. Glancing across the kitchen toward Jessica's schedule posted on the fridge, she swallowed, then said, "And, it was nice to have a huge support system when little Bryce died." Her fingers tightened on the tea cup. "Does it bother you if I talk about it?" She ventured a peek at his face.

"Not at all," Sam said, continuing to eat, but with his focus firmly on her.

She squeezed her eyes shut as the whole unspeakable tragedy came rushing back as if it had happened yesterday. "It was awful, Sam. Unbearable, really. There were some days when I could hardly drag myself out of bed, and it was a million times worse for Eamon and Susan."

"Your brother and his wife? The parents?"

She nodded. "And the kids, too. But, Eamon is a typical first born, too. Know what I mean?"

Sam sort of shrugged, noncommittally.

"He felt like he had to keep the world spinning for everyone, even though he'd gone through the biggest crisis any parent can face." She shuddered involuntarily. "It took a lot of time to convince him that his feelings and grief were just as valid as everyone else's, but he finally released a lot of that. It felt good for me to be his shoulder to lean on."

Sam's eyes narrowed just slightly, but he nodded.

Her nerves were on edge, but he was listening. Good sign. "A-and, once he worked through some of his grief, it was like the whole family was able to do the same. It's a strange phenomenon, how family members look to one certain person in order to school their own reactions. But, sometimes people don't know exactly *how* to react after a tragedy. We all do our best."

"Erin?"

"Yes?"

"Are you, by any chance, talking about me here?"

Whoops, busted. Her throat constricted, but she was able to maintain her expression. "No, of course not. I'm talking about Eamon. And maybe about me, about how I came to do what I do. I…just want you to understand my motives better."

After a moment of looking suspicious, he nodded once.

Phew. She moistened her suddenly dry lips. "It was a real trial and error learning experience for me when Bryce died."

"I can't even fathom how any of you held it together."

Good, he was starting to talk, at least, and his suspicions seemed in check. "Sure you can. Grief is grief, and you seem to have held together just fine."

He cocked an eyebrow, but said nothing.

She cleared her throat and fiddled with the woven placemat at her spot. "So...did your family rally around you after...?"

An odd shadow moved across Sam's face, and for several long moments, Erin felt certain he wasn't going to answer. Getting through to Sam was like tiptoeing through a minefield in the pitch black of a moonless night. She never knew if her next step would be the fatal one.

Finally, he set his fork aside and wiped his hands on the napkin in his lap. "No."

"I'm sorry."

"Don't be. Just count yourself lucky to have all those brothers who annoy you so much. And parents who love you."

She wondered what that meant. Did he have unsupportive parents, even during a tragedy so large as a fatal fire? She couldn't imagine, but she knew examples of that kind of familial distance happened with disturbing frequency in today's society. "My parents are great. And, I really do love my brothers, the big, annoying lugs. I just wish they'd see me as a woman and not a little girl sometimes."

His gaze darkened into something that made Erin's tummy swirl. For a moment, she forgot her mission to get Sam to loosen up and found herself fully suspended in a net of attraction for this man. She could hear a subtle whir of the kitchen clock, the ticking of the dishwasher on the dry cycle. Most of all, she could hear and feel her blood pulsing through her veins and traveling to various pertinent parts of her body. Her response to a simple look from Sam left her off-kilter and disconcerted. Gosh, she was in trouble.

"I can't imagine anyone not seeing you as a woman," he drawled.

Her heart fluttered, and white-hot embarrassment rushed to her face. "Well, thank you, but—"

"Then again, if I was your brother, I'd probably protect you just as ferociously as they do."

Erin bit her lip and tilted her head to the side. "You're a good man, Sam Lowery. But, thank you very much, the last thing I need is another brother."

He snorted, scooting back his chair to stand up from the table, then turned to carry his dish to the sink. "Thank you again for dinner, Erin. I really appreciate it, and I certainly don't expect it."

"It's no problem." She settled in and listened to the comforting kitchen clean-up sounds for a moment…water from the faucet, the clink-clank of dishes and silverware in the stainless steel sink. With effort, she shook off her distracting attraction to Sam and decided, once and for all, she needed to broach at least one difficult topic head on. "Can I ask you something, Sam?"

His shoulders braced from behind, she noticed. "Shoot."

"Jessica carries around the photograph of her

mother, but she's never said a word about it. Even when I ask her directly, she simply doesn't answer. Has this been your experience?''

Sam placed his plate in the dish drainer, along with his silverware, then turned, drying his hands on a thick, white bar mop towel. ''Not exactly.''

''How so?''

He pursed his lips, then sighed. ''Honestly? She never touched that photograph until you came into our lives.''

Shock zinged through Erin, and she sat back. Blinking a couple of times, she shored up her composure. ''Really?''

''Yep. I don't know what to make of it.''

''Sam, I think that's a positive sign. She remembers, but maybe she doesn't feel able to talk about it. Maybe—'' she held up a hand ''—and this isn't, in any way, a commentary on you.''

He nodded once.

''But maybe having a woman here is sort of of…freeing her up to remember Jenny. To acknowledge that she misses the mother she loved so much.''

A pained look crossed his face, but he propped the heels of both hands on the counter at his back and set his chin. ''She did love her. And Jenny loved that baby enough to die for her.'' His voice went husky with pain. ''There's no greater love than that.''

Erin's eyes stung with tears, and she lifted her clasped fists to her chest. ''God, Sam, I'm so sorry.''

''I am, too.'' A tense beat passed. ''So, what do we need to do about Jess?''

Stunned that he asked, she didn't answer right away. Instead, she thought about it a moment, tucking her hair behind her ears so she could rein in her emotions. "Do you...can I have access to some additional photos of Jenny? Maybe you and Jenny, or Jenny and Jess?"

Sam got that oh-so-familiar distant look in his eyes and rubbed the back of one hand thoughtfully against his jawline. "For what?"

She shrugged one shoulder. "Well, to tell you the truth, I'm not sure yet. Maybe I can scrapbook them for you, or maybe she and I can just go through them. She just seems so attached to that one photograph, maybe it will help to see how she reacts to some others."

He crossed his arms over his chest. "And if it upsets her?"

"Then I'll stop immediately and try another path. You have to know I would never do anything to hurt Jessica," she implored.

The faint lines around his eyes from working out in the weather seemed to deepen. "I just want her to be happy."

"I want that, too. So much. And I want her to be free to express her emotions. About everything. It's so necessary to the healing process." *I want it for you, too, Sam.*

Their gazes locked, and Erin could sense his internal war. It almost made her feel guilty pushing him like this, but he'd hired her for her expertise and her ability to connect so easily with Jessica. She'd been through the overwhelming fatherly grief ordeal with Eamon and she knew this prodding needed to happen. If she didn't force the issue a little bit, he'd stay locked up forever, and if that happened, little Jessica would stay just as tightly wound.

Finally, he expelled a breath through his nose and looked resigned. "I'll pull the box of photos down from the attic before I turn in."

"Thank you." She breathed easier, and her shoulders relaxed. She hadn't even realized they were so tense. "I know this is difficult for you. Understatement."

A muscle in his jaw jumped, and he looked away.

"If things go well with the photographs, perhaps we can introduce some of Jenny's clothing into Jessica's life."

The wariness returned. "There's not a lot. The fire…there was smoke and water damage to a lot of…well, everything. Especially the things in our bedroom."

"But you have some?"

"Yes."

"Any of her favorite comfy clothes? A sweatshirt, maybe?"

"Yes," he said, his voice choked.

"I have some ideas I gathered after watching other children grieve for their parents." She flipped her hand. "But one step at a time. Let's save the clothing issue for another day. We can start with the photographs."

Sam eased his muscular neck side to side. "Okay."

He glanced at the wall clock, then pushed away from the counter and stretched. "I'd better get to it if I want to be worth a damn at work tomorrow. Four-thirty comes early." He headed toward the dining room, with a friendly but dismissive nod.

As he passed her, Erin reached out and touched his hand. "Sam, wait."

He stopped, turning toward her with trepidation clear in his expression, his body language, everything. He was a bundle of nerves around her, and she wasn't sure if it was because he didn't like her or because he *did* like her.

Hoping to ease his mind, she smiled. "Thanks for talking."

Sam rested his free hand on the doorjamb. He hung his head. "Look, I've never been much of a talker. But I want to do everything I can to help my daughter, and I know you're trying to help, too. I'm sorry if I was…"

"Stubborn?" Erin teased, lightly.

One corner of his mouth lifted. "Yeah, that. This morning. I don't mean to stand in your way with this."

"We have plenty of time, Sam. No harm, no foul." She grinned. "Deal? We're in this together, and having been through a major loss myself, I know there are going to be advances and setbacks along the way. Don't worry. I'm not expecting you to be superhero."

"That's a damn good thing. If there's one thing I'm not, it's a superhero."

"Oh, don't be so sure."

He studied her briefly, his eyes both expressive and searching. Hopeful and bleak. Vulnerable and yet incredibly strong. The rest of his expression remained inscrutable. "I'll go get that box and leave it here in the kitchen for you. Goodnight, Erin."

"Night, Sam."

It hadn't taken Sam long to find the box of photographs up in the attic, since he was the only person who'd ever been up there, but he hadn't quite made it all the way downstairs yet. Instead, he'd been sitting numbly on the edge of his bed with the box on his lap for—he glanced at the alarm clock—a little over half an hour. Sweat slicked his palms and his heart pounded out a dull, dread-filled rhythm in his chest.

He wanted to look.

He wanted to never look again.

Why was he so afraid to open the box? To revisit his life before the fire had left it in tatters? More guilt? Sad evidence of the family he could've built but didn't?

And, if he couldn't bear to confront the old photographs, why didn't he just take the box downstairs and leave it in the kitchen for Erin like he'd promised? This box held captured moments of his family life, short-lived as it was. He shouldn't be afraid of them, he should cherish them, but the notion left him cold and distant.

Without warning, Sam's thoughts veered sharply toward thoughts of Lissa and Adam, his *other* family. Little Mark, too, with his grave health problems. He even thought briefly of Jared Cambry, who could've been a father to him, to all of them, but thoughts of that man just made him clench his jaw. Sam hated to dwell on what could've been. But, sitting there alone in his room, with a wife gone and buried, a traumatized daughter, and siblings who didn't know he existed weighing on his mind, he couldn't help it. Things might have been so different for him if Cambry had stepped up to the plate after their young mother had been killed. Who knows, Sam might have even been part of a family like Erin's.

His hands balled into fists.

He had built a good life for himself and Jessica. He shouldn't be feeling this way, but he couldn't deny it. A seemingly bottomless well of sadness opened up inside him, sucking him in. He set the box aside and laid back on his bed, propping his hands behind his head. Above him, the ceiling swirled in and out of focus as he ruminated about the whole, incredible mess.

The last news article he'd read about the blissfully reunited Lissa and Adam said the doctors were still waiting to see if little Mark's body had accepted the bone marrow transplant. Sam had never given much thought to a rejection. An image of Jessica floated into his mind, and to his surprise, he felt a sharp surge of compassion for Jared Cambry and the rest of the family. His heart ached for any parent who might lose a child. He hurt for Erin's brother and sister-in-law, for the scare he had with Jessica on the night of the fire, even for Lissa and Adam…and for himself. But, he came to the realization that, no matter how bitter he was about having been abandoned by Cambry when he was a baby, he still couldn't wish for anything but good health for little Mark.

His brother. God, he was just a kid.

He squeezed his eyes shut and felt tears threatening. *God, let Mark Cambry live. Let...my little brother...live. Please.*

After several silent moments of prayer, a weight seemed to have been lifted from his soul, and Sam sat up slowly. With a little lingering trepidation, he opened the box of photographs and started sifting through them. Photos of him and Jenny at the Justice of the Peace. Their first Christmas, with the mother of all Charlie Brown trees. They hadn't even been able to afford lights, and all the ornaments were handmade, but he'd thought it was beautiful. In lieu of a stand, the forlorn little tree sat in a bucket of generic kitty litter and was anchored to a nail in the wall with a length of red yarn. It had been one of the best Christmases he could remember.

He pulled a particular snapshot from the stack and his chest squeezed until he felt like he couldn't breathe. Moving to the side of the bed, he studied it under the light of the bedside lamp. A hospital photo from the day Jessica had been born, after a grueling twenty-six-hour labor. Jenny looked exhausted, like she'd run a marathon...or been hit by a bus.

But she also looked happy.

He hadn't remembered her being happy for so long, but on this day, during this captured moment, she had been. On one day, at least, Jenny Lowery had been happy, and the knowledge brought him a small measure of solace. A melancholy smile lifted his mouth and thawed some of the ice encasing his heart.

Erin was right.

It would be good for Jessica to have an album of these photos. In general, people only photographed the good times in life, and it would certainly help his daughter to be able to see snapshots of happiness from a babyhood she wouldn't remember otherwise. Who knew? Having his short marriage and Jessica's first few months of life chronicled might be therapeutic for him, too. He wondered if Erin truly wanted to tackle the project. If so, he'd have to tell her to keep all the receipts so he could reimburse her for any costs. He'd probably have to assist with the sorting anyway. And if Erin wasn't up for it, maybe it was time for him to undertake the job himself, to stop hiding from the past and begin looking toward the future.

Feeling better, Sam returned the photos to the box and carried them down the stairs. He left them on the kitchen table with a short note.

"Erin—Here you go. If you truly want to work on an album with Jess, let me know and I'll buy whatever supplies you need. A lot of the photos are labeled by date, but I'll help you sort the others. Thanks. Sam"

For the first time in six solid horrible months, Sam slept soundly.

Chapter Seven

Erin's first week as a nanny seemed to fly by once she and Jessica had a project to work on together. They spent every morning until naptime sifting through the photo box, an activity as enjoyable for Erin as it was for Jessica, although at twenty-four months, she had a limited attention span. They worked in fits and spurts, which was fine. It allowed Erin to get lots of other things done around the house, and it also allowed her to scrutinize the photographs at her leisure during the times when Jessica lost interest.

Erin noted that Jenny Lowery often seemed overly serious in the photos. She wondered why. What kind of woman had Jenny been? And why weren't there any photos of extended family? Not a single picture.

Maybe they were kept in a different box; Erin couldn't be sure. But it would be nice to incorporate multiple generations in the scrapbook project. She thought about asking Sam about it, but decided she'd pressed enough for one week. Maybe later, when he trusted her more, the conversation would come more easily.

Afternoons were dedicated to trips to the park, playing Barbies, fingerpainting, doing puzzles, baking cookies, and other fun Jessica-focused activities. Occasionally, they'd spend a half hour or so on the photo book project. Through it all though, Jessica still wasn't talking about her mother. Not one word. She would happily exclaim "me!" or "daddy!" when she came across pictures of herself or Sam, but photographs of Jenny were set quietly aside in a private pile. No one but she touched the precious photos; Erin didn't even attempt to work them into the layout. The one time she'd reached for the stack, Jessica had snatched it away, holding it against her little chest while tears welled in her eyes. Erin asked Jessie light, nonthreatening questions about the photos, but all were met with absolute silence.

That was going to have to change.

The thing was, Sam needed to be the one to change it, but he was still as closed off as his daughter when it came to the topic of Jenny Lowery, and none of Erin's attempts to bring them out of their respective shells had been successful. She was beginning to think she might be a fine "surrogate aunt," but she was proving to be a mediocre grief counselor, despite years of school and personal experience. The whole debacle was disheartening, to say the least.

On Friday afternoon, after putting Jessica down for a much-needed nap, her beloved stack of pictures within clear view on her dresser top, Erin settled onto the couch with a cup of orange pekoe tea and dialed her sister-in-law, Susan. She'd reached her wit's end and needed a brainstorming session big time. Her usual methods were falling flat. Most days, she prepped dinner during Jessica's early nap, then finished it during her afternoon nap, but that morning while Jessica still slept, Erin had whipped together chicken chili in the crock pot. She had at least ninety minutes free to ponder her dilemma and come up with a new and better strategy.

Erin had always marveled at the fact that Susan had lost a child in a most heartbreaking way, and yet she was able to come back to a place of serenity and continue raising the other kids. She was an amazing woman, and if anyone could help Erin figure out this situation, it was Susan. The phone only rang once before her vibrant sister-in-law picked it up.

"Hey, Erin! How's the new job?"

"It's absolutely wonderful," she said, with slightly feigned enthusiasm.

"Hmmm. Sure doesn't sound like it."

"Am I that transparent?" Erin sighed, running her fingers through her hair. "In so many ways, it is wonderful. I wouldn't trade this job for the world. But I'm just not making the progress I'd hoped with Jessica. I have a lot of work to do to get this baby—and her father—past their locked up grief and onto the path of healing. I'm pulling everything out of my bag of tricks but everything fails."

Her selfless sister-in-law was always ready to lend a hand, and her voice turned all business. "How so?"

She filled Susan in on every aspect of the situation, then said, "I can tell that little girl has all her feelings about her mommy bottled up somewhere I can't quite reach."

"Of course she does. She was so little when it happened."

"Yeah. But if she doesn't let it out in a healthy way, it's going to explode out sooner or later." Erin bit her bottom lip, wondering about the wisdom of forging ahead with her query. She decided to go for it. "Listen, I know it's hard for you to revisit, but do you remember how we got the kids to start talking freely about Bryce? I mean, Kellan was about Jessica's age, and if I remember correctly, he opened up after I started working with you guys. I just don't remember exactly how we made that happen."

"It's not so hard for me to talk about, hon." Susan sighed, but it was a sigh of peace, of contentment. "I've come to a place where I can celebrate Bryce's life rather than feeling bitter about his death. I miss him every day, no doubt about that. And I'll never fully heal from the sheer trauma and pain of it. But, I think of Bryce and smile now, whereas I used to think of him and weep."

"You're an inspiration."

Susan laughed. "Get out. It's called living one's

life. I'm dedicated to living my life because my son was denied that privilege. I live for him. Besides, we wouldn't be anywhere near this level of recovery if it weren't for you, so you're the inspiration.''

"If I'm so great, what am I doing wrong here?" Erin flopped her head back against the plush uphol- stery of the sofa. "Sam—he's the dad—is still so closed off and self-protective. It's like he's always on guard. Without him, I can't get Jessica to open up. She takes every single emotional cue from him.''

"Of course. Is he completely uninvolved?"

Erin felt terrible, like she'd inadvertantly been bashing Sam. "Oh, not at all. He's a great father." Erin regaled her quickly about the scrapbook project. "I mean, he stretched his boundaries giving me the photo box in the first place, and he helps me sort photos into chronological order in the evenings. It's relaxed enough. Sam is—" She couldn't hold back a sigh. "—such an amazing man, really. A truly good guy.''

"But overly guarded?"

"Yeah. I have a sense his little fortress of emo- tional safety was erected long before the fire, though. That tragedy just reinforced the walls. I'm struggling so hard to get through to him.''

"How do you know?"

"How do I know what?"

"That he went through some kind of trauma before the fire. That's what you meant, right?"

"Yes." She ruminated a minute. "I can't really say. Getting to know him, I just have a sense about him. He's so self-protective and such a loner. A little haunted, I guess. He epitomizes the strong, silent type, and I'm sort of piecing his psyche together as I go. He sure isn't telling me anything without my handy Erin pry bar, and even then, the information is scant at best.''

Susan was quiet a moment. When she finally spoke, she was hesitant. ''You know, when Eamon was so closed off, nothing I did could bring him out.''

Erin frowned, confused by Susan's comment. ''I know. But he's your husband. Sam's my boss. It's a totally different situation.''

''Well…could it be that you're feeling a little something for this boss of yours? That you've become emotionally invested on a romantic level, and it's getting in the way of your work with the two of them?''

''What?'' Erin protested.

''Just listen. Caring deeply can do that sometimes. God knows, I wanted to help Eamon, but I just couldn't.''

Erin sat up straight, eyes bugged. Mostly because her sis-in-law was so darned astute…or Erin herself was completely transparent. That scared her. If Susan could see it, Sam would surely catch on sooner or later, and she'd die if he knew of her crush when he didn't feel the same. She didn't want to out-and-out lie to Susan, so she settled for a half-answer that held some truth. ''Susan, for goodness sake, I am not having an affair with my boss.''

''Of course not, hon. That's not what I meant.''

She paused, and her voice softened. "But, you are attracted to him, right?"

Erin groaned. Darn, intuitive women. "Ugh. How did you know? I can't hide anything."

Susan laughed softly. "Well, it is pretty obvious."

"That sucks."

"No it doesn't. But, all I can say is, you'd better work on your poker face tomorrow morning at brunch. You know they're all going to grill you anyway, but Eamon's back from his business trip and he'll watch you like a hawk. He'll see it, Erin."

"Yeah, what's new? It's the bane of my existence. I can't blush without people in three counties knowing it, I can't hold back my emotions, and I can't evade my brothers. I'm a mess."

"Not even. You're refreshing and charming. It's better than being locked up and closed in."

Erin slumped in her seat. "I guess."

"Hey, look at it this way. You like this Sam guy. You know and I know there is absolutely nothing wrong with attraction between two consenting adults. Right?"

"Right, except my attraction isn't reciprocated."

"Give it time."

Erin bit her lip and tamped back a bit of hope. "You really think so?"

"Sure. Why not? But, for now, hide it. If your brothers get an inkling that you have a crush on your very eligible boss, they'll make your life miserable."

"They already do make my life miserable," Erin

said, with a grudging smile. "The jerks." A worrisome premonition tickled her spine. "Maybe I should skip brunch."

"That would be even worse, and you know it. Plus, the kids would really miss you."

"Good point. I'd miss them, too. I miss them already! But enough about my ill-fated and nonexistent love life. What about getting this little baby to open up about her mother?"

"Erin, I reiterate my advice. Give it time. Give Sam time, too. You've been there, what? A week?"

"Yes."

"You're trying to undo six months worth of pain and grief, and one week isn't going to cut it. Just relax."

Erin twisted her mouth to the side, wondering how much she should share. Sam was such a private person, and she didn't want to breach that confidence. Then again, if she could confide in anyone and have it go nowhere, Susan was the person. "You know, sometimes I get the feeling that family just isn't important to Sam, but then I see him with his daughter and I know that's not true. Well…at least with her. But he never talks about other family. Ever. Not even his late wife, if you can believe that. I just can't figure the guy out."

"So, don't try. If anything, show Sam how important family is by using our family as an example. Subtly, of course."

Erin tilted her head to the side and considered the advice. "That's a good idea, actually."

"Of course it is. That's why you called me," Susan teased. "I'm full of good ideas about how to fix other people."

Erin laughed. "So true."

"Bottom line, little sis, enjoy that baby girl and give her lots of love and hugs. She'll come out of her shell eventually. I can't imagine anyone resisting you forever."

Erin felt warmed by the love of her family. "And Sam?"

"Well, hey," Susan said, wryly, "if you get the opportunity to give him love and hugs, too, I say go for it. You're a modern woman, and it's high time you found the man of your dreams. Or at least *did* the man of your dreams."

"Susan! That's not what I meant." But Erin's tummy flip-flopped at the thought, and mental pictures of showering Sam with love and affection left her distracted and grinning like the village idiot. Her brothers were so intimidating to any possible dates, she didn't even have experience with men. Oh, what a joy it would be to gain that experience with Sam. "But, what a decadent, wonderful thought."

"I have to go," Susan said, through a laugh. "Kellan is wailing like he just lost a limb in a wood chipper, but I'm sure he just lost a toy to his brother. Kids." She sighed. "Call me any time you need to commiserate, okay? I'm here."

A horrible thought entered Erin's head. Didn't husbands and wives share everything. "But, don't—"

"Not to worry. I wouldn't rat you off to your

brother, hon, whether he's my husband or not. If it was up to the O'Grady boys, you'd be safely in the convent already.''

''How did you know that's what I was going to say?''

''Duh.''

Erin breathed easier and also found herself cheered by Susan's intuitive sense. ''Thank you for understanding.''

''Understanding?'' Susan laughed again. ''Hey, your brothers may keep you in a glass box like some untouchable princess, but your sisters-in-law have your back, girl. Don't forget that. And don't forget us when the wedding rolls around, either. No ruffles on the gowns!''

''Oh, be quiet!'' Erin chastised. But, she hung up with a smile on her face, the glow of familial love in her heart, and a renewed hope that she could make a difference with Jessica and, God willing, with Sam, too.

It had taken a full week of Erin's exuberant, nurturing presence in his world, but by Friday, Sam reluctantly admitted to himself that he enjoyed coming home to help her and Jessica with the scrapbook project—almost too much. Not that he did much more than put things in chronologial order, but still. It was getting easier and easier to look through the photos and remember the good times rather than focusing on the loss or the guilt, which seemed sort of amazing when he thought about it. He hadn't been able to get to that point for six months, then Erin shows up and things start to change in a matter of one week.

Most surprising of all, he simply looked forward to coming home now. Walking into a house redolent with the aromas of home cooked meals, soft lighting, and the sounds of music, laughter, and baby chatter smoothed out the sharp edges of a life that had always felt so cutting. Erin was like a sunbeam, warming and lighting the dark corners of his world.

He could seriously get used to the routine.

He found himself secretly glad that Erin wasn't involved in a relationship at the present time—not because he was interested himself, of course. He'd sworn off love and meant it. But, any smart guy would recognize the gem he had in Erin and secure a ring on her finger before she could blink. The happy couple would be off to the church, and he and Jessica would be back to square one. Alone. Floundering in the cold and dark.

He knew these thoughts were unfair. More than anyone, Erin deserved to find love and start that family she had her heart set on, but he didn't want to let her go now that she was here. He hoped she realized she had plenty of time. She was a young woman, only two years older than he'd been when he married Jenny, and Jenny had been a mere nineteen at the time. Looking at it from his current perspective, they'd been veritable children, far too young to take on the daunting task of marriage and family. Certainly he would've waited to marry until he was older if he hadn't been so damned lonely and alone.

He didn't want Erin to make the same mistake, rushing into a marriage before she'd gotten to fully know herself.

Who are you trying to kid, Lowery?

Altruism aside, he was beginning to need Erin, in so many ways. Not just for Jessica—although Erin's caring for his daughter had lifted a huge burden from his shoulders—but for himself as well. In the evenings after Jessica was down for the night, he and Erin had taken to sitting in the kitchen chatting about the day's events. If Erin had been too busy to clean up, they shared the task. If not, he sipped a cup of coffee or a beer, while she indulged in her favorite citrusy-scented herbal tea and regaled him with...well, anything and everything, if he thought about it.

Erin, in fact, did most of the talking. But, never having been much of a conversationalist, he preferred it that way. He loved the melodious tone of her voice, her easy windchime laughter. And he liked listening to all the stories about her full, fun days with his precious Jessica. Through the ages, men could never reach a consensus about the sexiest aspect of women, but he was beginning to think there was nothing sexier than a woman who loved a man's child like Erin loved Jessica.

He enjoyed hearing about her big, colorful family, too, although she didn't talk about them too much. In a way, he lived vicariously through her. Her life seemed foreign and exotic to him, but unfortunately, hearing about her siblings made him think about his own. He knew Adam and Lissa both had recently married their true loves. Soon they'd start families of their own, adding another layer to his secret, another level to something he'd never have. Not only was he a brother, but he might very soon be an uncle. The thought was, frankly, overwhelming.

Thankfully, he and Erin had moved away from the really hard topics—like his feelings—and he appreciated that, too. He'd learned young that being under the microscope's probing lens was not a place he enjoyed, so he'd honed his aloof, private persona until it had become second nature, until it had become the core of who Sam Lowery was. Erin was the first person ever to almost crack through it, and he had to admit, that made him nervous.

But, he still loved their lopsided conversations. Oftentimes, he had a hard time breaking away to go to sleep, even knowing he had to be up at the crack of dawn to start the grind all over again. Sleep deprivation was worth spending time with Erin O'Grady. He could listen to her talk forever, could stare into her brilliant blue eyes and bask in the warmth of her endearingly crooked smile until the sun came up and beyond. Oh yeah, he had it bad for Erin O'Grady, as much as he struggled against it. Her vibrancy was like a vortex, pulling him toward her every time they were together.

Luckily, he'd been able to keep his wholly inappropriate attraction under wraps, despite how long it had been since he'd shared intimacy with a woman. He couldn't say he didn't entertain notions of taking things a step further with Erin, wouldn't deny he fantasized about making love to her in the dark privacy of his own room at night, but he'd been able to resist. All he had to do was think of Erin's brothers and their low expectations of him—and any other guy interested in their baby sister—and he was able to say goodnight and escape to his bedroom without giving in to the singularly powerful urge to taste those beautiful lips of hers, to touch her skin.

It made for some relentless toss-and-turn nights, but at least his conscience didn't have another black mark on it.

His confusing feelings warred inside him that Friday as he pulled his truck into the garage. He sat in the cab for a moment, listening to the hot tick of the engine and strengthening his resolve to keep things professional. He was so glad to be home, he wanted to run up those steps and call for Erin and Jessica, pull them both into his arms and rain kisses on their faces. Bad choice. He could shower affection on his daughter all he wanted, but when it came to Erin, polite, platonic distance was his only choice.

Once he'd tamped down his eagerness enough to stay in control, Sam entered the house the same as always, but to his surprise, Erin and Jessica were waiting for him in the mudroom doorway, all smiles and shining eyes. His stomach contracted painfully, and he stopped short and glanced around. "What's with you two? Did someone win the lottery?"

"Daddy!" Jessica exclaimed, toddling over and lifting her arms toward him.

He swung her into a big bear hug, planting kisses on her face and reveling in the feel of her embrace. "How's my honeypot? Were you a good girl for Erin?" As per usual, she didn't answer, choosing instead to nestle her sweet smelling head into his neck. He glanced up at Erin, cocking one eyebrow questioningly.

"She was a perfect little girl, like always." She bounced on her heels, something she did when she was holding in good news, he'd come to learn. "And we have a great surprise."

"Yeah? What's that?"

"We finished the scrapbook," she said, with the same pride she might've shown for winning a marathon. Her face absolutely glowed with excitement. "Well, the first one, at least."

"That's great. I didn't realize there'd be more than one." He gave Jessica one last kiss on the top of the head, then set her down. She immediately became occupied with a used dryer sheet that had fallen onto the mudroom floor while he stooped over to remove his dusty, muddy workboots.

"Yeah, there will be a second one," Erin said, rather cryptically. "I hadn't planned for it to be that way, but…" Her eyes darted to Jessica. "We can talk about it more later."

Her words sent up a red flag in his mind, but he wanted to revel in the moment and worry about any problems as he came to them. "Okay." He stood and glanced over her shoulder toward the kitchen, inhaling deeply. "Something smells great. Did you cook again?"

Erin rolled her eyes playfully. "Don't pretend you're surprised. Need I remind you, I've cooked dinner every night since I've been here? Except that first night, when we had pizza."

"Yes, but—"

"I don't have to. I know, I know. We've been over this." She winked, beckoning him in with a sweep of her arm. "Come on. Let's eat before it gets cold."

He couldn't argue with that. His stomach growled in response to the enticing scents wafting out from the kitchen, and the whole tableau of "welcome home" warmed his soul. "What's on the menu tonight?"

"Chicken enchiladas, salad, and, to satisfy the sweet tooth in you, double chocolate layer cake."

Sam groaned, shrugging out of his jacket and moving over to the sink to wash his hands. "You know, if you keep this up, I'm going to get used to it."

"One would hope. Then you might stop telling me daily that I don't need to cook."

"That won't happen."

Erin looked pleased. "It's a celebratory dinner, anyway. When we're done, we'll unveil the scrapbook."

"Sounds really great, Erin," he said sincerely. "Thank you." He indicated his work clothes. "Do I have time to change? I hate to come to a special dinner with construction dust ground into my clothes."

Erin crossed her arms and tapped her foot playfully. "Oh, if you must, but hurry up."

Sam raised his eyebrows and stifled a smile. He liked the playful ease of their interactions. Such a change in a week. He'd gone from guarded to greedy for her attention. He wondered if she could read that about him and hoped not.

Forty minutes later, they'd finished the excellent dinner and had moved into the living room for the presentation of the scrapbook. Jessica's attention waned pretty quicky, so Erin laid down a nap mat and blanket in front of the television and popped in *Mulan,* Jess's favorite video du jour. When the baby was settled in and drowsy, Erin sat next to Sam on the sofa with a thick, maroon book clutched to her chest.

She peered over at him expectantly. "Okay, here it is. I hope you like it."

"I'm sure I'll love it." He held out his hand, tapping his fingers to his palm in a give-it-up motion. His heart began to pound, though. Sure, he'd grown more used to viewing the photos each day when he'd helped Erin sort them, but seeing them like this—a chronology of his married life—set his nerves afire.

Erin took in one big breath and released it, then presented him with the book. His throat constricted, and he took a moment to marvel about the fact that, less than a week earlier, he wasn't sure he could look at these photos ever again. The change wasn't his doing, for sure. He couldn't have reached this point without Erin's gentle prodding.

Bracing himself, he opened the cover.

"Daddy & Jessica" read the title page, in colorful cutout letters and framed by little matching squiggles and swirls. What about Jenny? he wondered. He peered over at Erin, but her gaze stayed firmly on the book. She had one corner of her bottom lip clamped between her teeth, and she looked uncharacteristically nervous.

Sam pushed away his confusion, cleared his throat, and turned the page. The photos, decoratively framed with pink, green, and yellow cutouts, were all of Jessica as a newborn. He smiled. "Isn't she a doll?"

"Oh, yes."

He turned the page again to find photographs of himself. Next page, photos of him and Jessica together. A curious frown bisected his brow, and he peered up to meet Erin's cautious gaze. "Where are the pictures of Jenny?"

Erin tilted her head toward Jessica, who was sucking her thumb, lids heavy, and rapidly heading toward dreamland. "Later," Erin said softly. "After she's asleep, we'll talk."

Worry pricked at Sam's soul. It obviously wasn't anything serious, or Erin wouldn't have thrown the celebratory dinner, but he still worried. When it came to anything having to do with his daughter, he always worried. He couldn't seem to help it. Hadn't Mia told him he acted like a mother to Jessica? Hey, he didn't take that as an insult. Quite the contrary.

"Is everything okay?" he whispered.

Erin's gaze slanted toward Jessica and back. "In a

global way, yes. But...well, give it a few minutes, and I'll try and explain.''

Sam nodded once and continued perusing the book. It didn't take long before Jessica's eyes were closed, her breaths coming steadily through a slightly opened mouth. She looked like an exhausted little angel who'd tucked her wings away for the night. Sam set the scrapbook aside and stood. "Let me just get her off to bed," he said in a quiet tone.

"Okay. Can I get you anything?"

"You've done enough for one night, Erin. Just re-lax."

"Relax? What's that?" she teased.

He scooped Jessica gently off the floor, waking her just enough so she could squawk her meek, sleepy protests. He started off toward the stairs with Jessica resting against his chest, but suddenly she reached out over his shoulder. "Erin, night-night."

Sam held her from him slightly. "What, honey-pot?"

"Erin go night-night." She stretched her little arms toward Erin and whimpered a little. It reminded him of the day Erin came for her interview, which seemed light years ago. Even then, Jessica had demonstrated an unusual attachment to Erin. The woman was like the pied piper of kids.

Sam pressed his lips together for a moment, but turned toward Erin. It's not like he could blame Jessie for falling in love with her. "Care to join us for a tuck-in?" he asked.

Erin sat forward on the couch, her eyes troubled

but hopeful at the same time. "Oh, Sam. I don't want to infringe on your routine or your time alone with her."

"Erin, go night-night," Jessica said again, more demanding this time. She was starting to wake up fully, and neither of them wanted that.

Sam smiled gently. "It looks like you've been outvoted. And it's okay. I don't mind."

"Really?"

"Really."

"I'd love to, then." Grinning at the baby, Erin stood and smoothed her palms down the sides of her jeans. She grabbed a packet of photographs in a plastic bag, waggling them at Jessica. "Okay, little miss. Let's go night-night."

Satisfied, Jessica relaxed against her father's shoulder, and together, the three of them ascended the stairs.

Sam might've been imagining it, but he could sense Erin's heat behind him. Her perfume wafted in the air, something vanilla and youthful. It felt right, he and Erin carrying Jessica up to her crib. He couldn't help but think, this is the way it's supposed to be. Two people who love a child, a man and a woman, tucking her in for a night of sweet dreams.

For the second time that evening he thought to himself, *I could certainly get used to this,* and it sobered him. Sure, he could, but he needed to resist the urge. He absolutely, positively had to pull back from Erin's magnetic draw. The last thing he wanted was to hurt her, and giving in to his attraction when their relationship was a guaranteed one-way ticket to hurtsville was one hundred percent wrong.

She wanted forever.

He wanted never again.

If that wasn't a big enough indication that they weren't meant to be, he didn't know what was.

Chapter Eight

It was probably ridiculous, but Erin could think of nothing sexier than a man who adored his child like Sam obviously loved Jessica. She'd been flattered to be included in the bedtime ritual for the first time, but she hadn't expected it to affect her feelings for Sam so profoundly. Before they left the nursery, she made sure to set up Jessica's stack of mommy photos where the baby could see them if she needed to, and then it took everything within her to walk on wobbly legs down the stairs, all while acting like everything was status quo.

Sam walked behind her, and a crazy part of her wanted to stop and just lean into his chest. She straightened her back and sped up.

"What's your hurry?"

She laughed nervously. "Oh, I just want to get things cleaned up and ready for you for the weekend, so you can enjoy your time with Jessica."

"I appreciate that, but you've done enough for one week. Let's talk instead and I'll clean up later."

"O-okay. I hate to leave a mess, though."

"I've got to meet this mother of yours," Sam joked, wryly.

"Well, she did have a big influence on me when it comes to housework." She flashed him a smile.

Sam settled back onto the sofa, so Erin chose an armchair across the room. Juvenile, she knew, but she didn't think she could trust herself sharing the same piece of furniture with the guy at the moment. Hey, she was only so strong, and he had her emotions in a delicious tailspin.

"So," he said, crossing one ankle over the opposite knee, "what's with the multiple albums? Something to do with that stack of photos you left on Jessie's dresser, I assume?"

Erin sighed, running a hand through her fiery hair. "Yes. She seems to be hoarding the photographs of Jenny."

He cocked his head to the side. "Hoarding them?"

"Yes. She pulls them out and keeps them in her private stack, then carries them around all day. I've tried to talk to her about them, but—"

"She doesn't respond."

Erin sat back in the chair and nodded regretfully. "Nope. And don't even try to take them from her."

Sam pondered this, feeling somehow like it was his

fault. Again. "Do you think it's just going to take time? I mean, she hasn't seen but the one photograph since that night."

Erin tilted her chin down and gave him a direct stare. "I think…Sam, I think you need to talk to her about the photographs. Not just the photographs, but about her mother."

"This again, huh?"

"Yes, this again. Let her know it's safe to love them—and Jenny—but also safe to let them go. Enough to preserve the pictures in a book and to mourn her mother however her emotions dictate. Then she can enjoy the album every day if she wants, and she can feel however she feels about her mother without thinking it's wrong or bad. Plus, the photos won't get damaged from being carried around."

Sam's eyes clouded over, and for a moment Erin thought she'd lost him. She'd said her piece, so she just waited.

He covered his face with both hands, pulling them down slowly. "God, I really messed things up by not talking about Jenny with her, didn't I?"

A rush of compassion filled Erin, and without worrying about her earlier skittishness, she moved to sit next to him on the couch. "No. You did what you needed to do, and there is no crime in that. Don't berate yourself."

He looked weary, older. "I don't know how to do it. I don't even know how to talk about her to…you. Or anyone."

Erin laid a palm on his knee. "It's okay. Just take

your time. Speak from the heart. You have all week-end. Well, frankly, you have your whole life, but…I'm sorry to push so much…the sooner the better. Jessica is fine on the surface, but she needs to learn that emotions are okay to express, even if they're difficult." A beat passed, during which she searched his face. "That's going to be up to you."

"Can I just tell her?"

"You have to show her."

Sam's conflicted gaze raised. He hated to ask for help of any kind, in fact he rarely did. But this situation was beyond him. "Will you help me figure this out? I've held my emotions in for so long, I hardly know how to show them."

"Of course, Sam. I'll do anything. But I think you'll be surprised. You're showing emotion right now. You just need to let it carry over into every part of your life." She gentled her tone. "Were your parents the unemotional sort?"

"Oh, Erin," he said, blowing out a breath. He sat forward, elbows on his knees, fists clasped beneath his chin. A muscle in his jaw flexed, and his eyes looked distant and haunted. Something told Erin to sit quietly and wait. If Sam wanted to talk, she needed to give him the room to do so.

"We weren't getting along, Erin."

She gulped. "You and…your parents?"

He shook his head. "Jenny and I," he answered, through gritted teeth. "Not just on the night of the fire, but for…God, for years before that. I can't believe I'm even saying this. She's dead and buried, for God's sake.''

''It's okay.'' Surprise zinged through her. He'd seemed so torn up about his wife's death, she felt sure he'd lost the love of his life. To learn it was otherwise came as a shock. But did anyone really know what went on behind the closed doors of a marriage? ''I'm sorry, though.''

Without acknowledging her words, he went on. ''I was working overtime the night of the fire. I didn't have to, but...man, this is hard.'' He grimaced, and his handsome face looked suddenly haggard and guilt-etched.

''It's okay. Take your time.''

''I didn't want to be home,'' he said simply, turning to look at her directly. ''There's the plain, ugly truth. Jenny wanted me home that night, and I told her I had to work mandatory overtime on the job.''

''Well, you can't help it if you had to work.''

''It wasn't mandatory.''

Erin swallowed, trying very hard not to move. She felt a thud of realization in her gut, but didn't want to do anything to interrupt Sam's revelations.

''I told Jenny I didn't have a choice about working when I actually did. Overtime was voluntary, and I rushed to volunteer, just so I didn't have to be home. That night she died saving our daughter.''

''Sam...I'm so sorry. Can you tell me...what happened?''

Sam's Adam's apple jumped a few times, and he curled his hands inward, rubbing the knuckles together. "From the fire investigation, it all started with a candle. Jenny—" His voice caught, and he pressed his lips together until he'd regained his composure. "Jenny loved candles. Burned them all the time. So much that, at eighteen months, Jessica already knew not to go near them. I hate the damn things."

Erin made a mental note to never burn candles in his presence again. She tried not to feel guilty for burning the utility candle during their first dinner together. This wasn't about her. She reached out and clasped Sam's hand in a show of support, and he allowed it.

"She and Jessica must've fallen asleep on our bed. There was a video, *Mulan,* melted in the VCR in our bedroom. I was so surprised when you put it in tonight."

"That's Jessica's favorite movie," Erin blurted.

Sam looked at her sharply. "So I noticed. She hasn't looked at it since the fire. I bought her that new copy, but—" He shrugged.

"Wow, Sam. She picked it out the first day I was here with her, and we've watched it every day since." They were both silent for a moment. "But, please, go on. I didn't mean to interrupt."

Sam nodded once. "By the time the smoke woke Jenny up, the carpet was on fire, blocking the bedroom door. There was no way out except the window." His eyes searched Erin's, and she found she was holding her breath. "We lived on the third floor."

"Oh, no." Erin released the breath in a rush and let her eyes flutter closed for a moment.

"Things may not have been perfect between Jenny and me, but God, Erin. She stood in that thick black smoke, with flames licking at her back, and held my daughter out the window until a firefighter got close enough to catch her, and then she dropped her to safety. By the time they got Jessica down and into the care of the paramedics, then went back up that ladder, Jenny was unconscious. They got her out and rushed her to the hospital, but her lungs were so burned and filled with carbon monoxide, she never recovered. She died saving Jessica. There is no bigger sacrifice a parent can make, and despite her faults and our disagreements, Jenny made that sacrifice."

"Sam..." Erin didn't know what to say.

"And I was at work. A little white lie, mandatory overtime when it wasn't mandatory. As a result, Jenny died a horrible death alone."

Erin squeezed his hand harder. "That fire wasn't your fault. You can't lay that kind of guilt trip on yourself."

Sam pulled away and stood, pacing the living room. "I should've been home. I was forever blowing out candles when Jenny left them burning." He clenched his fists. "I could've prevented the fire, or I could've found an escape route for Jenny, some-thing. I could've done something, Erin." He spun to face her, his face ravaged, his chest rising and falling with ragged breaths. "I didn't love her anymore, but I didn't want her dead. And yet, she is. Jessica's mother is dead because of my selfish choices. I've had to live with that for six months, and I'll have to live with it forever.''

"Oh, Sam." Erin did the only thing she knew to do, she did exactly what anyone in her family would do. She stood and crossed the room, wrapping Sam in a hug. "You can't blame yourself for what happened."

"I can. I do."

"But it wasn't your fault."

He snorted. "So you say. Want to know the worst part? I don't even know if I can tell you this."

"You can tell me anything."

He visibly struggled, clenching and unclenching his fists, which remained at his sides. "When I'd heard that Jenny died and Jessica lived, for a split second I was relieved it wasn't the other way around. I'm a monster, Erin."

"No, you aren't. You can work past this. I can help you." She felt his arms come around her and hold on, and it bolstered her courage.

"I don't know how. I don't know how to atone."

"You don't need to atone, Sam. You aren't a monster, you're human. You need to heal." Erin's heart thudded, but this was her perfect opening. "And you can do so by helping Jessica heal. Imagine how it was for her."

"Believe me, I imagine it every day."

"Then help her," she whispered.

"How?"

Erin pulled back, looking up into his tormented

face. "Talk to her about her mother. Talk to her about how much you miss Jenny, even if you don't."

"I do, just not—it's hard to explain."

"You don't owe me an explanation. But, Jessica." Erin shrugged. "Open the door for her to miss her mother, too. It's obvious she does, but she's holding it all in. That's not healthy for any person, but especially a little person."

After a moment, Sam pulled her back into a hug. They stood in silence, rocking in the embrace. Erin could feel his warm breath on the top of her head, the heat of his muscles through his T-shirt. She closed her eyes, reveling in the feeling, wanting it to never end.

"You're an amazing person, Erin O'Grady."

"So are you. And you're an amazing father. Don't you dare think otherwise."

Sam took his time reining in his emotions, but finally he released his grip on Erin and set her away gently. "Thank you for listening. I haven't told anyone…about that night. It's a bit of a relief to…admit it all."

"I'm honored you chose me."

"To dump on." He got a pained expression. "I'm sorry about that. I didn't mean—"

"Don't ever apologize for feeling, Sam." She smiled at him gently. "You're allowed to feel whatever you feel."

His eyes searched her face until his expression went from ravaged to resigned, then finally he reached out and tucked a lock of hair behind her ear. "Are you busy tomorrow night?"

Erin's heart jumped to her throat, and she blinked a couple times. "Um...no. I have brunch with my family in the morning, but my evening is free." A pause. "Why?"

"I'd like to take you to dinner. As a thank you for this week, for the scrapbook. And...maybe we can talk about how I can go about helping Jessica." He twisted his mouth to the side. "I know I can be stubborn, but I want that more than anything in the world, you know."

Erin smiled tenderly again, her heart taking flight. "I do know that. And I'd love to go to dinner."

Sam nodded once. "Good. I'll call my secretary to babysit. Mia will jump at the chance. She misses Jess so much now that she's not coming to the worksite anymore."

"I can imagine." Erin smiled. "She's a pretty amazing little person, your Jessica."

Sam's eyes darkened in a way that made Erin's tummy swirl. He reached out slowly, almost touching her cheek. She could almost feel his work-roughened hands on her face, and her skin tingled in anticipation. At the last moment, he seemed to think better of his actions. He curled his fingers against his palm and pulled away, stepping back. His eyes darted around. "I should go to bed."

"Me, too."

There they stood, strands of the unsaid stretching and buzzing between them like power lines, zapping them to the spot. He watched her. She watched him. Tension vibrated all around them, and some unspoken connection held them like a tether.

"Erin."

Suddenly, Erin could see her dream future laid out before her. Sam loving her and Jessica. More children, lots of them. She was way out of control with her fantasizing after just one week on the job, and she stumbled backwards into the reality of what was happening. This attraction wasn't real. Sam was merely grateful she was helping him and his daughter. She needed to keep things in perspective or risk a broken heart.

Sam reached out to catch her, leaving his hand wrapped loosely around her upper arm after she'd regained her balance.

"I-I'm sorry," she stammered. "Clumsy. I…should go."

He released her…but the action seemed reluctant. "Thank you for everything. And please, don't clean up the kitchen or anything else before you turn in. I mean it. You've done so much for us already."

Gratitude. It's just gratitude, Erin.

"I'll take care of it."

"Okay." She ducked her head, heat rising to her face. She'd agree to anything just to escape this moment where her feelings were undoubtedly plain as printing on her face. She was all about showing feelings, but she did not want to embarrass herself in front of this man. "Night, Sam."

"Goodnight, Erin."

"Sleep well."

He released a signature Sam almost-laugh. "Oh, I don't think there is much chance of that."

As she walked on wobbly legs toward her room, she wondered if she'd merely imagined the double entendre in his words.

"What's this I hear about you working for a single man?" asked Eamon the next morning, after he'd cornered her by the tea kettle when she'd gone for a refill. It was the first chance they had to talk in three weeks, since he'd been out of town.

Erin stood on tiptoe and planted a big, noisy kiss on his cheek. "Nice to see you, too, big bro."

Eamon pretended to be grossed out, making a big show of wiping the kiss away. "I mean it, Erin. If I'd been in town when you got that interview—"

"But you weren't," she told him firmly, popping a piece of cinnamon roll into her mouth. After chewing and swallowing, she said, "And your cohorts in crime went over and interrogated him before I moved in, much to my abject horror, so you have no basis for argument. Besides, he's a nice guy."

"Hmph." Eamon snagged a piece of the communal cinnamon roll and ate it himself. "I'd still like to meet the guy and be the judge of that myself."

Erin planted her fists on her hips and lifted her chin. "Maybe someday you will, Eam, but only if it happens in the natural course of things. He's already suffered the O'Grady male presence once. You're not going to put him—or me—through it again. I'm just starting to get in the groove of the job, and I don't want you messing it up.''

He frowned. ''When did you get so uncooperative?''

''Don't you trust me, Eam?''

''I do.'' He sighed, then pulled her into a hug. ''I just want the best for you.''

Erin gave him a squeeze, then pulled away. ''I know you do. But, listen. This job isn't about Sam. It's about his two-year-old, Jessica.'' Okay, so it wasn't entirely true, but Eamon didn't need to know that. Over the week, it had become as much about the man as the child.

Eamon's stony expression eased. ''Susan told me what they went through. I'm really sorry about that.''

Erin leaned her hip against the counter. ''Yeah. I'm hoping I can help them.''

''If anyone can, sis, it's you.'' Eamon grabbed her around the neck and gave her a giant noogie.

''Cut it out!''

He released her, then bent and kissed her on the cheek. ''Just be careful and be smart. And, I'd still like to meet the guy if it ever falls into place.''

''What did the others say about him?''

''I like to draw my own conclusions about a person, Erin.''

''What did they say?'' she insisted.

Eamon grumbled under his breath. ''They said he seemed like an okay guy.''

''See?''

Eamon jabbed a finger in her direction. "Folks said that about Ted Bundy, too, you know."

"Ugh!" Erin spun around and headed off. "I'm going to go hang out with the women and children, where people are sane!"

Luckily, Eamon's interrogation was the sum total of the grilling she received that morning at brunch, much to her surprise. As she drove back to Sam's, her heart felt light, and her anticipation about dinner had grown. If things went her way, Jessica would come out of her shell, Erin herself would break through Sam's wall of defenses, and her brothers would eventually do a lot more than meet Sam. They'd welcome him into the family.

Yeah. Right. Now, where had she placed that magic wand?

"So, you're the legendary Erin O'Grady," said Mia that evening, as she opened her front door to them. Erin could smell something spicy baking inside, and the sound of children's laughter wafted out on the fragrant air. She felt right at home and offered a smile to match the other woman's warmth. Mia was probably forty, a little round at the middle and radiating love and a motherly demeanor that felt both familiar and soothing. No wonder Jessica loved her so much.

"I don't know about legendary," Erin said, laughing. "Notorious might be a better word choice." She reached out a hand, and Mia shook it with enthusiasm.

"Well, come in, please." She stepped back, opening the door wider. "Hi, Sam."

"Mia," he said. "What's baking?"

"Gingersnaps."

"Yum. Those are my favorite," Erin said.

Mia winked. "Well, I'll be sure to pack up a little gift package for you to take home."

"How sweet of you."

Mia hooked her arm through Erin's and steered them into the living room. "I'm so delighted to have Jessica for the night. I've missed her."

"Understandable. She's such a doll."

Mia's gaze flicked to Sam, who carried a sleeping Jessica against his chest. "Hand her over, buddy. You're the boss at the worksite, but I'm the boss here."

Sam smirked, but rubbed a sleeping Jessica's cheek gently with his knuckle until her eyes fluttered open in confusion. Her hair was squashed down on one side and sticking up endearingly on the other. Sam kissed his daughter's forehead, then indicated his secretary. "Look who's here, honeypot."

Jessica turned her head, saw Mia, and broke into a grin. "Mi-mi!" Suddenly awake, she reached out.

Mia grabbed hold of her, smooching her fat cheeks. "How's my favorite little rascal?"

"She's doing great, thanks to Erin," Sam said.

"Oh, come on. Don't give me that much credit."

He flashed her a look of gratitude that flamed into something deeper, scarier and more exciting, and Erin caught Mia appraising them both.

Mia cleared her throat and lifted up Jessica's still-bandaged hand. "How's the boo-boo?"

"Owie," Jessica said.

"She gets the stitches out this week, right Sam?" Erin asked.

He nodded. "That ought to be a joy. I'm sure Doc will kick me out of the suture room again."

Erin and Mia laughed, and Erin reached out and laid a hand on his forearm. "Don't worry. I'll stay with her." She and Sam shared another private look that made her middle clench, and when she looked back at Mia, the older woman's eyebrows were raised sky high, her assessment obvious.

"Well," Mia said, in a tone like she'd just heard the year's juiciest gossip. "Don't let me keep you from dinner. And, remember. There's no hurry. In fact, if you want me to keep her overnight—"

"Mia," Sam said, in a playfully warning tone.

Mia shrugged and sniffed. "I'm just saying, the option is open. If you decide the evening is…getting late."

Erin's face flamed, and she stared at her feet. Did Sam's secretary think there was more to their relationship than boss and nanny? She wished.

"We'll be back to pick her up in just a few hours," she heard Sam say, in a firm tone.

"Whatever you like," Mia replied, in a sing-song, teasing manner. "So glad to finally meet you, Erin. It's nice to see Sam without that omnipresent scowl on his face."

Erin worked to keep her expression from betraying

her feelings about Sam and offered a wide smile. "Nice to have met you, too." She leaned in and kissed Jessica's cheek. "Bye-bye, sweetie."

"Bye, Win."

Erin shrugged. "She calls me Win."

Mia laughed. "That's adorable."

Sam stooped down next, cupping Jessica's face and giving her big smoochy kisses on her cheeks. "Be a good girl for Mia, honeypot."

"Yuv you, Daddy."

"I love you, too."

"Yuv you, Win."

A lump rose in Erin's throat and she splayed a palm on her chest. "Oh." She looked at Sam with moist eyes. "That's so sweet. She's never said that to me before." Returning her attention to Jessica, she touched the baby's cheek gently. "I love you, too, sweet girl."

"My sleepover offer still stands," Mia called out as they descended the stairs from her stoop.

Erin watched Sam out of the corner of her eye. He shook his head, but at least he looked amused.

"See you soon, Mia," he said pointedly.

Once they were in the car, Sam expelled a breath and started the engine. As he pulled away from the curb, he cast an apologetic look toward Erin. "Sorry about that. Mia is an unrepentant matchmaker."

Erin laughed nervously. "No problem. Hey, it's the opposite problem I have. She wants to fix you up, and my brothers want to lock me away in a convent."

"Now, that," Sam drawled, "would be a darn shame."

A flock of hummingbirds set loose in her tummy. It sounded like he was flirting, but she just couldn't trust her instincts. "So, um, where are we going?"

"Just a little neighborhood grill I like. Is that okay?"

"Fine."

"How was brunch, speaking of your brothers?"

"Well, they didn't hammer me too badly about working for a single man. But, my brother, Eamon, is back and says he wants to meet you for himself."

"Didn't he get the full report from the others?"

"That's what I asked." Erin rolled her eyes. "He said, and I quote, 'They said he was a nice guy. But people said that about Ted Bundy, too.'"

Sam held a fist to his chest. "Ouch."

"I know. I'm sorry."

He glanced over. "I think it's nice that they look out for you, Erin. Maybe…down the road, we can meet."

"I don't expect that, Sam, but thank you."

He reached over and patted her hand, sending tingles up her arm and all through her body. "It's no problem. Setting your brothers' minds at ease is the least I can do for you."

Erin smiled, then turned her attention toward the window. Man, was she ever falling for this man.

Chapter Nine

Dinner with Erin turned out to be one of the most pleasant evenings Sam had spent in a good long time. She counseled him extensively about how he should approach Jessica regarding Jenny, but she'd also shared stories of her brothers' antics and her big, raucous family life that left him smiling. Truly smiling, instead of that forced slash of a grimace he'd used in place of a smile for the past several months...or had it been years? Maybe Mia had been right—he did scowl more than smile.

Her stories also made him a little envious, and an insane part of him yearned to be a bigger part of her life. What would it be like to belong to a family like Erin's? To always know there were people who accepted you, who loved you so much, looked out for you to the point of exasperation? He'd always thought having that sort of connection in his life didn't matter to him, but being around Erin made him reconsider. Listening to her stories made him yearn for something he'd never have and made him regret his childhood in an acute, very real way.

It also made him wonder about his siblings. Lissa, Adam, and little Mark, but also Cambry's teenage children, Shawna and Chad. A whole family he'd never met, he marveled. Was he making a mistake keeping his identity secret from them?

Like it or not, Erin was melting the ice around his heart, making him question decisions in his life that had previously been cut and dried. He'd reached out for connections before, though, and been bitterly disappointed with the results. Of course, his previous attempts had always been with various foster families, not with blood relatives. Would that make a difference? He still couldn't believe he had *blood* relatives. No one would believe it—that was the thing.

But, bottom line, he had a lot of emotional work to do with Jessica in order to get their little two-person family back on track. For now, that's all he had room for in his life. He couldn't—wouldn't— even contemplate revealing himself to Lissa, Adam, and the whole world, mainly because he wasn't emotionally ready himself. He'd seen the two of them on television enough to know they were in a whole different place in their lives than he was in his.

The discussion with Erin over dinner had made him realize a lot of things about Jessica, but even more about himself. He wasn't a cold man, or bitter. Maybe on the surface, but that was mostly a self-protective thing. Deep down, he was one big ball of fear. Fear of rejection, of losing Jessica, of living a disconnected life. But, other than with his daughter, wasn't he doing that now? Maybe. Probably. But, he feared trying again, so he'd focus on Jessica and count his blessings.

Erin helped him see that he could take this journey with Jessica one step at a time, that there was nothing to fear in that respect. He hoped she was right, and he also hoped Jessica's recovery would have a ripple effect through his life.

The dinner had been a kind of awakening for him, and he'd always be grateful to Erin for it. In such a short time, she'd become one of those blessings he'd count during times he felt alone. If he felt emotionally healthier, more prepared to risk his heart, he could fall for Erin O'Grady in a red hot minute. Truthfully, he'd already begun to.

That didn't mean he planned on doing anything about it.

He'd woken the morning after their dinner to a sunny, bright Sunday and decided he and Jessica would take advantage of the weather and enjoy a few hours outside. Erin was spending the day with her parents, so it was up to him to broach the very difficult subject with his daughter alone. That's the way it should be, though. He had a whole day with Jessica, and he planned to use it wisely. A picnic in the park sounded perfect.

As he pushed Jessica in her little stroller, going over the dinner conversation from last night in his mind, he chastised himself for feeling the pressure. How could he fear talking to a two-year-old child—his own daughter? It seemed ludicrous. But, the little plastic bag filled with photos of Jenny burned a hole in his pocket, reminding him of the difficult discussion to come. With his whole heart, he wanted it to go well. Some strange part of him wanted Erin to be proud of him for how he handled this. He gripped the stroller handles tighter and glanced up at a puffy white cloud tripping through the sky.

Please let me do one thing right.

He truly wanted Jessica to feel free to open up about her mother. More than anything, he yearned to be a better father than Cambry had been to him—which wouldn't be too hard. Cambry hadn't been a father of any kind. And yet, how could he judge the man? Sam might not have physically abandoned Jessica, and he never would, but Erin made him realize he'd inadvertently abandoned her emotionally by closing off after Jenny's death and "keeping busy" to avoid the difficult conversations. Jessica had probably taken his silence to mean she couldn't talk about her mother, because she never, ever did. It just wasn't natural. He needed to right the wrongs, get past the pain, and set them on the path toward a better, closer family life.

Today was his chance.

He'd packed a little lunch of peanut butter and jelly

sandwiches, Oreos, and juice boxes, and he'd planned to broach the topic after Jessie had tired of playing and they'd shared the meal. When they got to the park, though, Jessica showed little interest in the playground equipment or the other children. Reverting to her post-fire timidity, she sat right next to him watching the fun from the blanket they shared. They sat in companionable silence while he shored up his courage. The air smelled of cut grass and the sweet promise of Spring, and exuberant children's chatter and laughter ribboned through their surroundings. Finally, he smoothed his hand through her wispy, baby soft hair, warm from the sun. "Are you hungry, honeypot?"

Jessie shook her head and nestled closer.

Okay, game on. He'd been stalling long enough. If he didn't jump in with both feet, he'd never get past his own trepidation. Taking a deep, steadying breath, Sam asked, "Want to look at some pictures with me?"

Jessica blinked up at him and nodded. She'd grown fond of flipping through photographs ever since Erin launched the scrapbook project.

He pulled the plastic baggie of photos from his pocket and opened it, carefully removing the stack of precious photos. "Do you recognize these?"

"Mine," she said, on the verge of a whimper. Her eyes grew wide and troubled.

"Yes, they're the photos you collected. They're yours." He waited until she relaxed. "Are these special pictures, Jessica?"

She nodded. On top was the photo of Jenny smiling, holding a newborn Jessica in her arms at the hospital.

Jessica pointed to the swaddled baby. "Me," she said, quietly. "Baby Jes'ka."

"Yes, that's you. The day you came out of mommy's tummy." He pointed at Jenny's face, trying not to let his hand or his voice shake. "Mommy was so happy. See?"

"Mommy," Jessica whispered, as though the word were a solemn prayer, not to be uttered aloud.

Sam's heart clenched. He slipped that photo to the back of the stack and showed her the next one. It was a snapshot of Jenny sitting with her feet curled under her on the edge of the couch in the apartment. He couldn't say when the photo was taken or why. It was just one of those photos people take to finish out a roll of film, an uneventful moment in a life taken for granted. But it definitely portrayed Jenny in her most common state. She looked pensive, darkly pretty. Deep in thought.

"Mommy," Jessica whispered again.

He swallowed, as blood pounded hot and loud in his ears. "Do you remember Mommy?"

Jessica nodded. "Our house." She pointed at the sofa.

"Yes, that was our other house." He paused. "I miss Mommy, Jess. Do you miss Mommy, too?"

"Mommy go bye-bye," she said, gravely, peering down at the picture with a calm, solemn acceptance.

Oh, God. Sam choked back an onslaught of grief. He struggled to keep his voice steady, then remembered that Erin told him he didn't need to hold in his pain. He'd do Jessica a bigger favor by showing his emotions rather than bottling them up. Tears sprang to his eyes, and he let them come, which was completely out of character for Sam Lowery. His voice remained thick with emotion when he spoke. "Yes, Mommy went bye-bye, honeypot, but she loved you very much." He reached out to stroke some wispy hair off her forehead. "She loved you as much as I love you. You know that, right?"

Jessica looked up at him, surprised. To his utter shock, she reached up and touched his cheek. "No cry, Daddy."

A tear escaped, and he sniffed. "It's okay to cry, Jessica. I miss Mommy, and sometimes I cry. It's okay."

Her tiny, chubby fingers awkwardly patted at the tear, and he could almost feel his heart expand to bursting in his chest with love for this tiny, compassionate person. "Do you miss Mommy, honeypot?" he asked again.

Jessica stared back down at the picture, reaching out one finger to touch the image of Jenny's face. "Mommy angel."

He blinked with confusion, smearing the wetness from his cheeks with the back of one hand. "What's that? Is Mommy your angel?"

"Uh huh. Mi-mi say, Mommy angel."

Sam closed his eyes for a moment. God bless Mia. At least someone had been talking to Jessica about her mother. It should have been him doing the talking, but he shoved away a pang of guilt. He needed to focus on the present and the future, not the past. God knew, there was nothing he could do about the past.

Sam pulled Jessica onto his lap, resting his chin on her head. He wrapped her in his arms and released a long, shuddering sigh. "Mommy *is* your angel, Jess. Mine, too. She watches out for us every day."

"Uh-huh."

"Do you—" he swallowed "—want to talk about Mommy?"

Jessica hesitated for a moment, then shook her head.

"It's okay if you do."

"No. I want Win," she said unexpectedly, her voice cracking as her bottom lip jutted out and trembled with emotion.

Erin. She wanted Erin. Jenny had become less real for her, but Erin was a flesh and blood woman who loved her. It didn't surprise him. This conversation was emotional, probably a little bit scary, and Jessica had come to depend on Erin. "Erin will be home tonight."

At that piece of news, Jessica began to sob. "No. I want Win now." She turned and wrapped her little arms around Sam's neck, weeping until the neck of his T-shirt was wet. He just rocked her and let her release it all. He had an inkling that she was crying for Jenny just as much as she was crying for Erin, but it was hard for her to express her pain, thanks to his piss-poor example. Finally, her sobs turned into hiccups.

"Yuv Mommy," she whispered.

He tightened his embrace. "Oh, Jess. I love Mommy, too." It wasn't a lie. He'd always love Jenny for giving him such a beautiful, special daughter.

Jessica twisted around and picked up the stack of photographs, clutching them to her chest. "Mine."

"Yes, they're your pictures. No one is ever going to take them from you, okay? You can keep them forever."

She studied his face for a moment, then nodded.

"Do you want to make a book of Mommy's pictures with Erin?"

Jessica pursed her little lips, then nodded. "With Win and you."

"Okay." He kissed the top of her head. "We'll all work on the book of Mommy's pictures together. I promise."

Jessica bit her lip for a moment, then implored him with pain-filled eyes. "Mommy scared. Mommy cry."

An anvil of dread dropped in his gut. Jessica had been little more than a baby the night of the fire. Could she possibly remember the horror of it all enough to discuss it? He almost went the route of, "Shhh, it's okay," but he remembered Erin telling him to let her talk. He swallowed back his own feelings of inadequacy and forged ahead. "D-do you mean the night of the fire, Jessica?"

She nodded.

Sam fought back a wave of nausea. "Was Mommy scared for you? Is that what you mean?"

Another nod. "Mommy cry. I fall, and—" she flipped her pudgy little hands palm up, in an oddly older looking mannerism "—Mommy go bye-bye."

Sam's tears returned. Jessica's matter-of-factness about the tragedy tore at his soul. "Were you scared, too?"

Jessica bit her bottom lip, and her big, liquid eyes met his. She nodded. "I no like fall."

It was so hard to discuss this in terms a two-year-old would understand. He felt like he was swimming in a dark ocean with a desperate need for air and yet no inkling of which way was up. "I know, honey. I was so scared when I heard that you fell, too." He smoothed the backs of his fingers down her cheek. "But you know, Mommy let you fall so the nice man could catch you. So you could get away from the fire. Mommy saved you. Do you understand what I'm saying?" Probably not.

Jessica just watched him.

"Mommy loved you so much. So much, sweetie."

Jessica nodded.

"And I love you, too." He dipped his chin. "When you get sad, when you think about Mommy, you can talk to me. Okay?"

"'Kay."

"And when I get sad, I'll talk to you, too."

"'Kay."

"And you can talk to Erin or Mia, too. We all love you."

"Yuv you," she said, squeezing both of his cheeks with her little hands. "No cry, Daddy."

"I won't cry anymore today, honeypot. But if I feel sad on another day, I might cry again. Is that okay if Daddy cries?"

She nodded, and then she smiled. "'Kay."

Sam's heart soared with love and a huge weight lifted from his shoulders. They could get through this, because they had each other, and finally, *finally,* they were talking about it. He couldn't wait to see Erin and tell her how it went.

"You seem distracted, honey," Erin's mom said. They were in the bright yellow, sunflower theme kitchen at her parents' house, side-by-side, finishing up a batch of cookies before Erin headed home to prepare for the week ahead.

"Hmm?" Erin glanced up, then checked the clock. "Oh. I guess I am."

"What's up?"

She quirked her mouth to the side. "Sam's talking to Jessica about her mother today for the first time since she died. I guess I'm just hoping everything goes well. He was pretty nervous about it."

Sarah O'Grady was silent for a moment as she dropped some dough onto a cookie sheet. "Tell me more about this Sam."

Erin tossed her a droll look. "Oh, you mean the boys didn't already give you the full run-down?"

"They did, but I want to hear it from you. You know how your brothers are." She reached out and smeared a dab of cookie dough on Erin's nose.

Erin laughed, wiping it off and eating it. "Yeah, how could I forget."

"So, come on. Dish about your boss." The older O'Grady woman slid the cookie sheet in the oven, set the timer, then turned back toward her daughter.

Erin took a seat on one of the wooden and wrought iron stools by the breakfast bar, hooking her heels on the upper rung. She rested an elbow on the counter and planted her chin in her palm. What to say? "Sam's a really good guy, Mom. Such a good father, too. But…I don't know. He has a deeply mysterious side." She looked sharply at her mom. "And don't tell the evil five that I said that, or they'll be pinning unsolved serial murders on the poor guy within minutes. That's not how I mean it, though."

Sarah laughed, but she shook her head. "Erin, they just care about you. Be happy your brothers look out for you."

"Oh, I am," Erin groused. "Thrilled to death."

"So, what do you mean, dark and mysterious?"

She squinted toward the ceiling. "It's just something I can't put my finger on. I feel like we connect on a lot of levels, but there are just some parts of him I can't reach." She blew out a breath. "I guess I have a feeling that losing his wife wasn't his first trauma, but I don't know what else could've happened. He doesn't seem to have very close family ties.''

"Really?" Sarah pulled up another bar stool and reached for two warm cookies, handing Erin one. For a minute, they both munched on them.

"Yeah. I mean, I've been working on that scrapbook I told you about, remember?" Her mother nodded. "Well, he doesn't have a single photo of his parents or any other extended family. And there were none of his wife's family, either."

"Hmm," Sarah mused. "Maybe they weren't big picture takers. Or maybe they didn't have the money to take photographs, Erin. We were very fortunate in that respect, but a lot of families weren't. Do you think he came from a poor background?"

Erin shrugged. "Could be."

"A lot of people who've pulled themselves up by their bootstraps don't like to discuss their humble beginnings.''

"Yeah, but I wouldn't care if he was poor as a child." She finished the cookie and wiped her fingers on a napkin. "I just wish I could get inside his head sometimes."

Erin's mother sat peering at her curiously, and suddenly Erin felt like a bug under a microscope. "What?"

"If I didn't know you better, Erin go lightly, I'd say it sounds like you're interested in the man."

Erin bit her lip and cast her mother a sidelong glance. "Would it be really awful if I were, Mom? I mean, I know he's my boss, but it's not like I'm doing anything unprofessional with him. I just…can't help but be attracted to him.'' She groaned. ''I never thought seeing a man be a good father would be sexy.''

Sarah laughed. ''Welcome to being a grown woman, hon. And no, it's not wrong. Just be careful. This is your job—''

''I know, Mom.''

''And you'd hate to jeopardize that for…a crush.''

Erin started to protest, but her mom held up a finger.

''However, if it's more than a crush, take it slow. Be smart. And protect your heart.'' She winked. ''You never know what might happen. Heaven knows, people have found love in stranger places.''

Erin reached across and hugged her. ''I promise I'll be smart, Mom, no matter what happens. And responsible. Jessica is my first priority.''

''That's my girl.''

''Besides, you don't really have to worry. Sam's not interested in me. This is a wholeheartedly one-sided crush.''

''Well, then, the man's got one gaping fault.''

''What's that?''

''Excruciatingly poor taste in women.''

Erin laughed, then jumped off the bar stool and started packing up her things to head home. ''I'll keep you posted on how things go with little Jessica.''

''And Sam, please. Pretty please. You're my only daughter. A old married woman like myself likes to experience things like falling in love again, however vicariously.''

"God, Mom, you embarrass me." At the door Erin and her mom embraced again.

"Embarrassing you is my duty as a mother, and my right." As Erin turned and headed down the walk, her mother called out, "Don't forget, dear. Next Saturday morning is Kellan's birthday party here at the house.''

"Oh, no." Erin spun back and pressed her palm to her forehead. "I've told Sam I'll work next Saturday. He and his crew are working overtime that day.''

"Well, just bring Jessica with you.''

Erin thought of Sam. He probably wouldn't go for that, as protective as he was of Jessica, but it sounded like a good plan to Erin. Jessica needed to get out more and be exposed to other children. Sometimes it was better to ask for forgiveness than permission. "I will think about it. I swear, you will love that baby girl.''

Sarah grinned, leaning her tall, lanky frame against the door jamb. "I have six children and fifteen grand-children, honey. I haven't met a baby yet that didn't steal my heart.''

"Now I know where I got it from," Erin said, blowing her mom a kiss.

Chapter Ten

The second week Erin lived with him and Jessica brought one revelation after another, largely because he'd finally broken through his own barriers and talked to Jessica—thanks to Erin's wise and gentle persistence. Sam could hardly remember why he hadn't wanted to hire her in the first place...except for the overwhelming attraction part. He was doing his best to keep that under wraps.

Despite Mia putting on the full court press matchmaking scheme every day since she'd met Erin, Sam went to work feeling happier and more hopeful, and he couldn't wait to come home and work on Jessica's very special Mommy scrapbook with her and Erin each evening. He'd grown to crave Erin's smiling approval, and the more time he spent with her and Jess, the more he received it. She'd been so proud of him when he told her about his groundbreaking talk with Jessica, she'd actually gotten teary-eyed. He had marveled at how freely she could show her emotions. Would that type of expression have been easier for him had he grown up in a family like hers?

She still tried, every so often, to probe for more details about his family life, usually in the evenings after Jessica was asleep, when the two of them sat in the kitchen together, sharing conversation and companionship. But instead of seeing her questioning as an invasion of his privacy, he began to tell himself it was because family was such a big part of her life. She talked about the O'Gradys all the time, and it probably seemed strange to her that he didn't talk about anyone at all.

He'd toyed with the idea of confiding in her on more than one occasion, but ultimately, Sam couldn't bring himself to tell her about his less than pleasant childhood. The last thing he wanted was anyone's pity. Plus, telling her about his beginnings might bring the issue of Lissa and Adam closer to the surface, and he couldn't risk that. Media attention on the reunited twins had ignited into almost daily updates as the world waited to hear whether the selfless bone marrow donation from Adam had been accepted by little Mark's ravaged body.

No gut-spilling, he thought. Too dangerous.

Even as close as he'd grown to Erin, the issue of his childhood would have to remain his secret.

The following Saturday, Erin had agreed to stay

home and care for Jessica while Sam and his crew pushed forth with a project that had seen more than its fair share of rain delays resulting in hundreds of thousands of dollars spent over the budget. Sam arrived at the worksite at four-thirty in the morning, hoping to power through his work and get home in time for Erin to have the rest of her weekend off. He wanted to make sure he kept her happy, because he and Jessica both needed her around.

By one o'clock that afternoon, though, Sam had finished for the day and headed home. He drove faster than usual from the site to his house, bouncing into the driveway as he hit the button clipped to his visor for the automatic garage door.

He smiled as the door rose, unable to remember ever feeling so eager to get home before. He liked to tell himself it was because Jessica was making such good progress recovering emotionally from the fire, and that was certainly a large part of it. But, he also rushed home to be with Erin. Vivacious, guileless Erin.

Seeing her, listening to her laughter and her stories, her lullabies for Jessica—all of it. He craved it. Sometimes he found it hard to think of her as merely his nanny. That was such an impersonal title, and she'd begun to feel like such a bigger part of his life.

How had that happened in such a short time?

And, anyway, it was just his little fantasy.

After pulling into the garage and cutting his engine, Sam hurried into the mudroom and stooped over to remove his work boots. He listened, but didn't hear anything from inside the house. Perhaps Jessica was down for a nap.

He took care padding into the kitchen quietly, in case Jess was, indeed, sleeping. Crossing the room, he rapped softly on the door to Erin's wing, but got no answer. For no logical reason, an alarm bell went off inside him. Moving quickly into the living room, he checked for Erin, but the room was empty. He took the stairs two at a time and peeked in the nursery. Empty. His heart grew heavy with dread, and he bounded back down the stairs. "Erin?" he called out, his voice sounding sharp to his own ears. "Jessica? Anyone here?"

No answer.

In the doorway to the kitchen, he stopped short. Of course. Erin's VW Bug hadn't been parked in the garage when he pulled in, but he'd been so lost in his happy thoughts about being home, its absence hadn't registered. Perhaps they'd just headed out to run errands. Sam took a deep breath and huffed out a laugh. When had he become such a worst-case scenario thinker?

He started toward the refrigerator to get himself a Pepsi and a snack, and that's when the note on the kitchen table caught his eye. He snatched it up and read Erin's neat handwriting.

Hi Sam,
Jessica and I are at my parents' house for my nephew Kellan's birthday party, which runs from noon to probably four o'clock. You are more

than welcome to join us if you get home in time. I know Jessica would love to have her daddy there. Directions, address and phone number are on the back. See you soon, I hope!

Erin and Jessica

Without warning, a flood of anger coursed through Sam's veins, squelching his earlier good feelings. Jessica was just starting to make progress overcoming her fears. How could Erin think she would be comfortable around hordes of people she'd never met? Strangers. Especially the undoubtedly boisterous O'Grady clan? Erin knew how skittish Jessica got simply going to the park.

Lips pressed together, he flipped the note over and read the address and directions. Tossing the note aside, he headed upstairs for a quick shower. Damn right, he'd meet them at the O'Grady's house. He'd retrieve his daughter, and later, when Erin returned home, he'd lay out exactly what he expected when it came to Jessica being thrown into strange situations or large groups of people without his approval.

A small part of him whispered, "Hypocrite." Hadn't he just been singing Erin's praises? Still, this was different. He'd been looking forward to seeing Erin, and yes, she'd begun to feel like a permanent fixture in his life. But, in reality, she was his *nanny*. She had absolutely no latitude when it came to decisions about his daughter's welfare. Dammit, she should've checked with him first.

Jessica was *his* daughter.

As he yanked off his work clothes and stepped into the hot steam of the shower, Sam watched his little fantasy life swirl down the drain like so many soap bubbles. Hey, it was his fault for playing mind games with himself, for picturing what it would be like if Erin were his lover rather than hired help. But, at the end of the day, Sam really was a single parent. Any greater connection he felt with Erin was nothing more than a figment of his hopeful imagination.

Story of his pathetic life.

All the O'Gradys, big and small, were gathered in the backyard of Sarah and Eamon Sr.'s rambling ranch style home, just the way Grandma Sarah liked it. She'd loved being a mother to babies, small children—even teenagers. But now that her kids were grown and gone, she found she loved being a grandmother even more. She enjoyed spoiling her grandchildren, thrilled to the fact that she could pass them off to their parents when they had meltdowns or potty mishaps. The grandmother perks completely validated all she'd gone through raising five rambunctious and often difficult boys and one thankfully sweet and obedient daughter.

A burst of laughter followed Sarah inside as she popped into the kitchen with an empty bowl to refill. She reached for a new bag of potato chips, tore it open, and started to pour them in, humming to herself. The buzz of the doorbell gave her a start. She glanced over her shoulder toward the living room. ''Just a moment,'' she called out as she finished.

Wiping her hands on her apron, Sarah wound her way through a chair-filled, toy-strewn kitchen and into the front entryway. She glanced through the peephole and got an eyeful of a very handsome, albeit a little stern-looking young man. Finally, she thought, feeling self-satisfied. She knew Erin would work her magic on Sam Lowery if it was meant to be, and based on looks alone, he was quite a catch.

With a grin on her face, she pulled open the door, eager to meet the mysterious man her daughter had fallen for, head over heels and then some. After meeting precious little Jessica, all Sarah could say was, bring on the daddy. Any man who had managed to raise such a precious little gem like Jessica, with all the hardships they'd faced, had to be an amazing person. Sight unseen, Sam Lowery had her vote as a potential partner for her Erin. Still, she was glad to finally meet him.

The door opened, and Sam found himself staring into the face of Erin…in about twenty-five years. Same crooked smile, same auburn hair, albeit in a more conservative style. Same kind eyes, but a generation older. For a moment, he suffered a complete loss for words. Erin's resemblance to her mother startled the anger right out of him.

He'd always been intrigued by genetic similarities between family members, since that had never been a part of his world. Until Adam Bartlett, of course.

Don't think about that.

"You must be Sam," said the woman, pushing

open the screen door and stepping aside. "I'm Sarah, Erin's mother. So glad you could join us. Come in, come in."

He smoothed his palms down the sides of his jeans. Sarah O'Grady's warm welcome left him suddenly awkward and a bit sheepish about his earlier temper flare. "Thank you. I...don't mean to intrude."

"Don't be silly. We're happy to have you." She tucked her arm into the crook of his elbow. "And Jessica, of course."

"Is she okay?"

"Why, she's fine. And absolutely adorable, Sam. You must be proud as punch of that little girl."

He allowed a small smile. "Thank you. I am. I thought I'd come pick her up and get her out of Erin's hair so you all can enjoy your party."

"Oh, you can't leave yet," Sarah said, sounding truly disappointed. "Jessica's having so much fun watching the other kids, and she just adores our dog, Olaf."

"Yes, but—" He inclined his head. "I don't mean to be ungracious, but Erin's been working all week. I thought she might like some free time."

Sarah laughed and leaned in toward him as though he'd just cracked the biggest joke of the century. "Believe me, it is not a hardship for my daughter to be with your daughter. I guess she hasn't told you just how much she loves children."

"Actually, she has."

"Just stay and enjoy yourself, Sam. Erin is fine. Jessica is fine. It's about time we got to meet both of you. Erin talks about you all the time, you know. What can I get you to drink?''

All the time? he wanted to ask. What does she say? Then he remembered Sarah's question. ''Any soft drink will be fine. Thanks.''

''Ice?''

''Straight up, and the can will do.''

''You'll fit right in,'' she said, laughing. She tossed him a blue can, which he caught deftly, then picked up a large yellow bowl filled with potato chips. ''Follow me. Everyone's out here enjoying the dry weather.''

Everyone.

The entire O'Grady clan in one fell swoop.

A sudden rush of anxiety nailed Sam's feet to the floor. He felt, once again, like the little orphan boy, standing on the fringes of a huge, loving family to which he'd never belong. He'd never truly be a part of such unconditional love, and he felt it like a dagger, all the way to the core of his soul. The familiar surge of futility and loneliness reminded him all too well of his earlier years, and for a moment, he wanted to bolt. Why put himself through this again?

''Sam?''

''Sorry.'' He gave her a tight smile. ''Do you mind if I use your restroom before I join the others?''

''Of course not.'' She pointed to the left, toward a small corridor. ''Second door on the right. Just come on out when you're ready.''

Locked safely in the small restroom, Sam splashed his face with ice cold water. He patted it dry with a lavender guest towel, then stared long and hard at his face in the oval-shaped mirror. He wasn't that unwanted little boy anymore, dammit. He was a grown man with a daughter of his own. A family, no matter how small. He wasn't going to run away or be afraid of the O'Gradys. Feeling more in control, Sam left the bathroom with his shoulders back and his head held high. He passed through the flowery yellow kitchen, then pushed open the sliding screen and stepped out onto the wooden back deck.

His eyes searched for and found Jessica, happily cuddled in the arms of Erin, who was talking animatedly with another woman.

God almighty, she was beautiful. Sam's throat went dry.

Erin wore a longish, black skirt that swirled gently in the breeze, and a emerald green halter top. Her slender back and shapely shoulders were beautifully displayed in the outfit, but the sexiest thing about her was how she held his daughter on her hip as though Jessica were her own. Jessica looked nothing if not comfortable, alternately nestling her head against Erin's neck and squealing happily at a tiny Jack Russell terrier who could, no lie, spring off all four paws about five feet in the air. Repeatedly. The little dog seemed as taken with Jessica as she was with him.

As though sensing his presence, Erin stopped talking in midsentence and turned toward him. Their eyes met, and Sam could swear the entire party went dead silent. A slow smile spread across Erin's face, and Sam felt an answering smile on his. For what seemed an eternity, Sam stood locked in the warmth of Erin's gaze, oblivious to the festivities carrying on around them.

"Daddy!" Jessica cried out, breaking the spell.

He lifted a hand to wave, then held his arms out for her.

Jessica wriggled down out of Erin's grasp and toddled over, arms outstretched. Sam swung her up into an embrace, kissing her chubby cheeks until she erupted in gales of laughter.

"How's my baby girl?" he asked, softly.

Her eyes went round, and she pointed vaguely over her shoulder. "See doggy?"

"I saw him. Do you like that doggy?"

She nodded vigorously.

"He sure can jump high for a little guy, can't he?"

"He sure can," Erin said, as she approached. "And yes, she seems to love Olaf. I think you've got an animal lover on your hands there."

He smiled down at Erin over Jessica's shoulder as he hugged her. "Hi."

"Hi," she said, almost shyly. "I'm glad you decided to come. I hope you don't mind if I brought her."

He toyed with his earlier angry thoughts then decided, no, he didn't mind at all. "It's fine. I'm glad you were able to join your family."

"How was work?"

"Busy. Dirty. Over, thank goodness."

Someone cleared his throat, off to the left of where they stood. Sam glanced over and saw a row of men—Erin's brothers, aka the evil five—gathered around a massive grill. More than that, though, he saw in their stony expressions that *they'd* seen what had just occurred between him and Erin. It wasn't anything blatant, just a crackle of attraction that any man who'd ever wanted a woman like he wanted Erin would recognize in a flat minute. Great.

First time at the O'Gradys and he gets busted by the menfolk casting lustful glances at their baby sister. Sam raised a hand to the men, and each one of them either reciprocated the action or lifted a chin toward him in greeting.

Jessica reached back for Erin, and Sam handed her over.

"Come on in. I want you to meet my oldest brother, Eamon. He's the only one you haven't met, and—" she leaned in, adding under her voice "—brace yourself, he's the worst."

"I'd love to," he said, wryly. "Thanks for the warning."

"And you can meet my dad, all my sisters-in-law, who are destined for sainthood for putting up with my annoying brothers all these years—"

"I heard that," called one of the brothers from his front position at the grill. He frowned at Erin before raising some barbecue tongs toward Sam. "Hey, Lowery. How's it going?"

"Fine, thanks. You?"

"Not bad. Hanging in. You hungry? We've got burgers, brats, chicken, and steaks."

"A brat sounds great."

The grilling brother nodded, turning back toward his domain.

"Which one was that?" Sam asked, out of the corner of his mouth.

"Mick."

"I'm never going to keep them all straight."

Erin laughed her musical, windchime laughter, then reached out and grabbed another look alike O'Grady male who was probably in his early thirties. "Eamon, look alive, buddy. This is Jessica's father, Sam. Sam, my oldest brother, Eamon."

"A pleasure," Sam said, reaching out to shake the other man's hand. "I've heard a lot about you."

"Likewise. You've got a great little daughter there." He tickled Jessica under the chin, and she giggled.

Sam looked at her with love. "Yeah, I think I'll keep her."

Eamon clapped a hand on Sam's shoulder. "Listen, I'm sorry about your loss, man. We lost our son, Bryce, a few years back, as I'm sure Erin has told you. I can appreciate what you're probably going through."

Sam swallowed a couple times, unused to such blatant, honest communication. He had to admit, though, it felt good to speak with someone who could relate, even in a small way. "Thank you. I'm…sorry about your son."

Eamon nodded, pressing his lips together. Clearly, the pain was still fresh. "Life. You just never know what it's going to throw your way."

''That's too true.''

Erin's father wandered over, and she went through introductions again. After that, Sam found himself passed from sister-in-law to sister-in-law, and before he knew it, he was seated in a lawn chair in the middle of this big, loving Irish family, feeling more welcome than he'd ever imagined possible.

He could get used to this if he wasn't careful.

Chapter Eleven

That evening, when Sam, Erin and Jessica left the party, Sam was imbued with a sense of safety and well-being, and he felt closer to Erin than ever before. They'd ended up hanging out and talking with the family until seven-thirty, and Jessica was so tuckered out, she'd fallen asleep immediately in Erin's car on the way home. After they'd pulled into the garage side-by-side, Sam released her from the carseat and carried her into the house. He glanced at Erin over his shoulder. "Would you like to join me in tucking her in? Then maybe we can have a cup of coffee—"

"—or tea."

He smiled. "Or tea in the kitchen. Unless you're tired."

"Not at all," Erin said, flashing a smile. "I'd love to."

They carried Jessica up the stairs together, tugged her playclothes off and replaced them with jammies, then laid her gently in her crib. Through all of it, Jessie remained solidly asleep. Both of them stood there just watching her breathe deeply for several moments. She looked like an angel.

"She's almost too old for this crib," Sam said, regretfully. "Something about that just makes me sad."

Erin touched his arm. "Yeah. If only we could keep them young forever. But, Jess is going to be such a cool kid and an even cooler teenager. I can't wait to see her grow up."

Sam peered over at Erin, repeating her words in his head. He liked the sound of them, as though she planned on being in their lives for a good long time. "Shall we head down to the kitchen?"

Erin unfurled her arm in the direction of the door with relish. "Age before beauty," she joked.

Sam snorted. "Sadly, that's true."

Several minutes of beverage preparation later, they sat at right angles to each other at the table, Erin sipping tea, Sam nursing a mug of joe. Their silences had become companionable in the past week, and Sam loved it.

"Thanks for today, Erin. I really like your family."

"Me, too." She rested one cheek in her hand, elbow propped on the table. "You totally passed the test with the evil five."

He balked. "There was another test?"

She rolled her eyes. "There's always a test. But you're an ace at doing and saying the right thing."

"I wasn't trying to be fake, you know."

"I know," she said softly. "That's what makes it so cool. You just…fit."

He'd never really fit anywhere, and the words warmed him from his heart out through the rest of his body. "Well, I'm just glad you're still allowed to be Jessica's nanny. I wouldn't want you to stay if you didn't have your family's approval."

Erin studied him through the steam rising out of her teacup. "Sam? What's your family like?"

The easy acceptance of the day had lowered Sam's guard, and suddenly he realized he didn't want to hide from Erin anymore. He wanted her to know where he'd come from, what had made him into the man he was today. A small part of him still dreaded her reaction, but he forged ahead regardless, ready to be done with the hiding. "I don't have a family, Erin."

A small, confused frown bisected her brow. "What do you mean?"

"I mean, I was orphaned at birth."

"Oh," she said, in surprise.

"Yeah. I grew up in a series of foster homes." He watched for her reaction and braced himself for her pity, which he feared would totally shatter the sense of well-being he'd cultivated over the day. Lucky for him, pity didn't seem to be a part of Erin's extensive repertoire.

"Well, that explains a lot," she said, matter-of-fact.

He cocked his head. "What do you mean?"

"I had wondered why there weren't any photos of you as a child, or any of extended family, when Jessica and I were working on the scrapbook. That's all."

Inside, he relaxed. "Well, that's why. The whole, unvarnished truth. I don't tell many people," he said, by way of mild warning.

"Don't worry. I'm not going to take out an ad in *The Oregonian.*"

Sam smiled, cheered by her joking.

"So, what was that like? Living in foster homes?"

To his utter relief, she didn't show one ounce of pity. Mild curiosity was the extent of it. He shrugged, sipping his coffee. "Part of me wants to say it wasn't so bad, but that would be a lie. It sucked."

"How so?"

He held up a palm. "Okay, to be fair, I guess not all of it sucked. I did have a few foster homes that were…fine, I guess. Some were awful. But, bottom line, during my whole childhood, I felt like a guest who just might have overstayed his welcome."

"That does suck."

"Yeah." He stared down into his mug. "I got out of the system at age sixteen and haven't looked back since."

"Do you keep in touch with any of your foster parents?"

"No. The only ones I really connected with were the Lowerys. They were older, and Dad Lowery passed away just months after Mom Lowery had an unexpected heart attack. Just like June Carter and Johnny Cash.'' He shrugged. ''They really loved each other, and I really loved them. I was crushed. I guess I didn't let myself get attached after that.''

''I'm so sorry you lost them. But can I just say, you're an amazing person, Sam Lowery.''

''Don't be silly.''

''No, really. Look what you've done with your life, how you've raised Jessica, even after having what some might call a difficult childhood.'' She shook her head with admiration. ''You're one of those resilient types who will overcome every obstacle thrown your way. I envy you, really.''

Sam pulled an incredulous face. ''Come on, Erin. You have a great family who loves you. What's to envy here?''

''Exactly. I have a great family, and despite my constant brother complaints, I've never been tested even mildly. I wonder how I'd do.''

''You were tested when your nephew died.''

''True, but that's different. I had a whole family system for support. I'm assuming you didn't have that growing up?''

''You guess right.''

''See?'' She smiled at him. ''Amazing.''

Sam smirked, shaking his head. ''Whatever you say.''

Erin wrapped her fingers around her mug. ''It's true, so just take the compliment.''

''Undeserved as it is, thank you.''

She sipped her tea. "So, what do you know about your birth parents? Anything?"

Sam's stomach lurched, and he slanted his glance toward the floor. He did *not* want to broach the topic of his genetic origins. He wasn't sure how much attention Erin paid to the news, but the stories about Lissa and Adam were rampant. All it would take was one person who knew him putting together the puzzle pieces, and life as he knew it would be over. "Nothing much," he lied, amazed that his voice remained nonchalant when his heart pounded so incessantly. "My birth mother was a teenager who died in a car accident, I guess. I don't even know her name. No info about the father."

"Wow."

"Yep." He took in a breath and blew it out slowly through his nostrils. "Oh well, what can you do?"

Erin smiled, true approval shining in her beautiful eyes. "You can overcome, leave the past behind, and build yourself a wonderful, successful life. But I guess you know all about that, don't you? Because you're a living example."

Heat rushed to Sam's face, and on impulse he reached across the table and took one of Erin's hands in his own. "You're an amazing woman, Erin. You've already helped Jessica and me in so many ways. And now...you always know just how to say the right things. I just don't know how to thank you enough." Against his volition, his gaze dropped to those full, crooked lips of hers, and all he could think about was kissing her breathless. God, how he yearned to do that right at this moment. The kitchen remained dark, save the pendant fixture just above the table, and the low lighting set a vaguely romantic mood. He could smell her spicy vanilla perfume, and her hand felt so damn soft against his. Maybe he should just go for it and kiss her.

Yes, he should kiss her.

He leaned closer, swallowing deeply and feeling overwhelmed by his desire for this spirited Irish spitfire.

Erin cleared her throat. Sam's gaze jumped to her expression. Eyes wide and serious, she looked nervous, skittish…almost cornered. A zing of guilt struck him, and he released her hand as though it had stung him.

"God, I'm sorry, Erin."

"No. No. It's okay." She ran a hand through her hair awkwardly, then pushed her chair back and stood. "It's just, I don't—"

"Please don't explain. I should never have let my thoughts run away like that. It's unfair to you. Forgive me."

"But that's not it. I—"

"Erin, listen. It won't happen again. I am not the guy your brothers warned you about. I promise."

She sighed. "Look, I should probably turn in, Sam." She raked her bottom lip through her teeth, and he could've been mistaken but she looked like she regretted the whole thing as much as he did. "Tomorrow starts early for both of us."

Sam stood, too, feeling like a jerk of colossal proportions. He'd been so wrapped up in his attraction to Erin, he'd forgotten that he was essentially her boss. Putting her in the position of kiss-or-don't-kiss was a very real form of harassment. How could he have been such a thoughtless idiot? "Yes. Okay. You go on."

Erin nodded, then spun and headed toward her rooms. At the doorway, she spun back. She looked conflicted and remorseful. "Sam, I'm sorry, but—"

"No, Erin." He held up a hand. "It's okay. I didn't mean to make you feel—"

"No, please. Don't apologize. It's just—"

"Goodnight, Erin," he said softly, closing the conversation. He didn't want her to feel like she had to explain anything when it was he who'd screwed things up so royally. "Thanks again for today. I'll see you tomorrow."

She pressed her lips into a thin line and hesitated. Finally, she nodded, and turned into her hallway, closing the door quietly behind her.

Sam released a long breath and closed his eyes, fists clenched by his sides. He needed to rein in his wild emotions about this woman before he did something they would both regret. He'd come so close to crossing a line he'd sworn he wouldn't even approach, and he had to make sure that didn't happen again. The last thing in this world he wanted was to make an impulsive, selfish mistake that hurt Erin or prompted her to leave.

Kissing was, therefore, out.

* * *

How could she have been such a gutless idiot? After Erin closed the door to her bedroom, she leaned her back against it and fought to catch her breath. God, she could've realized all her dreams and kissed the man right then, but no. She'd chickened out, and in doing so, she'd somehow given him the idea that she hadn't wanted the kiss to happen.

On the contrary. She'd wanted to kiss Sam Lowery almost since the first day they'd met. But clearly, he was a worldy man, and she was, unfortunately, as inexperienced as a sweet sixteen-year-old, thanks to the intimidation factor of her brothers. Just at the moment she'd known Sam was going to kiss her, she'd panicked. Panicked and destroyed everything, darnit.

Why, why, why hadn't she just kissed the man?

Surely the act of kissing was something that came naturally. He wouldn't have even known she was inexperienced with men. If she'd led with her feelings, the kiss would've been nothing short of spectacular. Instead she'd scurried into her rooms like a schoolgirl, all while Sam promised he'd never think about kissing her again.

Ugh, what an idiot.

She shoved off the door and scuffed through her room, removing clothes as she went. It was only when she'd changed into her nightgown and climbed into bed that she realized something incredible: Sam Lowery had wanted to kiss her!

There was hope, no matter what impression she'd left with him. No matter what he'd promised. There was hope for her and Sam, and knowing that, Erin fell asleep with a smile on her face.

Chapter Twelve

The following evening Erin and Sam had worked their way back into a semblance of normalcy with each other, and for that, Erin was grateful. She didn't want the awkwardness of the previous evening to color every interaction. That unspoken attraction bubbled just below the surface, where they could both keep it under control.

They were busily working on the Mommy scrapbook with Jessica when the phone rang. Sam was in the midst of gluing down some decorative elements on the current page.

"I'll get it," Erin said, jumping to her feet. "Just keep going."

Sam nodded.

Erin crossed to the phone and answered on the third ring. "Lowery residence."

"Erin Marie, it's your brother, Eamon."

She smiled, leaning against the kitchen doorjamb and winding the long, curly cord around her elbow. "Hey, Eam. What's up?"

"I'd like to talk to Sam."

Her smile melted into a scowl, and she turned from the living room, lowering her tone. "Eamon, don't tell me you guys are still on a witch hunt for my boss."

"No. We aren't."

"Why do you want to talk to him then?"

"If you must know, we're having a guys-only barbecue and poker day when all you yappy women go to that craft fair next weekend, and we wanted to invite him."

Surprise and pleasure zinged through her. She straightened up and laid a hand against her chest. "Really?"

Eamon sighed. "No, I'm lying. I have a habit of that," he said, in a droll tone. "Can you put the man on, please?"

"Well…okay. Hang on." Erin held a palm over the phone and glanced toward Sam, who looked so endearing as he bent over the scrapbook, doing his best to apply the decorative elements neatly. She bit her lip and once again thought, wistfully, of the kiss that had almost happened. "Sam?"

He peered up.

"It's for you. My brother, Eamon."

With a questioning look on his face, Sam drew a finger across his neck like a knife.

Erin laughed. "Nope." She held out the phone.

Sam kissed Jessica on the head, then stood and headed over, taking the phone from Erin.

Erin went back to helping Jessica, trying not to eavesdrop on the conversation as Sam and Eamon talked, but she had to admit it was difficult. Finally, he said his goodbyes and headed back into the living room.

Peering up at him, Erin asked, "What was that all about?" even though she knew already.

Sam looked, frankly, baffled. He scratched the front of his head for a moment before sweeping his fingers back through his hair. "Your brothers are having a get together next weekend when, apparently, all you women are off to some craft fair. Does that sound familiar?"

"Yes, it's a yearly thing. The craft fair, I mean. You can, of course, join us women if you'd prefer," she teased, with a completely straight face.

Sam snorted. "Yeah. Right." He indicated the scrapbook. "That is as crafty as this guy gets, and only because it's for my precious daughter."

Erin refocused on the nearly completed book, striving for a nonchalant tone. "So, you're going to go then?"

"Yeah, I think I will." He shrugged when Erin glanced back up at him. "I'm surprised they thought to include me, but hey, I enjoy their company, so why not."

"Indeed, why not?"

"Don't get me wrong. I'm sure they called in order

to find out if I have nefarious designs on their precious baby sister.''

''Gag me.'' Do you? she wondered, in spite of herself.

''But, I'd still like to go. To be honest, I haven't really had many male friends lately. Or…ever.''

''Reclusive?''

''You know,'' he said, with a look of regret on his face, ''maybe too much so. It might be nice to go do some guy stuff.''

Erin beamed up at him. ''I'm glad you're going. And I hope you don't mind if I take Jessica along to the fair. She'd love it, I promise.''

''I don't mind at all. Plus—'' he sighed ''—you're right. She does need to get out and be around other people. She knows your family now. I know your mother loves her.''

''My mother has never met a baby she doesn't adore.'' She winked. ''I think I inherited her genes.''

His gaze darkened into something that made her pulse race. ''I can think of worse things to inherit.''

Gulp. ''Me, too.'' A pause. ''Sam?''

''Yeah?'' He took his seat on the sofa again.

''I'm proud of you for stepping outside your comfort zone. Even if it is with the evil five.''

''Thank you, Erin. That means a lot to me. And I promise I won't let them pump me for info,'' he joked.

The day of the craft fair/guys-only event rolled around more quickly than they'd imagined. Sam, Jessica and Erin drove to Eamon's together, and Sam tried not to think of them as a little family unit, but that's how it felt to him. He wouldn't lie—he liked the feeling, and not just because he'd never had a true family before, but because it was with Erin. He'd grown closer to her every day she lived with him and Jessica. She was undoubtedly the most special woman he'd ever had in his life, and he felt lucky to have met her. In the dark of night, he allowed himself to imagine what life would be like if he and Erin were a couple. She was the kind of woman a smart man would hold on to with his whole heart and soul. That alternately drew him and scared the hell out of him.

As all the O'Grady brothers were dutifully kissing their wives goodbye, Sam fought the urge to follow suit with their baby sister. In fact, he fought valiantly to avoid even looking like the thought had crossed his mind, when in reality, he couldn't get it out of his head.

When the women had packed off in two minivans, the men headed off to the backyard. Mick clapped a hand on Sam's back as they walked. "So, what's it like having my annoying little sister underfoot 24/7, Lowery?"

"You know, Mick, she's not so annoying when she's not your sister. It's a strange phenomenon."

All the O'Grady men laughed, and then they settled down for a long afternoon of poker, grilled meat, football watching, and general guy bonding. After an initial awkward period, Sam found himself relaxing, even enjoying the camaraderie. Having male friends wasn't as threatening as he'd imagined it would be. In fact, he could get used to it with very little effort. Not for the first time, he yearned to be a part of the O'Grady family. But hadn't he had those kinds of wishes his whole life? It was better simply not thinking about things that wouldn't happen.

It wasn't until hours into the afternoon that he noticed Eamon watching him a little too closely for his comfort. He ignored it as long as he could, then glanced up at the man, lifting one brow in question.

"Sorry, dude," Eamon said, holding up one palm. "I can't shake the feeling that you remind me of someone."

Sam's stomach dropped, and he took pains to keep his face from revealing anything. "Yeah? Odd."

"Not so odd, actually," interjected the middle brother, Matthew. "I've noticed it myself on a couple of occasions, and I finally figured it out. I mean, it makes no sense…"

Hot blood rushed all through Sam's body as the fight-or-flight response launched, full bore, inside him. "What did you figure out?"

Matthew glanced around at his brothers. "I don't know if any of the rest of you have been following that story about the reunited twins, Adam Bartlett and Lissa Cartwright," he began.

Sam's entire life flashed before his eyes. Was this to be his undoing, then? Right here in Eamon O'Grady's home, over mugs of frosty beer and delivery pizzas? "I've seen a thing or two."

"Matt's a news junkie," Mick said. "Don't mind him."

That comment earned Mick a rude gesture on behalf of Matthew's middle finger, but he went on. "I just realized after Kellan's birthday party that you bear an uncanny resemblance to Adam Bartlett. Pretty freaky thing."

"Yeah," Sam said, playing off his horror with a nonchalant snort. "Too bad I couldn't resemble Brad Pitt instead. It sure would help me more in the female department."

Everyone laughed, but Eamon didn't let it drop. "You know, that's it. Matthew's right. You really do look like the guy."

"Huh. Stranger things have happened, I guess."

"For sure," Mick said, looking less than interested in the twin story. "And speaking of the female department, let's talk about my little sister for a bit, eh? I'm sure you know we're pretty protective of her welfare."

Relief rained through Sam at the change of subject. "I do know, and I respect all of you for it. But you don't have to worry about me. Erin is a gem, and I'd do anything to keep her as my nanny. I know that wouldn't happen if the six of you," he said, including Erin's father, "worried for her safety at my house. So let me set your minds at ease. I feel as protective of Erin as you do, and she couldn't be safer living in my household. That's a promise."

They assessed him for several tense moments, and then the party turned back into just that. Beer. Pizza.

Hot wings. Football. Adrenaline continued to pulse through Sam's veins for several minutes, but soon he looked around at the other men and breathed a sigh of relief. He'd successfully jumped through the flaming hoop of his resemblance to Adam Bartlett, and he'd passed another O'Grady men test. Now all he had to do was stay away from Erin.

That, he thought ruefully, would be an even bigger challenge.

Several days later, Matthew called Erin to see if she could babysit his son, Finn, a couple evenings later. Finn and Jessica were close in age and got along great, so she agreed readily. They chatted about family stuff for a bit, and then Matt switched topics.

"You know, we had an interesting conversation with your boss the other day at the guys-only gig."

"Yeah?" Erin was in the midst of preparing dinner while Jessica slept, so she just continued chopping vegetables, the phone tucked between her ear and shoulder.

"I don't know if you've kept up with the news lately—"

She huffed. "Like I have time."

"Well, maybe you should make time."

A niggling sense of alarm slowed Erin's movements. "Why? What's going on?"

"We think Sam bears an uncanny resemblance to Adam Bartlett, that software mogul who was recently reunited with his twin sister, Lissa Something-or-other."

"Oh, I know that story. Who doesn't? It's such a heartwarming tale."

"Haven't you noticed the resemblance?"

"I haven't really paid that much attention, Matthew."

"He looks just like him. It's interesting. You should have a look at the Adam guy and decide for yourself. I mean, it's not like they could be related. Adam and Lissa were both adopted as babies. But, still. It's just uncanny."

Erin's throat tightened, and she wobbled over and took a seat at the kitchen table. She fought to keep her tone light. "So, you brought this up to Sam?"

"Yep. He blew it off with a joke, but still it's a pretty cool thing. They say everyone in the world has a twin somewhere. I'd like to find the lucky guy who looks like yours truly."

"Yeah, I bet you would. Try the mental hospitals," she chirped. "You might have some luck."

"Very amusing, sis."

"Anyway, I'll have a look next time I see something about Adam Bartlett, but right now, I'm preparing dinner. I should go, so I can get this done before Jess is up from her nap. As you well know, it's ten times more difficult to do chores like cooking with a two-year-old underfoot."

"Okay." He paused, and Erin waited because it seemed like he had more to say. "You know, we really like this Sam guy. He's alright."

"I'm glad you approve, Dad," she quipped. "But, newsflash, there is nothing going on between us."

"I know, I know. But don't feel apprehensive about bringing him around, is all I'm saying. He's a good guy. And a good father. Fits right in with the O'Grady way of living."

"I'm glad the five of you finally realized what I've been telling you all along. Sam Lowery *is* a good guy. And I have a great job here."

"Yeah, yeah. You were right."

Erin smiled. "Mark this day on the calendar. One of the evil five said I was right!"

"Evil is a little much, wouldn't you say?"

"Talk to you later, Matt," Erin sang. After they'd hung up, she rushed into her sitting room and booted up the internet. She did a google search on the twin case and came to photos of Adam Bartlett. As the first photo downloaded, her stomach plunged to her feet. My goodness, Sam didn't just resemble Adam Bartlett, he looked like his double. She turned next to photos of Lissa Cartwright. Sure, the gender thing made a difference, but even Lissa resembled Sam around the eyes and mouth.

Erin checked on Jessica quickly—still out cold—then returned to her computer and watched a taped interview with the reunited twins. The more she watched, the more convinced she became that her brothers had stumbled onto something they didn't even realize. In addition to the physical resemblance, Sam's mannerisms mirrored those of Adam Bartlett. Lissa's slow, careful smile was uncannily reminiscent of Sam's.

Upon further checking, she learned that Adam's

and Lissa's birth mother was a teenager killed in a car accident. Their ages matched, birth dates matched.

The story Sam had told her about his mother matched.

He'd said there was no information about the birth father, when clearly Jared Cambry had come forward when his little son, Mark, contracted the rare blood disease requiring a bone marrow transplant. But maybe that said more about Sam than it did Jared Cambry. Hadn't Sam told her once that abandoning a child was the worst crime a parent could commit? Maybe he wanted to forget he had a birth father, especially now that he knew his identity.

She felt certain he knew. How could he not?

Even more curious, all the birth records for the day Adam, Lissa and Sam were born had been destroyed in a fire later that year. Could the teenage mother have birthed triplets instead of twins? Could this be one of the secrets Sam held so tightly to his soul?

Then again, if he was one of the triplets, why didn't he come forward and make himself known?

Erin didn't have answers for any of it, but she made a plan to watch Sam a little more closely and figure things out for herself. This could very well be another huge layer to the mystery that was Sam Lowery…a man she respected and cared about, a man she was beginning to love.

A man filled with secrets.

Sam couldn't stop thinking about the get-together at the O'Gradys' house in the days that followed.

Wasn't it Murphy's Law that Erin's suspicious brothers would be the ones to make the connection between him and Adam Bartlett, when neither Mia nor Erin had said word one? In any case, he'd skirted the issue as best he could, and now he needed to just lie low until the whole media circus ended. He didn't want to be "outed" by Matthew O'Grady, or any of them. He didn't want to have his hand forced when it came to meeting his siblings, because, bottom line, he didn't want his life exposed like theirs had been.

The whole event left him feeling like he was teetering on the edge of catastrophe…and he had vertigo. Erin had gotten him to lower his guard so much that now his anonymity, his life, his daughter's privacy—all of it was threatened. There was only one thing to do: raise that guard back up and live his life the way he had for years before Erin came along. Maybe it didn't work for her and the O'Grady family, but being a closed-off, unreachable person had served him well for twenty-seven years. It was high time he went back to his usual methods.

If it ain't broke, don't fix it.

Right?

Strangely, Sam seemed to retreat into his shell after the day he'd spent with her brothers. Gone was the open, smiling man he'd slowly become in the weeks Erin had lived there, and out came the thick shell he'd hidden behind when she'd first arrived. That would all be well and good, except his complete behavioral

180 was having a negative effect on Jessica and all the progress she'd made.

Like it or not, Sam's behavior had and would always have a huge impact on that little girl. Sam had seemed to forget that, and it was becoming increasingly more difficult to bear witness to the negative transformation in Jess's demeanor. Erin let it go long enough, until one night she'd had it.

Jessica wouldn't look at her Mommy scrapbook anymore, and she'd been teary and clingy at the park that day. Sam had stopped joining Erin in the kitchen for evening conversation, had avoided all opportunities for her to discuss Jessica's change in behavior with him altogether. As Jessica's nanny, she had a duty to keep him apprised of what was up with his daughter's life. If he planned to do his level best to avoid her, she planned to make it difficult if not impossible for him to do so.

That evening, Erin waited for Sam to come back downstairs after he'd tucked Jessica in so she could confront him, but he never materialized. That was fine. Maybe he'd had a rough day at work and wanted to turn in early. But wasn't it sheer politeness to say a simple goodnight? She *had* to talk to him about Jessica, and the sooner the better. If he was going to hide out in his room, she'd go to him. The heck with it.

Bolstered by her intent, Erin headed up the stairs and stood outside Sam's closed bedroom door. She raised her hand to knock…then hesitated. She drew her bottom lip in between her teeth and felt a twinge of apprehension. What in the hell was she thinking, coming to his bedroom like this?

Doubting herself, she padded softly down to Jessica's nursery and checked on the baby. Jessica slept on her back, mouth opened slightly. Erin looked around the room and didn't see her Mommy scrapbook anywhere. All her work, all the progress they'd made, down the drain. She pressed her lips together.

This was about Jessica, not about Erin.

She had to talk to Sam.

Whirling, she left the room, crossed the hallway quickly, and knocked on his door before she had the chance to rethink her actions, to doubt herself.

The door opened almost immediately, and Erin's throat went dry. Mistake. Sam stood before her in nothing more than his wear-softened blue jeans with the top button undone. No shirt, no shoes or socks. Her gaze dropped of its own volition to his work-honed, muscular chest, and attraction swirled low and hot in her body. *Oh, God.* Taking a step back, Erin lowered her gaze. "I—I'm sorry. I shouldn't have bothered you. I—I'll talk to you tomorrow morning."

Chapter Thirteen

Sam's hand around her shoulder stopped her from fleeing, and she reluctantly turned back. She tried to look anywhere but at the man's bare skin, but it was difficult considering his size and proximity.

"What's wrong, Erin?" He glanced down the hall over her shoulder, concern etched into the fine lines around his eyes. "Is Jessica okay?"

"Yes," she answered immediately, but then she reconsidered her answer. "I mean, she's sleeping fine, if that's what you're asking. But..." She sighed. "Sam, we need to talk."

"Now?"

"Now." Erin watched as a mask of remoteness fell over his expression.

"About what?" he said.

He sounded closed-minded and defensive. Even his body language exuded distance. He was about as open to this conversation as her brothers were open to letting her dance naked at a strip joint, and Erin's frustration exploded inside her.

Hot, healthy anger trumped her earlier embarrassment, and she was surprised to realize she was truly upset about Jessica's reversion. This wasn't about his bare chest, or her attraction to him. It wasn't about either of them. "About your daughter, Sam. About Jessica."

"What about her?"

Annoyance coupled with a lingering but unwanted, at this point, attraction fueled her to give him a piece of her mind. Her bottom lip trembled as she implored him, but with anger rather than fear or tears. "Has it escaped your attention that she's losing ground? She's back to being fearful and less talkative." Her voice rose slightly. "She hasn't looked at her book of Jenny's photos for days."

Sam stared at her for a moment, then stepped backwards into the room, indicating Erin should precede him. She did, spying a chair and side table set into a bay window area at one end of the large, very masculine room. She crossed over quickly and took a seat in the relative safety of the chair. She tried not to notice Sam's large, mission-style bed, or the fact that the entire room smelled like the spicy cleanness of the man. This was about *Jessica.*

Sam sat on the other available surface: the bed.

When he spoke, his voice was softer than it had been. "Tell me what's happened, Erin."

Good. At least one of them was focused totally on the important matter at hand. She lifted her arms and let them fall limply at her sides. "That's what I should be saying to you."

His eyes narrowed. "Meaning what?"

"I don't know, Sam." She scooted to the very edge of the chair and leaned into her words for emphasis. "She was making such progress. You both were."

"I've told you, this isn't about me."

"And, as I've told you, she takes all her emotional cues from you. You've completely closed up, and she's feeling it."

He crossed his arms over his chest, causing his pecs to bulge in a very distracting way. "But...I'm trying. I made the scrapbook, I talked to her about Jenny. I talked to you about Jenny, for Pete's sake, which isn't something I'd do on any given normal day."

"Yes, but over the past several days, you've reverted to the Sam I first met, and Jessica is following suit." Erin shot to her feet, threading fingers into the front of her hair as she paced the length of the room. "I just don't know what I'm doing wrong, Sam. One day, you and I are getting along fine, talking openly, sharing conversation after Jess goes to bed. The next day, nothing. It's as if you're avoiding me completely." She spun to face him. "Was it something I did?"

A muscle jumped in Sam's jaw, and he let his gaze slide away. "No. It's nothing."

"So, you're not going to talk about it, huh? Just bottle up whatever you're feeling so that Jessica sees you and thinks she needs to bottle up all her feelings, too?" She waited for Sam to say something, and when he remained stonily silent, she huffed. "What am I even doing here? If you don't help me, I can't help your daughter. Maybe this is a waste of both of our time."

Sam came off the bed and crossed the room in two long strides. He cupped Erin's upper arms gently. "It's not a waste, Erin. You can't mean that. Jessica loves you."

"Which doesn't much matter if you dislike me so much you avoid me." Erin smacked the back of one hand against the opposite palm for emphasis. "She takes her emotional cues—"

"From me. I heard you." Sam studied her face for a moment, than a sad, small smile lifted one corner of his mouth. "Erin O'Grady, the last thing I do is dislike you."

Her tummy tightened, but she concentrated on making her point. She squared her shoulders and hiked her chin. "Then what? What happened, Sam, to set you back?"

"I—" He released her arms and stepped back, and she stepped forward, closing the distance.

"Don't run from me, Sam. Don't run from this."

He peered down at her, looking so conflicted, so haunted. "I don't know if I can even explain it."

"Try."

Their gazes locked for several tense moments, then

he reached out and ran the back of his fingers down her cheek. "I can't, Erin."

She thought of the timeline, and suddenly everything fell into place. He might be hiding from his past, but he'd face up to it if she had anything to do with it. Everything had already gone so wrong, what would it hurt to ask? "Does this have something to do with Adam Bartlett and Lissa Cartwright?"

His eyes widened just long enough to let her know she'd hit pay dirt. For a moment, anger glittered in his eyes and he clenched his jaw. Finally, he released a long, defeated breath. "So, they told you?"

"Matthew called me." A beat passed. "None of them know you were a foster child, Sam. I didn't give up any of what you've confided in me."

"Thank you."

"But I'm asking you to level with me. Is it true? Are Adam and Lissa really two of a set of triplets?" She paused. "Are you the missing piece of that puzzle?"

Sam held his breath so long, when he finally let go, his shoulders seemed to sag with the action. "I think so. Yes."

"Oh, Sam." She lifted her fingertips to cover her mouth.

Sam raised a finger. "I don't want anyone to know. Ever."

Surprise riddled through Erin, and she blinked back her confusion. "But that's crazy. You have family, Sam. Blood relatives. A brother and a sister who seem like delightful people. Not to mention, those half-siblings.''

"Enough."

She almost winced as he barked out the word, and then she stared at him in silence for a few moments. "Why on earth wouldn't you want to meet them?"

"I'm a private person, Erin, if you haven't noticed. I don't want my life and my baby's life laid out on television like some reality TV show." He turned back toward the bed, sitting on the edge of it. His eyes looked troubled, his body language conflicted. "Besides..."

"Besides, what?" she prompted, moving over to sit in front of him on the bed, one leg tucked up beneath her, the other dangling off the side of the mattress.

When Sam looked up this time, his eyes flashed with resentment. "Lissa Cartwright grew up on a vineyard. Adam Bartlett is some fancy CEO. Clearly the two of them were adopted by loving families. Why on earth would I want to show my face as the triplet who no one wanted?" He flicked a hand, as if he were disgusted with himself, with the whole situation. "Not even Cambry, who could've been a father to us all those years ago, but he chose to ignore we existed until it was convenient for him to start a new family, a keeper family. With family like that, who needs enemies? No thanks. I want no part of it."

Erin absolutely ached for his pain, for the scars of a childhood he had not quite overcome, no matter how much he liked to pretend otherwise. She moved closer and took both of his hands in her own. Her realization at that moment smacked her so hard, she felt dizzy—she loved this emotionally scarred man so much, respected him incredibly, and he couldn't even recognize his own qualities.

"Sam Lowery," she said, her voice trembling with emotion she didn't even try to squelch, "you are one of the kindest, most gentle men I have ever been privileged to meet. You have an amazing daughter. You've overcome so much adversity and managed to build yourself a life you should be nothing but proud of. I feel like the luckiest woman in the world to be a part of your life and Jessica's life." He glanced up, and she smiled tenderly at him. "I completely respect the fact that you aren't up for media invasion of your life, but please don't avoid meeting your siblings just because you feel lesser, or slighted. You were infants when you were split up. They had no more control over what happened to them than you did." Releasing his hand, she reached up and traced his strong jawline. "Can't you see, it wouldn't be an honor for *you* to meet Adam and Lissa, it would be an honor for *them* to meet *you*." Leaning in, Erin did what she should've done days ago. She kissed him.

The feel of Erin's lips on his own, the memory of her sweet words, ignited a fireball of emotions inside Sam that he simply couldn't ignore. He'd wanted her for too long. When she started to pull back from the kiss, he tugged her closer and deepened it instead. She made a little sound in her throat, halfway between a gasp and a moan, but after a split second of surprised resistance, she melted into the kiss. Her soft hands came up around him and tangled in his hair as her tongue slipped over his. Sam heard a sound and realized it was a groan, deep in his own throat.

Erin tasted like sugary little gumdrops, sweet and smooth. Her skin felt like satin, smelled uniquely like her spicy vanilla perfume, with a hint of her own scent underneath. Mysterious, rich and inviting.

His body ached for her, and if her enthusiastic response was any indication, she ached for him just as much.

God, what was he doing?

Feeling drunk with wanting her, Sam nevertheless pulled back, pleading with his eyes for Erin to be the voice of reason in this situation. He just couldn't pull it off. "Erin?"

"No," she lifted his hand and placed it boldly on her breast, her own hand closing over it. "Don't stop, Sam," she whispered. "Please."

Sam felt the hard jut of her nipple against the center of his palm, the round softness of the breast he touched through her T-shirt. He struggled, but later he would be able to pinpoint the exact moment he began to lose grip and fall into the liquid pool of desire that shone from her eyes. He'd gladly drown there, and yet he found himself struggling for air, for reason, one last time.

On the one hand, why shouldn't he and Erin make love? They were both adults, both consenting. He wanted her, and thank God, she wanted him, too. Then again, she was his daughter's nanny. He'd initially resisted hiring her for just this reason—his instantaneous visceral reaction to her presence. But then, over the weeks, he'd fallen under her spell just like Jessica had, and now he was too far gone to resist her.

Sam nestled his face into her neck, inhaling deeply of her scent. Dammit, he deserved this. Hadn't he had enough pain in his life? Couldn't he take this moment of happiness and tuck it away for when things got lonely and cold?

"Yes," he whispered, against Erin's neck.

"Yes?" she asked.

"Yes, I want to make love to you, Erin O'Grady." He peered into her eyes, twisting his mouth to the side. "You've got to tell me if we're not on the same page."

Erin reached her hands up and cradled his face on either side. "Sam Lowery. Make love to me."

With a groan of surrender, Sam lowered his mouth to hers. This was no test kiss, no hesitant peck. He kissed her with a lifetime of pent-up need, with an urgency he'd never felt before, not even with his late wife. He kissed her like he meant it, and she pressed against him and reciprocated.

Before long, both of them were breathing heavily, arching and lifting to remove clothes that had become barriers. Once naked, Sam cupped and lifted Erin's small, firm breasts. "Beautiful," he whispered.

He lifted them to his mouth, licking and kissing each nipple in turn until Erin writhed and whimpered beneath him. When he took her left nipple gently between his teeth, she bucked and he felt her wetness against his leg, hot and inviting.

He couldn't wait any longer.

Reaching across Erin, he opened the drawer and removed a condom. He made quick work of slipping it on, grimacing against the ache of his need. He lifted himself above Erin, and she obligingly opened her legs, looking him directly in the eyes. He rubbed against her once, twice, and then plunged into her body, hard and deep.

Erin let out a short, sharp cry, then clung against him, shaking slightly. Sam himself had been stunned into immobility.

"My God, Erin," he whispered, his heart sinking. "Why didn't you tell me you were a virgin?"

She slowly opened her eyes, and he couldn't tell if she was in pain or if she felt guilty. He smoothed her hair back with a gentle hand. "Why?"

"Because you wouldn't have made love to me," she said, her voice wavering. "I did tell you I was inexperienced with men."

"That's not the same, and incidentally, I'm not going to make love to you." He started to withdraw as gingerly as he could manage, when Erin pulled him against her.

"No!" She implored him with watery eyes. "Sam, I meant it when I said I wanted to make love to you." She began to arch and rotate her hips beneath him. "I can't imagine a more perfect man to be my first. You can't destroy that memory for me, Sam. Please…make love to me."

Sam studied her face for a moment before blowing out a sigh and resting his forehead against hers. What could he do? She was right. If he stopped now, she would always have bad memories of her first time. She should've told him, but she hadn't. There was no way to get her virginity back, he realized with a sword-stab of guilt. The only honorable thing to do was to make her first time as pleasurable as possible.

And that's exactly what he did.

After Erin fell asleep in his bed, Sam, ice-cold with remorse for what he'd done, slipped from beneath the covers, grabbed some pajamas, and retreated to the upstairs guest room. His body felt fantastic, but his heart was heavy and his conscience was even heavier. Feeling physically sated just made things worse. He climbed into the full-size bed, propped his hands behind his head, and then stared up at the ceiling in a horrified daze.

She'd been a virgin, and he'd taken it.

Just like that, and rather roughly, too.

God help him. He would never have touched her had he known. She should've saved that gift for the man she married, the lucky bastard who got smart enough to hold on to her forever and give her the brood of children she desired. She deserved a devoted man, and she deserved to bear as many of his children as her big generous heart desired.

Sam Lowery was not the man to fit that bill. He'd tried the forever thing, and it had ended in the worst way imaginable. He wasn't going to risk his heart or

Jessica's heart again, hence he shouldn't have made love to Erin. With a surge of utter devastation, he realized he was exactly the man her brothers had always feared. A man who didn't love Erin, didn't plan on creating any kind of romantic, fairy tale ending, and yet he'd taken the worst kind of advantage of her. If the brothers got wind of this…but, of course, they wouldn't. Erin would never tell them, and he sure as hell wasn't making any phone calls tomorrow.

Sam threw an arm across his eyes and silently berated himself. What a selfish idiot he was. He didn't anticipate getting any sleep, but he had a lot to think about anyway. Now that he'd crossed the line with Erin, the only way to get things back on a professional track was to pull away completely. He couldn't stand the thought of losing the friendship and closeness they'd created, but there was no other way.

Sam had taken something precious from Erin.

He'd screwed up. Again. This time, royally.

Now he had to atone.

Chapter Fourteen

The morning after they'd made love, Erin woke up alone in Sam's bed, which should've been her first clue that all was not right in the Lowery household. Unfortunately, she'd still been blissfully drunk with passion, blossoming into her own sexuality, and she put his absence down to the simple fact that he'd had to go to work. In his own gentlemanly way, he hadn't wanted to wake her up, she reasoned, stretching her deliciously sore body and remembering every touch, every sound, every taste, every shudder. A thoughtful gesture, his letting her sleep. It didn't mean anything more than that.

That's what she chose to believe, at least.

By day four of Sam avoiding her at all costs, Erin admitted to herself that she'd been dead wrong. His absence that fateful morning after hadn't been a thoughtful gesture. More like panic. Remorse. Regret. Whatever you'd call it, Sam was most definitely not interested in a repeat performance of what had been the most special night of her life.

Clearly it had been a milestone moment only to her.

To him, most likely a mistake.

The crushing pain of knowing that sucked her breath away.

Men *were* cads, just like her brothers had always warned her. Maybe Sam had a logical explanation for his behavior, but as bad as she felt, she couldn't bring herself to see the situation objectively. The male point of view? Not so much. Clearly, she was Venus all the way, because it was lost on her. The house—same as always, really—seemed colder, silent, almost funereal with a gauzy film of the unsaid draping over everything like a drab, gray shroud. She had grown so comfortable living here over the past weeks, yet since she and Sam had made love, that level of easy comfort had dissipated like steam on a mirror.

Screw gender differences. It made no sense. How could a man make love to you and not *love* you? Especially when you loved him so incredibly much, loved his daughter, loved the prospect of the life you could share with them both, a life you could see in your mind like a vivid picture of perfection? How could Sam see and feel that deep, true, intense love coming from her and not reciprocate? Maybe she did see the world through rose-colored glasses, but it was a darn lovely view from where she stood. She didn't plan to change, broken heart or not.

Sam or no Sam.

Feeling hurt and a little bit depressed—and hating herself for the whole icky codependence of it all—Erin nevertheless found herself dialing Sam's cell phone that afternoon after putting Jess down for a nap. Erin wouldn't call him at work if she had any other choice, but she never saw him anymore, except in passing. He barely met her eyes then, and he always did his best to vacate the area as quickly as possible. She might be inexperienced with men and love, but his feelings were coming through loud and clear, and she was no dummy.

They were finished, even before they began.

In her heart, she knew it. But she needed to hear directly from him if what they shared had been nothing more than a one-night diversion, needed confirmation so she could move on.

The phone rang twice, all while Erin's heart did its best to pound its way out of her chest. She clenched the back of a kitchen chair in a death grip, rethinking this impulsive move. Just as she went to hang up, she heard him answer.

"Lowery," he said, in a clipped, businesslike tone.

Erin swallowed and closed her eyes, praying for strength. She never wanted to be one of those whimpery, needy women, but right now she felt like she needed something from Sam. Anything, even a polite kiss-off, if that's what it was going to come down to. "Sam? It's Erin. I'm sorry to bother you at work."

"What's wrong? Is Jessica okay?" His voice changed immediately, but not in the manner she'd wished it would have at hearing her voice. There was no private, loving tone, no indication whatsoever that they'd shared each other in the most intimate, special way possible.

Erin swallowed back a bitter pill of disappointment. "No. I mean, yes," she rushed to correct. "Jessica's fine."

"Oh." A beat passed, and when he spoke again his tone was calmer but still wary. "Okay, good. What's up?"

What *was* up? Why exactly was she calling? To confront him? She should've thought this through a little better, but since she'd always been a leap first, look later kind of gal, she fell back on the first thing that came to mind. "I was just wondering if you might be home in time for dinner?" Realizing how cloying and trumped up that sounded, she added, "It might be nice for you to have dinner with Jessica. She misses eating with you."

"I miss her, too, but I don't think so." He sounded so distracted, so not like the Sam who had whispered words of gentle encouragement in her ear as his body moved inside hers. "We're running behind schedule. I'll probably just grab something before I leave here."

Erin plunked down into the kitchen chair she'd been clutching. Exhaustion weighed on her. "But… we can hold dinner, if you can give me some kind of a time window."

"I thought you said it was important to keep Jessica on a schedule?" he asked suspiciously.

It's also important for her father to eat dinner with her now and then, Erin thought, quite snarkily, which wasn't like her at all. But she couldn't go back on her word at this stage of the game. "Yes, you're right," she relented. "I did say that, and it is."

"Then…go ahead and do that, Erin, okay?" Sam sounded impatient with the whole topic. "I've got a lot on my plate here at work and just about nothing's going right."

What was the point? He wasn't giving her an inch. "Okay. I'm…sorry to have bothered you." *Say something, Sam,* Erin pleaded silently, winding the long curly phone cord around her arm. *Acknowledge the fact that you and I were more than just employer and employee, even if just for one night. Something. Anything.* Tears stung her eyes, and she bit her bottom lip hard enough to cause pain. She gratefully focused on the pain in her lip rather than that of her slowly breaking heart, only easing up when she tasted blood, coppery and acrid. Reaching for a napkin from the holder centered on the table, she pressed it to her cut mouth, daubing the blood away.

"Is there anything else?" Sam asked, the trepidation and impatience clear in his question.

She thought about broaching the subject of their lovemaking and the subsequent distance, but decided his silence and irritation were comment enough. Why put herself through hearing it out loud? He didn't want her. He'd never wanted her in anything other than a physical way, and now that he'd reached that goal, he was moving on. No sense crying about it. In fact, she ought to take a lesson from Sam and move on, too. Her brothers had warned her that men did that sort of thing to women all the time. She never thought she'd admit this about the evil five, but she should've listened.

In that moment, Erin grew up just a little bit more.

''Erin?'' Sam prompted.

''No. Nothing else.'' She paused, knowing she was about to tread on dangerous ground and not caring much. ''Well, maybe one other thing.''

''Which is?''

Screw caution. If a destined love affair wasn't in their future, the least she could do was continue her work with Jessica *and* Sam, help them both to heal. That's what she'd been hired to do in the first place. Feeling stronger and imbued by a what-the-hell? sort of calm, she lifted her chin. ''Have you thought anymore about getting in touch with Lissa and Adam, letting them know they aren't twins after all?''

She heard Sam blow out a frustrated breath. ''Erin, I'm working. We're behind schedule and it's costing thousands of dollars a day. Thousands. You can't possibly think I want to get into this subject now.''

''But—''

''Or ever. I've made my wishes clear. Now I'd appreciate it if you'd just drop the topic altogether.''

She cringed, knowing she was stretching, looking for any reason to keep him on the line. ''You're right. This isn't the time. I'm sorry.''

Annoyance threaded into his voice. "Why do you keep saying you're sorry?"

Because I am, she thought. Sorry she'd ever thought there could be something deeper between them, sorry she'd pinned all her hopes on a man who'd flat out told her he never planned on marrying again. After all, Sam had never been anything other than brutally honest with her. He told her on numerous occasions that his life was Jessica and he had no room for anyone else.

Why hadn't she believed him?

Her family always told her she couldn't save the whole world, and again, they were dead-on right. Maybe she was the one who needed some sense knocked into her. Sam had even given her a chance to back out on the night they'd made love, but she hadn't taken it. She'd chosen to make love to him. Really, this was as much her fault as his, and it was high time she took responsibility for her own actions. She'd wanted to feel Sam inside her, to connect with him in a deep, visceral way, and she had. The whole thing had been a grown woman's choice, and it didn't go her way. Oh well. Life wasn't always fair. If it were, her nephew, Bryce, would still be alive. Jessica's mommy would still be alive. And Sam might just love her.

None of that was true.

She was logical and intelligent enough to know that not every tryst had a romance-novel ending. And, hey, at least she'd had one night. *Be happy with that, Erin, and get on with your life.* She still had her job, and her first lover had been a man she adored. That was more than a lot of her friends could claim.

Taking a deep breath, she felt stronger, resigned, more serene about the whole stupid situation. "Never mind. Everything's just fine. Go back to work, and we'll see you whenever we see you." She hung up before he could have the satisfaction of doing it first.

Sam flipped the face of his cell phone closed and muttered a vicious curse. He'd hurt her deeply; he could hear the pain in her voice. Knowing that lanced through his soul, but, dammit, there was no other way. He wouldn't marry Erin and drag her into the dark emptiness of his life. He couldn't bear to father a passel of babies, just to flounder in parenting them like he'd done with Jessica. A large family with a devoted husband and father were Erin's dream, and since he couldn't fill those daunting shoes, he had to let her go completely. If only she could understand it. She was all about family and he had absolutely nothing to offer but shoddy genes and poor parenting skills.

Not to mention all the emotional baggage.

Aside from all that, Erin's constant prompting for him to meet Lissa and Adam had begun to needle its way inside him, stirring up trouble and guilt and curiosity he desperately didn't want to feel. Why couldn't she let it drop? Not everyone needed a close family, for Pete's sake. Lissa and Adam didn't even know he existed. No harm, no foul. What Sam needed was absolution, peace of mind, and a happy, healthy daughter. He did not need more upheaval in his life, and meeting Lissa and Adam would cause him nothing but upheaval of the most stressful variety.

So would falling in love with Erin O'Grady, which he was doing his damnedest to avoid.

No thank you. Give him peace and anonymity any day.

He didn't need love.

He didn't need a bigger family than he already had, no matter how intriguing the concept.

Too bad he couldn't expel the feel of Erin from his soul or her gentle urgings from his conscience....

"Hi, Mom."

"Erin!" Initially, Sarah O'Grady sounded delighted to have heard from her youngest child, but with that uncanny, inexplicable maternal instinct, she homed in on Erin's mood immediately. "What's wrong?"

Erin bit the corner of her mouth. She dreaded this, but she needed someone to talk to. "If I tell you, do you promise not to tell Dad or the evil five? And do you promise to listen without judgement?"

Her mother sighed. "You've fallen in love with your boss, haven't you?"

Momentarily stunned, Erin's jaw dropped. "H-how did you know that? All I said was 'Hi, Mom.'"

"Erin, doll. Before I was your mother, I was also a young woman. I'm not so obtuse."

Erin groaned, and tears stung her eyes. Instead of holding them back, she just let them slowly trickle down her face unheeded. "God, I've made a mess of things."

"Tell me about it."

Erin filled her in on the whole scenario, including a Cliff's Notes version of their impromptu lovemaking but leaving out the long-lost triplet angle. She respected Sam's privacy in that respect.

"Goodness, honey." Erin's mother sighed, but thankfully didn't lecture her about crossing the line with her boss. "I'm so sorry you are learning this the hard way, but it sounds to me like you're going to have to cut your losses. There is no other way. And look at the bright side—you still have a job you love. Jessica really needs you in her life, honey."

"I know." Erin sighed, long and full of despair. "The whole thing really is my fault, but that doesn't make it hurt any less." Her voice wavered. "I love him, Mom."

"Love is always a blessing, even unreturned love. And if you really feel that way, let him go."

"How can I?"

"You have to. Give him the gift of caring for his daughter but release the rest. That's true love, baby girl."

"Why can't it be easy?"

She heard her mother's soft laughter carry across the line. "Nothing worth having is easy. You'll find the perfect man for you someday, Erin. You're young. You don't have to push it."

Erin glumly pondered this a moment and, even though she didn't want to hear it or admit it, she realized her mother was completely correct. She did have time, and she owed it to Sam to leave him with a healthy, happy Jessica.

And since she *would* have to leave him eventually, she made another split-second decision. If she couldn't have him, couldn't live the dream of being with him and Jessica forever, then the least she could do was leave him with one gift.

His siblings.

No matter what it took, no matter how much he wanted to throttle her in the end for all her pushing, she would convince Sam that meeting Lissa and Adam was the way to go. That way, if things worked out like she suspected they would, Sam would always remember her fondly. Remember her. Which meant she wouldn't be a part of his world.

Why did life rot so much some days?

By the end of the week, avoiding his attraction to Erin had morphed into a full-time, extremely difficult job, and Sam felt ready to crack under the pressure. He wanted to get away, to run fast and far from feelings he shouldn't be having, from desires for a future he couldn't even let himself contemplate. Erin had slipped into some annoyingly serene state of mind, tending to Jessica and being faultlessly polite whenever they collided. He, on the other hand, wasn't able to be so Zen about the whole jacked-up situation. His tension manifested itself in a case of extreme edginess, and he dared anyone to cross his path and come out alive. At the worksite, he'd become growly and unapproachable. At home, he'd retreated into a brooding, remote state. Sure, everyone from Mia to his employees to his own daughter had quickly read his evil mood, and everyone was giving him a wide berth. Everyone except Erin, of course. She'd suddenly felt the need to go full court press with this "reunite with your siblings" diatribe, citing the often logical reasons why and shooting down all of his—mostly self-protective and lame—excuses.

None of it helped.

On Saturday morning, he crept downstairs early, hoping to snatch the paper and a cup of coffee, then skulk back to the safety of his room until Jessica woke up or Erin left for her weekend off, whichever came first. No such luck. His heart dipped when he saw the glow from the kitchen light reaching out into the dark house beyond. He knew she'd be there, and he knew she'd press him to talk. He'd awakened from a disturbing dream about his little half-brother, Mark, and he wasn't feeling chatty. Not in the least.

Sure enough, Erin sat at the table, nursing her own cup of coffee and perusing several papers. His burst of uncontrollable joy at her presence warred with his fear that she'd start in on him again. No, not fear, knowledge. Erin hadn't let up about his "family" since he'd admitted the truth to her. Why should today be any different?

Erin glanced up from the article in which she'd been immersed. "Good morning."

He grumbled something that could've passed for a polite reply and stalked over to the coffee maker.

Please just let me get my coffee and go, he prayed silently.

"You should have a look at these new articles about Lissa and Adam, Sam," she said, with an excitement in her tone that was simply too much for the crack of dawn and his state of mind. "Due to the publicity, they're uncovering more detailed records from those the adoption agency lost in the fire. It's been a win-win for everyone."

Yippee. He said nothing. Couldn't she get the hint? Didn't care, didn't want to know, didn't like talking about it. Period.

And why did she smell so damn sweet in the morning, even before a shower? He remembered the distracting candy scent of her skin, the sugary taste with a primal jolt. All of it was pure Erin. No perfume company could bottle something so insanely erotic. He didn't want to think about her in that way, but with her so near, so sleep tousled, he could hardly help it. Good thing she kept ruining the mood by yammering on about the triplet thing, or he'd be in trouble.

"They haven't uncovered anything about you being a triplet, though," she added, oblivious to or ignoring his Grinchy silence. "I think that's something you're going to have to do yourself."

His jaw tightened. "Or not do myself." He crossed to the table and deliberately ignored the feel-good human interest sections of the paper she tried to foist on him daily. Instead he pulled out the sports section, world news, and the comics, tucking them under his arm. "I'll talk to you later. Have a nice weekend off."

Sam spun stiffly and started out the kitchen door, but Erin's palm around his forearm stopped him. It also sloshed hot coffee out of his mug onto his hand and the floor.

"Dammit, Erin."

"I'm sorry." She stood, crossing to the paper towel roll mounted below one of the cabinets. "I didn't mean to spill it."

Chagrined, he bent to help her sop up the mess. "And I didn't mean to swear at you."

"Hey, that's okay." She tossed her hair back, offering him a playful half-smile. "I know how you are before coffee."

"And how's that?"

"You know…growly."

He pulled back his chin. "I have never growled."

She rolled her eyes. "I'll set up a tape recorder tomorrow morning. Trust me. You growl."

"Can I give you a suggestion then?" He smiled, but the sharp slash of his mouth felt insincere, a little anger-induced.

"Sure."

"Stop jamming the Adam and Lissa stuff down my throat and perhaps I won't feel the need to growl so often."

Erin sat back on her haunches, wadding the soiled paper towels in a ball. "I'm not jamming anything. I just think it would be really good for you, and for Jessica, to know your extended family."

"They're not my family, Erin," he said, his tone bursting out angrily. "How many times do I have to tell you that? How many ways?"

She blinked at his raised voice, but didn't falter. "Oh, but they are. You can deny it all you want, deny them if you're stubborn enough to do so, but they are and always will be your family. A family you're choosing to ignore for God knows what reason, Sam Lowery. If for nothing else, your daughter deserves to know who her relatives are."

That did it. Sam could handle being told how badly he was screwing up his life, but he drew the line at being told he was also screwing up Jessica's. "Listen, Erin, because I'm only going to tell you this once. You are Jessica's nanny. Period. Not her mother, not my wife. When I want your opinion on how I raise my daughter, I'll ask for it." He stood. "Until then, do me a favor and butt out. I don't want to hear another word about Lissa Cartwright or Adam Bartlett. Do I make myself clear?"

Erin stared at him through wide, watery eyes, her lips shaking slightly with shock. He didn't think she could look more hurt if he'd reached out and struck her. Slowly, with pained dignity, she stood, too. "Perfectly clear, Sam. You couldn't be more clear if you printed it on a billboard, and believe me, I get the message." She lifted her chin. "I'm nothing more to you than hired help. What we shared that evening meant nothing to you, either."

"Erin, that's not what—"

"And as for Jessica," she went on, ignoring his

attempts to cut in, "as much as I love her, you're right. Maybe I do need to butt out." She smoothed the front of her robe. "Unfortunately, I care too much, and this Lissa/Adam issue is too much a part of her healing process. So the only way for me to butt out is to resign my position as Jessica's nanny."

Sam's heart lurched. "Erin—"

"Don't." She held up a hand. "It's my decision and it's final. I'll have my things out tomorrow by the time you get home from work. You'd better arrange for alternate childcare for Jessica tomorrow, in case you have another late night. Because I won't be here when you get home, Sam. I can't stand by silently and watch you destroy yourself, and I can't seem to get through to you. That's probably my failing and not yours, but rest assured, I won't be here ever again."

Chapter Fifteen

Erin spent her first two days back at her parents' mostly sleeping and avoiding everyone and everything—primarily her bruised feelings. Her mother had told her she would always have a loving place to return to if things didn't work out with the nanny job, and in a global way, that was true. Her mother hadn't even blinked when Erin told her she'd quit her job and would be moving home. The house was warm and cozy, food was plentiful, and she was surrounded by people who loved her unconditionally. Ironically, the only loving place she wanted to be was at Sam's house, in Sam's arms.

Fat chance.

The worst thing of all was how her brothers tiptoed around her, being extra nice, super solicitous. Not a single "I told you so," had been uttered, and although part of her felt relieved to have avoided the slings and arrows she'd expected, the rest of her was simply disconcerted.

These weren't her brothers. They were some weird shell-like brother stand-ins who were eerily in touch with their feminine sides. She preferred them annoying.

Clearly Mom had talked to them and threatened them with their lives if they bothered her, but that didn't feel right either. In fact, nothing felt right without Jessica and Sam.

On day three, she was taking a nap when someone knocked on her door. Turning groggily toward the sound, Erin croaked out, "Come in."

Eamon, the worst of the worst, entered, standing just inside the door, which he'd closed behind him. "Want to talk, sis?"

"No."

A long pause ensued. Erin finally sighed, dragging herself into a sitting position, knees pulled up against her chest. She wrapped her arms around her knees and flashed Eamon an undeserved venomous glare. "Fine, talk."

"I just want to make sure you're okay. We all do."

She toyed with the idea of lying, but decided not to. "No, I'm not alright."

"What happened?"

"I screwed everything up. I had the perfect job and I fell in love with my boss."

A muscle in Eamon's square jaw jumped, but to his credit, he declined to lecture. "And Lowery?"

"Not so much in love with me."

Eamon crossed the room and sat on the edge of the bed gingerly. He cast Erin a baleful, earnest glance. "Do you want us to beat him up, sis?"

The absurdity of the question dragged Erin out of the pits of despair in which she'd taken up residence, and she laughed. "No, geek. He's a nice guy—he just doesn't love me."

"That's enough of a fault to earn a beating, little sis."

"No beatings!"

Eamon made a regretful face. "I guess I'm glad about that. I liked Lowery."

Erin bit her lip and her eyes filled with tears.

Eamon reached out and took her hand in his. "Growing up sucks, little sis—"

"I'm already grown up."

"I know. But we continue to grow all the time. It doesn't end when we're suddenly legal to buy booze."

Erin felt a wash of affection for her stern, meddling brother, and she scooted closer to him and rested her head on his shoulder. "I know. Thanks."

"For what?"

"For not annoying me."

"I didn't annoy you? What a drag." A pause ensued. "You know, that woman from the agency keeps calling. She wants you for a temporary nanny job. You should call her."

"I know." Erin sighed, but the action quickly morphed into tears. "I'm sorry. This is so stupid. I just don't know if I'm ready to jump into another job. I miss Jessica so much."

"It's not stupid. That baby was one heck of a wonderful kid. But there are a lot of children who would benefit from being around you, kiddo. Especially your nieces and nephews." He let that sink in. "You can call her back whenever you're ready, but will you do me a favor?"

"What?"

"Come back to the land of the living. Take a bubble bath, have a glass of wine, whatever you need. But, after that, rejoin the family. We miss you, Erin. The kids really miss you."

Erin realized how right Eamon was. She might not have Jess and Sam, she realized with a stab of pain, but she was missing out on what she'd always had—the love of her big, boisterous family. It made no sense to take out her pain on them. "Okay, I'll come out there."

"Yeah?" Eamon beamed.

"After a bath, which was a great idea. Make yourself useful as well as ornamental, Eam, and bring me that glass of wine. I'll fill the tub."

Eamon squeezed her against his shoulder. "That's the Erin we know and nag. And hey, the offer of a beating still stands. You say the word and you've got ten meaty O'Grady fists on your side."

Erin pulled away and stood. "Duly noted, but I'm not so into the violence thing. Now, get."

Eamon left, and Erin stood up and stretched. Crossing to the bathroom, she pulled her favorite vanilla bath foam from the cabinet and set it on the edge of the tub. As the steamy water gushed into the tub, she looked at herself in the mirror and got philosophical. So, she'd fallen in love with an unattainable man. It happened to a lot of women. She'd get over it eventually, even though it didn't feel like it at the moment. But being cocooned in the arms of her family could do nothing but help the process along. She'd loved, she'd lost, she'd mourned. Now it was time to move on.

Though it was Monday morning, Sam had taken the day off to try to get a handle on this train wreck of a life. He had tried to go back to being Superdad after Erin left, simply as a matter of pride. He wanted to show the world—or maybe himself—that he could handle a full-time job and a two-year-old on his own. Heck, single mothers did it all the time.

As he filled the washing machine with light garments picked out of the monstrous mound of unwashed laundry and simultaneously threw together some pathetic excuse for lunch on the stove, he wondered how in the hell the single mothers pulled it off. He certainly didn't have a handle on the multitasking thing, not even a fingerhold. He was chagrined to admit that he hadn't had any clue exactly how much Erin did around that house to make things run smoothly, but the past several days had given him a hard lesson in the truth.

God, he missed Erin.

And, as much as he missed her, Jessica missed her even more acutely. His baby girl was utterly inconsolable, and Sam couldn't even deny that her unhappiness was his fault. Granted, the break with Erin had to happen, and he'd stand by it. Still, knowing that didn't make the days any easier.

Just as he started the wash cycle, the smoke from the burning lunch on the stove top set off the smoke alarms, and the shrill sound startled Jessica out of her nap. As she screamed and wailed from her crib, he alternated between running into her bedroom to console her and dashing to the various smoke alarms waving a towel at them in the hopes of stopping the heinous shriek. After he'd pulled open all the doors and the smoke had dissipated enough to silence the alarms, Sam, breathing heavily, pulled Jessica out of her crib and sank onto the floor of her bedroom. He cradled her in his arms until her sobs had mellowed into hiccups, all the while deciding that home cooking was overrated.

He washed Jessica's face, combed her soft hair, and buckled her into her carseat for a quick drive to McDonald's. They used to love impromptu lunches together at McDonald's, but after they'd gotten their food and settled at a table in the Playland area, all Sam could feel was the absence of Erin. Life was staid and drab without her, colorless and humorless. He stole a peek at his listless baby girl and knew she felt the same thing.

He remembered Erin's lessons all at once, and decided to give them a try. His heart started to pound, and he swallowed once and then cleared his throat. "I miss Erin, Jess. So much. Do you?"

Jessica blinked up at him in surprise, then nodded. "Want Win home. Make Win come home." She burst into tears and reached her chubby arms out. Sam went to her immediately, pulling her into an embrace on his lap.

"I don't know if Erin will come home, baby. But maybe you can go visit her. Would you like that?"

Jessica shook her head emphatically. "Want Win home!"

Sam sighed, tucking Jessica's head under his chin. "I know. Your old dad is a champ at screwing things up, honeypot. Did you know that?" She didn't answer, and he was grateful. "I don't know what to do to make things better."

"Win come home."

That would make things better. Just like peace would make the world better. Yeah. Right. He held Jess and rocked her for a few minutes, saying nothing. Finally, he patted her on the back. Somehow, they needed to move on. "Go eat your lunch, Jess. Okay?"

"Not hungry."

Hell, he wasn't going to force her. He hadn't had much of an appetite since Erin vacated their lives, either. "Do you want to go play, then?"

Jessica nodded unenthusiastically, then wriggled off his lap and toddled toward the multicolored play station.

To pass the time, Sam pulled a newspaper off an adjacent, empty table and began to peruse headlines. Most of the world news escaped his interest, he hated to admit. He finished the first section, checking on Jessica regularly, then slipped it behind the rest of the stack.

His eyes immediately fell to the article about little Mark, and his heart leapt. Most of the other articles centered on Lissa and Adam, so this had to mean—

Scanning it quickly, Sam learned what he'd hoped: the bone marrow transplant had taken. Finally. Little Mark was on the mend and his prognosis was great. Sam released a long breath, surprised to realize how much he'd been praying for this outcome. Everyone had cause for celebration because a beloved child had a second chance at life. He grabbed his cell phone on instinct, thinking he should call Adam and congratulate him.

Adam. A man he'd never met.

Not just his brother, but a brother who'd shared a womb. What had he done? He replaced the cell phone on his belt and scrubbed his hands over his face. Yes, everyone had reason to celebrate Mark's news except Sam himself, because he'd chosen not to know these people. His little brother. He *chosen* not to reach out for the one thing he'd always wanted. Family.

Without warning, the sting of tears blurred his eyes. Was he the most obtuse man who ever walked the earth? Erin had been right all along, and he'd punished her for it. He *should* be celebrating with his siblings, with little Mark Cambry, who was a com-

plete innocent in the whole drama of Sam's abandonment and childhood. If he chose to continue down
this path of denial, it was no one's fault but his own
if he remained lonely and bitter.

Adam. Lissa. Mark. Shawna. Chad.

How exciting would it be for Jessica to know she
had aunts and uncles, even one just a few years older
than she?

He'd been so selfish.

So stupid.

So deeply in denial.

Sam's hands trembled as the biggest realization
he'd had in maybe forever zinged through him like
an electrical charge. Part of him found it ironic, the
other part found it pathetic. Only Sam Lowery would
have a life-changing epiphany in McDonald's Playland.

But, surroundings notwithstanding, he couldn't
deny it.

Like a sledgehammer to the chest, Sam admitted
that he'd screwed up the most important chance he'd
ever been presented in his life. Not the delay in meeting his siblings, which he could remedy with a little
courage. But rather, his chance at a relationship with
Erin. Sure she'd goaded him, prodded him, pushed
him repeatedly to the edge of his comfort zone which
annoyed the heck out of him, but that was only because she loved him. No one had ever loved him like
that, and he'd turned that love away.

God knew, he loved her, too. With his whole heart,
soul, being, he loved Erin.

He might not be the perfect man or father, but his love for Erin O'Grady was poignant in its perfection, right and whole and complete. Why hadn't he seen it before? Instead, he'd done his very best to push away the one woman who'd loved him in that unconditional manner for which he'd always yearned.

Urgency filled him. He had to make things right.

Sam hastily stacked the paper and pushed it aside. He threw away their mostly uneaten lunches and then called for Jessica. Generally obedient, she came to him immediately, curiosity showing in her expression.

Sam squatted down before her, smiling. "Want to go get Erin, honeypot?"

His little girl broke into a huge grin for the first time in at least a week, and she nodded vigorously.

"Let's go get her, then." He kissed Jessica on the temple. "I love you so much, Jess."

"Yuv you, Daddy."

And I love Erin, he thought. I am in love with Erin O'Grady and there's no going back. He squeezed his eyes shut, trepidation riddling through him. Please, God, let her be a forgiving woman. Moreover, let her brothers be forgiving men.

Sam clung to Jessica a little tighter as he knocked on Eamon O'Grady's front door. He'd called ahead and asked for an emergency meeting with all the O'Grady men, including Erin's father, and the reception had been icy and grudging, but at least they'd agreed. He didn't know how much they knew about his and Erin's relationship, but surely they wouldn't pound him into cad dust if he had a baby in his arms.

Eamon yanked the door open. "Lowery."

"Eamon. Thanks for taking the time to see me."

Eamon inclined his head and stepped aside. He gave a wink and a smile to Jessica, who giggled in response.

Sam entered the house, heart hammering in his chest. He wasn't used to opening up, but if he meant to bring Erin back to him and Jessica, he'd have to suck it up and spill his guts in order to get past the nearly impenetrable wall of brotherly protection.

In the living room, Matthew, Miles, Mick, Patrick and Erin's father, Eamon Sr., took up most of the space. He nodded to each one in turn, ending with Erin's father. "Sir, thanks for seeing me."

Eamon Sr. turned his attention to Jessica, holding out his arms. "Come here, you bonny little lass," he said in a very grandfatherly tone. "I might have a bit of candy for a pretty girl." He patted his chest pocket.

Jessica giggled shyly and looked toward her father. Sam nodded, setting her on the floor. She toddled over to the senior O'Grady male, clambering up into his lap.

"Have a seat," Matthew said to Sam, indicating a straight-backed wooden chair they'd set in the middle of the room.

Sam eyed it warily, half expecting it to be an electric chair.

"Fill us in on what this is all about. Something to drink?"

"Hemlock?" Mick suggested, in a thinly veiled venomous tone.

"Mick, watch yourself," his father admonished.

Mick held up his hands and backed down. "Just a suggestion, Dad. That's all."

"It's fine. I understand his anger." Sam took a seat, smoothing his sweat-slickened palms on the fronts of his jeans. Once Eamon Jr. had joined them, Sam leaned forward, resting his elbows on his knees. He made sure to look directly at all of the brothers as he spoke. "What this is about is the fact I've been a total ass."

"We don't know details, but we gathered that," Matthew, the burliest brother, said. "We've told Erin we'd be glad to pummel you into the dirt, but you remain unscathed at her wishes."

Sam clenched his jaw with chagrin. "I'll be sure to thank her when I see her."

"You expect to see her?" Mick asked.

"Expect? No. But I hope to see her." He paused, formulating his words. "Mr. O'Grady? Eamon? Patrick? Matthew? Miles? Mick? The truth is…I'm in love with Erin. Granted, I've screwed things up, but Erin came into my life like a whirlwind and sort of—" he shook his head "—threw me off kilter."

"Erin has a knack for that," Patrick said, and he didn't sound murderous. Sam took that as a good sign.

"I screwed things up, no doubt about it," Sam continued. "But I'd like your blessing to make it up to Erin."

"You want her back as your nanny?" Eamon Jr. asked, his eyes narrowed suspiciously. "She's already found another nanny job. She can't be bouncing back and forth at your whim."

"No, not as a nanny," Sam told him, all of them, feeling more assured about his position the more he talked. "I want to make her my wife."

"What?" Eamon Jr. asked.

Sam nodded. "I'm very serious with my intentions. I just can't stop thinking that Mrs. Erin O'Grady Lowery rolls off the tongue like poetry, but I won't propose if you disapprove." He paused, gathering the last of his courage.

"What are you asking us, son?" Erin's father asked gently.

"I'd like your blessings to propose to Erin."

Erin sat on the floor with her new charges, twin four-year-old sisters, listlessly playing with Barbies. It wasn't that she didn't like the children; Erin liked all children. But her heart had been shredded, and all she could think about was Sam and Jessica, especially after having read the update about Mark's bone marrow transplant in the newspaper that morning.

Had he gone on with his life?

Did he even care that his little brother's life had been saved? Did he know?

"Erin!" whined Britney. "Your Barbie is wearing the shoes that go with my Barbie's outfit."

"I'm sorry, honey," Erin said, slipping off the minuscule plastic pumps and handing them over. Just then, the doorbell rang. Erin turned toward the entry-way with a frown on her face. She wasn't expecting anyone.

She glanced back at Britney and Blair, smiling. "Stay here, loves. I'll just go see who that is."

The girls were so caught up in their game, they didn't give the doorbell a second thought, nor did they respond to her comments.

Erin padded through the house, stopping to check her appearance in the foyer mirror. No two ways about it, she looked like death. Dark circles smudged the delicate skin beneath her sad eyes, and her cheeks seemed sunken. No surprise, since she hadn't been able to sleep soundly or eat appropriately since leaving Sam's house, but she didn't like the overall image. Her hair was wild and crazy, but then again her hair was always wild and crazy. She liked it that way.

She threw the deadbolt and pulled open the door, then stopped, stunned. Her throat closed. "Sam. What are you doing here?" The ache to pull Jessica into her arms reached all the way down to her bones. No, deeper. To her soul, her heart, her very being. She missed both of them so incredibly much, she momentarily forgot her manners. She wanted to laugh, to cry. She wanted to yell at Sam and then hold him close. Hope and wariness fought for top billing inside her. Her emotions were so jumbled, so overwhelming, she simply stood there dumbfounded.

"I need to talk to you," he said, his voice husky.

He looked terrible, as terrible as she felt. Clearly,

he hadn't been sleeping or eating either. Part of her rejoiced in that, another part wanted to take care of him. "You look awful," she blurted, unintentionally.

One side of his mouth lifted. "Sleep deprivation."

"I hear you." For a moment, they simply searched each other's faces.

"Erin, I—"

"Win!" Jessica stretched as far as she could without falling, and Erin glanced up at Sam for his approval.

He nodded, so Erin took Jessica into her arms, cuddling her close. She breathed in her baby smell, closing her eyes at the wave of emotions that washed over her, sucking her under. "I've missed you so much, Jessica."

"Yuv you, Win."

"Oh, gosh." Erin's voice caught, and she had to swallow several times to regain her composure. "I love you, too, Jess. So very much."

"Erin."

Sam's soft voice drew her attention back, and she read something new and enticing in his eyes. Her heart leapt with hope, fired to life by the look on his face.

"Can I come in? We need to talk."

"Of course."

They stood just in the entryway, and Sam reached out and touched her cheek. Softly, gently.

Erin swallowed. "What's this about?"

"The transplant took. Mark's. His prognosis is good."

Tears filled Erin's eyes, and she smiled up at Sam over Jessica's head. "I know. I read it this morning and thought of you. All of you."

She watched his Adam's apple rise and fall with emotion. "My first instinct after reading the story was to call Adam, Erin, and congratulate him."

"But—"

"But I don't know him. He's my brother, and I don't know him. He doesn't know I exist." Sam raked fingers through his hair, leaving some of it standing askew. It gave him a boyishly vulnerable look.

"You can know him. If you want to."

"I know." A beat passed, then he lifted his gaze to her face cautiously. "But there's one problem."

"Which is?"

"I don't want to meet…my family without you."

Her heart jumped. "W-what do you mean?"

Sam started to pace in the large foyer, and Erin moved to lean against the wall and get out of his way. "God, Erin, I've had so much time to think since you left, and everything's wrong."

"What do you mean?" She was repeating herself, she knew, but he wasn't making much sense.

Suddenly, Sam spun to face her. "What I mean is, I don't want to live without you, Erin. I'm a mess. Jessica is a mess, and she needs you."

Her stomach dropped. "You want me to come back and work for you? Sam, I don't know."

"No. I don't want you to come work for me."

"Oh."

"I want you to marry me, Erin."

The room swayed before her. "Excuse me?"

Sam moved close, smoothing his hands down her upper arms. "I'm in love with you, Erin O'Grady, and I was just too damned stupid or scared to admit it to myself. Too afraid of losing you to let you close. I want to marry you, Erin. I want you to be my wife and Jessica's new mother. Please say yes. I haven't begged for much in my life, but I don't want to face another day without you."

"Oh, Sam." Tears filled her eyes and spilled over.

Jessica, confused, reached up to pat her cheeks. "No cry, Win."

Erin laughed, a watery sound, and kissed Jessica on the head. "I thought you said you didn't have room for family in your life?"

"I'm an idiot. I was wrong. Scared, maybe. I want you and Jessica. I want all the other children we'll create together. I even want the evil five, who have, incidentally, given us their blessings. Your father, too."

Her jaw slackened. "You actually went to my brothers?"

He pulled his chin back. "Come on. Do you think any guy in his right mind would get near Erin O'Grady without first getting permission from the O'Grady men?"

Erin laughed, feeling bubbly and free. "You're crazy."

Sam pulled her into his arms, Jessica cuddled between them, and he kissed her softly on the lips. "I am. Crazy about you, and crazy without you. Please take me out of my misery and say you'll marry me.'' He glanced at his daughter affectionately. ''That you'll marry us.''

Erin smiled so widely, she felt like she'd never be able to stop. ''Of course I will, Sam. You know I will.''

He cupped the sides of her face in his hands and kissed her so gently, her heart ached. ''I love you, Erin O'Grady.''

''And I love you, Sam Lowery. I'll love you forever.'' They kissed for several moments, then Erin pulled back. ''There's just one thing.''

''Uh-oh. What's that?''

''You once told me you had no room for more family in your life. You *do* realize that marrying me means marrying my family, don't you?''

''I can't think of anything better. Well, except for introducing you to *my* family as my soon-to-be wife.'' He smiled slowly at her. ''Can you handle that?''

''I can handle anything as long as we're together.''

''So can I, Erin, love. So can I.''

Epilogue

Sam's throat was so tight, all he could do was grip Erin's hand and stare straight ahead as they walked down the hospital corridor toward Mark Cambry's room. His nervous solemnity belied the cheeriness of the giant purple stuffed elephant he carried, a gift for his recuperating little brother. Finally, after twenty-seven years, he was about to meet his siblings. He could hardly believe it.

Lissa and Adam had been floored when Sam first contacted them, but after he'd outlined all the facts and mailed a photo, they couldn't wait to meet him. The human heart, he learned, had an infinite capacity for love. They welcomed him into the fold just as they'd first welcomed each other, as they'd both welcomed Mark, Shawna and Chad. Even the father who had abandoned them all, Jared Cambry. Sam wasn't sure he'd quite reached that point of altruism, but he wanted to meet Mark, wanted to tell the little guy to hang in there.

Thankfully, both Lissa and Adam respected Sam's aversion to publicity, so they agreed to meet in private this first time. No one had alerted the press that a third sibling had come forward, and the hospital business carried on as usual, with no one giving Sam a second glance. Maybe in the future, they'd decide together to let the media in on this little twist in the reunited twins story, but for now, it was a family event, pure and simple. Family. He loved the sound of that.

Outside the threshold to Mark's private room, he glanced at Erin, and she sent him an encouraging smile full of love. Jessica, all prettied up, sat happily on Erin's hip. Sam took a moment to marvel that he had more family in this moment than he'd ever had, and he adored it. He couldn't wait until he and Erin added new babies to their family tree. The more the better. Jessica deserved to be a big sister, and she'd make a great one. And as for Erin's mothering skills, well, Sam only knew that their children would be extremely lucky.

"Go ahead and knock, honey," Erin said. "We're right here for you."

He nodded once, rather grimly, then raised his fist and knocked gently. Immediately, his heart began to thud in his chest and he had to fight the urge to bolt.

"Come in," called a feminine voice.

He raised his brows at Erin and took a deep breath. "Now or never," he murmured.

Sam pushed open the door and peered in.

"He's here!" Lissa cried, jumping up from the chair she occupied next to little Mark's bed. "My God, look at you. You look just like Adam."

Sam took in Adam's tailored, undoubtedly expensive suit and laughed wryly. "I wouldn't say we're exactly twins."

Everyone laughed.

Adam rose, too, and came over. Sam handed the giant purple elephant to Erin, who hung back, then both Adam and Lissa wrapped Sam in a huge, long-overdue, swaying hug. Tears filled the corners of Sam's eyes as they clung to one another. He didn't know what to say. How did people catch up on twenty-seven lost years? They had time for that. All he knew at that moment was, this felt right—it felt like he belonged at last.

When they pulled apart, all three of them had tears in their eyes. Adam grinned. "Can I just say, I hope we're not quadruplets? I don't think I can handle another shock like this in the near future."

Sam and Lissa laughed, then Sam glanced toward the solemn, observant little boy in the hospital bed. He moved over, taking a seat on the edge. "I'm going to take a wild guess and say you must be my brother, Mark."

The little boy nodded, then reached out for a hug.

Sam embraced the child, squeezing his eyes shut.

"I'm so glad you're doing well, little buddy. I read every story about you in the papers."

"Why didn't you come visit me earlier?"

Sam pulled back and sighed, holding one of Mark's hands in his own. "I was afraid. Not of you, but just—"

"Because you didn't know any of us?"

"How'd you get to be so wise in such a short time?" Sam asked, tilting his head to the side.

"I don't know." His eyes flickered toward the door. "What's with the elephant?"

Sam looked toward Erin, and she moved forward. "I brought him for you. But if you're too grown up for him, I'll get you something else. Whatever you want."

"No, he's kewl." Mark reached out for the elephant, and Erin handed him over. "Thanks, Sam." He peered curiously toward Erin and Jessica then. "Is this your wife?"

"She will be soon." Sam looked around to include Adam and Lissa in this conversation. "This is my fiancée, Erin. And Mark, this is your niece, Jessica. My daughter."

Mark looked momentarily stunned. "I'm an uncle?"

"That you are."

"That is so unreal." His little chest puffed out as he glanced at Jessica. "Hi, there. I'm your uncle Mark."

Again everyone laughed.

Jessica reached out for Mark, and Sam held out a hand. "Is it okay, Mark? Are you in pain?"

"Naw, I'm fine. She can sit on my bed."

Erin sat Jessica on Mark's bed, instructing her quietly to be gentle with her young uncle, and Jessica seemed to understand. As the children chattered, the adults gathered in one corner of the room, and Erin was hugged and welcomed into the family by both Lissa and Adam. They'd begun to talk about wedding plans when the door swung open.

Everyone turned.

Sam's gaze met that of the man who could only be Jared Cambry. To Sam's surprise, the man didn't look like a self-serving monster. He looked like a concerned father who'd gone to hell and back. Sam, nevertheless, stiffened.

Jared came right up to him and held out a hand. "You must be Sam. I'm your—" He pursed his lips. "I'm Jared Cambry. I'm so glad you came by."

Sam took the man's hand and shook it, then introduced Erin and Jessica.

Sam was shocked to see Jared's eyes moisten as he looked at Jessica. "I'm a grandfather?" Sam said nothing, and the older man cut a glance his way. "Would you rather I didn't refer to myself that way?"

Erin moved up beside Sam and curved her hand around his elbow. "Sam, wouldn't it be nice for Jessica to have another grandfather?"

"Yes. I guess that would be fine. Although you seem pretty young to fit that bill," Sam told Jared.

Jared eyed him, then laid a hand gently on his shoulder. "How about you and I take a walk, talk a little?"

Sam glanced toward Erin, feeling uncertain.

"Go," she told him softly, and the love in her eyes said she knew he'd handle everything just right. Her faith imbued him with confidence.

"That'd be okay, I guess."

Sam and Jared left the room side by side and didn't speak until they reached a private, family consultation room down the hall from Mark's. Jared peered into the oblong window in the door and, finding it empty, he opened the door. "After you."

Sam went in and took a seat on one of the plum-hued sofas. Jared chose a chair at a right angle to the sofa, and then he simply met and held Sam's gaze.

"I wanted to hate you," Sam said, through a clenched jaw. "But you're not quite the monster I'd made you out to be in my mind. You're just a father, like I am."

Jared expelled a long breath through his nose, and a lifetime of regret etched lines around his eyes. "I didn't know there were three of you, Sam. Didn't even know Olivia had died in the crash until Mark got sick and I got desperate to find a way for him to live." He wrung his hands. "There is nothing I can say to make up for not having been there when you three were growing up. But you're all adults now and you've built amazing lives. I'm proud of you, whether or not I have a right to be."

Sam swallowed thickly. "Thank you."

"Listen, can we just start from here? I don't expect you to call me Dad or to think of me as your father. But I would like to be a part of your life."

"I...I'd like that, too. I've been so damn angry at you since the stories about Lissa and Mark first hit the media."

"I understand. I don't blame you."

"But I want to let it go. I want to start fresh." Jared reached over and patted Sam's forearm, and surprisingly, the gesture felt consoling to Sam. He continued, feeling stronger. "Erin and I are getting married, and I'd like the whole family to be involved in the wedding."

"I'd like that very much."

"I may not ever refer to you as...Dad, Jared, but—"

"What is it, Sam?"

"I'd like to start anew. I'd like you to sit in the place of my father at the wedding. I've never had a father—" His voice caught, and he clenched his fists.

"Sam Lowery, I'd be honored to participate in your wedding in whatever manner you'd like. You may never consider me your father, but I think of you and Lissa and Adam as my children, just as much as I think of Mark, Shawna and Chad that way."

"I've never had a father," Sam said again, dazedly.

"Well, maybe we can start with friendship and work from there."

"I'm glad Mark's okay," Sam said.

"Sam, I'm glad you're okay."

Sam thought of Erin and Jessica. He thought of

Adam, Lissa and their spouses, whom he'd be meeting later that evening. He thought of Mark, Shawna, Chad, Jared and his wife. Lastly, he thought of Erin's family, the whole big, bustling bunch of them. And he realized, maybe for the first time, that he *was* okay. He had more family than he'd ever imagined and he felt surrounded, loved, included. "I am okay, Jared. I really am."

The two men shared a smile of understanding, then they walked, side by side, back to be with the rest of their family. They'd come full circle, and both were now ready to move forward. When they entered Mark's hospital room, Sam met Erin's eyes and shared a private look of love. Her pride and respect shone through and warmed him from the inside out. His precious baby daughter laughed happily with her young uncle on his hospital bed, and the siblings with whom he'd shared a womb for almost nine months sat smiling up at him as if they'd never been separated. Calmness and completeness knocked the chip that life had put on Sam's shoulder off, once and for all, and he smiled back at all of them.

He was crazy in love.

His baby girl was happy again.

And, most unexpectedly, he had siblings—a lot of them—bound by blood and all that kind of connection entailed. The good, the bad, the happy, the sad, all the rights and responsibilities that were part and parcel of belonging—he would gladly take all of it and give back in kind.

For so many years, Sam had built houses. It had

been his calling, his passion, to take raw materials and fashion them into houses of every style imaginable, but, standing in Mark's hospital room that afternoon, he realized he'd never built a home. Only love and family built a home, and he knew that now because he'd come home.

Finally and forever, Sam Lowery had a home—not the kind built out of brick and wood, but the kind made of love. The kind a man never lost...and never left.

The kind he never, ever took for granted.

* * * * *

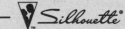

SPECIAL EDITION™

After *The Sons of Caitlin Bravo* comes...

BRAVO FAMILY TIES
Stronger Than Ever

From award-winning author
Christine Rimmer

FIFTY WAYS TO SAY... I'M PREGNANT

(Silhouette Special Edition #1615)

Starr Bravo had been in love with rancher
Beau Tisdale since she was sixteen, yet they'd
agreed that this "summer of love" was just that.
When September rolled around, they'd go their
separate ways—she to her glamorous job in
New York City, he back to the ranch.

But now she needed to get the words out—
Beau, I'm pregnant—before their baby did it for her!

*Available June 2004
at your favorite retail outlet.*

The scintillating MacKade brothers are back
in a special collector's volume!

#1 *New York Times* bestselling author

NORA ROBERTS

Devin and Shane

THE MᶜKADE BROTHERS

Sexy, charming and determined to stay single, Nora's
sexiest bachelors ever are about to fall in love....

"You can't bottle wish fulfillment but Ms. Roberts
certainly knows how to put it on the page."
—*New York Times*

Available in June 2004.

Silhouette®
Where love comes alive™

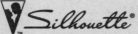 Silhouette®

COMING NEXT MONTH

SPECIAL EDITION

#1615 FIFTY WAYS TO SAY I'M PREGNANT—Christine Rimmer
Bravo Family Ties

Reunited after six long years, Starr Bravo and Beau Tisdale couldn't deny the attraction that had always sizzled between them. But when Starr discovered she was carrying Beau's baby, she panicked and fled the scene. Could Beau find—and forgive—his one true love so they could be a family at last?

#1616 ACCIDENTAL FAMILY—Joan Elliott Pickart
The Baby Bet: MacAllister's Gifts

When Patty Sharpe Clark set out to track down a child's missing father, David Montgomery, she was shocked to learn he'd been in an accident and had amnesia! She vowed to care for Sarah Ann until the girl's father recovered, but would Patty find love where she least expected?

#1617 CAVANAUGH'S WOMAN—Marie Ferrarella
Cavanaugh Justice

Deeply dedicated to his family and work, Shaw Cavanaugh didn't have time for the frivolity of life…until he met Moira McCormick. The charming actress came from a troubled past and longed to be part of a family, but would Shaw accept her into his life…forever?

#1618 HOT AUGUST NIGHTS—Christine Flynn
The Kendricks of Camelot

After CEO Matt Callaway and Ashley Kendrick shared a steamy one-night stand, the fear of scandal had separated them. Ashley had never forgotten the way Matt made her feel, but would he be able to forgive her for keeping their unborn child a secret…?

#1619 THE DADDY SURVEY—Janis Reams Hudson
Men of Cherokee Rose

Rancher Sloan Chisolm had never turned his back on a woman in trouble. So when beautiful Emily Nelson lost her job as a waitress, he was determined that she come work for him at the Cherokee Rose Ranch. He knew she considered being his housekeeper temporary, but their kisses made him hope that this might be a partnership…for life.

#1620 ONE PERFECT MAN—Lynda Sandoval

Years ago Tomas Garza's dreams of a family had fallen apart after his wife abandoned him and their daughter. He'd desperately tried to fill the void in his daughter's life, but the time had come when she needed a woman—someone like the beautiful event planner Erica Goncalves. She'd agreed to help him plan a party for his daughter, but would she be open to something more permanent?

SSECNM0504

SECOND THOUGHTS

Lizzie was sitting at her dressing table, brushing her hair. Matthew walked silently over to her and bent so that he could look at her in the mirror.

Lizzie, having heard nothing, almost fell off the bench, and then she rapped his hand with her brush when he tried to catch her.

"Matthew! What do you think you're doing? You have no business to be here!"

"I know that, Lizzie, Come dance with me!" he exclaimed, opening the music box so that the melody would begin.

"Dance with you? Have you quite lost your mind?" she demanded.

"No! I have found it!" he answered, sweeping her up from the bench and into the dance. "I have loved you all my life, Lizzie Lancaster—though I didn't know it until I thought it was too late to ever be able to do anything about it."

"And what do you think you're going to do about it now?" she demanded, clutching her dressing gown as they danced.

"I am going to marry you and take you home," he replied, folding her into his arms and kissing her firmly . . .

BOOKS BY MONA GEDNEY

A LADY OF FORTUNE

THE EASTER CHARADE

A VALENTINE'S DAY GAMBIT

A CHRISTMAS BETROTHAL

A SCANDALOUS CHARADE

A DANGEROUS AFFAIR

A LADY OF QUALITY

A DANGEROUS ARRANGEMENT

MERRY'S CHRISTMAS

LADY DIANA'S DARING DEED

LADY HILARY'S HALLOWEEN

AN ICY AFFAIR

FROST FAIR FIANCÉ

A LOVE AFFAIR FOR LIZZIE

Published by Zebra Books

A LOVE AFFAIR FOR LIZZIE

Mona Gedney

ZEBRA BOOKS
KENSINGTON PUBLISHING CORP.
http://www.kensington.com

ZEBRA BOOKS are published by

Kensington Publishing Corp.
850 Third Avenue
New York, NY 10022

All Kensington titles, imprints and distributed lines are available at special quantity discounts for bulk purchases for sales promotion, premiums, fund-raising, educational or institutional use.

Special book excerpts or customized printings can also be created to fit specific needs. For details, write or phone the office of the Kensington Special Sales Manager: Kensington Publishing Corp., 850 Third Avenue, New York, NY 10022. Attn. Special Sales Department. Phone: 1-800-221-2647.

Zebra and the Z logo Reg. U.S. Pat. & TM Off.

First Printing: February 2004
10 9 8 7 6 5 4 3 2 1

Printed in the United States of America

One

On the day that Matthew left for the war, the first daffodils starred the early golden-green of the garden. Even though Lizzie was only fifteen, her parents had permitted them a private farewell before the public one in the Lodge, for the couple's deep attachment was acknowledged and approved. As they strolled hand in hand through the spring garden, the world around them was awakening with a piercing tenderness, made more poignant to them because they soon would be hundreds of miles apart. For the first time, spring seemed a cruel time to Lizzie, mocking her with its promise of beginnings just as a part of her world was ending. She swallowed hard, determined to master the lump in her throat, and smiled at Matthew, who was looking down at her a little anxiously.

"Are you certain that you won't forget me once I've gone away, Lizzie? Perhaps you will find some dashing young fellow and not even be able to recall my name." Matthew's voice was teasing, but she could detect a hint of concern, too.

He had worn his Hussar uniform so that she could see him in his full military splendor. He looked magnificent, of course, in his blue jacket with the white facings and the white braid, the short fur-trimmed pelisse jauntily over one shoulder, but Lizzie could focus on nothing but the steady gaze of his gray eyes. That reassured her. He might look unfamiliar and rather stiff in his military regalia, but he was still her Matthew.

"Never," she replied firmly. "You know that I won't forget you, Matthew." She did her best to equal his teasing tone. "It is *I* who should be worried. You are the one going away into a new world, and I understand that the ladies of Portugal and Spain are lovely. Are you certain that you will remember *me* after a few weeks have passed and England is far behind you?"

"Absolutely certain," Matthew said, squeezing her hand and pulling her close to him. "And will you make time to write to me now and then?"

"Every day," she promised, "and I shall think of you every minute." She took from around her neck a chain bearing a golden medal of St. George slaying the dragon. She had ordered it months ago, and had worn it for a week herself before giving it to him, as though by doing so she could send something of herself with him.

"St. George is the patron saint of soldiers," Lizzie reminded him, standing on tiptoe so that she could slip the chain over his head. "He will bring you safely home to me."

"I will place my confidence in St. George, then—and in you." His voice shook slightly as he folded her close and kissed her.

The time had arrived for him to leave, and Lizzie knew that she mustn't cry. She had talked to herself firmly about that. Her duty was to send Matthew off cheerfully, to be a support to him rather than a source of sorrow and concern. She caressed his smooth cheek and then ruffled his dark hair, smiling up into his dear, familiar face.

"And now, dear heart, I fear that you must go in and

run the gauntlet of my family's farewells. I warn you now that Alice and Mama will cry, Papa will shake your hand gruffly and wish you Godspeed, Tussie will give you a book to improve your mind and keep your spirits up, and Cook will have sent out a basket of delicacies so that you may keep up your strength. She puts no faith in foreign food."

Cheered by her manner and forewarned by her words, Matthew went in with her to face the group awaiting him. All went just as Lizzie had told him it would. Mrs. Lancaster's handkerchief was already a damp ball of lace before he could hug her, and Alice, though only eleven, had already developed a fine theatrical sense and had to be borne away in hysterics by their governess, Miss Tussman. Tussie, also agitated by his leave-taking, slowed just long enough to press into Matthew's hand a slim volume of *Pilgrim's Progress* and to remind him that time would pass quickly and that soon he would be home again in the bosom of his family. Then she hurried from the room, pressing her handkerchief to her eyes and murmuring audibly, "So young, so young."

Mr. Lancaster cleared his throat several times, shook Matthew's hand firmly, clapped him on the shoulder, and finally said, "Godspeed, my boy. Come back to us safely." Then he turned and disappeared abruptly into the library.

Mrs. Clary, the cook, who had been awaiting her opportunity behind the door to the dining room, hurried out and thrust a large wicker basket into Matthew's arms, saying "God bless you, sir! Take care of yourself!" Then she too pressed a handkerchief to her eyes and bustled from the hall as Matthew called his thanks after her. Mrs. Lancaster retired tactfully, still sobbing, so that the pair could have their final good-bye in privacy.

Determined not to become a watering pot too, Lizzie hooked one arm through the handle of the basket. "I shall have to help you carry it, I know," she told him in a low voice so that she could not be overheard. "I watched Cook filling it. She began two nights ago and then kept thinking of things that you might need once you left British soil. If she had had another day, you would have enough here to sink the transport."

"It was very kind of Mrs. Clary to prepare this feast for me," said Matthew, smiling. "She always fed George and me in the most royal manner when we were young."

"And you know how she loved doing it. Nothing has ever pleased her more than feeding hungry boys who think that her kitchen is just one step down from heaven."

A small stable boy had brought Matthew's horse around and, casting an admiring eye at the glory of Matthew's uniform, handed him the reins and retired discreetly.

Lizzie inspected the basket and the horse in a businesslike manner. "Well, it is absolutely certain that you cannot carry this heavy basket on horseback, Matthew, even for the short distance back to Prestonwood." She removed the napkins covering it, opened the saddlebags, and began judiciously stowing the basket's contents within them. Touched, she saw that Mrs. Clary had even included a bottle of her famous blackberry wine—for medicinal purposes.

"I am afraid, Matthew, that you *shall* have to carry the steak and kidney pie back to Prestonwood with you. It simply will not survive a saddlebag, even for two miles."

He looked down at her gravely, but his eyes were merry. "You do realize, Lizzie, that carrying it will quite ruin my heroic exit. How can you possibly view me as the figure of romance I am attempting to be if I am riding away with my arms full of pie?"

"The pie will not interfere at all," Lizzie had assured him, laughing. "I shall be greatly struck by your heartrending exit—but be certain not to get it all over your uniform. That pie will not blend well with your colors."

Matthew kissed her lightly, then swung himself into the saddle, waiting as she handed him the pie.

"Do be careful with it, Matthew," she said anxiously. "After all her trouble, Cook would never forgive us if you dropped it right here."

"Tell Mrs. Clary not to fear," he assured her with becoming gravity. "I shall pack it up safely before I leave for the coast. This pie will accompany me to my ship and it will sustain me when England has slipped below the horizon and I can see her no more."

"I will tell her," Lizzie assured him with equal gravity. Then, to prevent matters taking a more serious turn, she dimpled and blew him a kiss. "A safe journey, love."

He returned the kiss, smiling, then turned and rode down the drive, stopping to wave—somewhat awkwardly, of course, because of the pie—before the road curved away into the grove of oaks.

"Good-bye, Matthew! Good-bye!" Alice was calling from the nursery windows on the third floor, where she and Tussie were frantically waving what appeared to be a white tablecloth in farewell.

Hearing them, Matthew stopped and waved once more, laughing, then rode on and disappeared among the trees.

Lizzie kept her pledge. She had indeed written Matthew every day, although the letters were posted only once each week. In return, he wrote to describe the new worlds he was encountering. His first letter told of the stormy seas on the voyage to Portugal. Virtually everyone on the transport had succumbed to seasickness, he wrote, but to his delight it had not affected him. Indeed, he had dined upon Mrs. Clary's pie with great gusto. Lizzie read and reread his account of his voyage and of the excitement of joining his regiment in the Peninsula. To his distress, he arrived in Spain too late to participate in the taking of Ciudad Rodrigo, but he was present for the dreadful battle at Badajoz and for the victory at Salamanca.

His letters were full of his admiration for Lord Wellington. "I would not say that the men love him," he wrote, "but they have confidence in him as a commander. They say that in battle they would rather see the Beau with his hooked nose and steely eyes among them than another commander who might later heap compliments upon them or supply them with extra gin. I only wish that I could be such a man. My chief comfort is that now that I have seen battle and held my own without turning tail, the others can no longer call me a Johnny Newcombe. I have at least proven myself to that extent."

Soon after this letter had come another, in which he wrote that he had had an unbelievable stroke of good fortune. At Salamanca, Wellington had seemed to be everywhere during the battle, with no regard for personal danger. At one point, his horse was shot from beneath him, and the telescope that he always carried to survey the progress of the battle had flown from his hand during the fall. Matthew had leaped from his own mount and called, "Take mine, sir!" and scrambled down a ravine to retrieve the telescope and restore it to him. Wellington, tall and spare in his plain gray frock coat, had sprung into the saddle, nodded at him, and galloped away.

Two days later, he had been surprised to be summoned to Lord Wellington's headquarters and thanked by him personally. Although he had not known Matthew's name, he had known at a glance his regiment, and had sent one of his aides-de-camp to make inquiries about the young officer who had lent him his horse. Matthew's mount was returned to him, and Lord Wellington had asked if there were any kindness that he might show him for the loan of an excellent mount at a critical time—and for retrieving the indispensable telescope. Gathering his courage, Matthew had taken his opportunity. He had asked to be taken as an aide-de-camp on Wellington's personal staff, knowing that such a favor was most unlikely to be granted. Although the commander had several very young men on his staff, Matthew knew that they had come from noble families. The famous cold gray eyes had appraised him narrowly—"I felt as though he could look right through me," he had written—but finally Wellington had nodded, saying shortly, "We shall try it."

And from that time, Matthew had served on his staff. Lizzie heard much about life at headquarters—of Wellington's days of hunting with his own pack of hounds, of the long days of work and the General's meticulous attention to detail, of the exciting reports of scouts and spies, of occasional theatrical evenings and supper parties. "We have excellent wine here, but the quality of the food is indifferent," he wrote. "Mrs. Clary would be horrified to hear that we often have cold meat for dinner when we are on the march, and at such times the General himself sometimes goes for an entire day with only bread and a boiled egg that he has carried in the pocket of his coat. On nights that we do sit down to dinner, it is the conversation and not the food that makes the meals memorable."

For two years Lizzie had looked forward eagerly to Matthew's letters, rich with the details of his days. When Alice demanded to know if she did not feel jealous, Lizzie had only been amused.

"Why should I be?" she had inquired, certain that Alice was going to tell her whether she asked or not.

"Why, it's as plain as a pikestaff, Lizzie! Because Matthew is having adventures—a perfectly wonderful time, in spite of the fighting—and you're still here in the same old place, doing the same old things!"

She scrutinized her older sister for a moment, then shook her head when she could see that her words had made no impression. "What do you do here?" she demanded. "The same boring thing every day—and you are satisfied with it!"

Lizzie had nodded with what Alice could only consider as the most irritating calmness. "You are right," she agreed. "I am indeed satisfied with my life here." And she had picked up the book she had been reading and moved closer to the fire.

Alice had given an exaggerated sigh of exasperation, thrown her hands into the air, and marched from the room. Once she was safely gone, Lizzie slipped Matthew's latest letter from her book and read it one more time.

She was grateful for each one that she received. For as long as she was reading a letter, she felt close to him once more. She could imagine him sitting here with her by the fire, recounting each of his adventures, just as he would when the war was over, and he came home once more. Then they would be married, and sit beside their own fire together, talking over all that he had experienced. Their children would grow up hearing the tales of their father's adventures with Wellington in the Peninsula as they worked to defeat the armies of Bonaparte.

When she was not reading one of his letters, the Peninsula and Matthew—and their marriage—seemed very far away indeed.

Two

On the morning that her world fell apart, Lizzie stood for a long time at the window, the letter still in her hand. She stared blindly at the familiar white sweep of gravel that appeared from the distant grove of oaks and curved gently to the front of their house. How many times had she stood in this same place, waiting anxiously for him to ride out of the shadows of the grove and into the sunlight? No matter what horse he had ridden, she had always been able to identify Matthew at a glance, by his dark hair and the easy manner in which he handled his mount.

Unbidden, recollections of him flooded her mind. One of her earliest memories was of him riding down the drive on a sturdy little pony. He had successfully evaded the company of the groom and, taking his first ride on his own, had come proudly over to see her brother George. George had saddled his own pony, and together the two of them had trotted away, off on one of their many escapades. A few years later, on one of the golden days of her life, she had been allowed to tag along with them. However, her mother had made short work of that, announcing firmly that no daughter of hers would be running gypsy-wild for all the countryside to see. Then George and Matthew had been sent away to school, and thereafter their larks—at least many of them—had been confined to holidays.

When she was fifteen, her parents had held a Christmas ball. Despite her age, she was allowed to attend because the guests were just the families of the neighborhood. Matthew, in the highest of spirits because his father had promised to purchase him a commission in the Hussars, had suddenly noticed her that night. He had been away for more than half a year, and when he saw her, his eyes had lighted with a sudden warmth, and she had known that the time she had been waiting for had come. He had walked directly across the room to her, ignoring pretty Bella Simmons, who had been attempting to flirt with him.

"Lizzie!" he had exclaimed, taking both her hands and smiling down at her. "How could it be? I go away for a little while, and when I come home, I find that you have grown up overnight!"

"Perhaps it is because I am putting my hair up now, Matthew," she had responded demurely, her heart beating so quickly that she had thought it might burst.

"Perhaps," he said, "but I see that I must keep a more watchful eye on you."

Hugh Simmons had come up just then to claim her for a quadrille, but Matthew had shooed him away, tucking Lizzie's arm through his own and announcing to the indignant Hugh that he had already engaged her for that dance.

"It could be, Lizzie," Matthew had added, looking down at her thoughtfully as he led her out to dance, "that we shouldn't have laughed at our fathers. Perhaps they were wiser than we knew." At his words, Lizzie had felt her cheeks grow warm.

Both their families, the Lancasters and the Websters,

had known for years—from the time Matthew was six and she was still in leading strings—that their fathers wished for the two of them to marry. The men shared a friendship as close as that of their sons, and it had appeared highly desirable to them that the families be officially united.

Like the others, Lizzie had always laughed at their old-fashioned notion, but she had been secretly delighted, even if everyone treated it as a joke. She had always loved Matthew Webster, but to him she had merely been George's little sister. Then, on the night of that Christmas ball, he had danced with her three times and had kissed her under the mistletoe.

From that time on, when Matthew came to call at Lancaster Lodge, he came to see Lizzie, his gray eyes lighting up whenever she walked into the room. By the time he left for Portugal, the talk of their eventual marriage was a serious matter rather than a family joke. She had been too young to become engaged at the time, of course, and Matthew had been going away to fight in the war, but it was understood that they would one day marry.

She had been able to think of nothing more deeply satisfying than marrying Matthew and settling at Prestonwood, here in the neighborhood where they had grown up together. For a brief time she had thought that their marriage might come more quickly than she had ever imagined. Poor Mr. Webster had died only two months after his son's departure for Portugal. As the heir and only son, Matthew could have sold out and returned home when he received the news, but he had chosen to remain with his regiment. Nevertheless, Lizzie knew that he would eventually return and that their children would grow up at Prestonwood.

After a year had gone by, her mother had suggested that

she have a formal coming-out in London during the Season, but Lizzie had refused. She had no great fondness either for London or for society life and, since she already knew that she was to marry Matthew, she told her mother that she had neither the desire nor the need to be a part of the Marriage Mart. Although Alice had criticized her decision passionately, her parents had accepted it, and she had remained peacefully at Lancaster Lodge, waiting for the war to be over and for Matthew to come home.

"But of course you should go to London!" Alice had insisted. "Don't be such a pea-goose, Lizzie! Matthew is off seeing the world. Why shouldn't you have a little fun instead of poking around here? What harm could having a Season possibly do? You can still marry Matthew!"

Lizzie had patted her sister's arm. "There's no need to worry about me, Alice. I'm perfectly happy as I am, and Matthew will be home once Bonaparte is defeated."

How confident she had been about her future.

As she stood looking out over the drive, a sudden sharp pain shot through her, scattering the memories and leaving her unable to draw a breath. The day was warm, but she was shivering uncontrollably. Turning from the window, she stared blankly about the room. Nothing in the cheerful drawing room, with its Turkey rugs and curtains of gold velvet, looked familiar.

She sat down abruptly, the letter fluttering from her hand to the floor. With a curious detachment, she reflected that she felt exactly as she had last winter when Red Rover had balked at a fence and pitched her headlong to the frozen ground. She had lain there for what had seemed like forever, unable to catch her breath as she watched the world spinning around her. Although she was now in a warm and comfortable room, she felt as cold and lost as she had then.

"Lizzie?" The door opened and her mother bustled in, the ribbons on her tidy lace cap streaming behind her. "Lizzie, Walton tells me that you've had a letter from Matthew. How *is* the dear boy? Does he say when he will be coming home?"

Here Mrs. Lancaster paused, taking in her daughter's blank expression and the letter on the floor.

"What is it, Lizzie?" Her mother's voice was filled with concern. "Is he ill? Has something happened to Matthew?"

Lizzie nodded stiffly, and Mrs. Lancaster's eyes filled with tears. Through all the months that Matthew had been away in the war, they had feared for his safety daily. Now it appeared that the proclamation of peace had given them a false sense of security about his well-being.

"Oh, my dear child," she said gently, sitting down next to her daughter and slipping her arm around Lizzie's shoulders.

To Lizzie's relief, there were no more questions, and they sat in silence until Alice hurried through the door with Tussie following in her wake.

"What does Matthew say, Lizzie? Is he still with Wellington in Paris or has he already gone to Vienna? Where is he now and why hasn't he come home to see us? Will he be here for Christmas?"

The barrage of questions stopped only because Alice had to pause for breath. Tall and slim now, she was quick in everything she said and did and impatient with those who could not keep pace with her.

Taking advantage of the interval, Mrs. Lancaster glanced gravely at her younger daughter and Tussie, then shook her head slightly. "I think we should talk about this a little later, my dear."

"Yes, of course," agreed Miss Tussman hurriedly,

putting her hand on Alice's shoulder. "We should finish your French lesson, Alice, so that you have time to practice on the pianoforte before we take our walk."

Hearing her sister's unladylike snort at this plan for her afternoon would usually have won a sympathetic smile from Lizzie, but today there was no response. Noting this, Alice shot a puzzled glance at her mother, but she reluctantly allowed Tussie to guide her from the room.

As the door closed behind them, a tear slid down Lizzie's cheek. Mrs. Lancaster saw it, and stroked her hair gently. This was the calm child that never gave way to tears, so her fears for her daughter's happiness sharpened. What could have happened to Matthew, she wondered. The war was over, with Napoleon safely tucked away on the island of Elba, but accidents occurred, of course, even to young men—especially, she feared, to young men living abroad. Everyone knew that life on the Continent was more dangerous than life in England. How dreadful it would be if Matthew had come unscathed through two years of battle and rough living only to be taken from them after the return of peace.

Whenever news had reached them of each of the Peninsular battles, they had waited anxiously for Matthew's letters, assuring them that he was well. Mrs. Lancaster now waited uneasily to hear the worst, wishing that she could protect her children from all the pain that she knew life held in store for them.

Finally Lizzie leaned over and retrieved the letter from the floor. To her mother's astonishment, she crushed it into a tight ball and flung it across the room. Mrs. Lancaster stared at her daughter, shocked. Not only did Lizzie treasure all of Matthew's letters, packing each away in a rosewood box, but she also never made an exhibition of her feelings. Lizzie never allowed her emotions to run away with her. Alice was the daughter who gave way to anger and tears, Lizzie, the one who kept the household steady.

"How could he do it, Mama?" she demanded, brushing away the traitorous tears with her hand. "How could Matthew dream of doing such a thing?"

Mrs. Lancaster, who had been preparing to comfort her for the injury or death of her fiancé, stared at her. "What do you mean, Lizzie? What has Matthew done? Is he not injured?"

"Injured?" Lizzie's pale face flushed and her fingers curled together to form two small fists. "I should say that he is not—although I promise that he would be if I could place my hands upon him! *I* am the one who has been injured! It is our family that has been injured!"

Lizzie stood and began to pace the floor, stooping to pick up the crumpled ball of paper so that she could crush it once more, then she threw it down and attempted to grind it into the carpet with the sole of her slipper. "Matthew, on the other hand, appears to be in fine fettle!" she said, her voice bitter.

"That's good news, is it not?" inquired her mother cautiously. "That he is in good health, I mean." Mrs. Lancaster was so taken aback by her daughter's unusual behavior that she was almost afraid to ask the question.

"I daresay that all of his friends are delighted for him!" snapped Lizzie. "Particularly Miss Teresa Blackwell!"

"I see," murmured Mrs. Lancaster and, unfortunately, she did. The introduction of the name of an unknown young lady into the midst of Lizzie's distraught diatribe had exposed the heart of the problem. More unwilling than ever to probe an open wound, she sat and waited for further information. It was not long in coming.

When Lizzie began to speak, her words fairly tumbled over one another.

"To think that I believed him, Mama! When he wrote that continuing to serve on the Duke's staff, even after the war, was too great an honor to refuse, I believed him! What a blind fool I was!"

"But it is indeed a great honor," ventured her mother. "There was nothing foolish in believing that."

"But that is clearly not why he accepted the position! I should have known something was amiss when he wrote to me so seldom these last months. Even when he didn't bother to come here to see me while he was back in England this summer, I was goose enough to think that he still loved me and still planned to marry me! I must have feathers for brains!"

The speed of her pacing had increased as her voice rose. To Mrs. Lancaster's dismay, her daughter's anger was rising to a fever pitch. So concerned was she about such uncharacteristic behavior that she could not spare a thought for the serious consequences that Matthew's defection would have for their family.

The failure of the last two harvests and of some of Mr. Lancaster's investments during the war years, coupled with the outrageous gaming debts that George had acquired, had placed a severe strain upon the family's finances. Only a week earlier, just before leaving to bail George out once again, Mr. Lancaster had observed to his wife that Lizzie's wedding could come none too soon. Matthew's father had provided a substantial settlement for Lizzie and her family in his will. It was, however, payable only upon her marriage to Matthew.

"But you know that the Duke kept Matthew busy during the short time he was in London," she reminded Lizzie consolingly. "There were all the celebrations and

Matthew doubtless had work to do to prepare for the Duke's removal to Paris."

The Duke of Wellington had been appointed British Ambassador to France, as well as Commander-in-Chief of the army of occupation in Belgium, and Matthew was serving on his staff. "And it is a two-day journey here from London," she added, playing her trump card. "Why, he didn't even plan to come home to see his own mother."

"No, he did not," agreed Lizzie grimly. "Mrs. Webster went to London hoping to see him—and now we know precisely why she hasn't yet returned home, even though Matthew has already gone back to the Continent. Undoubtedly the poor woman has been waiting for him to inform us that there will be no wedding so that she doesn't have to come home and do it herself."

Here she kicked the wad of paper across the carpet. "Since this letter comes from Vienna, I daresay he has also written to tell her that it is safe to come home again."

Mrs. Lancaster shook her head. It was true enough that Letitia Webster had been gone for over two months. She had traveled to London in June for the lavish entertainments celebrating the defeat of Napoleon. She had not been certain that she would even see Matthew, for as a junior member of the Duke of Wellington's staff, he had remained behind in Paris to prepare for the Duke's imminent return as ambassador. Still, his mother had hoped that he might be in London for at least a week or two, and had gone to stay in the home of Lord Bradbury, a distant cousin of her late husband.

She had invited Lizzie to accompany her, but she had declined. Although Lizzie was fond of Letitia Webster, she had had no desire to spend several weeks constantly in her company, nor had she wished to be a country miss in a great London household. What she had wanted was to see Matthew at home, where they might have at least a little time alone together. In London, she doubted that there would be such an opportunity, for Mrs. Webster was naturally anxious to be with her son, too, and there Matthew also had the responsibilities of his position to fulfill.

Alice, in a voice of great disgust, had announced once again that Lizzie had lost her mind. "I would have gone in an instant!" she had assured her sister. "Why, you might even have gotten to see the Iron Duke himself had you gone! Half the country is going on pilgrimage to London to see the man who defeated Napoleon, and you choose to stay at home like a stick!"

Even Mrs. Lancaster, who was well aware of the reasons for Lizzie's reluctance, had felt that she was making a strategic error, but Lizzie had remained firm. And Matthew had not come to her—even though she had learned later that he had been in London for at least two weeks, so that he could have made the journey had he truly wished to do so.

Now she knew why he had not.

"Perhaps this is all a tempest in a teapot," suggested Mrs. Lancaster hopefully. "After all, what do we know of this young woman? Young men often lose their hearts— or at least think that they have—to completely inappropriate females. Why, my brother Robert once fancied himself deeply in love with an opera dancer, and it cost our father a thousand pounds to show him that his ladylove could be bought and had no real affection for him. Matthew has probably already had time to reconsider his letter to you and to regret it."

Lizzie shook her head stiffly. "He is to marry Miss Blackwell," she replied, not meeting her mother's eye.

"Her father is a colonel, recently retired from the 18th Hussars. Matthew writes that they are to marry in Paris as soon as Matthew returns there from his assignment in Vienna."

Mrs. Lancaster shook her head in dismay. If that were true, the young lady was undoubtedly an acceptable partner for a young man of comfortable means and respectable family. If it had not been for the embarrassment of his earlier connection to Lizzie, she had no doubt that Matthew's mother would be delighted with the match. As it was, her situation would be awkward for the moment, since all of their local society knew that the pair had been informally engaged for years. Indeed, since the end of hostilities in Europe, many of the neighbors had begun to talk of Matthew's return and the long expected wedding.

Lizzie had now reached the more than marriageable age of eighteen, but Matthew, having been away for two years and busily engaged on Arthur Wellesley's staff for the majority of that time, had made no recent reference to a wedding in his letters. She had not set eyes upon him since her seventeenth birthday, when he had unexpectedly appeared at her party and danced with her. They had not even known that he was in the country, but he had been sent with a delegation to London to present the Prince Regent with the baton belonging to Marshal Jourdan and with King Joseph's sword, both seized after the triumph of Vitoria. Matthew was to return to Spain immediately, but he had ridden nonstop, rather than resting, so that he could see her and his mother.

That night he had presented her with an exquisite music box that played the haunting melody of "Greensleeves." He had danced with her to that same song at the long ago Christmas ball, when she had been wearing a gown of green silk, and he had whispered to her that the green of her eyes would put emeralds to shame. Since then, the small gold box had held the place of honor on her dressing table, solid, reassuring proof that he still loved her and had not forgotten her.

After that evening, she had half expected him to appear without warning once again, this time to announce their wedding, but he had not come. After a few months, she had received fewer letters, even after Napoleon's surrender and consignment to Elba. As a matter of fact, his letters had grown briefer and more impersonal with the end of the fighting, just at the time she thought he would have more time for her and would write of coming home to stay. She had begun to fear that Matthew found his work too exciting to leave and that, when they married, she would have to move with him to Paris. She had thought at the time—innocently enough—that he did not wish to upset her by telling her such a thing, knowing how she loved it here.

"Why do you think he has not come to see me, Mama?" she had asked just that morning.

"He will come to you soon enough," Mrs. Lancaster had replied calmly. "You have said that the Duke is sending him to Vienna, to report upon events happening there. After they have settled everything in Vienna, I am certain that he will be coming home, at least for a while."

Only this morning, her mother's explanation had seemed reasonable to Lizzie. She knew how excited Matthew was to be singled out by Wellington himself and sent to Vienna. The Iron Duke, held in awe by the members of his staff as well as by what seemed to her the vast majority of Europe, had assured Matthew that he needed all of the trustworthy intelligence possible. The meeting in Vienna was a most important affair, a congress of nations to determine the fate of Europe now that Napoleon had been removed from power.

The Duke would, of course, remain in Paris for most of the time, but he would be in close contact with England's representative to the congress, Lord Castlereagh, by means of their flying dispatch service. Moreover, Wellington had chosen those on his staff for their loyalty, and having a trusted junior officer present in Vienna would allow him to hear gossip that might not be repeated to more important and powerful men.

All of this, she knew, was heady stuff indeed to a young man like Matthew. The gathering in Vienna was the greatest assembly of statesmen and royalty that Europe had ever seen. And it was also to be the most glittering gathering, for many fashionable members of European society who were to play no active part in the negotiations also planned to be present. For the first time in decades, travel on the Continent was safe once more, and thousands were flocking to Paris and Vienna and Brussels. The whole world, Lizzie thought bitterly, seemed to be celebrating.

Exhausted by the revelation of Matthew's letter, Lizzie finally retired to her own chamber, refusing company and food. She would not light a candle as the sun went down, nor would she allow a maid to light a fire for her. Instead, she sat at her window, looking out into the darkness and waiting for the coldness to melt from her heart. Anger had comforted her briefly, but she could not sustain it. Misery had returned, and she knew that she faced the future alone.

Suddenly, however, an idea occurred to her, and for the first time since reading Matthew's letter, she felt a brief rush of hope. She did not go to bed but, wrapping herself in a blanket, waited for the dawn.

Three

Lady Thalia moaned and pulled the covers up over her head. The room was dark, although a thread of pale light shone at one window where the curtains had not been properly drawn together.

"Have you gone *mad*, Beavers?" she demanded of her maid in a muffled voice rigid with reproach. "You know *perfectly* well that I wasn't to be disturbed before noon today! I shall turn you out without a character! Go and pack your things immediately!"

Unruffled by the threats of her mistress, which she knew were made for the sake of drama rather than truth, Beavers regarded the lump in the bed patiently. "There seems to be a pressing problem downstairs, ma'am, so I thought that you would wish to be told."

Lady Thalia sat up abruptly amid the covers and stared at her, wide-eyed. "What has happened, Beavers?" she demanded. "Is the stable on fire?" She spoke her worst fear first but, to her relief, Beavers calmly shook her head.

"Then is it the house that is afire?" she asked, collapsing back against a sea of lacy pillows. "Should I be running for the stairs or the window? Are they bringing a ladder for me?"

Again Beavers shook her head, unmoved by any of

these dramatic possibilities. "It is Miss Lancaster, Lady Thalia," she replied. "She rode over from the Lodge and asked to see you immediately."

"Miss Lancaster?" repeated Lady Thalia blankly. "Here before *dawn*? Has someone died?"

Again Beavers shook her head comfortably. The peculiarities of those she served—save for cruelty—never troubled her. She was forty years old, and had begun her life in service when she was seven. Thus far she had waited on four women, and Lady Thalia had been her mistress for the past ten years. If Beavers had anything to say about it, she would stay with her until she died. The members of the *ton* might consider Lady Thalia Stanhope an eccentric, but, in Beavers' opinion, she was a good mistress. Her manner was theatrical, and her behavior was often unusual, but she had a generous heart. So far as Beavers could see, that made up for everything.

Lady Thalia groaned again, then demanded her dressing gown. "I suppose you must have her come up—but *do* bring us some chocolate, Beavers. *Something* must atone for getting me out of bed at this ungodly hour."

She stumbled to her dressing table and brushed her dark hair, already threaded with gray although she was only thirty. She had long ago chosen never to marry, having her own fortune and her own tastes and not wishing to subordinate herself to anyone else. Nonetheless, she was still a woman of distinctive appearance and took great pains to remain so. She was by now considered a spinster by the rest of society, but she was also considered an interesting paradox. She was fashionable but well-educated, frivolous but well-read—and, most important of all, she was well-funded. She spoke her mind with disarming—and sometimes alarming—candor, and she expected others to do the same. Her drawing rooms in the country and in London attracted an unusually rich and entertaining variety of guests, for Lady Thalia hated to be bored.

She had become a local fixture since moving to Hayworth Manor five years ago. It was a small property belonging to her family, one that had become her possession at the age of twenty-five. The manor, although well kept by her family's staff, had seldom been visited until Lady Thalia had taken up residence there. The Stanhope family was highly respected, and it was not long until she herself had made her own reputation in the district. Her house parties were elegant, if somewhat irregular in nature. Most of the guests came from a considerable distance and were clearly people of fashion, but she always had a healthy mixture of poets and politicians and artists. To be invited to one of her parties, the guests had to be intelligent, entertaining, or discerning— discerning because they recognized the worth of others. She preferred, naturally, that they possess all three characteristics. Guests at her parties could speak their minds with little fear that they would hear their words repeated elsewhere. She herself had often been the subject of gossip, but that bothered her not at all.

Lady Thalia had met Lizzie Lancaster shortly after setting up housekeeping at the Manor. She had encountered the young girl, just turned thirteen, at a lending library in town, and had been immediately attracted by her choice of reading. Aside from More's *The Shepherd of Salisbury Plain* and Godwin's *The Life of Lady Jane Grey*, and several gothic novels, Lizzie had a small book entitled *A Vindication of the Rights of Woman* by Mary Wollstonecraft. Lady Thalia had looked at Lizzie curiously.

"Do you mean to read all of these?" she had asked. After all, the girl looked more likely to spend her time selecting fabrics for gowns than selecting thought-filled reading materials.

Lizzie had regarded the newcomer closely, clearly surprised by the question. "Of course," she replied. "I wouldn't take them with me if I didn't mean to read them." Then, feeling that she been somewhat abrupt, she added in an interested tone, "Will you read all of yours?" And she had indicated with a nod the books Lady Thalia had stacked on a nearby table.

Far from being affronted, Lady Thalia had been pleased with Lizzie's response. "A very fair question," she said approvingly. "I shall indeed read them all—unless, of course, I find that I do not care for some of them."

"Even if I don't like one, I feel that I should read it straight through so that I can think about why I don't like it," Lizzie had responded seriously. "That is a good thing, don't you agree?"

"Why, yes, I do," Lady Thalia had answered, more surprised than ever. "And after you finish reading your books, I would very much like it if you would come to call upon me at Hayworth Manor and tell me what you think of them."

Lizzie, unaccustomed to having adults—or children, for that matter—interested in her opinions, had flushed with pleasure and promised gravely that she would do so. Accordingly, a few days later she had ridden over to Hayworth Manor and spent a delightful afternoon with Lady Thalia, enjoying the gothics, discussing the oppressively good and contented shepherd, the impressive scholarly accomplishments of Lady Jane Grey, and the unheard of matter of the rights of women.

Both ladies found it such a wholly satisfactory experience that they had repeated it many times during the next five years. Lizzie's grave manner contrasted sharply with Lady Thalia's lively one, but they enjoyed one another's company tremendously. The girl promised to be a lovely young woman, but, to Lady Thalia's pleasure, she was anything save self-absorbed.

After Lizzie's seventeenth birthday, she had been allowed to attend a number of parties at Hayworth and had met there a host of interesting people. Lizzie had enjoyed them far more than she had expected, and Mrs. Lancaster, although doubtful at first about the wisdom of allowing such visits, had decided that the outings might help to take the place of a Season.

Lady Thalia was determined to broaden Lizzie's experience as much as possible, and she had enjoyed watching her protégée grow into a promising young lady. Although she had regretted Lizzie's deep attachment to Matthew Webster, she had been forced to admit that it was only to be expected, and that he was, at least, a likable and reasonably intelligent young man.

"I am so sorry to disturb you at such an hour, Lady Thalia," Lizzie said earnestly as Beavers shepherded her into the room and directed her to a chair by the fire. "But I simply had to talk to you as soon as it was possible to do so. I could not wait."

Her hostess could see that her guest was not overstating the matter. Lizzie leaned toward her, her gaze intent. She looked not at all like herself, Lady Thalia thought uneasily.

"What do you need to talk about, Lizzie? What has happened?"

"I've had a letter from Matthew," she replied. "He will be marrying someone else very soon."

Although Lady Thalia's first reaction was that Lizzie had received a merciful deliverance from marriage, she did not allow herself to say so or to show it by so much as the flicker of an eyelash. Instead, placing her hand on Lizzie's, she said with all sincerity, "I know how this must hurt you, my dear. I am so *very* sorry."

Lizzie shook her head. "That isn't why I've come, Lady Thalia—not for sympathy. Mama can give me that—although I truly don't want it."

Lady Thalia sipped her chocolate thoughtfully and waited. After a few moments, Lizzie took a deep breath and continued.

"I know that I am presuming greatly upon our friendship, Lady Thalia, and upon the kindness that you have shown me—but I *must* ask you. When you leave for the Continent on Friday, may I accompany you as your companion?"

Lizzie's gaze was still fixed on her friend, who carefully put down her cup and cleared her throat. "Go with me as my companion?" Lady Thalia repeated.

Lizzie nodded eagerly. "I could do whatever you or Beavers tell me to, and I could read to you when you're tired, or bring you your tea. I have listened to your stories about your travels to Italy and Portugal and Spain and Greece—and even to Paris during the Peace of Amiens. I should love to see those places for myself."

"And yet, Lizzie, you did not think to mention your longing to see them until just *this* very morning," observed Lady Thalia.

Lizzie colored and looked away. It was true enough that she loved the stories about foreign places, but she preferred hearing or reading about them to traveling to see them herself. She had frequently announced that she was a homebody, content to have her adventures vicariously.

"I know that you also plan to go to Vienna, and I

should like to see Matthew again—preferably before he marries," she admitted in a low voice.

"My dear child, what will you do if you *do* see him?" Lady Thalia's voice was kind, but one eyebrow was lifted quizzically. "After all, Lizzie, you can *not* force a gentleman to love you if he has given his heart elsewhere. And indeed I should not think you would *wish* to have him under those circumstances."

"Oh, I know I must sound ridiculous, but—but, you see, Matthew did not say in his letter that he had stopped loving me. He said that—"

Here she broke off and took a very wrinkled piece of paper from her pocket and tried to smooth it. Then she read from it carefully.

"Here is what he said."

Had I been content to remain at home and ruralize, then I might not have outgrown our relationship and been satisfied to settle at Prestonwood and raise a family. Now, however, I realize how much more the world has to offer, and I know that I should only make you unhappy by forcing you to live a life in which you would be uncomfortable, or make myself unhappy by coming home and trying to pretend to be satisfied with such a life. We have, I fear, grown too far apart to be comfortable together.

At this point she paused and folded it back up again, then continued in a low voice. "Matthew goes on to say that the lady he has fallen in love with is quite my opposite and that it is with her that he desires to live the rest of his life."

Lady Thalia, thinking that she could have cheerfully

throttled Matthew Webster for such a pompous, patronizing letter, held her silence so that she would not say something that they would both regret.

Misinterpreting her silence, Lizzie sighed and shook her head. "I do apologize for burdening you with my problems, Lady Thalia. It is just that I do not think myself such a dowdy little dab of a thing as Matthew seems to, capable only of living in the country. Even though I have always preferred life here, I daresay that I could be just as polished and sophisticated as Miss Blackwell, were I given the opportunity."

"I am quite *certain* that you could," Lady Thalia agreed firmly. "After all, during the past year your parents have permitted you to attend several of my evening parties, and you have become quite comfortable moving amid a *very* distinguished company. Why, I have watched you discuss art with Thomas Lawrence and poetry with Lord Byron and everything under the sun with Henry Brougham."

She did not add that she had been delighted to see that Lizzie, always rather quiet and self-effacing, had grown more and more self-assured. She felt that Matthew Webster would be quite shocked were he to encounter his Lizzie now. She smiled to herself at the thought.

Lizzie's face brightened perceptibly at Lady Thalia's words. "That is so," she agreed. "Perhaps I would not be at a complete loss in an assembly such as those Matthew attends."

"Of *course* you would not!" said Lady Thalia encouragingly. "Or at least not so long as you had anyone *intelligent* with whom to talk. Assemblies are not necessarily rife with such people."

She studied her guest with a speculative eye. "Of course, we shall have to provide you with a more suitable wardrobe. After all, we shall be keeping *very* fashionable company on the Continent."

"I'm afraid that I cannot afford to be extremely fashionable," Lizzie replied hesitantly. Then her eyes lit up as the full import of Lady Thalia's statement burst upon her. "May I indeed go with you, then?" she demanded, throwing her arms around the neck of her benefactress.

"*Indeed* you may," Lady Thalia replied, wondering if she would soon regret this hasty decision. "We must first get your parents' permission, however."

"Only Mama's," replied Lizzie. "Papa and George will not arrive home for a sennight." She found herself unreasonably grateful for this, for she knew that she could persuade her mother far more easily than her father.

"Then by all means take yourself home, my dear," said Lady Thalia. "I shall call upon your good mother as *soon* as propriety will allow. At least *I* will wait until the sun has fully risen."

Lizzie sprang from her chair, hugged Lady Thalia once more, then hurried from the room, transported by her good fortune.

Lady Thalia eyed her bed longingly for a moment, then shook her head briskly and rang for Beavers. There was much to be done before Friday.

Four

Daniel Thoreau studied his fellow passengers with interest as the old French diligence lumbered along the road from Calais to Paris. He was keenly aware that the ladies had wished to have the coach to themselves, but unfortunately it had been the last Paris-bound vehicle available. He had been to Calais to see off a friend of his on a packet bound for Boston—if it could thread through the British blockade—and so he had already noted the general squalor of Calais. He had had no intention of being forced to wander about its streets the rest of the day and put up at some filthy inn for the night, so he had cheerfully made himself one of the party in the diligence, ignoring their protests. The French postilion had silently accepted the money that he offered, and had ordered Thoreau's luggage loaded onto the coach.

The ladies had been assisted into its vast interior, eyeing its cracked leather seats with disfavor and pressing perfumed handkerchiefs to their noses to ward off its musty smell. Thoreau had climbed in behind them and seated himself next to an older woman attired in a plain dark pelisse, who appeared to be a servant.

"*Really*, sir, if you must *insist* upon forcing your presence upon us for the journey, you might at least ride on top of the coach. My footman is riding there in order that we may have our privacy," observed the sharp-eyed lady seated across from him. Self-assured and elegantly dressed, she appeared to be in charge of the other two.

"Surely you would not be so cruel as to deny me such charming company," he replied pleasantly, ignoring the fact that he had been placed in a category with her footman and quite certain that she would deny him anything that was within her power—particularly their company. "And, quite apart from that, it appears to me that it might well rain soon. I would prefer not to arrive in Paris soaked to the skin."

When there was no immediate reply other than a chilly glance, he added, "Since we are to be traveling together, allow me to introduce myself. My name is Daniel Thoreau, and I am originally from New York, most recently from Ghent."

"An American," said the sharp-eyed lady, nodding. "Yes, that *would* explain it, of course."

In Thoreau's experience with the British, which this lady clearly was, such an observation was not a complimentary one, so he was surprised to see her look amused and offer her hand.

"I am Lady Thalia Stanhope and this is Miss Lancaster." The dark-haired young lady seated next to her nodded and smiled. Miss Lancaster was, Thoreau thought, quite charming in appearance, even though she was not as modishly dressed as her companion.

When no other introductions were forthcoming, Thoreau raised his eyebrows and glanced briefly at the lady seated next to him.

"And this is Miss Beavers," added Lady Thalia, who did not usually introduce her maid, even one as highly valued as Beavers. But then, she reminded herself, the Americans that she had met had most unusual ideas.

They were, she had found, often amusingly refreshing—
if undeniably provincial—in their thoughts. Beavers
nodded comfortably and almost immediately lapsed into
a gentle doze.

"For the sake of polite conversation, I would ask you
ladies where you are bound, but since you are obviously
on your way to Paris, I suppose I must think of something
else."

They rode in silence for a few miles, while the gentleman studied the toe of his polished boot reflectively,
apparently devoting himself to the consideration of
other conversational gambits. Eventually, he glanced up
and grinned at Lady Thalia. "It must be a great relief to
your countrymen to be fighting only one war now."

Lady Thalia was surprised by his choice of subject, but
she was certainly equal to commenting upon it. "It was,
of *course*, a relief to see Bonaparte defeated," she conceded. "Naturally, little attention could be paid to such
a *minor* fray as the one with your country while we faced
such a serious threat."

He nodded in appreciation at this home-thrust. "I noticed, however, that as soon as the French were taken
care of, thousands of Wellington's troops were shipped
off to North America to assist with that fray."

"That could well be," she replied, with the air of one
who had paid no attention to such unnoteworthy devel-
opments. "On the whole, I find war a *tiresome* subject. The
Jacobin threat and Bonaparte belong to the past, and *soon*
the problem with your country will be resolved as well."

"I quite agree," he said amiably, not committing himself
to any observation as to what that resolution would be.
Judging by the newspapers, no one in Britain appeared to
be aware that the government there was presently negoti-
ating a peace with American representatives at Ghent.

Lizzie, who had been paying little attention to this exchange, drew their attention to the passing countryside. "The dwellings do not look nearly so—" She paused a moment as she searched for the word. "They are not nearly so tidy-looking as they are in England."

Lady Thalia laughed. "Very true, my dear. In *fact*, when so many of the French came to London this summer to celebrate the end of the war, some of them believed that we had cleaned up the villages and farms along the Dover Road ex*press*ly for the purpose of impressing our visitors. They could not imagine that such places *always* looked so well-kept and orderly."

Gazing at the crumbling chateaux and down-at-the-heels farms and remembering the dirt and beggars of Calais, Lizzie could understand why the visitors would have thought such a thing. The English farms and villages looked clean and well cared for, but the countryside in this part of France was quite the opposite. She was beginning to wonder if she had made a serious mistake in coming on this journey. They would be gone for months, she knew, and suddenly home seemed even more attractive than it always had. Aside from grieving for Matthew, she was now assailed with a painful longing for home.

Seeing her forlorn expression and guessing a part of the reason for it, Thoreau remarked, "This certainly doesn't remind me of the country around New York either. I have been away from home for well over a year now, and I confess I look forward to seeing it again."

"I should imagine that you *do* long for it, Mr. Thoreau. I know I should after so long a time," said Lizzie. She paused for a moment, then added, "How do you keep yourself from always thinking of it?"

He had hoped that she would ask, so his reply was ready. "I look more closely at everything about me—at the people and what they are saying and doing and probably feeling, at the details of the place and its appearance and sounds and smells. Once I have focused my attention outside of myself, the longing passes because my mind is fully occupied. Then there is no space left for unhappiness."

"What a *very* sensible idea," said Lizzie, her eyes bright for the first time since they had met. As though he had prescribed a medicine, she turned her gaze once more to the passing landscape and firmly forced herself to take it all in. Wallowing in despair would certainly do her no good, and Lizzie was always practical.

Lady Thalia gave him an approving glance, took up her book, and began to read. They had suddenly become, Thoreau thought, a very domestic party. Miss Beavers was still sleeping, Lady Thalia reading, and Miss Lancaster was watching the world go by, occasionally remarking upon a particularly fine apple orchard or an interesting ruin. Comfortable now, he took out a newspaper he had brought with him from Ghent and began to read.

They traveled in such a manner for a number of miles before it began to rain. At first there was a spattering of large drops like gunfire, then a blinding downpour. The team slowed to a walk and the diligence rolled painfully onward. After a mile or two more, it creaked to a halt. The rain was still lashing down, so they could see nothing and hadn't the least notion what was happening outside. Finally, the wheels turned once more, and Lady Thalia sighed in relief.

"I feared for a moment that we could go no further, and I can think of *nothing* more dreadful than being stranded in this abominable coach."

"We are in complete agreement on that point," said Thoreau, and Lizzie nodded fervently. Beavers was snoring gently, the feather in her bonnet keeping time with the rise and fall of her breathing.

All too soon they again came to a stop, and the three of them waited anxiously for the coach to move forward once more. This time, however, the door opened and a gust of rain blew in over them.

"I'm afraid we can go no further, my lady." At the door stood Henry, Lady Thalia's footman, holding his greatcoat. "We have stopped at an inn and the coach is as close to the entrance as possible."

With Henry's assistance, Lady Thalia stepped down under the protection of the greatcoat. One by one he shepherded each of the ladies inside, and Thoreau splashed in behind them. The inn was a tiny one, no more than a single serving room and a kitchen, but it was moderately clean and there was a fire. The travelers gathered in front of it, grateful for its warmth against the damp chill of the autumn afternoon.

One other gentleman had arrived before them, a slender young man with dark hair curling from the damp, who emerged from the kitchen with a bottle of brandy.

"It's the very devil out there, is it not?" he demanded cheerfully, shaking hands with Thoreau and bowing to the ladies. "I very nearly drowned getting here after my chaise got stuck just down the road. My poor driver led the horses in, and he is out there now, prying the rig out of the mud." He glanced down at the bottle in his hand. "Since the landlord is the entire staff and he is putting up the cattle, I decided that I would assist him within. Gregory Mansfield, at your service."

As the introductions were being made, Beavers and Henry disappeared into the kitchen to inspect the possibilities. The gentlemen pulled the settles closer to the fire to block the drafts and placed a table between them. Mr.

Mansfield poured brandy for them all to keep out the cold, and in very short order Beavers and Henry appeared with hot coffee and a crusty loaf of bread.

"That is all that we could find, my lady," Beavers told her mistress apologetically, "but there are fresh eggs, so there must be chickens, too. We shall do better for dinner."

"Don't forget, Beavers, that Mrs. Clary sent a basket with me from the Lodge," said Lizzie. "It is still in the diligence."

The company made very short work of the bread and the coffee, laughing and talking with the genial Mr. Mansfield as they were revived by food and drink and warmth. Soon, however, Thoreau saw that Miss Lancaster's eyes were closing and that she was beginning to sway slightly. He caught Lady Thalia's eye and nodded toward the young lady.

To Lizzie's surprise, she awakened some three hours later, stretched out on one of the settles. Henry had brought in one of Lady Thalia's trunks, so Lizzie now had a pillow in a silken case under her head and a soft woolen blanket tucked around her. Lady Thalia was seated beside her, and she and the gentlemen were still talking.

Lizzie lay there, listening drowsily and trying to follow Mr. Thoreau's advice. She concentrated intently on the scene before her. The wooden settles, high-backed and unyielding, had been polished to a glossy sheen by the countless people who had sat there over the years. The flickering of the wood fire—apple wood, she noted appreciatively—and the two guttering candles cast shifting shadows on the walls and on the faces of the people across from her—Mr. Mansfield, well-bred and lively, giving the impression of movement even when he was seated; Mr. Thoreau, solidly reassuring, talking with the ease of an educated man—but in an American accent, of course. The wood smoke from the fire and the savory scent of roasting chicken, the faint cold dampness from the stone floor and the smell of melting tallow from the candles, all mingled with the rose-petal sweetness of Lady Thalia's perfume.

Mr. Thoreau was correct, she mused dreamily. She had been grief-stricken and homesick earlier in the day, and the inn where she found herself now was strange and uncomfortable—so much so that awakening there had again filled her with unhappiness. Nevertheless, giving her determined attention to the details of the scene that was her world for the moment *did* fill her mind and crowd out thoughts of the Lodge and her family.

"I believe that Miss Lancaster is rejoining us," observed Mr. Thoreau. "She appears to have been drifting in and out of sleep for some minutes now. Perhaps dinner will restore her to us completely."

"I know that it will do so for me," agreed Mr. Mansfield. "Only the fear that I might slow the cook's work has kept me out of the kitchen. The smell of that chicken roasting has been driving me to distraction."

As though on cue, the door to the kitchen swung open and Henry emerged, carrying a platter bearing three roasted chickens. Beavers followed on his heels with a hot steak and kidney pie, made with Mrs. Clary's own hands and firmly sent with Lizzie to sustain her on her journey to foreign places. Their meal was rounded out with toast made from Mrs. Clary's bread, a tart made from apples that Beavers had discovered in the kitchen, slices of cheese, and more hot coffee.

"I could not be happier if I had just eaten a meal prepared by the great Carême himself," announced Mr. Mansfield, leaning back as comfortably as the settle would allow.

"I don't believe that he would trouble himself with such simple fare, however," observed Mr. Thoreau. "Perhaps if we had been served larks encased in pastry lined with chicken livers or turbot in a lobster sauce—or, more likely, a dessert of cake and spun sugar, shaped like the Parthenon—*then* we might think of Carême."

"I am impressed that an American would even *know* of such a famous chef," said Lady Thalia. "I thought that in *your* country people confine themselves to eating whatever they can shoot."

"Oh, that is true, of course," he replied easily. "We are much like the English in that respect, you see." He glanced at her briefly and was pleased to see that she acknowledged the hit with a smile. "As to my knowing about Carême, I pride myself upon being well-informed, and I took note of him when Talleyrand first employed him some years ago."

Talleyrand had then been the French Foreign Minister. As the Bishop of Autun, he had participated in the opening of the Revolution, but he had left France just before the execution of the king, seeking safety first in France and then in America. After a few years, his friends at home had managed to remove his name from the list of *émigrés* so that he could safely return to his country. Aside from being a most astute politician, managing to survive and prosper during most of the changes in government, Talleyrand was also a noted gourmet.

"An extremely interesting man, Talleyrand," mused Mr. Mansfield.

"As crafty as they make them," agreed Thoreau. "His mind moves like quicksilver. It will be fascinating to see how the fox manages in Vienna. No doubt he will find a way for France, the nation defeated, to do more than hold her own during the negotiations."

Lizzie's attention was completely captured by the mention of Vienna, and she leaned forward attentively, eager for what crumbs of information she could gather.

Gregory Mansfield nodded. "He will be facing a master of manipulation in Metternich, however. And then Tsar Alexander will, of course, provide an erratic element to the mix. One can never be certain what he will do. And the Prussians are the very devil to work with."

Mansfield again shook his head. "I don't envy Lord Castlereagh the weeks of meeting with them. Even though he believes the Congress will last only a few weeks at the most, I am glad that I am merely a lowly member of the staff, fit only to fetch and carry."

"You are on Castlereagh's staff?" demanded Thoreau, clearly impressed. "That *is* good news! I have been reading about the Congress and there are some matters I'd like to discuss with you."

"And will you merely be *reading* about Vienna, Mr. Thoreau?" inquired Lady Thalia, before Mr. Mansfield could respond. "Or, like *us*, do you plan to travel there as well?"

Thoreau ignored the thorn in her question. "Both," he replied. "But I didn't realize that you and Miss Lancaster were traveling beyond Paris."

"We stop in Paris for only a few days," she said, not adding that a little time was needed to outfit Lizzie more appropriately.

"I had already been looking forward to my Viennese experience," said Mr. Mansfield, with a flattering sincerity, "but now I shall expect my pleasure to be tripled."

The gentlemen's discussion lasted far into the night as they talked of the difficulty of Castlereagh's position as he tried to achieve a balance of power among the nations of Europe that would be acceptable to the English.

"No doubt he would like to unite Austria and Prussia so that they provide a barrier for Russia," Lizzie heard Mr. Thoreau observe.

"That would be sensible," agreed Mr. Mansfield. "Of course, Talleyrand would like that as well, since it would provide a buffer between France and Russia."

That was her last recollection of the evening's conversation. Beavers and Henry had made makeshift beds on the settles for the two ladies. The servants were sleeping in the kitchen, and, when the gentlemen retired, they planned to roll themselves in their greatcoats and sleep close to the fire.

"It is unorthodox, of course," Lady Thalia had said matter-of-factly to Lizzie, "but in *these* circumstances, it will answer very well."

Lizzie had been unperturbed by the arrangement, which seemed both sensible and as comfortable as possible. Hearing the murmur of now familiar voices as she drifted off to sleep was reassuring.

And tomorrow she would see Paris. She had heard Mr. Thoreau and Mr. Mansfield talking over the arrival of the Duke of Wellington in Paris a few weeks earlier. Lady Thalia had told her that they would both be attending a reception at the British Embassy and that she would actually get to meet the famous Peer. Lizzie smiled sleepily to herself, thinking of what Alice would have to say when she wrote to her that at last she had met the Iron Duke.

Then she sighed. She knew that she would not see Matthew there, of course, for he had written that he would be in Vienna, but she would at least see the place where he worked and the people with whom he spent his time.

As sleep washed over her, she imagined Matthew— unexpectedly called back to the Embassy just in time for the reception, of course—walking toward her with outstretched arms. "Lizzie," he said to her, folding her close, "Lizzie, I've been the most awful fool! Can you ever forgive me?"

Finally, the last candle burned out, its flame drowning in a puddle of melted tallow, and the fire burned low. Even the gentlemen gave up their conversation and their brandy, wrapped themselves warmly in their coats, and fell asleep.

And Lizzie dreamed happily—for tomorrow she would be in Paris, and that much closer to Matthew.

Five

They did not make an early start the next morning, for the examination of the two vehicles by their postilions took some time, and then the gentlemen in question strolled out to inspect the road in order to be certain that it could be safely traveled and the vehicles not become too deeply mired in mud. A lengthy discussion followed, and the postilions required fortification, so they retired to the kitchen and drank deeply. Mr. Thoreau, finally becoming thoroughly annoyed, told them bluntly—in his best French—that *he* could see no problem with the road.

The two postilions were deeply offended by his lack of confidence in their expertise, and it required the more tactful approach of Mr. Mansfield to move them. He assured them that he could appreciate the difficulties that they faced in making their decision, knowing that they must consider both the well-being of their passengers and that of the equipages by which they earned their livelihood. Their expressions lightened noticeably as he soothed them and beckoned to the innkeeper to refill their glasses.

Finally, under the guidance of Mr. Mansfield and after the exchange of several folded notes, it was decided that only the diligence, as the heavier and more trustworthy vehicle, should brave the rest of the perilous journey, and

Mr. Mansfield's rented chaise should return to Calais. The postilions, pleased both by the extra money that they had received and by the appreciation of a gentleman for their delicate position, were then eager to depart.

"But there is no danger connected with this journey!" protested Thoreau, as Mansfield climbed into the diligence after him. "There is only inconvenience—and mud!"

"Naturally," said Mansfield agreeably, settling himself next to Thoreau and smiling at the ladies. "But there is no honor or excitement in inconvenience, my friend. It is necessary that they invest their lives with some drama, you see."

"Well, I do see, but I don't approve!" grumbled Thoreau. "We would never tolerate such an attitude at home."

"But you are not in America," Mansfield pointed out to him. "This is France, and there must be honor—and danger, of course."

Finally, to everyone's relief, they were under way. Lizzie watched the passing scene carefully, listening to the gentlemen only now and then. They seemed to find much to talk about, which pleased her, both because she liked to see others happy and because she had no wish to be engaged in conversation herself.

It seemed to her that the oddest thing about their journey, as they grew closer and closer to Paris, the very heart of France, was that she saw so few other vehicles. She had been to London several times, and one of the things that had overwhelmed her was the traffic, which was thick even before they reached the city. Paris seemed to be a different matter—or at least it was now, so soon after the war.

She was pleased with the windmills and vineyards of

Montmartre, and at last, just at dusk, they could see Paris in the distance. Finally they reached the *barrières* that fenced in the city and made their way slowly along behind a wagon of hay. Despite the oil lanterns swinging in the wind, the scene seemed very dark to Lizzie as the diligence wound through narrow streets toward the hotel in the Saint-Germain quarter where Lady Thalia had reserved rooms for them. Very soon after entering the city, both ladies were forced to take perfumed handkerchiefs from their reticules and press them to their noses once more. They had grown accustomed to the staleness of the air in the diligence, but the present stench almost overcame them.

"I fear that the Grand Canal is an unpleasant aspect of the city," conceded Mr. Mansfield apologetically. "However, Paris has other charms that will atone for it."

"The Grand Canal?" said Lizzie weakly from behind her handkerchief.

Lady Thalia nodded. "A sewer that circles the city. Unfortunately, much of it is open—not at all like what we are accustomed to in England."

Seeing Lizzie's eyes, horror-stricken above the handkerchief, she patted the girl's hand reassuringly. "We shall *not* be troubled by it at our hotel—unless, of course, they gave away our rooms when we did not arrive yesterday."

To Lizzie's great relief, their rooms had been held for them—and there was no trace in the air of the malodorous Grand Canal. The gentlemen engaged to meet them for dinner the next evening and bade them good night, climbing back in the diligence to be borne away to their respective destinations. Soon Beavers was making up the beds with Lady Thalia's own linens and pillows. Lizzie was too weary even to eat dinner and fell gratefully into a deep and dreamless sleep.

The next morning their first call was upon a dressmaker. "Although I haven't been here in a decade," said Lady Thalia, "I understand that Madame Delacroix still maintains her establishment. She does *wonderful* work and she is very quick, which is important since we do not have much time here. If we are fortunate, she will have time to make up half a dozen gowns for you before we leave Paris."

"For me? But, Lady Thalia, I cannot afford a new wardrobe!" She had managed to push the family's financial problems, aggravated by Matthew's defection, to the back of her mind.

"There is *no* difficulty," Lady Thalia assured her. "Wonderful fabrics may be had for a pittance in Paris, and you must remember, Lizzie, that, as my companion, you will be more in company than you have been accustomed to at home. I must *insist* that you allow me to gown you appropriately so that you are a credit to me."

Lizzie had not considered this aspect of the matter, so she reluctantly gave way to Lady Thalia. However, any lingering guilt that assailed her was swept away by the delights of the next three hours. Surrounded by a battery of tall mirrors, she was measured, then draped with fabrics of all hues and textures so that Madame Delacroix and Lady Thalia could determine those that were most becoming. By the time they left, two new morning gowns, two handsome walking dresses, and three evening gowns had been ordered. She was overwhelmed, both by the number of gowns and by the diaphanous fabric Lady Thalia and Madame Delacroix had chosen for one of the evening dresses. When she expressed some doubt about the suitability of the gauze-like gown, Lady Thalia had overridden her objection, reminding Lizzie that she was better acquainted with the society in which they would be moving.

Then, feeling that she had perhaps been a little too overbearing, Lady Thalia shepherded Lizzie to a *pâtisserie* for cakes and cheerful gossip about the people that she would soon be meeting. They would, she told her charge, take some time to look about the city before doing any more shopping for other necessities of her wardrobe.

Paris was a revelation to Lizzie. Accustomed to the gentle pace of a life in the country, the constant movement of Paris overwhelmed her. She had been to London, of course, but even there her senses had not been assaulted as they were in Paris. The crowds of people that swirled by them in the streets were by no means all French in nationality. They were of a variety of origins; she could hear them speaking many languages other than French or English, and their varied complexions and dress composed a rich human tapestry that seemed to surround her. Also, she noticed to her surprise that even when they were in the elegant Place Vendôme, the people on the pavement were not just the fashionables that she would have expected to find in such a place. Ragged porters and women in threadbare gowns also made their way through the front entryways of the tall stone houses.

"Do you suppose he really lives there?" she whispered to Lady Thalia, nodding in the direction of a man in a ragged frock coat far too large for him and boots that were caked with dried mud.

"It is possible."

"But how could that be? Would it not be too expensive for him? One would never find such a thing happening in Mayfair!"

Lady Thalia smiled. "That is very true. Here, however, living accommodations are arranged differently. In a house such as the one he entered, the poorest rooms with the lowest rent are to be found on the highest floors, the best ones with the highest rent are nearest the ground."

"But there is only one door! Do they all enter the same way?"

Lady Thalia nodded. "And they very likely share the same stairway as well. Sometimes the common area in such a place is a *fearful* mess, but then a door opens and you step into a set of rooms as well appointed as any you would find in Grosvenor Square."

"I don't believe I would care to live in such a way, no matter how well-appointed the rooms were," said Lizzie. "I greatly prefer the way we live at home."

"I've no doubt of it. I like England very well myself. However, you must remind yourself, my dear, that you are learning about the way *others* live their lives. After all, if you wish to make Matthew sorry that he is not marrying you, will you not have to show him that you are no longer a mere country miss?"

Satisfied by Lizzie's sigh and her despondent expression that she had made a home-thrust, she patted the girl's hand briskly. "Never mind that, my dear—but *do* promise me that you will try to enjoy yourself."

Remembering how much she owed to Lady Thalia's generosity, Lizzie had the grace to blush. "Forgive me," she said penitently. "I am *indeed* enjoying myself. I promise that I shall be better company."

Again she concentrated on taking Mr. Thoreau's advice, and turned her attention outward. With great determination she studied the faces of those passing by them, wondering why the old man with the white beard and the stiff gait was smiling to himself and why the pretty little flower girl, with a face as delicate as the lilies she was selling, looked so despondent. Strolling along one of the leafy boulevards in the September sunlight, they saw a small knot of people and paused with them to watch a nimble little terrier perform a battery of tricks, all at the command of his young master. Stalls filled with books and prints also slowed their progress, and it was with some surprise that she realized that it was time to return to the hotel and dress for dinner so that they would be ready when Mr. Thoreau and Mr. Mansfield came to call for them.

"And, my dear, you will be *amazed* by the place where we are going to dine!" Lady Thalia told her gleefully. "Just wait until you see the Palais-Royal! I do promise you that you have seen *nothing* like it in your life!"

Later that evening, as they strolled down the covered walks of the brightly lighted Palais-Royal, past busy cafés and *pâtisseries*, elegant shops and infamous gambling hells, Lizzie could see that Lady Thalia had not exaggerated. It was a little, she thought, like seeing Paris condensed. Once she had surrendered herself to it, she had been delighted by the sensual onslaught of daytime Paris, but evening at the Palais-Royal did indeed amaze her. She was grateful that Mr. Thoreau was at her side, for the bold glances of some of the gentlemen told her clearly that she and Lady Thalia would have been approached if they had not been escorted.

"Don't let them distress you," said Mr. Thoreau in a low voice, after he had caught her anxious glance at two swaggering young blades who had stopped to gaze at her with unabashed interest. "They won't trouble you at all."

She clung a little more tightly to his arm, careful not to look the young men in the eye. She was extremely uncomfortable and once again wished herself safely home at the Lodge.

Mr. Thoreau, determined to help her overcome her

homesickness and her natural timidity, began a dissertation to divert her thoughts from her unhappiness. "During the Revolution, they called this place the Maison Egalité, you know. It was a center for public debate."

He felt her shudder at the mention of the Revolution. "That is too awful to think about," she replied. "So many people dying needlessly."

"That is true," he conceded. "There was a terrible waste of life. It is unfortunate that their revolution could not, in the end, have been as successful as our own in America. They have a constitution now, but they also once again have a monarch."

She looked at him with wide eyes. "Are you a Jacobin, then?" she asked. "You do not think that the king should have had his throne restored after Bonaparte's defeat?"

Thoreau shrugged lightly. "You must remember, Miss Lancaster, that I am an American. We do not think so highly of kings as the English do."

He paused to chuckle a moment over what he had just said. "Naturally, with your old king incapacitated by his madness at the moment, and the Prince Regent making such a spectacle of himself in so many ways, I daresay a good many of the English feel that they could also do without kings."

Lizzie was a little indignant at this jab at her country, but she was forced to acknowledge the truth of it. "At least King George has no control over his problem," she responded. "He cannot help his fits of madness."

"Very true," he acknowledged. "At any rate, some of the French, like the Americans, have felt that men should have no king at all. It is a great shame that Bonaparte seized power and made himself emperor. Now the poor French are just exchanging one supreme power for another."

She pondered his comments and glanced about her a little more. "And so they met here to talk about their government?"

He nodded. "And the talk was not all of bloodshed. Understandably, the people wanted a better life for themselves, and they wanted a voice in the government so that they could achieve it. That has not been a priority for their kings or for most of their nobility—or even for their clergy."

With the arrival of their group at the café where they were to dine, the conversation moved to other topics, and Lizzie found herself drawn into it, feeling comfortable with the easy give-and-take among the four of them. During a momentary lull, she leaned back in her chair and surveyed the other three and the busy café in which they sat.

"A penny for your thoughts, Miss Lancaster," said Mr. Thoreau, smiling at her abstracted expression. "You suddenly look very far away."

"Forgive me," she said smiling. "It simply occurred to me that a week ago I could not have imagined myself in such a place as this, enjoying myself completely with Lady Thalia and two gentlemen who were so recently total strangers to me."

"I am glad, of course, that you are enjoying yourself," returned Mr. Mansfield, "and, as for myself, a week ago I could not have imagined that I would be spending my first evening back in Paris with two such lovely ladies."

"Very gallant," said Lady Thalia approvingly.

He inclined his head to her slightly, smiling. Then, turning back to Lizzie, he added, "and I am gladder still that you no longer consider Mr. Thoreau and myself strangers. I trust that all three of you now count me among your friends."

There was a murmur of agreement from the other three, and the evening had ended on a very satisfactory note, with all of them, even Mr. Thoreau, agreeing that they would see one another at the reception at the British Embassy the next evening.

"Even though our countries are at war?" Lizzie had asked him, a little surprised.

"I shall be inconspicuous," he assured her. "I am attending as one of La Fayette's party. I am a guest in his home, and he has insisted that I attend with him."

After they had said good-night to the gentlemen at the hotel, it suddenly occurred to Lizzie that she had spent very little of the day thinking of Matthew and home. And that, she decided, was not such a bad thing at all.

Six

The next day Lady Thalia and Lizzie returned to the Palais-Royal, this time to investigate the shops. Lizzie protested when she realized that Lady Thalia was again engaged in making purchases for her, but she held up a warning finger to Lizzie and reminded her lightly that her companion was to be a credit to her. Giving way once more, Lizzie entered into the shopping expedition with pleasure. To her delight, she was soon the proud possessor of three pairs of slippers, two of kid leather and one of Denmark satin; several pairs of silk stockings; two fetching bonnets; a cashmere shawl; an embroidered silk reticule; a seal muff; and a pair of pearl combs for her hair.

When she prepared for their evening at the British Embassy, she donned a simple white crêpe evening gown, for none of the confections being created by Madame Delacroix would be ready until the following day. She clasped a string of pearls round her neck and, with the help of Beavers, arranged the new pearl combs in her dark curls. Lady Thalia had lent her a handsome sash of red satin that matched her new red slippers, and she slipped on a pair of new white evening gloves. Well satisfied with the effect, she added the final touch, a dark blue shawl trimmed with the red of the sash.

The reception that evening was a crowded affair, held

in the house on the Rue de Faubourg Saint-Honoré that the Duke of Wellington had selected as the site for the British Embassy, purchasing it and its contents. The Hôtel de Charost had belonged to Bonaparte's young sister, the lovely Princess Pauline Borghese, whose portrait, rumor said, still hung in the Duke's chamber.

"How awkward it must be for him," Lizzie murmured in a low voice to Mr. Thoreau, watching the Duke in the center of a crowd of people. Lady Thalia had already been led out to dance, and Lizzie and Mr. Thoreau were engaged in inspecting the crowd.

Immaculate in the white breeches, white stock, and scarlet coat of his field-marshal's uniform, complete with ribbons and orders, the impressive Peer welcomed his guests. The salon in which they stood was filled with a throng in evening dress, studded generously with other jewel-like military uniforms.

"You know that some of these people were his enemies just months ago, and now he must stand and make polite conversation with them," she continued.

"And undoubtedly some still are his enemies," he murmured in return, "but I understand that the Duke has little trouble dealing with them. I imagine that he will do very well as ambassador. And I am certain that he keeps in mind the fact that all of the French army still keep their tricolors safely at hand, even though they now wear the Bourbon white cockade on their shakos."

"Do you mean they are still loyal to Napoleon?" Lizzie asked, her eyes wide. "But he has been exiled to Elba."

"Very true. And we must hope that he decides to remain there."

"Is there any doubt?" she inquired anxiously. The specter of a Bonaparte returning to France conjured a nightmare for all who had feared him.

"He promised his friends that he would return with the violets—and it is said that his supporters refer to him now as Caporal Violet and use the violet as their emblem."

"So he promised that he would return next spring?" Lizzie asked, her eyes wide as she considered this possibility. "Do you think it could be so?"

Mr. Thoreau shrugged and smiled. "Napoleon promised many things—and he has always seen himself as larger than life—so I doubt that you should let the thought of springtime and violets keep you awake nights, Miss Lancaster. After all, the Duke is here to stop him should he decide to put in an appearance."

Mr. Mansfield joined them just then, and pointed out some of the more famous figures in the room—among them the Duchesse d'Angoulême, the beautiful wife of the King's younger brother; the formidable and very intelligent Madame de Staël; Charles Talleyrand-Périgord, that master of duplicity; the wicked Duke of Cumberland, fresh from England; and the Comte de Chateaubriand, an egotistical, dangerous writer and politician.

"How fascinating this all is," remarked Lizzie. "It seems amazing, sir, that you should know so many important people in this foreign capital."

"You must not give me too much credit, Miss Lancaster. All of Paris knows those that I have pointed out to you. They would scarcely recognize me."

"You are modest, sir," she said, smiling up at him. Then, hoping that her tone was suitably disinterested, she added, "I suppose, Mr. Mansfield, that you know all of the Duke's staff here in Paris as well?"

Mr. Mansfield looked mildly surprised. "Why, yes—at least I believe that I do unless he has had occasion to take on someone new in the past few weeks."

Lizzie colored slightly. "Then I suppose you must be acquainted with Matthew Webster."

"Webster? Why, yes—indeed I am. A capital fellow! Is he a friend of yours, Miss Lancaster?"

She nodded, choosing her words carefully and keeping her tone light. "Indeed he is! I have known him all my life. He and my brother George were companions from the time they were in leading-strings."

"I am afraid that you will have to wait until you reach Vienna to renew your friendship with Webster, Miss Lancaster," he said regretfully. "I learned today that the Duke has ordered him there for the duration of the Congress—to be his eyes, so to speak."

"Well, at least I shall see him there," she managed to say with credible carelessness. "You have given me something else to look forward to, Mr. Mansfield."

He appeared to be struck by a sudden thought and turned to look about the crowded room once more. "Webster may not be here, but there *is* someone that I can make known to you immediately. He is recently affianced to Miss Blackwell, and I am certain that she is present tonight."

"Oh, that is not necessary, Mr. Mansfield!" she protested with convincing earnestness. "I don't wish to inconvenience you."

"Nonsense! No inconvenience at all! I shall be most happy to do it, ma'am. Allow me just a moment to search her out."

Before Lizzie could stop him, he had hurried away in search of his quarry. She could feel her heart sinking to the soles of her slippers at the thought of meeting the young woman whom Matthew found so irresistible. Mr. Thoreau was studying her with a quizzical expression.

"Do you not wish to meet Miss Blackwell?"

When she did not answer directly, he added gently, "There is no need to do so if you do not wish it, Miss Lancaster."

Lizzie made no pretense of hiding her feelings. "But how can I avoid it? If he finds her, then I must meet her."

"Not if you are no longer here. I can make my excuses to La Fayette and escort you back to your hotel. If Lady Thalia is not ready to depart, I am certain she would not mind your leaving. I could hide you behind a potted palm while I make the arrangements, and we could disappear in an instant."

"You are very kind, sir," she said gratefully, managing a shaky smile for his plan, "but indeed I cannot be so rag-mannered as that. But I do thank you for offering to rescue me."

In a few minutes, Mr. Mansfield reappeared at her side. "I am afraid that I must disappoint you again, Miss Lancaster. It appears that Miss Blackwell has already departed."

Lizzie found that she could breathe again, and did her best to look disappointed. "That is unfortunate, but I thank you for your effort, Mr. Mansfield. I am certain that I will have the pleasure of meeting her at another time."

"Yes," he agreed, brightening. "Since you and Webster are old friends, it must be so—and you will be delighted with her, I assure you. She is a charming young woman, much admired by everyone. Her father is an officer in the 18th Hussars, and I believe that I have heard some refer to her as the sweetheart of the regiment."

"Yes, I am certain that she must be delightful. I shall look forward to meeting her." Lizzie was able to speak with greater conviction now that she knew that she did not have to face Miss Blackwell.

After a few minutes, Mr. Mansfield was called away once more, and she turned to Mr. Thoreau a little self-consciously.

"You must think me very odd," she said, not looking up to catch his eye. "I feel that I owe you an explanation."

"I do not think you odd at all—and you assuredly owe me no explanation. In fact, I forbid you to offer me one." Offering her his arm, he deftly steered her toward a table placed in a palm-filled alcove and pulled out a chair for her. "I am going for refreshments so that you may recover your strength, Miss Lancaster. I shall return immediately."

Relieved to be tucked away in this private place so that she could regain her composure, she leaned back in the chair and surveyed the glittering group before her. How very comfortable Mr. Thoreau was, she thought—and how very perceptive. Knowing that he truly expected no explanation made her feel that she would unquestionably give him one. Even though she had known him for so short a time, she was certain that she could safely confide in him.

So lost in her own thoughts was she that she did not realize she was no longer alone until she heard a deep voice, and saw a tall figure bend over her, taking her gloved hand and pressing it to his lips. A dark man, attired in white breeches and a military coat of green and yellow, bristling with medals and ribbons, was speaking to her very attentively.

"Ah, mademoiselle, one so lovely as you should never be left alone. Allow me to present myself—Capitaine François LaSalle at your service, lovely lady. I implore you to allow me to join you here."

"And we would be delighted to have you join us, Capitaine. We shall only have to find another chair." Mr.

Thoreau had arrived, carefully balancing a plate of fruit for Lizzie and two glasses of champagne.

Chagrined, Captain LaSalle bowed to the newcomer. "Forgive me. I did not realize that I was intruding upon a *tête-à-tête*. I shall, of course, remove myself immediately— but most regretfully."

He turned to Lizzie, again taking her hand and pressing it to his lips. "Allow me to express my deep gratitude, mademoiselle, for wearing the colors that honor the flag for which I fought."

He bowed deeply once more to Lizzie, his dark eyes lingering upon her, and then turned back to the crowded salon.

"Well, well, Miss Lancaster," murmured Mr. Thoreau appreciatively. "A conquest! I turn my back for only a few moments and you have snared a prize from the French Dragoons."

"What nonsense!" said Lizzie, flushing, but mildly gratified. She had been grateful for Thoreau's appearance, for the French officer had been so imposing in appearance and so intense in manner that she had been quite overcome. "You could see that he is a practiced flirt, and I merely happened to fall into his path."

"I do not believe that for a moment," he said, smiling. "You are quite out of the way over here. I believe the captain was merely biding his time until you were alone."

"But what did he mean about my wearing the colors for which he fought?" she asked, eager to change the subject. As soon as she had said this, however, the truth dawned upon her and she clapped her hand over her mouth. "But he is correct! I *am* wearing the colors of the flag of the Revolution! The French flag is once more the fleur-de-lis."

Thoreau nodded. "Of course, I choose to think that you

are wearing the colors to honor *my* country, but I understand that the captain might not see it in that light."

"Splendid! One country we have been at war with, and the other we are at war with still! I was not thinking of that at all when I dressed for the evening! I wonder that Lady Thalia did not think of it."

"I doubt that it would occur to anyone other than those obsessed by such patriotic notions. As I told you, the French soldiers may wear the white cockade now, but they have saved their tricolors."

"What a goose I was! I shall be careful not to wear this color combination again."

"Nonsense! You look charming, Miss Lancaster. Merely pass off such remarks with a smile and a pretty shrug of your shoulders, and everyone will be satisfied. No one will charge you with disloyalty."

He watched her for a moment, the laugh lines around his eyes deepening. "Of course, there is one other option I have not mentioned—and this would not be nearly so gratifying to either the captain or me—you *could* be wearing the colors of your own country."

Lizzie stared at him for a moment, then started to laugh. "You must think me the most complete goose! I did not even think of my own flag."

"Miss Lancaster, I think you the most completely charming young woman I have met in some time."

"At least the most nonsensical one," she amended, still laughing.

They sipped their champagne in companionable silence for a few moments, watching the shifting kaleidoscope of the crowd.

"He was a member of the Dragoons, you said," she ventured at last. "It is possible, I suppose, that he fought in the Peninsula."

Thoreau nodded. "It is very likely." He watched her for a moment. "Have you a particular interest in that portion of the war?"

Lizzie was silent for a moment, then nodded without meeting his eyes. "A most—a most particular friend of mine fought there."

"Mr. Matthew Webster?"

Another minute or two passed as they watched the crowd, then she nodded, still looking straight ahead as she spoke.

"Matthew and I were not formally affianced, but we had an understanding that when he returned, we would be married. He has been gone now for well over two years. Just a fortnight ago, I received a letter from him that told me of his engagement to Miss Blackwell."

Mr. Thoreau remained silent, but he continued to regard her with a steady gaze. She could feel his eyes upon her and finally felt pressed to say something more.

"I know that I am foolish to think that seeing him again will make any difference. I daresay I shall only feel worse and appear ridiculous to everyone."

Mr. Thoreau seemed to be thinking the matter over, and she waited for his response. It should not be so, she knew, but she felt somewhat lighter in spirit after telling him about Matthew, and the lightness was not due to the champagne she was sipping.

"No, I don't think that you are being foolish. As a matter of fact, I think that you are quite courageous in going to face your fear."

She shook her head ruefully. "You notice that I did not wish to meet Miss Blackwell. I don't think that is an example of my being able to face my fear."

"Ah, but she is not the one you must face. It is Matthew Webster."

She straightened her shoulders and sat a little taller as she thought about his words. It was quite possible that he was right. She had been focusing her fears upon the young lady, but it was not, in truth, Miss Blackwell who was the source of the problem. It was Matthew. Had he truly loved her, he would not have put her by for some other woman, no matter how lovely. The decision had been Matthew's.

It was well that she had had the opportunity to think the matter through, for the crowd in front of them parted, and Mr. Mansfield appeared once more.

"Ah, Miss Lancaster! I knew that I should find you if I kept searching." With a theatrical flourish, he added, "And I would like to present to you Miss Blackwell, the fiancée of your good friend Matthew Webster."

And he stepped aside to reveal a dainty young woman in a filmy blue gown, its fabric too gauze-like to conceal any of the charms of her figure. Her pale curls shone in the candlelight, framing a perfectly heart-shaped face.

Both Lizzie and Mr. Thoreau rose automatically from their chairs, and the ladies dropped a curtsey to one another, then Mr. Thoreau was duly introduced and made his bow.

"But how delightful to meet a friend of Matthew's from home," said Miss Blackwell, two deep dimples showing in her creamy cheeks. She spoke to Lizzie, but her eyes were fixed upon Mr. Thoreau.

Lizzie's heart sank. Her nemesis was undeniably alluring. The Sirens of Ulysses could not have been more inviting. She could see that Mr. Mansfield was hanging on her every word, and she had no doubt that Mr. Thoreau would respond in much the same manner. There were some women, she knew, who appeared to have a fatal attraction for men. Matthew would have been helpless before her, and Lizzie wanted to do nothing so much as to turn and run from the room. Nonetheless, she caught herself in time and stemmed the rising tide of desperation. It was all over in a moment. She steeled herself, then gently returned the smile.

"You are very kind, Miss Blackwell. I understand that I am to wish you happy."

Miss Blackwell inclined her head demurely, dark lashes sweeping her cheek as she glanced up sidewise at Mr. Mansfield, who responded quickly.

"I must tell you that Webster has broken half the hearts in Paris with this engagement." He did not seem to be able to remove his gaze from Miss Blackwell, who smiled at him sweetly, then tapped his shoulder with her fan.

"Only half the hearts?" she quizzed him.

"Allow me to correct myself," he amended quickly. "Webster has broken the hearts of *all* the men in Paris."

"Ah, much better," she said, turning a roguish gaze upon Mr. Thoreau. "I believe that I see one gentleman whose heart has not broken, however."

Mr. Thoreau bowed. "You must forgive me, Miss Blackwell. I have been told upon the best authority that I have a heart that is impervious to romance, so you must not let the matter trouble you."

"Indeed?" she murmured. "Perhaps, Mr. Thoreau, you simply have not been in Paris long enough."

"Nor will I be. Soon I shall be safely in Vienna, with no need to guard my heart."

Miss Blackwell's lower lip protruded in a pretty pout that clearly enchanted Mr. Mansfield. "Everyone seems to be leaving for Vienna, and Paris will become deadly dull. Perhaps I shall have to go to Vienna as well."

"How wonderful that would be! Do you really plan to do so?" Mr. Mansfield's face was alight at the notion.

Miss Blackwell glanced up at Mr. Thoreau through her lashes. "If everyone felt as you do, I would feel that I *must* go. I could not bring myself to disappoint so many."

"I am certain that Mr. Webster would be delighted to see you there, ma'am," observed Mr. Thoreau, "and that must be all in all to you."

Her pretty mouth drooped slightly at this reminder of her fiancé, but she caught herself and, once again displaying her enchanting dimples, tapped his wrist with her fan. "How very good you are, dear sir, to remind me of my obligations. Perhaps I shall come to Vienna so that you may counsel me."

If she had hoped for a flirtatious rejoinder, she was disappointed, and Mr. Thoreau was saved from further attack by the arrival of several of Miss Blackwell's admirers. Under cover of the ensuing confusion, Lizzie and Mr. Thoreau made their escape.

He looked down at her, the trace of a smile in his eyes. "Miss Lancaster, I may well have been incorrect in saying that you must face only Matthew Webster. Miss Blackwell is more formidable than I had imagined. Nonetheless, now you have at least faced one of your dragons."

"Yes," Lizzie sighed, "but not slain her, I fear—although the notion holds a certain appeal."

He laughed and patted her hand. "Never mind, Miss Lancaster. Tomorrow is another day. Promise me a little time in the afternoon, and I shall show you something to take your mind from your troubles."

"Gladly," she responded gratefully. "What will you show me?"

"It will be a surprise—a most agreeable one," he assured her.

Before she and Lady Thalia departed that evening, Mr. Thoreau had received permission to call for Lizzie the next afternoon for a Parisian expedition. He had taken Lady Thalia by surprise with his invitation, but she had, after a moment of thought, agreed.

"I cannot spare Beavers, but my footman can accompany you," she had replied, nodding in Henry's direction.

"What will you do in the morning, Miss Lancaster?" he asked, as Henry was closing the door of their carriage after the ladies.

"I believe that I shall purchase a fan," said Lizzie, looking at him thoughtfully.

Her sally was rewarded by his sudden shout of laughter, which followed them as the carriage pulled away. Lizzie leaned back against the leather squabs of the carriage, pleased with herself.

Mr. Thoreau, still laughing, strolled away from the line of carriages. He was looking forward with considerable pleasure to spending the afternoon with Miss Lancaster. What a fool that young Webster must be, he thought, turning his steps toward the salon once more.

Seven

Lizzie did not allow herself to linger over thoughts of Miss Blackwell and Matthew when they returned to the hotel. Grateful that the day had tired her, she fell swiftly to sleep. The next day dawned bright and, to her surprise, she was in far better spirits than she had expected to be. Despite the lingering memory of Miss Blackwell enslaving virtually all the males that came within her range, she recalled with pleasure the fact that Mr. Thoreau had not fallen prey to her charm. Instead, he had appeared amused by the charade.

She was looking forward to trying on the gowns that Madame Delacroix had completed, and Lady Thalia had decreed that more shopping was in order after that, followed by a carriage ride to Notre-Dame. In the evening they were to attend a ball given by the Marquis of Belgrave at the Hôtel de Crillon on the Place de la Concorde. Most of all, however, she found that she was looking forward to her late afternoon outing with Mr. Thoreau. Lady Thalia seemed to be reading her mind.

"Mr. Thoreau is being *most* attentive to you, Lizzie," that lady observed idly, as they rode to the Delacroix salon. "If I did not know better, I would think that he is forming an attachment for you."

Lizzie experienced a slight sinking feeling at Lady

Thalia's words, but she spoke lightly. "And why should he not?" she inquired.

Lady Thalia looked at her with raised brows. "In part, because you are in love with Matthew and don't care a fig for Mr. Thoreau."

"You say that is in part. What are your other reasons for thinking that he will not form an attachment to me?" Lizzie was careful to speak casually, as though the whole matter was of no consequence to her—which, of course, it was not, she assured herself.

"Unlike us," Lady Thalia replied, "Americans are very direct in their manner. Although that lends them—or lends at least *some* of them—a certain charm, it does mean that they often say more personal things than we might say under similar conditions—but they mean very little by such intimacy. It is simply their manner."

Lizzie thought this over. "So you mean that I might misinterpret what Mr. Thoreau says to me because his manner is informal?"

Lady Thalia nodded, pleased that she had made herself clear. "Exactly so."

Lizzie shook her head. "I don't think that is the case, Lady Thalia, but I will think about it and be on my guard."

Lady Thalia was forced to be satisfied with that. She was pleased that Lizzie had not sunk into a deep melancholy over Matthew's defection, but she was not anxious to see her charge's affections quickly transferred to an unknown young American, no matter how charming.

Hoping to divert Lizzie's thoughts, she said, "Now *do* tell me what you meant by wanting to purchase a fan, my dear. Whatever made you wish for one?"

To her surprise, Lizzie began to laugh. "I had not realized until last night that fans could be used as tools of conquest."

"How *very* intriguing, Lizzie!" Lady Thalia's eyes brightened at this promise of entertainment. "Who did you see using one so effectively? Recount the scene for me precisely. Do not omit a single detail."

Lizzie gave her a vivid account of Miss Blackwell's performance, not missing the flutter of one eyelash, one sidelong glance, or one arch tap with a fan.

"You are quite in the right of it," Lady Thalia agreed, laughing when Lizzie had finished her tale. "You must by *all* means have a fan and learn to use it to advantage. We shall see to it directly."

Although fans were still used by ladies of the *ton*, their use was by no means as prevalent as it had been before the arrival of the simple, columnar gowns on the fashion scene. The old fashioned-gowns with voluminous skirts very effectively hid numerous pockets so that a lady could keep her hands free, while still carrying everything she needed upon her person. Modern gowns, however, offered few prospects for pockets, so ladies had begun carrying reticules to hold their personal effects. Thus fans had become one more item to carry and were not so likely to be included.

When they arrived at the Delacroix Salon, Lizzie tried on the gowns that were ready, Lady Thalia approved them, and Madame Delacroix boxed the dresses and sent them to the hotel. With that business taken care of, she and Lady Thalia set about their shopping. Aside from some ostrich plumes dyed a lovely shade of gold that would match one of her evening gowns, Lizzie's most delightful purchase was a trio of fans—a gauze fan ornamented with spangles and two brisé fans, one of tortoise shell and one of ivory, pierced so delicately that it looked like lacework.

"*Very* nice," said Lady Thalia approvingly. "Now you must practice using them."

"Practice? Do you think that is necessary?" asked Lizzie, surprised. Using a fan seemed simple enough to her.

"Of course! You must be graceful in your movements. Lead with your wrist." Picking up the tortoise shell fan, she demonstrated. "*Always* with the wrist. Your gestures must be artful so that you do not look as though you are about to jab the gentleman with the fan."

"Which in some cases might be a very good idea," Lizzie replied—but she took up the ivory fan and began to practice.

"And you must remember, Lizzie, not to behave coyly with your fan. Flirting—capturing a man's attention—with one is fine, but do not be too coquettish or you will lose the fan's effect."

Lizzie looked doubtful. "It seemed to me that Miss Blackwell was certainly being coquettish, but Mr. Mansfield seemed to find it most appealing." And that, she thought, was a case of understatement. Mr. Mansfield had been enchanted by Miss Blackwell and her annoying fan.

"You may count upon it that he was already infatuated *before* he encountered the fan," Lady Thalia said in a very positive tone. "Gentlemen do not care for young ladies who act too precious."

Remembering Miss Blackwell, Lizzie was far less certain, but she did not argue. Instead, she enjoyed practicing during the whole of their carriage ride to Notre-Dame, although she did relinquish it when they left the chaise. She decided that she would not carry a fan on her afternoon expedition with Mr. Thoreau. It would be more enjoyable showing him her new acquisition in the proper setting, where she felt certain he would appreciate its effect—and enjoy the reason she was carrying it. Since he was a guest in the home of La

Fayette, who had also been invited to the ball, she knew that she could count on seeing him that night.

When she and Lady Thalia arrived back at the hotel, Mr. Thoreau was waiting for her. Lizzie apologized hastily for her tardiness and hurried to her chamber to set herself to rights before going out with him. On her dressing table was a handsome bouquet of red and white roses, wrapped with a broad blue ribbon. The card was lying beside it, and it was, as she immediately suspected it would be, signed in the bold, black scrawl of Captain LaSalle, pledging his undying faithfulness and promising to call upon her the next day.

Lady Thalia opened the door between their chambers and gasped at the roses. "But they're *wonderful*, Lizzie! Who sent them to you?"

Lizzie told her about her encounter with LaSalle at the reception, and she was both amused and pleased. Her charge might have been jilted, but it was satisfying to know that she was not likely to waste away and die of a broken heart.

"A captain in the Dragoons! I must say, Lizzie, that you are doing *very* well! I am *most* impressed!"

"I wish you would not joke so about it, Lady Thalia. His attentions make me very uncomfortable."

"But why should they? *Every* young woman should have admirers, Matthew or no Matthew. You must remember that *he* has Miss Blackwell, so you must enjoy yourself, just as he is doing."

Lizzie nodded slowly. "That does sound fair," she agreed, "but it does not seem natural to me."

"It will," Lady Thalia assured her. "After all, why should Matthew be the only one to enjoy himself? *You* deserve to have some pleasure, too. Besides," she added sagely, "a young man, even Matthew, is *much* more likely to regret the loss of a young woman who is admired and full of life than he is one who is dying of love for him."

Having hastily splashed water on her face, straightened her bonnet and her sash, and applied a little of Lady Thalia's devastating perfume, Lizzie went down to join Mr. Thoreau. As they strolled out together, with Henry following at a discreet distance as chaperon, he looked down at her and smiled.

"You are looking very well today, Miss Lancaster," he informed her.

"Thank you, Mr. Thoreau. You are kind to say so," she replied demurely, tripping lightly along beside him. She paused a moment, thinking, then went on. "I realize that it is not discreet nor ladylike of me to tell you this, sir, but I know you will appreciate it."

"I am fully prepared to appreciate whatever it may be," he returned, straightening his shoulders, as though in preparation.

"I received a bouquet of roses—red and white—tied with a dark blue ribbon!" She looked up at him and waited expectantly.

"The captain of the Dragoons!" he exclaimed. "I told you that you had made a conquest, Miss Lancaster, but you would not believe me!"

She colored. "It was kind of him to send such lovely flowers, but I knew that you would appreciate the joke. I hope that you do not think it immodest of me to tell you." She would, she thought, have preferred that he not be quite so enthusiastic about her acquisition of an admirer.

"Not at all," he said comfortably. "I am delighted that he brightened your day. I daresay that I should have sent you a nosegay myself, but I am afraid that I do not usually think to do such gallant things. While your captain was ordering your roses, I was in the gardens at the Palais-Royal."

At her look of surprise, he added, "You can rent a morning chair there and read the newspaper."

"Ah, the newspaper." Lizzie nodded. "I have noticed how eager you are to keep abreast of the latest news."

His pleasant expression grew grim, and she looked at him curiously. "Was there something in the newspaper that upset you?"

"It appears that the British set fire to Washington," he said grimly.

"Your capital?" she gasped. "How terrible! Did the fire do great damage?"

"The capitol building and The White House—that is great damage." He looked down at her and made a visible attempt to lighten his expression. "However, in all fairness, I must say that the British are not the only ones to resort to burning. Both armies have done their share."

It seemed very peculiar, Lizzie thought, that they were talking together like this when their countries were at war. They walked on in silence, leaving the unhappy topic alone. Eventually, she became quite confused by the tangle of narrow medieval streets down which they had wandered.

"Where are we going?" she inquired, looking about her curiously.

"You will see in just a moment," he said, "and I believe you will think it well worth the walk."

They walked on silently for a few minutes more, and then they suddenly emerged from the warren of narrow dark streets into a space filled with the golden light of the late afternoon sun. It was the Place du Carrousel. Before them lay the Tuileries and the Arch of Napoleon, crowned by the bronze horses taken from St. Mark's in Venice. Everything they saw had been turned to gold by the light of the setting sun.

Finally Lizzie spoke. "I could say that it is lovely, but that simply does not do justice to this. I do not have the words."

They stood there gazing at the scene before them for a few minutes more, and then Mr. Thoreau led her to a small café on the sidewalk, where they ordered coffee and continued to look about them.

"This is the oddest city," said Lizzie finally. "Parts of it are so old and dark and dirty, and then there are the boulevards and parks—and now this."

Mr. Thoreau nodded. "Voltaire said that Paris—like the statue of Nebuchadnezzar—was built of mud and of gold."

"Well, I know nothing about Nebuchadnezzar's statue," she replied, "but I can quite see his point about Paris."

As twilight began to fall, the pair roused themselves from the reverie into which they had fallen.

"I must get you back to your hotel. After all, Miss Lancaster," her companion observed, tactfully avoiding any reference to Miss Blackwell, "you must array yourself in all your splendor tonight. It is always possible that your captain might appear."

"You overwhelm me. Perhaps I should wear one of his roses." She watched from the corner of her eye to see how he received this sally, but to her disappointment, he merely smiled.

When they said good-bye at the hotel, Lizzie held out her hand to him. "Thank you, Mr. Thoreau. This afternoon was a gift I shall treasure always—quite the nicest that I have ever received." Until recent days, the music box that Matthew had given her, now packed away in her trunk, would have held the place of honor.

"It has been entirely my pleasure, Miss Lancaster," he told her, holding her hand a little longer than necessary. "I can think of no one else with whom I would have cared to share it."

Lizzie was humming as she prepared for the ball. The gown was one of the confections prepared by Madame Delacroix, a sea-green silk edged thickly in white lace. Once again Beavers helped her put up her dark hair with the pearl combs, and before she left, she slipped the ivory fan into her reticule. She would practice upon the gentlemen tonight, and she looked forward to the laughter she expected to see in the blue eyes of Mr. Thoreau when she delicately tapped him with her fan.

She saw Mr. Mansfield first, and, to her pleasure, he led her out for Weber's "Invitation to the Waltz," the number which began the ball. Lady Thalia had insisted that she learn how to waltz, and Lizzie had been delighted with the graceful movements of the dance. When Mr. Mansfield escorted her back to Lady Thalia's side, Lizzie was gratified to find that her dance card filled almost at once. A handsome young lieutenant in the British Lancers was her partner for a quadrille, and the evening seemed to slip by so easily that she scarcely noticed it. The ivory fan frequently came into play, sometimes as a fan and sometimes—as she had seen Miss Blackwell use it—as a flirtatious device so that she could lean closer to a gentleman. She was amazed to discover how much she was enjoying herself, and how completely self-possessed she felt—not at all nervous or shy.

Mr. Thoreau had engaged her for a waltz and for supper, and as he led her onto the floor, he said, eyes crinkling in amusement, "I believe, Miss Lancaster, that you indeed have a fan."

Lizzie whipped it to attention. "Very true, Mr. Thoreau. And, if you will notice, dear sir, the management of the fan is all in the wrist." Here she demonstrated, first fluttering the fan before her face and then tapping him winsomely with it.

"I am overcome by your expertise," he confessed, sweeping her into the dance. "And I fear for the many hearts you will break with that fan."

"Do you think I could do so?" she demanded, cheered by the thought.

"Assuredly. Your conquests will be many."

"But you will not be one of them?" she inquired, eyes bright.

"Not because of the fan," he said, holding her securely as they moved lightly around the floor.

When the dance was over, he led her to a table where they would be having supper together. Settling her comfortably, he excused himself to retrieve their refreshments. All too soon, Captain LaSalle appeared at her side.

"Dear mademoiselle, did you receive my tribute?" he asked, bending low over her hand once more.

She smiled up at him. "They were beautiful, Captain. You were very kind to send them to me."

"They could not come close to your beauty, Mademoiselle Lancaster, but they were the best that my poor efforts could manage today."

"Why, Captain LaSalle, you have come to join us once more," said Mr. Thoreau, drawing close. "We seem to meet like this with somewhat painful regularity."

LaSalle bowed to him. "And once again I must proffer my apology for intruding upon a private supper." Turning back to Lizzie, he said, "I shall do myself the honor of calling upon you tomorrow at your hotel, mademoiselle. I hope that I shall find you in."

"I hope that I am there when you call, Captain," she said. "However, since tomorrow will be our last day in Paris, I am not certain what Lady Thalia's plans are for the day."

"You are leaving Paris so soon? I am devastated, Miss

Lancaster! Can I not persuade you to stay longer? Paris has so many delights that I am certain you have not yet enjoyed."

"I am certain that Paris has much to offer that I haven't yet seen, sir, but Lady Thalia and I have plans to travel to Vienna. I must not slow her."

He bent his head as though in acceptance. "Very well, Mademoiselle Lancaster. If it must be so, then it must. However, should you return to Paris, I beg that you will allow me to show you my city."

"I shall look forward to that," said Lizzie, plying her fan gently and looking up at him over its lacy edge.

After Captain LaSalle had bowed himself away, Mr. Thoreau turned to Lizzie, his eyebrows high.

"And what were you doing with that fan, Miss Lancaster?" he asked. "Were you flirting with our Captain of the Dragoons?"

"Only slightly, Mr. Thoreau," she responded. "I needed to practice, you see."

Before he could comment, Miss Blackwell and Mr. Mansfield appeared beside their table.

"Miss Lancaster, how delightful you look," said Mansfield, bowing low. "I am looking forward to our dance together."

Lizzie smiled at him automatically, but she could not respond to him because her attention was focused on Miss Blackwell. Around that lady's throat was a gold chain with the medal of St. George that she had given to Matthew.

"Miss Blackwell," she said, her voice sounding strained even to herself. "What a charming medallion."

"Is it not attractive?" she agreed. "It was Matthew's, but he *insisted* upon giving it to me." She lifted the medal with one finger so that she could see it and admire it. "It is not suitable with this gown, I know, but the dear boy was so anxious that I wear it. He begged me to think of him whenever I have it on." She looked at Lizzie and smiled. "But then, that isn't really necessary because I think of him all of the time."

"How commendable," replied Lizzie stiffly. "I am certain that he is grateful."

Miss Blackwell smiled at her again, then turned the full warmth of her charm upon Mr. Thoreau. "Perhaps, Mr. Thoreau, you might be able to call upon me tomorrow and tell me a little about America. I have always been so fascinated by your country."

"Delightful though that sounds, Miss Blackwell, I will be leaving Paris early tomorrow, so I fear your curiosity about America will have to wait for another time to be satisfied."

Miss Blackwell leaned closer to him and tapped his hand with her fan. "I shall look forward to that time, sir," she said, looking up at him through her lashes before Mr. Mansfield led her away.

Mr. Thoreau glanced at Lizzie, his eyes bright, to enjoy with her the matter of Miss Blackwell's fan, but he could not draw an answering smile from her. Lizzie found that she was so upset that she could not even enjoy Miss Blackwell's byplay with the fan. Instead, she focused on Mr. Thoreau's departure.

"You leave tomorrow?" she asked, her voice flat. "You had not mentioned it to me."

"No, although I was planning to do so," he assured her. "I shall see you very soon in Vienna. I will be going first back to Ghent, then I will be traveling to Vienna."

"But that will take quite a long time!" she protested.

"It will go quickly," he assured her. "You will have many new things to see there—and you will, of course, see Matthew."

When she did not answer, he looked at her gravely, then patted her hand comfortingly. "You will be able to face him, Miss Lancaster," he said in a reassuring voice.

Lizzie was not comforted, however, and the days ahead suddenly looked bleaker than they had. She said a sad good-bye to Mr. Thoreau that night, and when she returned to the hotel, she discovered that she could not sleep.

All she could see was the gold medal of St. George that she had given Matthew as protection, her parting gift to him, around Teresa Blackwell's neck. He had given it away.

And she would not be able to laugh with Mr. Thoreau for an unknown number of days.

Eight

Lady Thalia groaned with pleasure as she sank into the warm bath that Beavers had prepared for her. A hip bath had also been filled for Lizzie in her chamber.

"Every bone in my body has been jarred loose by that infamous journey, Beavers! How could Timothy Holywell *dare* to tell me that coming to Vienna would be no different from a journey from the Scottish highlands to Brighton? I thought that sounded grim enough, but it doesn't even bear comparison! Not only did this trip take *eons* longer, but I *can* not believe that the lowest wayside inn found anywhere in Britain could be as bugridden and noisome as the one where we stopped in Württemberg! The first two stops were dreadful, but that one was *unspeakable!*"

At that inn, the innkeeper and his wife, as well as the chambers themselves, were clearly unwashed. Bedbugs had crawled freely among the dingy bedcovers, and the entire place had smelled of boiled cabbage and unemptied chamber pots. Lady Thalia had taken one look at the place and marched her entire party back to the carriage despite the fact that the hour was late and no other accommodation was available.

"I prefer that we starve and go sleepless," she had told the others firmly. Although Lizzie, Beavers, and Henry were not inclined to argue, being quite as disgusted as Lady Thalia, the driver and postilions, being hungry and less nice in their tastes, had grumbled. She had allowed them to purchase their own dinner there before driving on, but Lady Thalia's party went hungry that night, except for some fruit and a handful of Mrs. Clary's cookies still kept fresh in a tin. Lizzie had divided those equally among the four of them.

After that horrifying experience, Lady Thalia had decided that for the duration of the journey they would sleep in the carriage and stop only to eat, to change horses, or to stretch their legs. Beavers and Henry were dispatched to the best-kept farmhouses they passed to purchase food so that they would not have to depend upon finding an inn or café with a decent kitchen.

Munich, at least, had been respectable—which was just as well, for they had broken an axle there and been forced to leave the carriage while it underwent three days of repairs. She had been forced to admit that Bavaria was really quite charming and she had discovered that she had a regrettable fondness for *strudel.*

After a fortnight of travel, they were all heartily weary of picnic meals and the confines of the carriage. Fortunately, though, the weather had been fine and they had encountered only one storm. Poor Henry, riding outside with the coachman and postilions, had borne the brunt of the bad weather. It had been with the deepest of gratitude that they had at last seen Vienna in the distance.

"I wouldn't be too put out with Mr. Holywell, ma'am," observed Beavers pacifically, handing her mistress a bar of the scented soap that she preferred and that Beavers had carefully packed in quantity. "After all, it has been a good many years since he last made this journey. I daresay he has forgotten just how hard a trip it can be."

Lady Thalia was unmoved. Timothy Holywell, some twenty years her senior and possessed of a wicked humor, was also one of her dearest friends. She was more than certain that he had willfully misled her.

"I should imagine that he is sitting at his comfortable fireside, chuckling to himself every time he thinks about us trundling along that miserable road! If I had the wretch here, he would pay *dearly* for that lapse in memory! As it is, I shall have to wait for months to avenge myself and must be content to playact the scene in my mind! I had *never* imagined traveling through such a dark, depressing countryside! Even the villages put me in mind of witches, and no doubt they were there, lurking inside those dim little houses, stirring their evil brew!"

She smiled suddenly as she lathered the soap across her shoulders, her mood brightening as she remembered that their situation was now quite different. "At least this hotel appears to be well run, and Vienna seems a pretty enough place. Don't you agree, Beavers?"

"Indeed I do, ma'am." Pleased with the shift in mood, Beavers was determined to encourage it. "There was so much green as we rode into town that I wasn't certain that we had really arrived in a city. It seemed more like we were driving through a great park."

Lady Thalia nodded in agreement, her irritation fading completely as she soaked in the warm, perfumed water and thought about the final part of their journey.

Seeing Vienna in the distance had been an agreeable experience for all of them, not just because they had almost reached their destination, but also because it presented such a pleasant prospect. They had driven up to the tollgate at the Linienwall, an outer wall of the city that once protected the suburbs of Vienna from the Turks more than one hundred years ago. Then they had made their way through the suburbs and across the Glacis, through vast green meadows with tree-lined alleys, to the Bastei, the old wall that surrounded the city itself and upon which the sociable Viennese strolled to look out upon nature. Inside the Bastei they had found a cheerful, bustling city, a highly ornamented tribute to the baroque era.

Lady Thalia had been most fortunate in her living arrangements, for Lord Danvers, a good friend of hers, had reserved three floors of a hotel close to the Hofburg, the vast home of Emperor Francis and the center of activity for the Congress. When Lord Danvers had heard that she too planned to travel to Vienna, he had insisted that she take one of the floors that he had reserved.

"For, my dear Thalia," he had told her, "you will find no other place at this late date, and you must not be left to the mercy of innkeepers."

Remembering his words now—and her experience with the dark little inn along the way—she shuddered, then opened her eyes and looked about her gratefully. A fire crackled below the marble mantelpiece, red velvet curtains heavily crusted with gold lace were closed against the autumn night, a gilt mirror upon her dressing table reflected the glow of firelight and candlelight, thick rugs covered the floor, and the bedcovers were turned back to reveal fresh, crisp linen. Their rooms were delightfully luxurious, and she felt that this augured well for their stay in Vienna.

"How was Lizzie when you left her, Beavers?" she asked. "She had gotten so *very* quiet as we grew near to the city that I thought she might have had the headache."

"I daresay she was just bone-weary, ma'am," replied Beavers. "She was about to take her bath, too, and when

I told her that you had ordered supper, she said that she would eat it if she were still awake."

"Once she smells the food, she will be able to eat. I should imagine that we have all lost weight during the past fourteen days, in spite of all the *strudel* I consumed. Lizzie ate very little, even in Munich. I shall go in to be certain that she dines with me tonight, for I don't want her gowns to hang upon her."

After wrapping herself in a warm red dressing gown, Lady Thalia sent Beavers off to her own chamber to bathe and prepare for supper. Henry had gone downstairs to order their meal and to supervise its delivery to their drawing room, where a table had been set by the fire. Lord Danvers had provided for them very well indeed, she thought, setting forth to shepherd Lizzie to the drawing room for supper.

Lizzie looked freshly scrubbed, but Lady Thalia noticed at once that her expression was nonetheless unhappy.

"What is wrong, my dear? I *told* Beavers that you did not look well, and she said that you were doubtless just bone-weary."

"Oh, indeed I am," she replied, grateful for Beavers. She had no desire to tell Lady Thalia about the medal of St. George nor to admit to her that she found herself missing the security that Mr. Thoreau's presence had offered her. "All that I care to do is to go to bed immediately."

"And so you shall—just as soon as you have had something to eat," said Lady Thalia firmly. "I can *not* allow you to go to bed when you have had so little real nourishment in the last three days. I have not seen you eat more than an apple and a few bites of bread in that time."

Lizzie shrugged. "I had no appetite."

"Well, you will in just a moment. Henry is setting out

our food in the drawing room now, so come along with me. As soon as you have dined, you may retire to bed and sleep for *just* as long as you wish."

Seeing that she had no choice, Lizzie allowed herself to be led down the passage, which was thickly carpeted like the rest of the rooms. However, as they neared the entry to the drawing room, the fragrance of well-cooked food greeted them. To her own surprise, Lizzie worked her way briskly through a bowl of nourishing beef soup, thick with vegetables in a dark brown broth, and then moved on to *Wiener schnitzel*—veal scallops breaded and fried to a golden brown—mashed potatoes, and beet salad. The meal was rounded out with cups of strong black coffee and *Bublanina*, a sponge cake topped with sweet dark cherries.

"That was delicious," sighed Lizzie. "I did not think that I wanted a bite to eat, but I have left nothing at all on my plate."

"Of course you haven't," said Lady Thalia, surveying her charge with satisfaction. "You have been *starving* for days without even noticing it."

Reaching to a silver salver placed on the table behind her, she picked up three letters, two addressed to her and one to Lizzie. "And now that we have fortified ourselves, we may read the messages that have been left for us." And she handed Lizzie her letter.

Lizzie turned it over and stared at it, puzzled. "Who would be sending me a letter? It is not from my parents, and no one else knows where to find me."

"Well, open it and find out, my dear."

Lady Thalia opened her first letter. "How *very* considerate! It is from Mr. Mansfield. He says that he is looking forward to our arrival. Such *pretty* manners in a young man!"

"Yes, he is very pleasant," agreed Lizzie absently, her letter still in her lap.

Lady Thalia smiled as she broke the wafer on her second letter and read the few lines scribbled on the heavy paper. "Danvers says that he is *delighted* that we have arrived at last, and that we should plan to attend a ball tomorrow night at the Redoutensaal. Everyone will be there and he has invitations for us." She folded the note. "Such a *dear* man! We will have a splendid time, Lizzie."

Lizzie was staring at her. "Everyone will be at the ball?" She hesitated a moment, then added, "Do you suppose, then, that Matthew will be there?"

"He might well be," said Lady Thalia briskly. "And if he is, that is a *good* thing, is it not? You want to see him, and what better place than a ball?"

"Yes, I suppose so," replied Lizzie slowly. "I just hadn't thought that I would see him quite so soon."

"Soon? You have waited *weeks* for this, and we have been preparing you for *just* this moment, Lizzie. You will look splendid, and Matthew will regret that he ever considered *glancing* at Miss Blackwell!"

Lizzie smiled. "I wish that it would be so simple."

"Who knows how it will be? There is no way of telling until you see him again." Lady Thalia looked at the letter lying in Lizzie's lap. "Aren't you going to open *your* note?"

Lizzie broke the seal and, as she saw the signature on the note, her expression grew bright. "It is from Mr. Thoreau!" she exclaimed. "I had thought that he would not be here for at least another week, but he writes that he was able to take care of his business much more quickly than he had planned and that he made excellent time on his journey to Vienna. He arrived here last night."

"Did he indeed?" remarked Lady Thalia dryly. "How *fortunate* he was not to have been traveling with us."

She studied Lizzie's face for a moment, then added, "*You* seem very happy to hear from our American friend."

"Of course I am! He has been a good friend to me, and he writes here that he will call at the hotel each morning until we arrive. He would like to be present to support me when I meet Matthew. How very kind he is!"

"Yes, quite extraordinarily kind," remarked Lady Thalia more dryly still. "I did not realize that *he* knew about Matthew—*nor* that the two of you had grown so close."

Lizzie flushed at her tone and the implication of her words. "As I said, Lady Thalia, he has been a good friend to me, and it would indeed be reassuring to have him present when I meet Matthew for the first time."

When Lady Thalia remained silent, Lizzie went on. "It seemed very natural to confide in Mr. Thoreau. He has been kind to me, and he appeared genuinely interested in my situation. After all," she added, seeing that her friend's expression had not lightened, "we know that he is not interested in me because of my fortune. He cannot have some hidden agenda."

Lady Thalia smiled at her remark. "We really know *very* little about Mr. Thoreau, however," she said slowly. "I can see that I shall have to remedy that."

"Well, I am certain that everything you discover will be to his credit," replied Lizzie.

"We shall see" was the answer that she had to be content with, and the two ladies took themselves off to bed, Lizzie to fall gratefully into a deep and dreamless slumber, Lady Thalia to lie awake for a little longer, considering the troublesome matter of Mr. Daniel Thoreau.

Nine

It was as well that Lady Thalia had reflected upon the matter of Mr. Thoreau before sleeping because that gentleman appeared the next day just as she was finishing her chocolate. She had slept later than usual, enjoying the luxury of a good bed and clean linen.

When Beavers announced his arrival to her, her first reaction was to have Henry send him about his business, saying that the ladies were unavailable. However, recollecting that she needed to have a private conversation with him, she decided that this would be the perfect moment. Lizzie was still asleep, and she would have the opportunity to speak with him before they took up their new life in Vienna.

She was satisfied that Mr. Thoreau had at least acted the part of the gentleman thus far and that he apparently had an adequate income to support him. She did not know much more than that about him, however, and his marked attentiveness to Lizzie was beginning to trouble her. She had not minded his attentions to the girl in Paris because it had seemed such a brief interlude—a period when all of them were more or less "between lives." However, she had not expected him to seek her out so pointedly once they reached Vienna.

As Lizzie had said, he could scarcely be a fortune

hunter since Lizzie had no fortune, but it was not unknown for gentlemen to prey upon innocent young women, particularly in unusual circumstances such as those their travels had imposed upon them. Too, since Lizzie was so distressed about Matthew, she might well be more vulnerable to developing a *tendre* for an attractive, attentive man—and Lady Thalia was forced to admit to herself that Mr. Thoreau possessed both of those qualities.

"Have Henry tell Mr. Thoreau that I will join him in the drawing room in a few minutes, Beavers," she said decisively. "And then see if you can find a morning gown less wrinkled than the others." Beavers had been unpacking her trunks, and she had a formidable amount of work to do if her mistress and Miss Lancaster were to be presentable at the ball that night.

In very short order, Lady Thalia entered the drawing room, where Mr. Thoreau was passing the time by staring out the window at the passers-by, three stories below him. Upon advice from Viennese friends, Lord Danvers had been careful to reserve his apartments well above the level of the street, where the bustle of the crowd in the narrow medieval streets would not trouble him and where his windows would catch what sunlight there was to be had.

"Mr. Thoreau, how *very* good of you to call upon us," she said brightly, entering the room and dropping a brief curtsey.

Mr. Thoreau bowed. "I had assured Miss Lancaster that I would see her as soon as she arrived in Vienna. I left a letter for her here at the hotel." He looked over her shoulder toward the door as though in search of Lizzie. "I trust that she is in good health after such a difficult journey."

"She is indeed," Lady Thalia assured him, seating herself and inviting him with a wave of her hand to do the same. She noted with a touch of annoyance that he had not inquired after her own health, which he apparently felt appeared satisfactory. "She is exhausted by so many days on the road, however, and will doubtless sleep the clock around. She will be sorry to have missed you."

"I am glad to hear that she is resting," replied Mr. Thoreau, crossing his legs and leaning back easily in his chair. "She will need to recruit her strength if she is to dance at the ball tonight."

His hostess looked at him in a mixture of surprise at his mention of the ball and irritation at his habit of making himself at home wherever he was. "*You* will be attending the ball at the Redoutensaal, Mr. Thoreau?"

He nodded, amused at her irritation. "No doubt you are wondering how I managed an invitation, being a mere American awash in a sea of Continental peers."

She decided to dispense with politeness for the sake of information, and her reply was brisk. "As a matter of fact, sir, I *am* surprised. I understood, of course, the connection between the Marquis de La Fayette and America, but here things are quite a different matter. I admit that I *have* wondered just what has brought you to the Continent at such a time—and why you have chosen to mix with, as you put it, 'a sea of Continental peers.' It *does* seem curious to me."

"I am flattered that I have been so much in your thoughts, Lady Thalia. And you have put your finger very astutely upon one of the reasons for my travels," he replied.

When she looked at him blankly, he prompted her. "Curiosity, Lady Thalia. With Napoleon defeated, what better time to travel to the places that war has made difficult to visit? And why not come to Vienna for the most illustrious gathering in history?"

"And so you are merely an interested observer, Mr. Thoreau?"

"Like yourself, Lady Thalia—but without the title, of course."

"You said that curiosity is *one* of the reasons for your travels," she remarked when he did not continue. "May I ask the others?"

"I fear, ma'am, that you would not find them of great interest—nor are all of them mine to reveal."

"How very *mysterious* you make it all sound, Mr. Thoreau! I have heard that Vienna is *thick* with spies. Are you perhaps one of them?" Possibly, she hoped, making outrageous speculations might serve to draw him out.

He chuckled, the lines around his eyes deepening in amusement. "I'm afraid that I must disappoint you, Lady Thalia. As I said, you would not find them at all interesting."

"Then may I inquire, sir, what you do when you are at home in America? We have heard so little of your life there."

Frustrated by her failure to extract any useful information thus far, she was quite determined to wrest something from him, but thus far it had been rather like attempting to prise open a particularly stubborn oyster.

"And may I inquire, ma'am, just *why* you are inquiring?" he asked, his eyebrows high. "As I said, I am greatly flattered by your interest, but you must admit that you have shown very little concern for my background until now."

"And for that, Mr. Thoreau, I must admit culpability." She had decided that frankness was the only possible response. "While in Paris, I should *indeed* have made a very thorough inquiry into your background instead of accepting you as what you appear to be—a gentleman of means. I thought, you see, that ours would be a transitory relationship, over in a few days. However, my only *real* excuse must be that I am not accustomed to being responsible for anyone except myself."

Mr. Thoreau's brow cleared. "Ah, you refer to Miss Lancaster! Now I understand your sudden intense interest, Lady Thalia." He executed a brief bow from his chair. "I apologize for failing to understand the reason for your questions."

She nodded an acceptance of his apology and waited for him to continue.

"My family has an importing business in New York," he explained, "and for the past ten years I have been in the habit of looking after some of the company's business interests abroad."

"And so you have traveled widely?" she asked, prodding him to say more. That his family was in trade scarcely surprised her. He was, after all, an American.

"Quite extensively," he agreed, "to the Orient and the Mediterranean and South America—and I have hopes of soon re-establishing our business ties in England."

"You believe that the war between our countries will soon end?" she inquired, momentarily diverted by his comment. "I had not heard as much."

"I am quite certain that peace will come quickly, and I plan to remain on the Continent until such a time."

Suddenly realizing that she had been successfully sidetracked, Lady Thalia took up her quest again. She was determined to learn more. "And are you not needed by your family at home or by your business there? After all, you have already been gone for quite some time."

He smiled at her, and she noticed again what an open, pleasant manner he had—precisely what she had warned

Lizzie to be wary of, and yet here she was, in some danger of succumbing to it herself.

"It is kind of you to be concerned, but my family is accustomed to my absences and they manage very nicely without me. The day-to-day business of our firm is largely run by people who have been in our employment for years."

He studied her face for a moment, then added, "If you are inquiring as to whether or not there is a young lady waiting at home for me, the answer is no. I am without romantic attachments."

"And since I am responsible for Miss Lancaster, I must ask you, sir, just what your intentions toward her are."

Here, most unexpectedly, he gave a brief shout of laughter, as he had on the night in Paris when Lizzie had announced that she was going to purchase a fan. Lady Thalia, who had been expecting a serious reply to her very serious question, looked mildly shocked.

Recovering quickly enough from that, she was irritated with herself for being caught by surprise, and more irritated with him for managing to throw her off guard once more. She prided herself upon being in charge of most situations, and she had planned to conduct this interview in a brisk and businesslike manner, discovering what she wished to know while putting the gentleman firmly in his place.

"*In loco parentis,* Lady Thalia?" he asked, his expression and his tone merry. "Forgive me for laughing, but I had no notion that you took your responsibility as seriously as that. You looked as stern and grave as any head of the family possibly could. Next you will be asking me what my fortune is and how much I plan to allot for quarterly pin money."

"A young lady's future does not seem to *me* to be a joking matter, Mr. Thoreau," she replied with some asperity, wondering how she had allowed herself to get into such a predicament. She had no desire whatsoever to play the role of a parent, yet here she was, as proper and prim as any careful matron of the *ton*. Her intimate friends would never believe their ears if they could hear her now. She who was prone to laughter reduced to a humorless watchdog!

"Nor do *I* consider Miss Lancaster's future a joking matter, Lady Thalia," he assured her, his tone more serious now. "I think that she is a most charming and courageous young lady. She faces a difficult situation, and I look forward to being of what assistance I can be to her while I remain in Vienna."

"So she informs me," said Lady Thalia dryly, "but I did not realize that she had made such a confidant of you, sir, in the *exceedingly* short time that we have known you. You must understand that I need to be certain that you will not take advantage of a young girl's vulnerability."

"Miss Lancaster is quite safe with me, I assure you, Lady Thalia. I must tell you, however, having seen some of the gentlemen that she will be meeting in Vienna, that you will need to be watchful. She is a lovely young woman, and doubtless will be a target for many flirts."

"How *excessively* comforting it is to have you put me in mind of my responsibilities, Mr. Thoreau! Since I have been so remiss in guarding her interests thus far, I daresay that I would *never* have arrived at such a conclusion myself, so I must thank you for cautioning me!"

Enjoying the tartness of her tone, he added, "And I would suggest that *you* take care yourself, ma'am. You also could fall easy prey to some of the gentlemen that I have encountered here."

Mastering the desire to pick up a book from the table

beside her and fling it at his head, she managed to reply with commendable restraint. "I comfort myself with the knowledge that we do not travel in the same circles, Mr. Thoreau."

Before he could respond in kind, the door opened and Lizzie hurried in. "I thought it must be you, Mr. Thoreau, when I heard the laughter. How very good it is to see you again—and you were so kind to leave me a letter. I cannot tell you how it cheered me to know that you were thinking of me."

He rose and bowed to her. "I am delighted to see you looking so well after a difficult journey, Miss Lancaster."

And she did, Lady Thalia noted with some concern, appear to great advantage today. Last night she had looked quite hagridden, but now, upon seeing their guest, her eyes were bright and her color good. Clearly she was in spirits as well. Lady Thalia frowned to herself as she watched the two of them together. Say what he might, Mr. Thoreau obviously found Lizzie quite as appealing as she appeared to find him. She could gladly have rattled his teeth for creating such a problem. *In loco parentis,* indeed!

It appeared quite clear to her that she had traveled hundreds of miles to a scene of glittering gaiety where she had planned to enjoy herself excessively, only to discover that she was going to be obliged to play mother hen to a pretty young woman. Without a doubt, countless days and nights of worry and watching lay before her. She sighed. It was all more depressing than she could abide.

Deep in her own dark thoughts, she glanced up and caught Mr. Thoreau's eye, bright with amusement. She could have sworn that he was reading her thoughts, and finding them most diverting. She found herself purposefully fingering a small crystal vase, and had to fight the impulse to do him immediate bodily harm.

"Dare I hope, Lady Thalia, that you too will save a waltz for me tonight?"

It needed only that, she thought bitterly, immediately attempting to mask her thoughts with a bright smile. He had asked her to waltz—and she actually wished to accept.

"I shall look forward to it, Mr. Thoreau," she assured him with a small, dignified nod. Gently, she restored the crystal vase to its rightful place on the table beside her.

Perhaps she might find other means, less violent and infinitely more satisfying, to cause him to regret making light of her.

Ten

By the time they left for the ball that evening, Lizzie was so tense that she had to make a conscious effort to relax her jaw enough to smile. Now that the time had arrived when she would undoubtedly see Matthew, she could scarcely bring herself to face the ordeal.

Both Beavers and Lady Thalia, knowing how difficult the evening would be for her, had helped her dress for the event, and she realized as she looked into the glass that she looked very well indeed. The new gold gown was most flattering, Beavers had tucked the golden ostrich feathers into her carefully dressed hair, and Lady Thalia had insisted that she also wear a diamond necklet and earbobs that belonged to her.

"They are the *very* thing that is needed!" Lady Thalia had exclaimed, as she had fastened them in place. "They are dainty enough so that they don't overpower you, yet they add *just* the proper touch of glamour! They will catch the candlelight and frame your face beautifully!"

"You are too kind," murmured Lizzie, not able to do much more than allow herself to be dressed like a doll. She felt absolutely frozen with fear. Not even her new seal muff nor the cashmere shawl could keep her from shaking as they prepared to leave.

Lady Thalia, seeing her state, regretted thinking for a

moment that Lizzie might be falling in love with Mr. Thoreau. It was obvious that her feelings for Matthew Webster threatened to overwhelm her at any instant. Indeed, Lady Thalia found herself wondering if she should even allow Lizzie to attend the ball in such a state. If she were to break down in front of Matthew and a roomful of strangers, the effect upon the child could be devastating.

Nonetheless, when Henry announced that Mr. Thoreau had arrived to escort them, she turned to Lizzie with an attempt at briskness. "Well, we had best be on our way. We don't want to keep our guest waiting for us—particularly when our first Viennese ball awaits us. Do you have your fan, my dear?"

She had hoped that this final pleasantry would lighten the mood somewhat, but Lizzie merely nodded, her movements as stiff as those of a marionette. Seeing Lady Thalia watching her closely, she added, "Yes, I've brought the gauze one—although I shall never be able to use it with such fatal effect as Miss Blackwell."

As they joined Mr. Thoreau, Lady Thalia murmured to him, "Do what you can to help her. She is so distraught that she can scarcely move."

Their carriage drive was not a long one, for the Redoutensaal was in the Hofburg Palace.

"It will doubtless be a crush," said Mr. Thoreau. "Not so dreadful as some, I have been told, but crowded nevertheless."

"Good!" said Lizzie desperately. "Perhaps I will not see Matthew there after all. Perhaps we should stay only a few minutes and then come directly back to the hotel."

"Think of your dragons, Miss Lancaster," he responded encouragingly. "One down and one to go."

"What dragons?" demanded Lady Thalia. "What are you talking about?"

Mr. Thoreau, who had hoped for at least a mild expression of amusement at the reference to Miss Blackwell as a dragon, was disappointed. Lizzie did not respond at all—or rather she did, but not in the manner he had expected.

"How can I slay my dragons? I cannot possibly face him!" she exclaimed, tears suddenly streaming down her cheeks. "*She* was wearing *my* St. George medal—the one I gave to Matthew before he went to the Peninsula! It was to protect him, but he gave it away without a thought of me!"

All of the unhappiness that she had kept dammed inside her for the past fortnight suddenly burst forth, and she collapsed into a heap on the seat of the carriage, sobbing as though her heart would break.

"That *miserable* boy!" murmured Lady Thalia through gritted teeth. "I hope that *I* see him tonight! I shall certainly tell him what I think of his behavior!"

This served to rouse Lizzie, who shook her head violently. "No! No, please, Lady Thalia, you *must* not say anything to Matthew! *Promise* me that you will not!"

"But why ever should I *not*, Lizzie?" she demanded. "Just look at yourself! You would not be so distraught if *he* had not behaved so badly! Why should *his* feelings be spared when yours have been lacerated?"

Lizzie scrubbed her cheeks with her hands and sat up. Although she hated having lost her composure in front of others, even friends like the two who were with her now, she was surprised to discover that she felt better after the sudden outburst of pent-up emotion.

"Because your fussing at him for me would make me look like the pitiful little squab that he thinks I am. *I* will let him see that I can manage *wonderfully* well without him, and I shall make him regret the day that he wrote that letter to me!"

"Brava, Miss Lancaster!" applauded Mr. Thoreau, taking

out a large white handkerchief and handing it to her. "Repair the damage that you have done with your tears, and we will escort you into the ball to slay all the dragons present! You have no need of St. George to help you. You can do it very well on your own!"

Giving him a watery smile, she patted her cheeks dry and Lady Thalia helped her to smooth her hair and readjust the feathers, which had been knocked awry. "The air is cool, my dear. If we walk for just a minute or two before we go in, you will have a little color in your cheeks."

By the time they made their entrance, Lizzie was firmly in control of herself and no one seeing her would have suspected that just minutes ago she had been sobbing. She glanced coolly about the room, her hand resting securely on Mr. Thoreau's arm. Lord Danvers appeared to collect Lady Thalia for his dance, and Mr. Thoreau led Lizzie onto the floor.

"It is quite a striking scene, is it not, Miss Lancaster?" he inquired, glancing up at the orchestra playing in the gallery above them, where fashionable guests strolled or sat on small gilt chairs to watch the dancers below. A magnificent double staircase rose to the gallery, which was lined with tall Palladian windows. From the high ceilings hung huge crystal chandeliers, the candlelight gleaming on their lustrous pendants and reflected in the countless windowpanes. Around them whirled the other dancers, and Lizzie found that the best way to keep from growing too dizzy in the crush of colors and movement and sound was to focus firmly upon her partner's blue eyes.

"Should you wonder what I am doing, Mr. Thoreau, I shall tell you. I am not merely staring at you, mesmerized by your gaze. I am taking your advice."

"My advice?" he inquired lightly, pleased to see that

she had so completely regained her composure. "And what advice was that?"

"Why to focus on the scene before me, of course," she replied, surprised. "To focus outward. Do you not remember?"

"I do indeed, and I am delighted to see that the advice is having a beneficial effect, ma'am. I confess it is a little disconcerting to me to find myself the focus. I feel rather like a bug caught on the end of a pin for a naturalist to study."

Lizzie laughed. "I am sorry that I make you so uncomfortable. I promise that I shall look away now and then—as soon as I have found my balance in the midst of this sea of movement."

She was pleased to discover that she was feeling almost lighthearted, and she gave herself up to the enjoyment of the final measures of the dance. As the last notes faded and Mr. Thoreau led her toward the edge of the throng, she looked away from him at last, and the first person that she focused upon was Matthew.

"Lizzie!" he gasped, looking her up and down in disbelief. "It *is* you, Lizzie! I did not believe Mansfield when he told me that you were here. You had not written to tell me that you were coming."

"No, I had not." Lizzie smiled at him sweetly. "But Mr. Mansfield was quite correct, Matthew. I am most certainly here."

She turned toward Mr. Thoreau. "Mr. Thoreau, this is Matthew Webster. And, Matthew, I should like for you to meet Mr. Daniel Thoreau, a most particular friend of mine."

Matthew bowed briefly in Thoreau's direction, although he did not take his eyes from Lizzie. "Your servant, sir," he muttered.

Mr. Thoreau bowed in return and nodded to acknowledge the greeting. Then he offered his arm to Lizzie. "Miss Lancaster, would you care for some refreshment after our dance?"

She slipped her arm confidingly through his. "That would be delightful, Mr. Thoreau."

As they took a step to move away, she glanced up at Matthew and smiled. "It was good to see you, Matthew. Perhaps our paths will cross again before the end of the evening. If not, I am certain that we shall meet elsewhere. I shall be in Vienna for at least the next few weeks."

Matthew stared at her, astonished. "But, Lizzie, I wished to speak to you—It is very important and we've had no opportunity to talk to one another in so long!"

"I have discovered that balls are poor places to attempt a serious conversation, Mr. Webster," said Thoreau over his shoulder. Then he winked at Matthew. "But they are wonderful for flirtations."

As the pair strolled away together, Lizzie realized that her fingers were digging into the sleeve of her partner's jacket. "Forgive me, Mr. Thoreau," she apologized, releasing her grip, "but thank you, too. You were wonderful with Matthew!"

"I must confess that I thoroughly enjoyed myself. I was half afraid that he was going to run after us as we walked away."

"Yes," said Lizzie, satisfaction thick in her voice, like the purr of a cat that has just been into the cream pot. "I thought that myself. I daresay that we shall see him again very soon."

"I have no doubt of it," replied Mr. Thoreau. "And I see that Lord Danvers is coming over so that we can switch partners. I fear that we shall have to wait for refreshments—and Matthew will have to wait until after this dance before he can try his luck again."

After Lord Danvers had claimed Lizzie's hand and they had glided away to another lilting melody, Lady Thalia took Mr. Thoreau's arm and shook it lightly.

"Well?" she demanded. "Tell me what happened! I could see the three of you from across the floor, but I couldn't tell just what was taking place."

"It was brutal," he assured her, guiding her to a place among the other dancers. "Webster never knew what had hit him. He didn't know that she was not still in England until Mansfield told him this evening. And Miss Lancaster handled the situation masterfully—she was as cool as a cucumber, treating him as though he were a distant acquaintance. She dismissed him very casually, saying that they might cross paths again during the next few weeks. He wanted to speak with her at that very moment, and insisted that it was most important—but she strolled away without a backward glance."

"Good for her!" said Lady Thalia with satisfaction. "I hope that he is *completely* overset by this evening. It would please me *tremendously* to know that he is suffering."

"Oh, I think there can be no doubt of that. Only look." Here he nodded toward Matthew, who was standing where they had left him, quite frozen in place as he watched Lizzie whirl around the floor with Lord Danvers. "Miss Lancaster is getting a little of her own back again this evening."

"And this is only the beginning," responded his partner, smiling. "And it only just occurred to me that Matthew probably does not even know positively that Lizzie has received his letter. He must suspect it, of course, because she was so cool toward him, but since she has not mentioned it, he cannot be certain. *He* will be forced to speak of it himself!"

"If I were not personally involved, with my allegiance naturally given to Miss Lancaster, I would almost find it in my heart to feel sorry for Webster," said Mr. Thoreau, looking at Lady Thalia's expression. "He will be shown no quarter."

"Most certainly not!" she agreed. "It is quite time for *him* to discover just how it feels to suffer!"

"Miss Lancaster is a charming girl, Webster," said Mr. Mansfield, clapping his friend on the back as Matthew watched her dancing. "You must be delighted to see her again!"

"Oh yes, yes, of course I am," murmured Matthew.

"You should have seen your face when I told you! I'm delighted that I was the one who got to surprise you with the news of her arrival."

"Yes, I was most certainly surprised," Matthew agreed unhappily. "I believed that she was still at home in England."

"She was disappointed not to find you in Paris, of course, but it cheered her, I think, to be able to meet Miss Blackwell. I was pleased to be able to introduce them to one another."

"She met Teresa?" demanded Matthew in horror.

Mr. Mansfield looked at his companion with concern. "Are you feeling quite the thing, Webster? You are as pale as megrims."

"I am fine!" He glared at poor Mansfield with ferocious intensity. "Tell me about their meeting! What did they say to one another?"

Mansfield began glancing about him, hoping to see a

friendly face, for Webster was clearly feeling unwell. His tone was carefully conciliatory as he answered.

"Only what young ladies say to one another upon such an occasion. Miss Blackwell told Miss Lancaster that she was glad to meet a friend of yours from home, and Miss Lancaster wished Miss Blackwell very happy—then we all chatted."

Webster clutched his arm, and Mansfield watched him nervously. "Lizzie wished Teresa happy? Are you certain of that?"

"Yes, of course I am! What could be more natural than that?" demanded Mansfield, who was beginning to grow slightly indignant. "That is quite usual for one young lady to say to another who has become engaged."

"Yes—yes, of course," murmured Webster, his gaze fixed once more on Lizzie.

"As to what we talked about the next night, I'm not certain I can remember—"

This was an unfortunate observation on Mr. Mansfield's part, because he discovered that Matthew once more had him by the arm.

"The next night? They saw one another again?"

"Yes—naturally, that was to be expected since they attended the same *soirées*—and of course I had gotten to know Miss Lancaster and Lady Thalia so well on our journey to Paris."

Webster stared at him, trying to piece all of the information together. "Lizzie is traveling with Lady Thalia Stanhope?"

Mansfield nodded happily. "Yes, she is a lovely woman. I quite enjoyed our conversations in the carriage."

"You traveled in their carriage with them?" It seemed to Matthew that his world had suddenly been turned upside down.

Again Mansfield nodded. "And Mr. Thoreau was already in their company, of course."

"Thoreau also traveled with them?" Matthew's voice was growing somewhat hollow.

"Yes, it was one of the most enjoyable trips that I have made, despite the discomforts of the carriage and of all of us sleeping in the taproom of the inn. We—"

Here he suddenly snapped his fingers, his eyes aglow. "And I *do* remember what we talked of the second time Miss Blackwell and Miss Lancaster met! Miss Blackwell was wearing the gold medallion that you presented to her, and Miss Lancaster was admiring it!"

He looked brightly at Matthew, proud that he had managed to remember the conversation at last.

Matthew, however, looked even paler than before, and Mr. Mansfield steered him carefully to the nearest chair.

"It's doubtless the heat in here, old fellow!" he said reassuringly. "I shall just go and find you something cold to drink and that will set you to rights."

He hurried away and Matthew remained in his chair. In the distance he could see Lizzie, smiling in the arms of Lord Danvers as they waltzed. She no longer looked like his Lizzie, he reflected—but then, of course, she was not *his* Lizzie any longer at all. He was engaged to Teresa Blackwell now, and Lizzie had no part in his life any more. Still, he sat and watched her, hoping for an opportunity to speak with her. He needed very badly to talk with her, to tell her how sorry he was for the pain he had caused her.

Except that she did not appear to be in any noticeable pain.

Eleven

The next morning Lady Thalia was pleased to see that they had received flowers from Lord Danvers, Mr. Mansfield, Mr. Thoreau, and two other young men with whom Lizzie had danced at the ball. The drawing room had become a veritable bower of roses and lilies, and their fragrance and color filled the room. She was delighted to think that Lizzie would begin her day with these visible signs of her success. Despite its inauspicious beginning, the evening had, on the whole, been a very satisfying experience.

Her pleasure was considerably diminished when Henry announced that Matthew Webster had come to call. Although she had been very pleased with the way in which Lizzie had dealt with him last night, she could not forget nor forgive the pain he had caused the girl. She nodded to him very coolly when he walked into the room.

"Good day, Mr. Webster. I had not expected to see you here."

Matthew flushed at this somewhat daunting greeting, but he bowed and took the chair that she indicated with another brief nod. He decided that he must dispense with the civilities and be direct, even though he had always stood in considerable awe of the lady before him. He felt an overwhelming need to speak with Lizzie, and he was willing to brave Lady Thalia's wrath in order to do so.

"I am certain that you know why I am here, Lady Thalia," he said earnestly. "I had hoped to speak with Lizzie at the ball last night, but she gave me no opportunity."

"Nor can I think why she *should* have done so, sir," replied his hostess, her tone growing arctic. "Your behavior has scarcely been such that she should feel *any* obligation to speak with you."

He sat there rigidly, distressed by her words but recognizing that she spoke no more than the truth. Watching him, Lady Thalia thought regretfully that it was a pity that such a promising young man should have proven to be such a disappointment. He had been an engaging, handsome boy and, although she had not particularly wished for Lizzie to form a serious attachment at so young an age, at the time she had been forced to admit that she could see no harm in the boy. It had seemed to her then that, though Matthew was not as highly intelligent as she would have liked Lizzie's partner to be, he atoned for that lack with loyalty and a pleasant, easy manner. She had believed that he understood Lizzie's worth and could be trusted to be a faithful and loving companion. "Which is more than most marriages achieve," she had told Beavers one evening just before he had left for the Peninsula, "so we must be grateful for that, I suppose."

"No, she owes me nothing, Lady Thalia," Matthew answered quietly, his gaze steady. "I quite realize that—but I feel that I owe *her* an explanation of my behavior."

She could see that his pain was genuine—but then so was Lizzie's, she reminded herself, and he was the cause of it. She hardened her heart against the appeal in his anxious gray eyes and the nervous twisting of his hands.

"I believe that you have already explained your behavior in a letter to her, sir. As I recall, you told her that you have fallen in love with someone much more so-phisticated than she, someone better suited to the life you now lead. I am certain that you made the reasons for your rejection of her *perfectly* clear, and I cannot imagine what you would be able to add to what you have already told her, Mr. Webster."

Matthew looked at her miserably. "Your choice of words is harsh, Lady Thalia. I assure you that I didn't mean to re-ject Lizzie, for I shall always love her. I *do* sound like the most awful cad in your version of the matter."

Lady Thalia's eyebrows arched nearly to her hairline at this comment. "In *my* version of the matter? Are you suggesting that there is a second version and that I have in some way altered the facts of the situation, Mr. Web-ster? Did you *not* write to her that you had found another young lady—a Miss Blackwell, I believe—whom you wished to marry in preference to Lizzie? That *is* what is commonly termed a rejection of your fiancée."

"No, what you say is true," he admitted, "but you make it sound so very heartless when I did not mean for it to be so. That is why I *must* talk to her!"

"And just how do you think that you can make your behavior appear *less* heartless, Mr. Webster?"

"By telling her that I still *do* love her—just not as a husband should love his wife." Matthew was extremely pale now, rather than flushed, but she could see that he was in earnest.

"In fact, I suppose that you mean to say that you love me as you would a sister, Matthew." Lizzie spoke quietly, standing just inside the door that she had closed silently behind her.

Both Matthew and Lady Thalia rose and turned toward her, Matthew going eagerly to take her hand.

"Yes, yes, that is precisely what I mean, Lizzie! You *must* know that I will always love you—you are a part of my life."

Lizzie gently removed her hand from his. "Not any longer, Matthew. You have a new life. You told me so in your letter."

"Well, yes—naturally I have a new life, Lizzie," he answered, looking at her unhappily. "But I mean that you are a part of my *old* life, which I must always remember with fondness, and that I wish to remain your friend."

"I see." Lizzie sat down on the sofa, calmly folding her hands in her lap. Both of the others returned uncomfortably to their chairs and watched her uneasily, Lady Thalia worried that Lizzie might give way to tears once more, Matthew hoping that she would smile at him and forgive him, making him feel easy once more. He had discovered that he did not like living with guilt, and here sat the one person who could assuage it.

"And just what would you have me say, Matthew?" she inquired, after the silence had continued for a painful minute or two. "That I shall dance at your wedding?"

Matthew, seeing no irony at all in her question, nodded eagerly. "Yes indeed, Lizzie! I should like it above all things to have you there—and to hear you say that you wish me happy."

"But of course I wish you happy, Matthew," she answered mildly, her tone and expression that of someone ordering a cup of tea instead of speaking of an event that had shaken her whole life. "How could I not when I have always cared for you? And naturally I plan to attend your wedding."

Lady Thalia stared at her as though she had taken leave of her senses, but Matthew leaped from his chair and hurried over to take her hand once more.

"Thank you, dearest girl!" He leaned over and kissed

her forehead. "How good you are to forgive me and make things comfortable between us once more!"

He took her hands and pulled her to her feet, enveloping her in a hug that she did not return. "I cannot tell you, Lizzie, what a weight you have lifted from my heart! I have wished to talk with you for the longest time! Do say that you will come out with me today so that I may show you Vienna!"

"Not today, I fear," she replied, slipping smoothly from his embrace. "Mr. Thoreau has already engaged me for an excursion and he will be calling for me at any moment."

"Thoreau? The fellow whom I met last night?" His voice was sharp.

She nodded, and he frowned at her. "Are you not spending too much time with him, Lizzie? How long have you known him, after all?"

Lady Thalia responded quickly so that Lizzie would not have to do so. "You must remember, Matthew, that Lizzie is traveling with *me*, and that *I* have given my approval to her outing with Mr. Thoreau."

"Will you be there to chaperone her?" he asked, his concern for Lizzie overriding his reticence with Lady Thalia.

Lady Thalia bristled visibly at his abrupt question. She had been planning to send Henry with them once again, as she had in Paris, but she greatly disliked being dictated to by anyone—particularly someone she considered little more than a beardless youth and someone who had jilted Lizzie to boot. Her rejoinder was quick.

"There is no need for me to do so. I have *absolute* confidence in Mr. Thoreau. You must remember, Mr. Webster, that you no longer have *any* claim on Lizzie other than friendship."

"Yes, but as a friend, I must—"

"As my friend, you wish what is best for me," inserted Lizzie smoothly. She was well pleased to hear that she was to have no chaperone. She disliked the awkwardness of worrying about Henry, who was forced to tag along behind them. "I quite understand, Matthew. And perhaps you can show me Vienna another time."

"Of course I will," he replied, happily reminded that they were friends once more and that he no longer had to carry his heavy load of guilt. As she turned toward the door, he remembered her engagement and took the hint, bowing to both ladies and taking his leave cheerfully.

"It is so *very* good to feel comfortable with you once more, Lizzie," he said before closing the door behind him.

Lizzie looked at Lady Thalia for a moment, then smiled. "Do not worry about me, Lady Thalia. I am perfectly well. I have not, as your expression indicates, lost my senses. I *do* plan to dance at Matthew's wedding, as I promised. Only I plan to be dancing with him as his bride."

Lady Thalia was watching her with concern, and it did not comfort her when Lizzie added, "But between that time and this, I plan to make Matthew Webster the most *un*comfortable young man in Christendom."

And then she smiled—but it was a smile of grim determination, and the expression in her eyes was one that Lady Thalia had not seen before.

By the time Mr. Thoreau arrived, Lady Thalia was deeply grateful to see him. Although she would not have thought it yesterday, she was delighted that he would be spending time with Lizzie, hopefully diverting her thoughts from taking vengeance upon Matthew Webster. She would not even mind now if there were a mild flirtation with Mr. Thoreau. Lizzie's statement about making Matthew the most uncomfortable young man in Christendom—and her expression as she said it—had made her profoundly uneasy.

"The flowers that you sent are lovely, Mr. Thoreau," remarked Lizzie as they walked downstairs to the waiting chaise. "But I thought that you told me that you never sent nosegays."

"That, Miss Lancaster, was before I met you," he answered cheerfully. "And it seemed to me that you deserved some sort of accolade after your performance yesterday evening. You were remarkable."

She dropped him a curtsey, smiling. "Matthew has already come to call this morning," she informed him, offering a brief account of what had happened. She did, however, omit her final comment, feeling that Mr. Thoreau might inquire into it more closely than she wished.

He offered no comment about Matthew's revelation that he wished to be friends again, but he gave her a comforting pat on the arm and turned the subject to happier topics.

"I am glad to see that you and Lady Thalia have such delightful accommodations, Miss Lancaster. You appear to have all the comforts of home."

"Yes, we were most fortunate that Lord Danvers had room to spare. I suppose not everyone has been so fortunate."

"That is undeniably true," he agreed. "I have discovered that there are far more visitors than there are beds in Vienna. Too many people have tried to crowd into the city for the Congress."

"Do you think most of them are attending the Congress?" she asked curiously. "Or are many of them like us—just come to see it all?"

"A great number have come chiefly to enjoy themselves,

Miss Lancaster—which means, of course, that you shall have a very fine time because there will be countless dances and entertainments of all sorts."

"Yes, Lady Thalia had promised that we shall have quite a wonderful time here." She glanced at him curiously. "What about *your* rooms, Mr. Thoreau? Where are you staying?"

He grinned at her. "It would be more accurate to speak of my *room*, Miss Lancaster—or rather, my *portion* of a room."

"Do you mean that you have to share a room with someone?" she demanded.

"Indeed I do. Fortunately, he is a very pleasant-tempered Greek and we get along well. He also wished to be present as the future of the Continent is decided—the Greeks, after all, have a vital interest in all of these proceedings."

"I'm glad that you like him, but I'm certain that it must be very uncomfortable for the two of you to live in one room."

"George and I get on very well together," he assured her. "We have many interests in common."

"That is his name? George?" she asked. "How very disappointing! That doesn't sound in the least Greek."

"George Andronikos," he amended.

"Ah, much better," she said. "Now he definitely sounds Greek. Andronikos gives him an air of romance that plain George simply doesn't provide."

"He will be glad to hear that you approve," answered Thoreau. "I will be able to tell him so this afternoon when we meet him at the Prater."

"I am going to meet Mr. Andronikos?" she responded, pleased. "I shall enjoy meeting someone from Greece. And what is the Prater? A café?"

He laughed. "Not exactly. But I promise that you will like it even better than the Palais-Royal."

As they rode through The Inner City, she could see that the dwellings of the rich and poor were all jumbled together, palaces standing cheek by jowl with crowded apartment buildings, many of the dwellings as tall as five or six stories, all elaborately ornamented. It seemed to Lizzie that there were statues everywhere, and on the streets wandered singers and barrel-organ players and magicians, all stopping to perform at a moment's notice and taking full advantage of the golden autumn day.

The Prater, she found, was a world apart from the rest of Vienna, and Mr. Thoreau proved to be correct—she did indeed prefer it to the Palais-Royal. Not only was it far larger, but it also seemed to her a far friendlier, far more inviting place. Innocent though she was, she had been uneasily aware of the dark worlds that existed on the floors above the cafés and shops of the Palais-Royal. Although she had been fascinated by it all, she had also been a little afraid. Here everything was more open—there were meadows and gardens and woods—and scattered everywhere were cafés and taverns and entertainment of all sorts. The Prater was also decidedly rural in character—there were even beehives and, at the entrance, a dairy bar that served milk to passers-by.

They stopped at Herr de Bach's "gymnastics circus," where Lizzie was enthralled by the ease of movement of the young performers. She was amazed by it all, having never seen such a thing before, but Mr. Thoreau informed her that gymnastics was growing popular in Prussia and Switzerland as well.

"You are very fortunate," the Englishman seated next to Mr. Thoreau told them. "This has been closed for several weeks so that they could rehearse a new show that would be worthy of performing for the visiting dignitaries."

"Do they come to the Prater?" Lizzie asked. "I thought perhaps they would spend all of their time meeting together."

"Scarcely that, I should imagine, ma'am," he replied, laughing. "In Vienna, everyone enjoys life—and *everyone* comes to the Prater. You will find countesses and coachmen, duchesses and duelists—even royalty mixes with the rest of us."

It was with some difficulty that Mr. Thoreau coaxed Lizzie away from the gymnastics performance, for she would gladly have sat through everything twice. Finally, only a reminder that they would keep George waiting caused her to leave.

"That is very true. I should not wish Mr. Andronikos to think me rag-mannered," she agreed, and at last they walked briskly to a nearby coffeehouse. The gentleman they were to meet was already seated and drinking a cup of coffee, but he rose as soon as they appeared, making a deep bow to Lizzie.

"Good afternoon, Miss Lancaster. I am delighted to meet you, for I have heard so very much about you."

His bright, dark eyes were fixed upon her and his smile was, Lizzie thought in admiration, simply dazzling. Everything about him seemed intense and very much alive. She dropped a brief curtsey, then held out a small hand to him and he clasped it eagerly.

"You are as lovely as I expected, Miss Lancaster—so I must believe that you also possess the other qualities I have heard attributed to you—charm and intelligence and courage."

He pressed her hand for a moment before she could reclaim it, but she glanced quickly at Mr. Thoreau, surprised by his companion's words. It was a gratifying description, she thought, and it could only have come from Mr. Thoreau.

Thoreau merely raised his eyebrows and smiled at her in response. Then he pulled out a chair for her, and Mr. Andronikos called a waiter over to take their order.

When they were settled, the young Greek turned to her once more. "Miss Lancaster, I am most eager to hear what you think of Vienna. I understand that you are visiting here for the first time."

"It seems a lovely place," she said, "but of course I have only just arrived. I have seen only a very little of it."

"Daniel and I shall remedy that very quickly!" he assured her. He turned to Thoreau and clapped his hand on his shoulder. "It is good that this is such a warm autumn, my friend. We can take Miss Lancaster to the *Heuriger* tomorrow! I shall engage to bring the sausages and bread!"

"What is the *Heuriger?*" she asked, eager for another adventure.

"It is the name the Viennese have given to small vineyards where this year's wine is drunk," replied Mr. Thoreau. "There are many such places close by, and they are open in the spring and summer, serving only their own new wine. Even this late in the year, I believe there are a few with wine still left. We shall check the list that is published each day in the newspaper—and then we shall go!"

"Most definitely we shall! Tomorrow! And we shall have our supper there!" agreed Mr. Andronikos with great enthusiasm.

"Perhaps we should invite Lady Thalia to accompany us," said Mr. Thoreau. "Like you, Miss Lancaster, she has never visited Vienna before, and she might enjoy seeing something that is off the beaten track."

"That will be delightful! We shall most certainly invite Lady Thalia!" agreed Mr. Andronikos, who clearly had only the vaguest notion of her identity.

"Do you think she will come?" Mr. Thoreau asked Lizzie.

She looked at him doubtfully, a little surprised by his suggestion. "I don't know what she might say. However, I suspect that she might feel that I need a chaperone other than Henry for such an adventure."

"Well, we shall make it our business to find out what she will say," replied Mr. Thoreau, smiling.

Mr. Andronikos, seeing a friend passing by the coffeehouse, excused himself for a moment and hurried over to talk with him. Once he was gone, she could not restrain her curiosity. "You seem on very good terms with Mr. Andronikos. Did you know him before you came to Vienna?"

"Yes indeed. I have known him for a very long time, Miss Lancaster. My family owns an importing firm, and they have done business with the Andronikos family for decades. I met him first when we were just boys, and I was on a trip to Greece with my father. George and I are about the same age, and his father decided to send him to school in America for a few years."

"His father sent him to school in *America?*" demanded Lizzie, clearly astonished. "Why would he do such a thing?"

He looked at her with amusement. "Try not to make America sound like the back of beyond even though you believe it is, Miss Lancaster. We do have schools and people *do* receive educations there."

She colored. "Well, yes, I know that, of course," she replied hurriedly. "I mean, you yourself are clearly an educated man. It is just that I would not have thought of anyone in Greece sending his son specifically to America for an education."

"Yes, I can see that. However, times in Greece were very unsettled, and George's father wished for him to have a more stable situation. He also had a great admiration for our revolution and the government we have established in America. He thought that George could learn about those, as well as learning a little more about our business since he would one day be taking his father's place."

Lizzie nodded. "So that is why he speaks English with such ease. I had wondered about that."

"He had no difficulty in making the change because he found many connections between our countries. George was delighted to learn that the ancient Greeks had greatly influenced many of the men who framed our Constitution. It made him feel much more at home among us."

They sat in silence for a few minutes longer as she considered what she had just learned. "And so our Mr. Andronikos—George—is he like his father? Also very interested in establishing a democracy in Greece?" she asked.

Mr. Thoreau hesitated for a moment, then nodded. "Yes—he is, Miss Lancaster."

Lizzie thought that over for a moment. "But the Turks still rule all of that part of that world," she remarked, "so naturally they would never agree to such a thing. Creating a democracy would more than likely require a revolution like yours—or like that of the French, would it not?"

Again he nodded slowly. "It is possible. We must hope that it would be more like our own and less like that of the French."

She sat and studied him for a few minutes. "It appears to me, Mr. Thoreau, that you are much more actively involved in politics than I had realized. I had thought that you contented yourself with reading about such matters in the newspaper. You are not really in Vienna just to observe, are you?"

He smiled at her. "I am like the majority of people who have come to Vienna, Miss Lancaster—eager to see and hear firsthand what is taking place at the Ballhausplatz, and equally eager to enjoy myself."

"You sidestepped my question very neatly, sir," she observed approvingly. "Very nicely done."

"I am happy that you are pleased, ma'am," he returned, inclining his head in a brief bow.

"So I do not really know more than the fact that you are interested in politics, Mr. Thoreau," she said, "and, as you say, most certainly Vienna is filled with people who share your interest. I will be careful, however, not to mention to anyone that Mr. Andronikos wishes for a democracy."

"I only wish that Mr. Andronikos would be as discreet," responded Thoreau dryly. "That is why I felt that I could tell you about his beliefs—because he will undoubtedly tell you himself very soon. He is not as careful as he should be."

"But is it really so dangerous for him to speak his mind?" she asked. "After all, he is in Vienna, not within the Ottoman Empire."

"Metternich and the others are here to decide how they can establish a balance of power so that they can look forward to a long period of peace. They do not want to hear ideas that might bring about revolutions. That could upset everything that they are trying to achieve."

She found herself mulling over that conversation as she prepared for sleep that night. How exciting it was to be in Vienna at a time such as this, when powerful people were making decisions—many of them, she was

We'd Like to Invite You to Subscribe to Zebra's Regency Romance Book Club and Give You a Gift of 4 Free Books as Your Introduction! (Worth $19.96!)

If you're a Regency lover, imagine the joy of getting **4 FREE Zebra Regency Romances** and then the chance to have these lovely stories delivered to your home each month at the lowest price available! Well, that's our offer to you and here's how you benefit by becoming a Regency Romance subscriber:

- **4 FREE Introductory Regency Romances are delivered to your doorstep (you only pay for shipping and handling)**

- **4 BRAND NEW Regencies are then delivered each month (usually before they're available in bookstores)**

- **Subscribers save almost $4.00 every month**

- **You also receive a FREE monthly newsletter, which features author profiles, discounts, subscriber benefits, book previews and more**

- **No risks or obligations...in other words, you can cancel whenever you wish with no questions asked**

Join the thousands of readers who enjoy the savings and convenience offered to Regency Romance subscribers. After your initial introductory shipment, you receive 4 brand-new Zebra Regency Romances each month to examine for 10 days. Then, if you decide to keep the books, you'll pay the preferred subscriber's price, plus shipping and handling.

It's a no-lose proposition, so return the FREE BOOK CERTIFICATE today!

Say Yes to 4 Free Books!
Complete and return the order card to receive this
$19.96 value, ABSOLUTELY FREE!

If the certificate is missing below, write to:
Regency Romance Book Club
P.O. Box 5214, Clifton, New Jersey 07015-5214
or call TOLL-FREE 1-800-770-1963
Visit our website at www.kensingtonbooks.com.

FREE BOOK CERTIFICATE

YES! Please rush me 4 Zebra Regency Romances (I only pay for shipping and handling). I understand that each month thereafter I will be able to preview 4 brand-new Regency Romances FREE for 10 days. Then, if I should decide to keep them, I will pay the money-saving preferred subscriber's price for all 4...that's a savings of 20% off the publisher's price. I may return any shipment within 10 days and owe nothing, and I may cancel this subscription at any time. My 4 FREE books will be mine to keep in any case.

Name _____

Address _____ Apt. _____

City _____ State _____ Zip _____

Telephone ( ) _____

Signature _____
(If under 18, parent or guardian must sign.)

RN122A

Terms and prices subject to change. Orders subject to acceptance by Regency Romance Book Club.
Offer valid in U.S. only.

Treat yourself to 4 FREE Regency Romances!

A $19.96 VALUE... FREE!

No obligation to buy anything, ever!

llı..ı.ı..ıllı.ı.ıl.ıl.ıl.ı.ı.ıl.ıll.ı.ıl.ıll...ıl

REGENCY ROMANCE BOOK CLUB
Zebra Home Subscription Service, Inc.
P.O. Box 5214
Clifton NJ 07015-5214

certain, in secret—that would determine the shape and the future of the Continent. Just how an American and a Greek fit into the picture, she was less certain—but it was all very exciting, nonetheless.

Thinking about such matters with great concentration helped her to keep at bay unhappy thoughts of Matthew, who now wished to be her friend. As she drifted off to sleep, she thought with pleasure of his irritation when he discovered that she was going out with Mr. Thoreau. She had thought that perhaps she had caught a glimpse of him at the Prater, and it had crossed her mind that he might have followed them.

The thought pleased her. She would deal with Matthew in her own good time but in the meantime, as she had told Lady Thalia, she was going to make him exceedingly uncomfortable.

Twelve

Lady Thalia, overwhelmed by the passionate entreaties of Mr. Andronikos, who had returned with his companions from the Prater to beg her company on a visit to the *Heuriger*, had reluctantly agreed to become a member of the party. He had pleaded for the pleasure of sharing a charming aspect of Vienna with a charming lady, assuring her that it was a beloved institution of the Viennese people.

"It is *of* the people, dear lady!" he told her, taking her hand and fixing her with his glittering black eyes. "To see the *Heuriger* is to see the soul of the common people! You must see it now, Lady Thalia, for soon the winter winds will blow, and your golden opportunity will be swept away with the autumn leaves! I could not bear to see that happen!"

Seeing that she had no way of regaining her hand nor of ushering this vibrant but most insistent young man from her drawing room until she agreed that she and Lizzie would accompany them the next day, she gave way. She watched uneasily as they made their farewells and turned to go, fearful that Mr. Andronikos would descend upon her once more.

"But after *this*," she told Lizzie firmly when the door had closed safely behind Mr. Thoreau and Mr. Andronikos,

and she was feeling somewhat stronger, "you must *not* be
so involved with just *one* gentleman. Mr. Thoreau's attentions to you have been *very* particular and we would not
wish to give the wrong impression. Besides," she added
happily, gesturing to a tray upon which rested a gratifying
heap of cards, "we have already been invited to so many
soirées that after tomorrow you will have no time for jun-
keting about with Mr. Thoreau and Mr.—with his Greek
friend."

Wisely, Lizzie did not object, knowing full well that Mr.
Thoreau would manage to see her whenever she asked
him to do so—or whenever he wished to see her himself.
Instead, she cheerfully joined Lady Thalia in going
through the invitations and filling out their engagement
calendar. Heartened by this demonstration of interest,
Lady Thalia was confident that she had made her point.

"We *must* go shopping once again," she said, deeply
satisfied by the promised whirl of activity and the interesting individuals she expected to meet. "Just look at the
balls and breakfasts and theater parties we shall be attending! You most certainly will need additional outfits,
Lizzie, and I am going to have to add to my wardrobe as
well or I will be forced to appear in the same gowns so
often that they will soon be in rags. I have made inquiries
about a reputable dressmaker and we are going to see
her tomorrow."

True to her promise, the ladies enjoyed a very satisfying
shopping expedition the next day, and Lady Thalia was
well pleased with the dressmaker she had selected. "Her
work is absolutely exquisite!" she remarked to Lizzie afterward. "I have *never* seen ball gowns so delightful, even
in Paris! And it is so *very* gratifying to know that when we
attend Dorothée de Périgord's breakfast next week, we
shall be impeccably gowned. Not having to think about

what I am wearing because I am certain that all is as it should be is such a *great* comfort to me. A lady's attention should *never* be concentrated on her apparel. Now I shall be free to enjoy all that is going on about me."

Lizzie could not disagree with her. She too was learning to enjoy everything that was happening around her in this new place—and, like Lady Thalia, she had been impressed by this particular invitation. Dorothée de Périgord was the daughter of the Duchesse de Courlande and her husband was the nephew of Talleyrand himself. Separated from her husband now, she had come to Vienna with Talleyrand to act as his hostess. Lady Thalia was eager to inspect the lady in question, about whom she had heard much.

"She is said to be a *wit* as well as a beauty," she told Lizzie. "It is Danvers, of course, who has managed the invitation for us. It should be *most* amusing to see some of the notables that we have only heard about thus far."

Lizzie encouraged Lady Thalia to talk more about the coming breakfast, for doing so would keep her from fretting over their engagement with Mr. Thoreau and Mr. Andronikos. She did not wish for Lady Thalia to become distressed enough to cancel it.

"I *can* not imagine how I came to allow myself to agree not only to allow *you* to go with them but also to attend myself!" she had told Lizzie earlier that morning. "The two of us going out to some rustic café with two gentlemen we scarcely know does not seem at *all* proper."

"But we do know Mr. Thoreau," she had reminded Lady Thalia. "And you have often told me that you don't particularly care what others think of you or of what you do."

"And I don't—but I *do* care what *I* think—and that is my problem," Lady Thalia replied crisply. "While I am certain that our evening will be amusing, I am *far* less certain that it is suitable for us to be going. And what I might accept as appropriate for *myself* is not necessarily appropriate behavior for you as a very young lady, my dear."

"Pray don't fret over it, Lady Thalia," Lizzie had begged her. "You know that Mr. Thoreau would not do anything that would expose us to embarrassment—although I daresay that Matthew would disagree with that."

As she had intended, bringing up Matthew put Lady Thalia immediately in mind of his unfortunate attempt to interfere in that lady's affairs.

"Well, I suppose that *one* evening cannot do any lasting harm," she conceded after a brief pause, and Lizzie turned toward the window so that Lady Thalia could not see her smile. Matthew had unintentionally done her a kindness, and it pleased her to think how distressed he would be to know that she was making use of his error.

And so it was that the four of them set forth in the late afternoon, three of them in high spirits.

"Ah, Lady Thalia, you will love the *Heuriger*!" Mr. Andronikos assured her, blithely ignoring the fact that her expression indicated that she felt such a possibility was extremely unlikely. "And, just in case ours does not serve its own food, I have provided all the necessities for dining *al fresco*." Here he happily indicated a wicker basket, neatly covered with a checkered cloth.

"How do we know which vineyard we will go to?" inquired Lizzie. "Did you consult the newspaper, Mr. Thoreau?"

"Can you doubt it?" demanded Mr. Andronikos before he could reply. "Daniel lives with the newspaper in his hand!"

"Yes, I have noticed that he does," said Lizzie, amused.

"In other words, Miss Lancaster," said Mr. Thoreau, unruffled by his friend's remark, "I did indeed consult the newspaper, which listed several *Heuriger* as currently open. We will merely have to choose the one we prefer. As we drive by them, we will be able to tell at a glance which ones are open because a fir branch or a circle of straw will be placed above the entrance to the house. The owner takes it down once all his wine is gone."

"That seems a very curious practice," observed Lady Thalia without enthusiasm. "Has it always been done in such a manner?"

Encouraged by even this mild display of interest, Mr. Thoreau nodded. "The Viennese vine-dressers have done so for many years. However, Emperor Joseph II gave them the legal right to sell the wine that they had pressed, along with any provisions prepared on the same property."

His friend's expression darkened for a moment. "What a great kindness of the emperor," Mr. Andronikos noted bitterly, "to give them the right to sell what they themselves have made! Someday things will be different for the people."

Lady Thalia looked at him in surprise, and Lizzie glanced nervously at Mr. Thoreau, who changed the direction of the conversation immediately.

"It is unfortunate, Lady Thalia, that we are here so late in the season. During the spring and summer, people flock to the *Heuriger*, and you can see the trees in blossom and smell the perfume of the flowers as you sip your wine."

"Visiting the *Heuriger* is a favorite Viennese pastime," Mr. Andronikos assured her, managing to put aside his grievances for the moment. "Soon you will see why it is so, even though it is now autumn."

The vineyard where they finally stopped was a small one, no more than a few acres in size, and they were soon seated at a rough wooden table in a diminutive garden, shaded by a linden tree glowing in the late afternoon sun. The light that filtered through its bright leaves washed the scene in gold, and Lizzie, noting this, thought that until this trip she had never paid the least attention to the powerful effects of light on a scene. She glanced at Mr. Thoreau gratefully, for without him, she might never have begun to appreciate such things.

Lady Thalia saw Lizzie's quick glance and, misinterpreting it, frowned. She looked around her in irritable dissatisfaction. "Is this all that there is to it?" she asked crossly. "It seems like a great deal of fuss about very little."

Embarrassed by her rudeness, Lizzie said hurriedly, "It seems quite charming to me. Will you show us now what you have brought in the basket, Mr. Andronikos?"

That gentleman stood and whipped off the checkered cloth cover in a most theatrical manner, smoothing it over a portion of the wooden table as a cloth, and then he took out a small wooden cutting board.

"Behold! Here we have cheese!" And, with a flourish, he lifted out two blocks of cheese, one pale and one golden, and arranged them on the board. "And we have sausage!" A long brown sausage, redolent of spices, joined the cheeses. "And we must, of course, have olives! These, dear ladies, are from my own trees and are like no other olives that you will ever taste!" And he placed a brown crock of brine-soaked dark olives on the cloth beside the board.

Nor was he finished. A crusty loaf of dark bread and a crock of fresh butter joined the rest and then he paused dramatically until he had their attention once more. "And now I present the *pièce de résistance—an apfelstrudel!*" And he placed the golden pastry, lying on its own lace doily, on the cloth.

"*How* delicious it looks!" exclaimed Lady Thalia involuntarily. She had not meant to express any pleasure in the meal or the wine or the trip so that she would discourage any further invitations, but her newly acquired fondness for *strudel* proved to be her downfall.

"I am so glad that you approve," replied Mr. Andronikos, bowing. "It was my desire to please."

"And indeed you have done so," Lizzie assured him. "It all looks delicious, and we shall probably have to leave the *apfelstrudel* entirely for Lady Thalia."

"Not *all*," Lady Thalia assured them, "but very possibly half." She decided that, having already spoiled the arctic manner with which she had intended to freeze the evening, she might as well enjoy herself. She was, at any rate, tired of playing the virtuous chaperone. For just this one evening, she would forget her responsibilities, allow herself a holiday from worrying about Lizzie, and be herself.

"Should you wish more, dear Lady Thalia, I shall leap upon my horse and ride back to Vienna to fetch it for you," said Mr. Andronikos gallantly.

"Very pretty, George, but you have no horse," Mr. Thoreau pointed out practically. "We came in a chaise."

His friend was not fazed. "I shall take one of those horses should it prove necessary," he assured Lady Thalia. "Or, if that fails, I shall take one from a passer-by."

"And then we shall all attend your trial and subsequent hanging," said Mr. Thoreau, slicing the pale cheese carefully and offering slices to the ladies. "Even the easygoing Viennese frown upon horse thieves."

Mr. Andronikos shook his head sadly. "Ah, my poor Daniel, you have no romance. You have no *soul!*"

He turned to the ladies. "That has always saddened me," he confided to them, ignoring Mr. Thoreau. "I must apologize for my friend, but it is true that I have found that many Americans seem to lack that sensitivity to romance that we Greeks possess. It is, perhaps, because their country is so new, and they have not had the opportunity to cultivate some of the more delicate feelings."

Unperturbed by his criticism, Thoreau responded cheerfully. "If I were to give my life, George, it would be for something I believe in—not for an *apfelstrudel,* no matter how delicious."

Mr. Andronikos continued to shake his head dolefully, as though all of his worst suspicions had been confirmed. "It would not be for the *apfelstrudel,* Daniel—that is not the point," he said patiently. "The point is that you are doing something gallant to serve a fair lady." And here he bowed to Lady Thalia, who acknowledged this pretty byplay with a smile and a nod.

Mr. Thoreau grinned at them. "An American would not be foolish enough to steal a horse in order to fetch a pastry for a lady—no matter how fair she might be. He is far too sensible for that. Now, he *might* be moved to appropriate a horse for a *truly* important cause—like warning other Americans that the redcoats are coming."

Mr. Andronikos put his head into his hands and groaned. Then, looking up at the ladies, he shook his head once more. "I must apologize for his appalling lack of gallantry, dear ladies."

"There is no need to do so, Mr. Andronikos," said Lady Thalia. "One cannot expect it of Americans. And I am pleased that Mr. Thoreau realizes that Americans *should* be worried if our soldiers are coming."

Mr. Andronikos threw up his hands in a gesture of despair, but before he could continue, they all looked up at the sound of new guests arriving. There were four other tables in the tiny courtyard, and only theirs was oc-

cupied. Two men entered, both of them obviously gentlemen, and Thoreau glanced sharply at his friend. Mr.
Andronikos did not, Lizzie noticed, meet Mr. Thoreau's
eyes. Instead, he bowed to her and to Lady Thalia, and
murmured his profuse apologies.

"I must, you see, have a word with these gentlemen on
a matter of business. It will take only a moment, and I
will return to you immediately."

He joined the two men at their table, and they began
to talk earnestly, their voices low.

"Well, so much for Greek gallantry," observed Thoreau
lightly, but his eyes remained for a moment upon his
friend. "I believe, ladies, that we should give our attention
to our meal, and make George regret that he was gone
from us for even a moment."

"Your friend seems to be very sociable," said Lady
Thalia, watching Mr. Andronikos. "How unusual it is for
him to stumble upon friends in such an out-of-the-way
place."

"George knows many people in Vienna," returned Mr.
Thoreau. "There has been a large Greek community
here for years."

"Yes, but I don't believe those gentlemen are Greek,"
she said. "I am quite certain that they are speaking Russian. Princess Lieven acquainted me with some of the
phrases from her language, so I do recognize the sound
of it."

"Princess Lieven!" said Mr. Thoreau appreciatively.
"You do move in rarefied circles, Lady Thalia—or at least
the Princess would think so."

Lady Thalia smiled a little at his reference to Princess
Lieven's pride. "I did not say that we are good friends,
sir," she pointed out. "Merely that she taught me a few
phrases of Russian. During a particularly boring house

party, we both sought sanctuary in the library one afternoon, and she entertained me with tales of Russia and a brief language lesson."

"I am only surprised that she was satisfied with an audience of one," he observed. "From what I have heard, she prefers to hold center stage with an audience of hundreds."

"I did not say the lady was modest and self-effacing," Lady Thalia reminded him. She glanced again at the gentlemen talking with Mr. Andronikos and back to Lizzie and Mr. Thoreau. "It does seem to me that I have seen one of them before."

"Very possibly at the ball last night," suggested Mr. Thoreau.

She shook her head thoughtfully. "Not there. In London, I believe. Perhaps he was there for the celebration of Napoleon's defeat. There was quite a large Russian contingent present."

"Very naturally, I believe," he replied. "Drawn there, no doubt, by the charm of your Princess Lieven."

Lady Thalia laughed. "Or perhaps by that of the Grand Duchess Catherine—even Princess Lieven would have to give way to her."

Catherine was the younger sister of Tsar Alexander, and both she and her sister Elisabeth had accompanied him to Vienna. Each of them had private apartments in the palace of the Austrian emperor, while the Russian delegation had taken up residence at the Paar Palace. Catherine was much accustomed to admiration and considered it her due, just as Princess Lieven did.

"Very reluctantly, though, I should imagine," observed Mr. Thoreau. "I saw her in Paris, and she behaved very much as you have described. The lady is also very clever. She was, I believe, born for intrigue."

"Is she a schemer, then?" inquired Lizzie with interest.

Just then, a rustle of movement drew their attention back to the table they had been observing. The three men had risen and appeared to be saying their farewells. Lizzie and Lady Thalia were watching so intently that they did not realize that anyone else had entered the courtyard. Therefore, it came as a shock to Lizzie to realize that someone stood at the corner of their table, just between her and Lady Thalia.

It was Matthew, and he was gazing at her reproachfully. "I told you, Lizzie, that you must be more careful—yet here you are."

"How did you find me?" she asked blankly.

Matthew shook his head. "I had not expected to. I simply happened to come along at the right time."

It was Lady Thalia's turn to shake her head. "There is not the least prospect of your coming upon us like this by accident, Mr. Webster. You might consider telling the truth, sir."

Mr. Andronikos rejoined them at their table as the other two men left the *Heuriger.* Seeing Matthew there, he paused for a moment, then smiled and bowed briefly. "Good evening, Mr. Webster," he said pleasantly.

"Do you know each other?" Lizzie exclaimed in surprise.

"Indeed we do," said Matthew, returning his bow very briefly. "I have discovered that Mr. Andronikos is a gentleman with many interests, and our paths have crossed several times since he has been in Vienna."

Mr. Andronikos continued to smile. "But of course they have, and I look forward to the time that they will cross again, Mr. Webster."

Matthew did not appear amused, and he appeared still less so when the young Greek turned to Lizzie and offered his arm.

"Shall we take a stroll in the garden, Miss Lancaster? I believe a little exercise may be in order before we return to our picnic."

She placed her hand on his arm, and together they strolled through the gate that led from the courtyard and into the garden, which was now growing thick with shadows.

"Lizzie!" Matthew called after her. "Don't do this simply because you are angry with me! Come back!"

"Mr. Webster, pray remember your present relationship with Miss Lancaster, and conduct yourself accordingly," said Lady Thalia, her tone short. "It can be of no consequence to you whether or not she walks in the garden with Mr. Andronikos."

"She is doing so simply to annoy me," observed Matthew grimly, staring at the backs of the retreating couple.

"What complete rubbish you talk, Webster!" snapped Mr. Thoreau. "Miss Lancaster does not require your permission for anything that she does, and you place too great a value upon your own importance if you believe that she acts out of a desire to irritate you."

"You take a very great interest in her affairs," replied Matthew, looking at Mr. Thoreau with obvious dislike. "For one who has known her so short a time, you seem to have grown much too intimate."

Here he directed his gaze to Lady Thalia, who had been listening to his remarks with mounting anger. "As for you, ma'am, I fear that the Lancasters placed too much confidence in you when they allowed Lizzie to come here in your company."

"How *dare* you say such a thing to me, you impertinent boy? I will thank you to take your leave of us now, and I assure you that you will *not* be welcome to call upon us until you have mended your manners and given me an apology!"

Matthew looked at her for a moment, unmoved by her anger. Then, after glancing briefly into the dark garden at the sound of Lizzie's distant laughter, he bowed to Lady Thalia and to Mr. Thoreau, then departed without another word.

"He takes far too much upon himself!" said Lady Thalia, deprived of her quarry and still angry.

"Indeed he does," returned Mr. Thoreau pacifically, "and I only hope that you will not take out your anger upon me, ma'am."

She relaxed slightly at his words and forced herself to smile. "I hope that I am not so rag-mannered as that. I shall force myself to think of other things."

Lady Thalia took a sip of her wine and looked thoughtfully at Thoreau. After a few moments, she said, "It does seem *excessively* odd that Matthew would know Mr. Andronikos."

"In Vienna these days, everyone knows everyone," he answered. "I daresay that both of them have made countless new acquaintances during the past weeks."

"Mr. Andronikos smiled at Matthew, but they didn't seem to like one another at all," she observed.

"No," agreed Mr. Thoreau, "no, they did not."

After a moment he added, "Perhaps we should join the others in the garden, ma'am. Would you care to accompany me?"

Standing, he offered her his arm. To her own surprise, she rose and took it, and then the two of them strolled into the shadows.

Thirteen

After that evening, Lady Thalia put aside all thought of Matthew and Mr. Andronikos, for she and Lizzie were swept up in a whirl of social activities that scarcely left them time to sleep. Lizzie, however, did not dismiss the gentlemen from her thoughts. In fact, within hours of their disagreement, she had another meeting with Matthew that Lady Thalia fortunately did not discover.

The morning after he had encountered them at the *Heuriger*, Lizzie was awakened by a young maid who worked for the hotel. The girl dropped Lizzie a brief curtsey, then handed her a folded note, smiled, and hurried from the room. Puzzled, Lizzie opened it and saw at a glance that it was from Matthew.

A few minutes later, she slipped quietly from her chamber so that no one would realize she had awakened and then hurried downstairs and out the main entrance of the hotel. She was half afraid that Matthew was bringing bad news from home, but the greater likelihood, she knew, was that he planned to continue the scolding he had begun the night before. Although she had dressed quickly, she had chosen her dress carefully—a gown of gold merino, trimmed with ribbon and cord of deep emerald green, and a pelisse of the same green. Perhaps, she thought, he might see it and remember that other gown of green and how they had danced together to "Greensleeves." At least it could do no harm to try.

"Lizzie!" Matthew was waiting beside the entrance, and he swiftly tucked her hand into the crook of his arm and walked her across the street.

"Matthew, is there something wrong?" she asked. "You said that it was an emergency. I thought perhaps that there had been an accident or sickness at home."

That had been her first fear, but now she had had time to realize that such news would naturally come to Lady Thalia rather than Matthew.

He shook his head. "The emergency is here, Lizzie, not at home."

Annoyed with him for having frightened her, she glared at him. "And just what is the emergency, Matthew?" Then, giving him no opportunity to reply, she went on. "I suppose that the emergency is that I am seeing Mr. Thoreau and Mr. Andronikos and that they do not meet with your approval! May I remind you, Matthew, that you are no longer my fiancé?"

"I know that, Lizzie," he replied quietly, "but I cannot stop caring for you simply because—"

He hesitated a moment, and she finished the sentence for him. "Simply because you have inconveniently fallen in love with someone else. Yes, you have told me that, Matthew, but it does *not* give you the right to interfere in my life!"

"I'm not trying to interfere in your life, Lizzie. Truly, I'm not. Or at least I wouldn't be if you were seeing someone more worthy of you." His tone was earnest, and she knew that he meant what he was saying. Unfortunately, what he was saying infuriated her. He would apparently be completely satisfied to hand her over to some gentleman he deemed "worthy" of her. She felt like a package that could be handed from one to another—at Matthew's discretion, of course.

"Mr. Thoreau *is*, as you put it, 'worthy of me'—and I admire him and enjoy his company! It doesn't matter to me that he is an American. As for Mr. Andronikos, he is *most* amusing—and, as a friend of Mr. Thoreau's, he must be perfectly acceptable to me. Whether or not you think him acceptable is not of the *least* consequence to me, Matthew! Really, you *do* take too much upon yourself!"

Despite her anger, a part of Lizzie was secretly amused to hear herself speaking in exclamation points as Lady Thalia did. She was pleased, too, to see that Matthew was astonished that she had spoken to him in such a manner, for at home she had always been in agreement with all that he said and did. When they were children, she had been too young to quarrel with, and later they were too much in love—over too brief a span of time, she thought regretfully—to quarrel. Also, she had known he would be going away to war, and she would never have done anything to distress him under those circumstances. At any rate, he was not accustomed to such a reaction from her, and she discovered that she felt better after saying it. Lady Thalia's approach had much to commend it, she decided.

They had been walking briskly and by this time they had reached a coffeehouse, its large windows polished and proclaiming to the world its name—*Hoffmann's*—in elegant gold letters. Just inside the coffeehouse, she could see an enormous espresso machine of white and gold porcelain ensconced on a marble counter, and as the door opened, the heavenly fragrance of freshly brewed coffee and baking bread floated out to her. For a moment at least, her attention was diverted, and Matthew was able to guide her inside without resistance.

"This is *wonderful!*" she exclaimed, breathing deeply

and glancing about her at the customers, all happily engaged in drinking and eating. The atmosphere was friendly and conversation was brisk.

"I thought you would like it," he said, smiling at her.

His familiar, affectionate gaze gave her heart a sudden wrench, and she looked away quickly so that he would not suspect it. "And I do," she said, quite calmly. "Who could not enjoy such a place?"

"I could, of course, have taken you on down the street for a *Frühstückgulash*," he said casually, "but I thought that you would prefer Hoffmann's."

"A *Frühstückgulash*? What is that?" she demanded, just as he had intended she should.

"A breakfast goulash," he returned, as they settled themselves at a table.

Before she could inquire more closely into this, a waiter arrived to take their order, and she had to wrestle with the delectable decision. At last, after careful consultation, she settled upon *Faschingskrapfen*, lovely golden brown rounds of fried dough, filled with apricot jam and dusted with sugar.

After the waiter left, she spent a few minutes watching the other customers, particularly one frail little woman who was having as much trouble making up her mind as Lizzie had. After serious consideration, she ordered what appeared to be cherry *strudel*, and Lizzie reflected briefly that Lady Thalia should have been there with them. She would love Hoffmann's.

"This is really a charming place, Matthew," she said at last. "Thank you for bringing me here—even if it was in order to lecture me."

"I'm glad that you like it, Lizzie." He had been watching her carefully. "To be truthful, I am surprised that you have been enjoying yourself in Vienna. After all, you are hundreds of miles from home, and you said that you never wished to leave there."

She shook her head. "I was wrong," she replied. "I may well wish to return there after a time, but for the present I am, as you say, enjoying myself tremendously."

Remembering his letter to her, she would have said as much whether it were so or not, but as she said it, she realized that it was true. She was indeed having a wonderful time. She would not have wished herself at home without the experiences she had had during the past weeks. Without quite realizing it until now, she had become, in some ways, a different person.

Matthew was still studying her. "I can't quite place my finger on what is different about you," he commented, "but I know that you have changed. You are not the same Lizzie that I have always known."

"Well, I scarcely could be after all that has happened, could I?" she asked gently and was pleased to see that he looked uncomfortable. "But you still have not told me, Matthew, why I should not spend time with Mr. Thoreau and Mr. Andronikos."

Matthew looked even more uncomfortable at this. "I can't tell you just what I know, Lizzie. I wouldn't be permitted to do so because of my work—but I can tell you that you *must* be careful here in Vienna. There are all sorts of dangers you could fall into, and you are such an innocent that you would never see them coming. I don't want you to find yourself in trouble."

"I shall be careful, I assure you," she answered, cheerfully addressing herself to the apricot buns and her coffee. "And if I find myself in trouble, I know that I may always call upon you—or upon Mr. Thoreau."

He had nodded encouragingly at the first part of her

comment, but at the mention of Mr. Thoreau, his brows drew sharply together.

"You seem to think very highly of a man that you scarcely know!"

"You are wrong, Matthew," she said, keeping her tone level. "I have come to know him quite well. Sometimes, I have discovered, when you are thrown together with strangers, you can establish friendships that are quite as strong as those that have existed for years. I trust him absolutely."

He shook his head in disgust. "Very well, Lizzie! I see that you have grown headstrong and that you will do whatever you wish to do, and the devil take the hindmost! I have done my best to warn you!"

"Indeed you have," she agreed pleasantly, "and that must be a comfort to you—so now you may put me from your mind, Matthew. You have done your duty."

He put out his hands and took hers in them, including the last bit of apricot bun, whose stickiness he ignored as he looked into her eyes.

"Lizzie! Why must you be so infuriating? *Do* please listen to me!"

"Good morning, Miss Lancaster. How fetching you look this morning," said a familiar voice, and she looked up to see Mr. Thoreau smiling at her.

He turned his gaze to Matthew, and his smile faded. "You, Mr. Webster, look somewhat less fetching." Before Matthew could respond, he continued. "And it would seem to me, sir, that for someone who expressed such concern for Miss Lancaster's reputation, you are being quite irresponsible in your behavior this morning."

Matthew flushed darkly and started to rise from the table, but Mr. Thoreau put a hand on his shoulder and pressed him firmly back into place. "And making a spectacle of yourself just now would compound the damage," he said gently. "You must know that you should not have brought her out alone so early in the morning to such a public place. Anyone who saw you and knew you might well misunderstand the situation."

"You have no business to speak to me about appearances nor about Lizzie—" began Matthew, trying to rise again. Mr. Thoreau's hand, however, held him firmly in place.

"On the contrary, Mr. Webster, unlike you, I have every right. I am a friend of Miss Lancaster and *I* am not engaged to another lady."

Lizzie could see that the muscle of Matthew's jaw was quivering, always a certain sign of scarcely repressed anger. She had seen it often when he and her brother George had quarreled, and she recognized it now with pleasure. It was satisfying to know that he was feeling at least a portion of the distress that she had felt.

Mr. Thoreau again smiled at Lizzie. "Miss Lancaster, I would like very much to escort you safely home."

"I would be delighted by your company, sir," she said, tidying away the last evidence of apricot buns with her heavy napkin.

"I brought you here, Lizzie, and I will see you home," said Matthew, finally rising successfully from the table and glaring at Mr. Thoreau.

"And I am certain that you asked permission of Lady Thalia before escorting her here, did you not, Webster?"

"You heard what Lady Thalia said to me last night!" retorted Matthew.

"My point exactly, sir," replied Thoreau, holding out his arm for Lizzie to take. She did so with what seemed to Matthew an irritatingly trusting air.

"*I* shall also see you home, Lizzie," he informed her grimly, offering her his arm as well.

"I am overwhelmed by such attention," she said sweetly, delighted to see him so irritated.

Together, the three of them made their way out the door, and they paused in front of the coffeehouse window because Lizzie stopped in her tracks to admire the great espresso machine once more.

"What a lovely creation," she said. "I am *so* glad, Matthew, that you brought me here. I quite enjoyed it."

Matthew glanced at Thoreau with a trace of satisfaction. "I was certain that you would like it, Lizzie. After all, I have known you for so long that I must by now know your likes and dislikes."

Lizzie turned to Mr. Thoreau and her face brightened. "Do you remember our afternoon in Paris, Mr. Thoreau?" she asked.

He nodded, both of them acutely aware that Matthew was staring at them, his attention fully engaged. "I am not likely ever to forget it, Miss Lancaster."

"I told you then that you had presented me with the loveliest gift I had ever received. That will always be true."

"Gift? What gift?" demanded Matthew. "Lizzie, you know that you have no business accepting gifts from men you scarcely know!"

When she looked up at him, she was no longer smiling. "But Mr. Thoreau isn't a stranger, Matthew. I have told you that. In fact, I feel that I already know him better than I ever knew you."

Silence descended upon all three of them, and it was maintained until they reached the hotel once more. The gentlemen bowed their farewells outside the entrance, and Lizzie disappeared within, pausing on her way to stop and lift her hand in a tiny wave to Thoreau.

For the next two weeks Lizzie did not see Matthew at all, nor did she see Mr. Thoreau more than twice, each time at a party where she scarcely had the opportunity to do more than speak to him. Mr. Andronikos she encountered once at a ball, where he danced with her twice, assuring her that he had never met any woman who was not a Greek that so fascinated him. However, she noticed that he had also danced with Lady Thalia, and she wondered if he had told her precisely the same thing. Smiling to herself, she thought that he probably had. He was quite an incorrigible flirt, which was a part of his charm.

And so the time slipped by, with Lizzie staying too busy to give overmuch time to thinking of the three gentlemen in her life. The days and nights were filled with engagements, and she was so exhausted by them that when she went to bed, she fell immediately into a deep sleep.

"How *very* satisfactory this has been," sighed Lady Thalia, slipping out of her shoes very early one morning as their carriage was rolling home through the dark streets. "I had the most *interesting* conversation imaginable with Prince Talleyrand. I *do* think that having his niece invite us to her breakfast was the most fortunate occurrence. He may not be a handsome man, but he *is* a fascinating one."

Their invitation from Dorothée de Périgord had opened other doors for Lady Thalia and Lizzie, as well as begun a friendship between Lady Thalia and Talleyrand, who always had an eye for an attractive lady, particularly one no longer young.

"Yes, I have noticed that the two of you deal very well together," returned Lizzie. "You had best be careful or the Duchesse de Courlande may grow jealous." Everyone knew that the Duchesse had been Talleyrand's mistress for years.

Lady Thalia laughed. "Oh, she would not do so. She is *very* well aware of what he is and how well he manipulates people. I am certain that much of his political information comes from ladies with whom he has had liaisons over the years. He *always* keeps his contacts and I understand that they are astonishingly loyal to him."

"And what were you two laughing about tonight as we were preparing to take our leave?" inquired Lizzie idly, listening to the wheels of the carriage thump over the cobblestones.

"He was telling me about his preparations for Vienna. When he was conferring with the King, Talleyrand said to him, 'Sire, I have more need of *casseroles* than written instructions.' He *knows* how much can be accomplished at social events. *Most* of the political maneuvering takes place away from the meetings at the Ballhausplatz. He is nobody's fool."

"And what did King Louis say to that?"

Lady Thalia laughed. "He *agreed.* And so Talleyrand brought along his chef, prepared to entertain *lavishly.*"

"And so he brought Carême? The one that Mr. Thoreau and Mr. Mansfield were discussing when we first met?"

"The very same. They no doubt have found that *most* amusing!"

Lizzie hesitated a moment before responding. "We have seen Mr. Mansfield several times, but it has been a week since we encountered Mr. Thoreau, I believe."

"I daresay it has," returned Lady Thalia with a marked lack of interest. "No doubt he has other obligations with *other* friends—perhaps with Mr. Andronikos."

"Perhaps," agreed Lizzie, trying not to sound too interested herself. Then she smiled. "I am surprised, Lady Thalia, that you remember his name."

"Why should I *not* remember Mr. Thoreau's name?"

she asked, sounding surprised. "After all, we have met him upon many occasions by now."

"Oh, I didn't mean Mr. Thoreau—I was referring to Mr. Andronikos," replied Lizzie mischievously. "But then, as I recall, you *did* dance with him recently."

"Yes, I really had *no* choice, but I was pleased to find that he was quite passable upon the dance floor—*except*, of course, that he does talk a very great amount of nonsense."

"Does he indeed?" said Lizzie, feigning astonishment. "What sort of nonsense?"

Lady Thalia sounded annoyed. "You know *very* well what I mean, Lizzie, so don't try to pretend that you do not. Precisely the kind of thing that he said at the *Heuriger*. If *ever* a young man dealt in false coin, it is George Andronikos."

She was silent for a moment, then added with laughter in her voice, "But he is still a *most* charming young man."

Lizzie laughed. "I knew that you thought so. Judging by your expression, I was only surprised when the two of you did not elope before the end of the dance."

Lady Thalia gave up all pretense of propriety at this point. "Yes, it is *all* very well to laugh at me, Lizzie. I *do* admit that I find both Mr. Andronikos and Mr. Thoreau very personable young men."

"You should not make them sound as though they are mere boys," objected Lizzie. "After all, they are your own age, ma'am."

"Yes, that is all very well," she replied, eager to change the subject. "What we *must* be planning for, Lizzie, is the fancy dress ball at the Spanish Riding School. We have only a fortnight to think of appropriate costumes and find what we need to create them."

"Two weeks is a world of time," said Lizzie. "We will

have no problem. I thought perhaps I might go as a shepherdess."

"Very pretty," returned Lady Thalia approvingly. "And I believe that *I* shall be Cleopatra."

Lizzie's eyes opened wide at this. "Why, your costume must certainly raise eyebrows, ma'am. You will be the talk of the evening."

"I should *greatly* enjoy that," she admitted. "I seem to have grown *dull* and I need to do something to stir myself up."

"Never dull!" denied Lizzie. "But if you would enjoy scandalizing Vienna, then you must by all means do so."

"Those are *my* sentiments exactly, my dear!"

Soon enough they arrived at their hotel, and the ladies retired to their chambers. Lizzie mulled over their conversation as she was preparing for bed. She had not wished to be a shepherdess, but Beavers had suggested it to her and, since she had not been able to think of anything else, she had accepted it. As she thought about it now, her choice seemed pitifully bland and unexciting. Surely, she thought, there must be something else.

She had just dozed off when she had a blindingly brilliant—or so it seemed to her—idea. She could picture herself in the costume. Better than that, she could picture Matthew's horrified expression when he saw her. She had only managed to aggrevate him a few times in the past weeks, and she needed to think of something that he would find completely unsettling.

Lizzie smiled. He would be thoroughly unsettled. She pulled the bedcovers up to her chin with a satisfied sigh.

She would send for Mr. Thoreau in the morning— or, she thought, remembering the time and correcting herself—later this very morning.

Fourteen

Only a few hours later, Lizzie wrote her billet and sent it to the inn where Mr. Thoreau was staying. In it, she told him that she would be in attendance at a ball at the Redoutensaal that evening and asked him to meet her there, telling him that she had a favor to ask of him. Satisfied that he would come, for she had acquired great faith in his reliability, she then gave her attention to the activities of the day—a late breakfast given by the Countess von Veermann, a ride in the Prater with Lady Thalia and Lord Danvers, the ball—and finally a late supper given at the Palm Palace by the Duchess von Sagan, the older sister of Dorothée de Périgord.

Lizzie had discovered that life in Vienna was rather more complicated than anything she could have imagined when she lived safely at home at the Lodge. For instance, she had been astonished to learn that the Duchess von Sagan was the lover of Prince Metternich of Austria—but then so was the Princess Bagration, who occupied the other wing of the Palm Palace. And both ladies also apparently received payment from Tsar Alexander for their assistance with Russian political interests. She looked forward to the supper that evening, for she very much wanted to see the Duchess more closely than she had thus far—and she was also very curious to see just who would be in attendance at the supper.

She arrayed herself carefully for the ball, choosing the diaphanous gown she had feared so greatly when Madame Delacroix had made it for her. She had not yet worn it, both because Lady Thalia had ordered so many new gowns for her after their arrival in Vienna and because she had still been uncomfortable at the thought of wearing it. Tonight, however, having made up her mind about her costume for the approaching fancy dress ball, she felt that she could face the gown, a gauze-like confection with the same soft golden glow of the late afternoon sun in the Place du Carrousel in Paris. She surveyed herself in front of the cheval glass in her chamber and smiled at what she saw. If she were fortunate, Matthew would be present this evening, too. She was certain that he would disapprove.

Lord Danvers escorted them to the Redoutensaal that evening, and he led Lady Thalia out to dance first. Lizzie's hand was requested by a pleasant-faced young man on Metternich's staff, but their conversation was difficult, for Lizzie's mastery of French was far from perfect, and she knew no German whatsoever. She was distracted, too, by her desire to see Mr. Thoreau. Given his dependability, she had really expected to be dancing first with him, but as yet she had not caught any glimpse of his sturdy form.

She was rescued from the young Austrian by Mr. Mansfield, who claimed the next dance. When she explained her language predicament to him, he laughed.

"Then you find yourself in the same predicament as most English," he laughed. "We have the same problem even in our delegation to the Congress."

"But you speak French, Mr. Mansfield," she protested.

"I remember being very impressed when you spoke to the French postilions when we were on our way to Paris."

"Oh, I do well enough with speaking it," he said lightly, "but writing it is quite another matter. We could do with having Wellington here, for not a one of us in the delegation can manage to write it well enough to maintain our correspondence."

"But then what do you do?" inquired Lizzie, surprised by his comment. French was the language of diplomacy, so it appeared to her that they labored under a great handicap.

"We have Gentz, Metternich's assistant, to help us. He comes around regularly to do our translations for us."

She looked at him doubtfully. "But is that quite safe, Mr. Mansfield? After all, English interests and Austrian interests are different—even I know that."

Mansfield laughed. "You are correct, Miss Lancaster, but you worry far too much, I assure you. Lord Castlereagh is a cautious man, and he keeps our affairs secure and, amazingly enough, running quite smoothly."

The movement of the dance separated them just then and when he joined her once again, he said, "I am delighted that you finally got to see your good friend from home, Miss Lancaster."

"Yes, I was pleased, naturally, to see Matthew once more," she replied smoothly. "He appears to be staying very busy in Vienna."

Mansfield nodded. "One sees him everywhere. It is just as well that he remains occupied, of course. Otherwise he would doubtless be troubled by his long separation from Miss Blackwell."

"Yes, I am certain that he is grateful for his schedule," said Lizzie, not betraying her thoughts by even the slightest change in expression.

"I had hoped that Miss Blackwell was sincere when she said that she might come to Vienna," he continued, "but I suppose that was too much to hope for."

"Yes," Lizzie agreed, thinking how very glad she was that Miss Blackwell was safely contained in Paris. She thought of her oftener than she would like, even at that distance. Having to see her with regularity would be still less pleasant. "It is a pity, but perhaps Matthew will be able to go to Paris soon and see her."

She was grateful for the end of the dance, and more grateful still for an interruption that saved her from Mr. Mansfield and further discussion of Matthew and Miss Teresa Blackwell.

"Ah, Miss Lancaster! How delightful it is to see you once again," said Mr. Andronikos, appearing suddenly beside her and bowing low over her hand. "I am devastated to be late! I had so wished to dance with you first this evening!"

"You are very kind, sir," she replied, smiling. She found it impossible not to enjoy him, even though she knew that he spoke only in hyperbole.

She turned to introduce him to Mr. Mansfield, but she was forestalled.

"Mr. Andronikos," he said, bowing. "I did not realize that you were acquainted with Miss Lancaster."

The Greek smiled and returned the bow. "And how could I fail to be acquainted with the loveliest lady in Vienna?"

Mansfield, clearly not wishing to converse with Mr. Andronikos, turned to Lizzie and bowed. "I thank you for the dance, Miss Lancaster. I can see that I leave you in good hands." And then, having inclined his head slightly in the other gentleman's direction, turned and walked across the floor to join another group.

Lizzie glanced about them, then asked, "Did Mr. Thoreau not accompany you tonight?"

He shook his head regretfully. "I fear that Daniel was called away unexpectedly and will not return for at least another sennight."

"But he did not tell me that he was going!" she exclaimed before she could stop herself.

Mr. Andronikos regarded her seriously, still holding her hand in his own. "And I must bear the blame for that, Miss Lancaster, for Daniel left with me a letter to deliver to you so that you would know of his absence—but I myself had to leave Vienna soon afterward. I have only returned this very afternoon, and I found your note waiting for Daniel."

She stared at him for a moment. "And did you open my letter to Mr. Thoreau?" she demanded.

He nodded guiltily. "I felt that I must, you see, for I had been remiss in getting his letter to you. I feared that you might have an immediate problem with which I might be able to help."

Forgetting for the moment the danger of wrinkling her gown, Lizzie sat down abruptly in one of the tiny gilded chairs that edged the dance floor. Concerned by her suddenly forlorn expression, Mr. Andronikos sat down next to her.

"What is wrong, Miss Lancaster? In what way may I be of service to you?" His voice was coaxing, but it took a minute for her to think about what he was saying.

She stared at him for a moment. Her problem was not really such a great one after all, she reflected. She should not feel so suddenly empty at discovering that Mr. Thoreau was far away instead of here in Vienna where she could call upon him whenever she needed him. And here was his friend, graciously offering to help her. The difference between depending upon Mr. Thoreau and depending upon Mr. Andronikos, however, seemed the difference between a rock and a grasshopper.

Mr. Andronikos was still watching her closely. "Shall I bring you something to drink? Do you have your smelling salts in your reticule?"

Lizzie smiled. "Thank you, sir, but I have no need of either. I am really quite well—only surprised, you see."

He nodded in relief. "Yes, of course it must be a shock to you to see me instead of Daniel—but I assure you that I will do my humble best to help you with any problem that you may face, Miss Lancaster!"

He straightened his shoulders and stood taller still. "Merely ask of me what you will, dear lady, and I will do my best to satisfy your request!"

In spite of herself, Lizzie laughed at his serious expression and pose. "And I assure you, Mr. Andronikos, that my request is not one that will threaten your health or well-being! I have a very small problem that I wished for Mr. Thoreau to help me with."

He sighed and relaxed his military stance. "I can only wish that it were a difficult one, Miss Lancaster, so that I could show you my devotion. What is it that you would like for me to do?"

"Do you plan to attend the fancy dress ball at the Spanish Riding School a fortnight from now? The one given by the English delegation?"

"But of course! Everyone will be there!" he responded.

"Exactly so! But, you see, I need help with my costume, Mr. Andronikos. I need to travel to another part of town to find it, and I have no one to take me there."

"But where do you wish to go, Miss Lancaster?" he asked. "What is the costume you have in mind?"

Lizzie laughed. "I shall be a gypsy!" she responded. "You

need to take me, I think, to the Prater, where I heard a gypsy fiddler playing when I was there this afternoon with Lady Thalia and Lord Danvers. I heard the music when I was there with you, too."

Mr. Andronikos stared at her in astonishment. "You wish for me to take you to see the gypsies, Miss Lancaster?" he demanded. "But you must know that I cannot do that. Lady Thalia assuredly would not allow it!"

"Well, we need not tell her," Lizzie pointed out. "I can make arrangements to slip away and you can meet me outside my hotel."

She glanced at him and he still looked extremely doubtful, so she added, "I knew that I would be able to rely upon Mr. Thoreau to help me with this, but perhaps, Mr. Andronikos, you feel that this would be asking too much of you. If that is so, I certainly understand. After all, this is not at all like stealing a horse to fetch another *apfelstrudel* for a lady."

Thus forcibly reminded of his offer at the *Heuriger*, as well as his ragging of Daniel Thoreau for his lack of gallantry, Mr. Andronikos straightened his shoulders, took a deep breath, and bowed to Lizzie.

"Dear lady, I will most certainly do as you request— although I am quite certain that I shall be reproached not only by Lady Thalia, but by Daniel as well."

Lizzie did not try to conceal her delight, and she leaned toward him, rapping his arm lightly with her fan without even realizing that she was doing so and causing him to bend down, since he expected her to say something private. Instead, she kissed his cheek lightly.

"You are a dear man, Mr. Andronikos," she said lightly, smiling at him. "And you are truly helping me, whether it seems so to you or not. In time, you will see."

He had no opportunity to respond because Matthew

bore down upon them just at that moment, bowing stiffly to Andronikos and glaring at Lizzie.

"May I request the pleasure of the next dance, ma'am?" he asked, his tone closer to that of a command than a request.

Mr. Andronikos frowned, but Lizzie again tapped him lightly on the arm, saying, "Then I may count on you, sir?"

He bowed to her deeply. "Indeed you may, dear lady. I shall see you very soon." Then, casting a dark look at Matthew, he added, "And I trust, Mr. Webster, that you will address Miss Lancaster in a more gentlemanly tone."

He turned and walked away before the startled Matthew could reply.

"Andronikos certainly takes too much upon himself!" he said sharply.

"Does he indeed?" inquired Lizzie mildly. "Asking you to treat me as you would a lady and not to speak to me as though you were giving me a command instead of making a request? You think *that* is taking too much upon himself, Matthew?"

"You know very well what I mean, Lizzie!" he snapped. "Don't start trying to play word games with me. You know precisely why I spoke to you like that!"

Lizzie paused for a moment, surveying the young man before her. He was still her Matthew, and he presented a well-dressed, polished façade to the world, but in his gray eyes she could see none of the old tenderness. She had seen it there when he took her to Hoffmann's to talk to her, and she had seen it at odd intervals since then— twice when he had danced with her, once when he had encountered her by accident upon the street. Now, however, it seemed to have disappeared all together. The only warmth there was clearly the result of irritation.

"What do you mean, Lizzie, by getting yourself involved with Andronikos and Thoreau after I expressly told you that you should avoid them?" he demanded. "You are behaving no better than Alice would, and we have always laughed about how headstrong she is!"

"Perhaps we simply see the whole situation differently, Matthew," she replied, not allowing herself to become ruffled in the least. "I, naturally, know none of the secret things about them that you claim to know, but I *do* know that I like them immensely—and that *they* go out of their way to befriend me."

"Of course they do!" he retorted.

"And what does that mean?" she demanded, her irritation beginning to get the better of her. "Is that supposed to imply that there is a reason that they would be kind to me, other than the fact they enjoy my company?"

They were beginning to attract a little attention from those about them and, noticing that, Matthew said in a lower voice, "Come along, Lizzie. Let's find a place where we can talk. We cannot possibly dance and discuss this."

"And if I don't wish to talk to you?" she asked sharply, thoroughly annoyed that he was once again trying to take command. "What will you do then? Drag me along with you?"

"Of course not, Lizzie! Please don't act so missish! It doesn't become you!"

"*Missish*? Because I disagree with you? I *never* thought I would say such a thing to you, Matthew, but you have become too set up in your own esteem! You were always such a merry, loving boy, and look what you've become! High-handed and completely careless of my feelings!"

They had been walking briskly, his hand at her elbow, guiding her, as they talked. Both of them were flushed and angry, but they paused for a moment in their argument because they could see that they were still drawing interested glances from passers-by.

"Where are we going?" she finally demanded, as they grew close to the entrance.

"To my carriage," he said.

"Without telling Lady Thalia?" she asked, shaking his hand loose and stopping to look at him.

"We will not be gone so long that she will miss you—unless, of course, Andronikos makes it his business to tell her that we left together." Once again he took her arm and guided her toward the door.

"Well, it doesn't seem to me that I should be going anywhere alone with you in a closed carriage, Matthew. It certainly has the appearance of impropriety."

"Honestly, Lizzie, if that is not being missish, please tell me what is!"

Fighting down the impulse to box his ears, she swallowed hard and forced herself to sound at least moderately calm. "And so you would not object if Miss Blackwell were to ride alone with a gentleman? At night and in a closed carriage?"

"Certainly I would object, but that would be quite another matter from the two of us getting into a carriage together. You know that, Lizzie."

They had by then walked out onto the street, and Lizzie suddenly realized that she had left without her wrap and the night air was sharp. Matthew noticed that she had begun to shake, and, without a word, he stripped off his jacket and put it around her shoulders. They turned a corner and continued to walk, the line of waiting carriages still stretching some distance. To her relief, they finally stopped beside one of them, and he opened the door and handed her in, calling to the coachman as he did so.

"You keep a carriage of your own in the city?" she

asked, curiosity for the moment overcoming anger. "Isn't it very expensive?"

"Emperor Francis is paying for it. He provided 300 carriages, complete with liveried servants for visiting royalty and dignitaries."

"But you're neither of those things, Matthew, so why do you have one?"

"Because I am here under Wellington's orders, and I occasionally have need of one," he replied briefly.

She was mulling that over as they started down the street. "It is still very cold, Matthew," she pointed out. "And I am most uncomfortable."

He picked up a carriage robe and started to lay it over her knees.

"Don't do that! You'll crush my gown and probably get it dirty as well!"

He dropped it back on the seat. "Very well. But you wouldn't be nearly so cold if you would wear sensible gowns instead of one made of fabric so thin that you might as well not be wearing a gown at all! I can't imagine why Lady Thalia allowed you to wear it!"

Lizzie ignored for a moment the fact that she had had her own private doubts about the gown, but she had certainly seen those that were much more daring than hers. And then she thought of Miss Blackwell, who appeared to live in diaphanous gowns.

"And I suppose you point that out to Miss Blackwell, too," she ventured.

"Of course not," he returned. "She always looks most attractive and it is scarcely my place to tell her what she should wear."

"But you are telling *me*. And you are about to be *her* husband, not mine, Matthew. The things that you are saying do not fit together very logically."

He sat in silence for a few minutes, and Lizzie, feeling that she had made her point, decided to press it. "And why should it be acceptable for *us* to be alone together in a carriage when you do not think it would be proper for Miss Blackwell to do so?"

He reached over and took her hand. When she tried to withdraw it, he held it still more firmly.

"I *do* owe you an apology, Lizzie," he said at last.

It was her turn to sit in silence as the carriage creaked through the dark streets.

"For jilting me?" she asked finally, her voice flat.

"Don't use language like that, Lizzie. It isn't becoming— and it isn't like you at all."

"And just how would you *like* for me to say it, Matthew? That you discovered someone else whom you loved and just dismissed me? That I am too much a homebody for you to marry and that you very much wish that I had stayed at home?"

She was furious, and she was determined that her anger would sustain her so that she wouldn't give way to tears. This was the first time that they had mentioned Miss Blackwell, and she longed to tell Matthew just what she thought of his giving away her St. George medal to his new love. She could not do it now, however, for she knew that she couldn't speak of it without crying at his betrayal, and she refused to do so.

"In truth, I *do* wish you had stayed at home, Lizzie! You have done nothing but complicate matters for me here! I cannot be worrying about you and still give all my attention to the work that I am here to do!"

"And why *should* you be worrying about me?" she demanded. "What have I done that should cause you such concern?"

"I have already told you, Lizzie," he replied, his voice

sounding as though he were trying to retain a semblance of patience. "I *warned* you that you should stay
away from Daniel Thoreau and George Andronikos, yet
you have clearly done nothing of the sort. If anything,
you have made a point to stay in touch with them—as
you demonstrated tonight."

"They are both perfectly gentlemanly in their conduct, Matthew, so why should you be so worried about
my seeing them?"

"Thoreau is as wealthy as Croesus, so he *should* be
able to play the part of a gentleman perfectly well!" he
retorted.

"As you very well know, it is his behavior that I am referring to, Matthew, not his pocketbook! And I know
that his family is in trade, so you needn't mention that
either! He is a delightful man!"

She paused a moment and then, before he could
reply, she added, "I knew he was well-to-do, of course,
but I had no notion that he was so very wealthy." She
glanced at Matthew from the corner of her eye. "Perhaps I shall set my cap for him! It is not often that one
finds such a happy combination of fine appearance and
disposition linked with a fortune."

She was aware that Matthew had no knowledge of her
family's present precarious financial situation, for her father had been careful to keep the matter secret. However,
he also knew that their circumstances were modest and
that a comfortable marriage settlement for Lizzie would
be more than welcome.

"Yes, that would be perfect, Lizzie! Choose someone
from a country with which we are at war! Marry a
wealthy American who believes in revolutions and sup-
ports them! The two of you can trundle around the
world together, throwing money to the lower classes in

order to encourage sedition! What a pretty life you would make for yourself by marrying him!"

"Naturally he believes in revolution! As you say, he *is* from America! As for supporting revolutions, the French one is over!"

"So we would like to believe," he replied.

Before he could continue, she said, "And Mr. Thoreau detests Napoleon for betraying the cause of the French people and making himself emperor, so don't think for a moment that he would support him! If Napoleon comes back with the violets as he promised, it will not be with Mr. Thoreau's assistance!"

He looked at her sharply. "You seem to know a great deal about all of this, Lizzie. I did not realize that you were so much in Mr. Thoreau's confidence."

She was somewhat taken aback by this, and quickly reviewed her words. She had not, as far as she could see, said anything that could damage Mr. Thoreau. "Not at all," she said stiffly. "It is simply that he is my friend, and that we *do* talk about things that are of interest to us both. And as for Mr. Andronikos, he has also stood my friend— even if he is the most accomplished flirt in Vienna."

"I cannot believe that you could call a man your friend and in the next breath admit him to be a dedicated flirt. What has happened to you, Lizzie?"

"Perhaps I've begun to grow up, Matthew. You told me in your letter that we had grown apart and should not marry. I know now that you were right and that we would no longer suit." As she said it, she realized with a flicker of pain that she might be speaking the truth. "As it is, we are both free to go our own ways—and it appears to me, Matthew, that you yourself have chosen a most accomplished flirt as your fiancée, so your own tastes have clearly changed as well."

She had not been able to resist that final jab, and Matthew bristled indignantly just as she had known he would. "How unjust you are, Lizzie! You have scarcely done more than meet Teresa, and yet you judge her in such a manner! Such behavior does not become you!"

"Miss Blackwell is not a flirt, then? If I spent more time in her company, I should see that she is nothing of the sort?"

He hesitated a moment before answering. "Teresa has a natural buoyancy of spirit—and a pleasure in others—that might make some who do not know her feel that she is a flirt. Anyone who truly knows her as I do, however, realizes that taking such pleasure in others is merely a part of her nature and not an artificial behavior."

"I see," said Lizzie, as though she had made a sudden startling discovery, "so a natural flirt is not to be criticized, while one who has learned the art should be. In that case, Mr. Andronikos is not to be condemned either, for he has undoubtedly had his happy manner from the cradle. I am certain that it was not acquired later."

"Miss Blackwell and Mr. Andronikos are not to be compared in any way. She is a refined young lady, a lady of quality, while Andronikos is—" He broke off, as though searching for words.

"A gentleman of quality?" she offered helpfully.

"A revolutionary who can be trusted to do nothing except foment trouble for all connected with him!"

Lizzie, remembering her conversation with Mr. Thoreau about his friend George, made no immediate reply.

The carriage paused for a moment in the light offered by an uncurtained window above it, and Matthew turned to look at her. "You know that is true, don't you, Lizzie?" he asked, his voice filled with disbelief. "And yet you like him and spend your time with him."

"I know nothing of the sort!" she said quickly, but she did not sound convincing, even to herself. "But even if what you say were true, how could it be so terrible for someone to long for freedom?"

"It depends very much upon what that person is willing to do to achieve it," he responded grimly. "And also how his actions might affect others. After all, Lizzie, the reason that we are here is to try to establish a lasting peace."

"And all of Vienna knows that every country represented here has its own notion of how that should happen—and they all have to do with carving up other countries, whether they agree to it or not!"

Even at the social gatherings, she had not been able to miss the rumblings of discontent from the Poles, who wanted their country back; from displaced German nobility, who wanted their estates back; from the Prussians, who wanted Saxony; from the Austrians, who wanted to limit the power of Russia and France; from the Russians, who wanted to keep Austria and France under control; from the French, who did not want an alliance of Russia and Prussia. And of course there was present an assortment of tiny kingdoms and principalities, all lobbying for their own concerns. Among the British, feeling blissfully that the war was over and they were safe once more, only Castlereagh and some of the members of his delegation appeared to have any notion of what the interests of their own country were. Lizzie had reflected that attending parties in Vienna sometimes felt like being in the midst of a bubbling pot, one that was about to come to a rolling boil.

"Lizzie, matters are growing more serious than you know. The French are increasingly unhappy with their king, and they feel that we are the ones that are keeping him in power. There is talk of insurrection there, and attempts have already been made on Wellington's life."

She stared at him in horror. "The Duke has been attacked?"

He nodded. "The problem is a very real one—which is precisely why you must not be mixing with those who support revolution in any form."

"But surely you are not saying that Mr. Thoreau and Mr. Andronikos are involved in encouraging France to rise again or in attacks against Wellington?"

Matthew shrugged. "There is always that possibility," he said gravely.

"Possibility? In other words, you have absolutely no proof that they are connected to the affairs you have been telling me of!" Anger came boiling up again as she realized that he was trying to control her and that his accusations had no foundation. "If you did, you would tell me so, instead of giving me ominous warnings based on nothing save your own suppositions!"

"You know very well, Lizzie, that all I wish is your safety." He sounded weary now, as though tired of arguing with a child who could not follow his reasoning.

"We are no longer engaged, sir, so you have no business at all to be concerned in my affairs!"

"But I still care about you, Lizzie, even though we aren't engaged! I feel that you are in some sense still my responsibility and I have told you that! I cannot stand by and see you involve yourself in matters that you do not understand!"

"I am not involved in *anything* save having a good time, Matthew—and you seem determined to keep me from having one!"

"Honestly, Lizzie, you would try the patience of a saint!" he exclaimed, giving way to anger once more. "It is a blessing twice over that we are not to be married!"

"I believe that we are quite in agreement with your last

statement, Matthew! And it is you who is interfering in my affairs without so much as a by-your-leave! I should like to see you try to treat Miss Blackwell in this high-handed manner!"

"Teresa has no need of being reprimanded! She knows how a lady should conduct herself—and you are either too young or too headstrong to behave sensibly!"

"And I am delighted to hear that you are marrying such a paragon, sir! But I will tell you now that if you don't take me back to the Redoutensaal immediately, I shall open the door and jump from this carriage!"

"That would be sheer idiocy, Lizzie. You would only hurt yourself and create a scene."

"And you would be the one who would have to explain that to Lady Thalia—and to any interested passers-by!"

"I *can* not believe the change in you, Lizzie. It is most disheartening. You used to be so reasonable."

However, he apparently took her at her word, for he ordered the coachman to turn back. They rolled back to the Hofburg in silence, each of them too angry to speak. Lizzie was profoundly grateful for the anger, since it kept the tears at bay.

After reclaiming his jacket and escorting her back into the ballroom, Matthew bowed to her, turned, and walked away without a word.

Lizzie, in the meantime, smiled mechanically at the eager young Frenchman who asked for the next dance and laughed as they tried to talk, using his limited English and her limited French. She was determined that she would enjoy the evening. After all, she still had the Duchess von Sagan's supper to look forward to—and Mr. Andronikos would soon be taking her to see the gypsies.

She had intended to make Matthew excessively uncomfortable and she had clearly managed to do so. Now, however, she could no longer determine just how her pleased she was with her success, and she was very grateful that she was too busy to be able to think about it.

The supper given by the Duchess von Sagan was fully as interesting as she and Lady Thalia had expected it to be. Even Prince Metternich came for a short time, although it was whispered that he went immediately across the courtyard to the wing of the palace belonging to Princess Bagration. They saw, too, the men that Mr. Andronikos had met at the *Heuriger*.

"They are Russians, just as I thought," Lady Thalia whispered. "Why do you suppose he is interested in them?"

Lizzie, naturally, had not the slightest idea, and they had no time to discuss the matter because she soon found herself engaged in conversation with a lanky young Englishman. Mr. Bakersfield had no official reason for being in Vienna, but he was well connected and had thus managed invitations to many of the most exclusive gatherings.

"This is the most marvelous place!" he informed her enthusiastically. "Always something going on or something new to see! And riding in the Prater is grand! Do you ride, Miss Lancaster?"

She was forced to admit that she was an indifferent horsewoman, and he looked mildly deflated for a moment. "I had thought perhaps we could ride out together," he said, "but if you would not be comfortable—"

"I'm afraid that I should spoil it for you," she replied.

For a moment she thought longingly of the velvet riding habit that Lady Thalia had insisted upon having made for her, despite her protests that she would never use it. Still, she did not wish to go riding, and most particularly she did not wish to go riding with Mr. Bakersfield.

"Nonsense, Miss Lancaster. I am certain that you are

being too modest," he assured her. "And if you were in need of help, I should assuredly be there to offer my assistance—and I can supply you with a very gentle mount."

"You are very kind," she said, "and I am certain that seeing the Prater from horseback is delightful. Tell me, sir, have you ever seen gypsies during your rides?"

If he was slightly taken aback by this turn of the conversation, he did not show it. "Have indeed," he told her. "Saw an encampment just at dawn a few mornings back. They were cooking their breakfast and grooming their horses."

"Have you seen them since then?" she asked.

He shook his head. "But I know that there are some gypsy fiddlers that play now and then at the cafés in the Prater, or at places around the city—sometimes in the little wine cellars, I believe. Interested in gypsies, are you?"

She nodded. "Yes, they are such romantic figures, are they not?"

Mr. Bakersfield's expression revealed both his doubt about that and his reluctance to disagree with a lady. Honesty won out, however. "Seem a little shiftless to me," he said, "and perhaps not as clean as they could be."

"But think of their music, Mr. Bakersfield! Think of their dancing and their joy in life! Think of their freedom!"

"Well, yes, there's that, of course," he admitted reluctantly. "Still, not to my taste, you see."

"Yes, naturally tastes differ, Mr. Bakersfield." Then, turning the conversation before he could return to the matter of the ride, she indicated with a nod of her head one of the gentlemen she had seen with Mr. Andronikos at the *Heuriger*. "Do you know the tall gentleman in the green waistcoat?" she asked idly. "He looks rather familiar to me."

"Yes, one sees him a great deal," agreed Mr. Bakersfield. "I can't remember just what his name is, though—a Greek chap, it seems to me. Difficult name."

"Greek?" she asked in surprise. "I had thought that he was Russian."

Mr. Bakersfield shook his head. "From Corfu," he said. "But he works for the Tsar. Quite a favorite, I hear."

"Indeed?" responded Lizzie thoughtfully. "That is very interesting."

Mr. Bakersfield looked doubtful. "Suppose that it is, but I haven't the least notion why."

Lizzie laughed. "How very enjoyable it is to talk with you, sir. It is refreshing to speak with someone from home."

"How relieved I am to hear you say that."

Lizzie and Mr. Bakersfield both looked mildly startled by this statement since neither of them had made it.

"Webster!" exclaimed Mr. Bakersfield. "Didn't see you come in. Miss Lancaster, allow me to present Mr. Matthew Webster." He paused a moment, looking puzzled as he thought about Matthew's comment. "Do you know each other then? Were you speaking to Miss Lancaster when you sneaked up on us?"

"I confess that the lady and I are acquainted," replied Matthew. "For many years, in fact."

"Indeed!" said Mr. Bakersfield, his brows rising and his voice teasing. "And what will Miss Blackwell think of your having a friendship with such a striking young lady as Miss Lancaster? I daresay she will be so jealous as to set a watch on you."

Not waiting for Matthew to reply, he turned to Lizzie

and added, "I met Webster's fiancée when I stopped off in Paris. I daresay you know what a prize he has won."

"Indeed I do," replied Lizzie. "They are, I think, very well suited to one another." She looked directly at Matthew as she said that, then turned back to Mr. Bakersfield and smiled. "If you will excuse me, sir, I see someone whom I need to talk to just now."

They scarcely had time to bow before she left them, walking boldly across the room to introduce herself to the Greek gentleman in the service of the Tsar.

Fifteen

By the time a few days had passed, Lizzie had managed to put Matthew out of her mind so that she could concentrate on the pleasures at hand. She and Lady Thalia had been engaged on a daily round of engagements, including as many Russians as possible since she felt that doing so would cause Matthew the maximum amount of distress (although she naturally was not thinking about him). Walking across the room to receive an introduction to the Greek Kapodhístrias that night at the Duchess von Sagan's supper had appeared to inflame Mr. Webster quite satisfactorily, and she could think of no reason not to fan those flames.

She kept herself busy, always smiling and enjoying every moment so that when she went home to England, she would have stored enough memories to keep her warm through her declining years—which she felt she would most certainly face when she went home, for no eligible young man would be likely to marry a young woman with no dowry. A letter from her mother had disclosed the unhappy news that her father had been obliged to use the money set aside for that purpose in order to solve some of their financial woes.

Perhaps she would have to go home and face life as a spinster, perhaps even become a governess, with Lady

Thalia's help. It was even possible that if she became desperate enough, she might marry some poor man who had no expectations of a dowry. Naturally, her life would be a much more difficult one under those circumstances, but it did not appear to her that she had many choices. In the meantime, she intended to make the most of each present moment.

She had discovered, to her amazement, that here in Vienna she had a following of young men—and of some older ones, as well—and she had begun to enjoy herself tremendously. So, for the moment at least, she put depressing thoughts away and reveled in the attention she was receiving—although knowing very well that there was no chance that any of them were thinking of making her an offer. They were simply doing what all the other visitors to Vienna were doing—enjoying themselves. It was, Lady Thalia had said, rather like attending a vast, extended house party.

She had almost given up hope of hearing from Mr. Andronikos and had resigned herself to attending the fancy dress ball as a shepherdess when he appeared one morning to call upon her, bearing a large bouquet that he presented to her with his customary flourish.

"Ah, dear lady, a thousand pardons for making you wait so very long," he said, bowing low over her hand. Then he lowered his voice and asked, "We are quite alone, are we not?"

"Yes, Lady Thalia is recovering from influenza and is still in her chamber, so we shall be able to speak privately, Mr. Andronikos. Have you had any success?"

He nodded, his dark eyes glowing. "But of course! How could you think otherwise, Miss Lancaster? It took somewhat longer than I had expected, since the weather has turned and the rain had caused the gypsies to move their camp. But tonight we shall meet them!"

"Are we going to their camp?" she asked, feeling slightly overwhelmed by his success and wondering if she really wanted to do this. Riding out to their camp in the dark and the rain suddenly held very little appeal. It did not seem nearly so enticing as going to see them on a sunlit afternoon.

Mr. Andronikos shook his head. "I did not think that would be suitable. I have made arrangements for them to play and dance at a tavern I know, and we shall talk to them afterward."

"At a tavern?" Lizzie faltered. This also seemed to her more than she had bargained for. Then, however, she had a sudden vision of Matthew's disapproving expression should he hear of such an excursion and that caused her to straighten her shoulders and continue. She wished to see how horrified he would be when she appeared in her gypsy regalia at the fancy dress ball.

"Yes. It is, of course, not usually appropriate to take you there, but I have also arranged for a private place for you. We will sit where you can see them perform, but there will be a screen so that you have some privacy from the others in the room—and naturally I shall remain at your side."

"Thank you, Mr. Andronikos," she said gratefully. "I know that this must seem foolish to you, but it will give me great pleasure."

"You could never seem foolish to me, Miss Lancaster—and if doing this gives you pleasure, that is all that I must know. And I assure you the tavern is safe. I often go there, as do many Greeks."

They settled their plan quickly. He was to meet her at a ball and supper being given that evening by a wealthy young Viennese couple. The couple appeared to have invited a goodly portion of the better-known visitors to their city, and the crush at the party would be tremendous. Lady Thalia, improved but still not feeling particularly well, had elected to stay at home resting. Lord Danvers had agreed to escort Lizzie.

"Nothing could be better," she told Mr. Andronikos, "for Lord Danvers will disappear into the card room immediately and stay until it is time to leave. No one will notice if I am gone for hours."

In fact, before Mr. Andronikos had come, she had been thinking of staying home that night. Even though she knew a number of people by now and never lacked for partners in the dance, she had not been happy at the thought of a long evening spent in a large crowd with no particular person accompanying her. Now, however, she had a reason to go.

All went as they had planned, and very soon after Lizzie's arrival, the two of them slipped out to the carriage that Mr. Andronikos had procured. This time she took her wrap with her, so the cold was not such a problem. The rain had abated for the moment, and the carriage rocked comfortably through the streets. Although she did not feel as absolutely secure as she did with Mr. Thoreau, she was assured that her companion would look after her well, and she was anxious to watch the gypsies perform.

When they arrived at the tavern, he helped her down and guided her quickly through the main door. The room was rather dark and smoky, but she could see that it was quite full. The others paid no particular attention to them, however, for they were talking and laughing loudly, and through it all was threaded the haunting strains of a gypsy tune. He led her down one side of the room to a small table behind a carved wooden screen. Although she was hidden from the eyes of the rest of the audience, she could see the pair of gypsy fiddlers. One was an older man, his hair shining white in the flickering candlelight as he bent over his fiddle, intent upon his music; the other was a thin, dark young man whose features and manner made her think of a hawk.

"May I bring you something to drink, Miss Lancaster?" Mr. Andronikos asked her in a low voice.

She shook her head, smiling. She felt that drinking something here would be tempting fate. Besides, all that she really wanted to do was to listen to their music and watch the dancer when she performed.

In only a few minutes, a young woman stepped out onto the floor where the fiddlers were. A few tables had been cleared away so that she would have space to move, and she swept into a sinuous dance, her movements more graceful than Lizzie could ever have imagined. All conversation stopped now, and she became the center of attention. Her dark hair hung loose, and her body seemed to follow every note of the music, responding to the shifts from joy to sorrow and a deep longing. Her eyes were bright and her gold earrings and bangle bracelets glowed against her dusky skin. Sometimes she whirled so quickly that the bright turkey red of her skirts and kerchief seemed to merge with the gold, so that it seemed to Lizzie that she resembled one of the gleaming tops that children played with at holiday time. Her feet were bare and around one ankle she wore a gold anklet hung with tiny bells.

There was applause when she finished and the three of them bowed under a shower of coins tossed by the audience. The older man looked toward Mr. Andronikos, who nodded and rose. Bending over Lizzie, he said, "I shall be back in just a moment, Miss Lancaster. You will be quite safe here."

He followed the three of them out of the room as soon as they had collected their money, and on the far side of the screen, the conversations resumed. She could follow none of them, for they were, she assumed, mostly in Greek. After a few minutes, however, they began a song of their own. She could see through the screen that they were standing and they sang with such fervor that the very room shook. Lizzie saw Mr. Andronikos slip back into the room. He nodded at her, but he stood with the others and sang until the song was over. Then he came to join her once more.

"What was the song, Mr. Andronikos?" she asked. "What were you singing about?"

"It is a song about freedom," he said. "Not just freedom from the Turks for us, but freedom for everyone. It is a clarion call to men to remind us of what we are and of how we should live. It is an oath never to act as a tyrant and never to allow ourselves to become slaves. Rígas wrote that it is better to live one hour in freedom than to live forty years as a slave."

Lizzie was shaken, both by the forceful singing and the intensity of Mr. Andronikos' words and gaze. "And it was a man named Rígas who wrote the song?" she asked.

When he nodded, she added, "Is he here tonight?"

"Dead," he replied, shaking his head. "Murdered!"

Lizzie stared at him, and he leaned toward her, taking her hand. "Forgive me for speaking so abruptly of such a terrible thing, Miss Lancaster, but, as you see, this a matter of great importance to me—to all of us who come here."

"Who murdered him?" she asked, horrified. "And when did it happen?"

"He died sixteen years ago," he replied. "He was born in Thessaly, but he did much of his work here in Vienna during the last nine years of his life. He studied the rights of man as they were proclaimed in America and in France, and he worked to write a constitution for the Greeks. All of his work, including his call for revolution against the Turks, was printed here in Vienna, but it had to be done secretly because this government would crush anything that threatens stability."

"And so what happened?" she demanded. "Did they find him out?"

"He was betrayed. He and a companion traveled to Trieste, and he had sent ahead to a friend boxes containing copies of his constitution, his freedom hymn, and his call for revolution. His friend was away and the boxes were opened by someone else, who reported him to the authorities. He, along with a number of others, was arrested and brought back here to be questioned. Those like Rígas, who were Turkish nationals, were sent to Belgrade, where they were murdered and their bodies thrown into the river. The authorities said that they drowned during an escape attempt, but we know it was not so."

Lizzie sat in silence. Anything that she could think of to say seemed too inconsequential a response to such a story. After a few moments, Mr. Andronikos appeared to remember that she was still sitting there and that he was holding her hand. He gave it a quick pressure, then released it.

"Forgive me, Miss Lancaster, but he was a great man. It still grieves me to think of it."

"And so it should," she responded, "but at least you still sing his hymn."

"It is sung everywhere there are Greeks," he assured

her, "and his work is widely read. Soon we will be able to establish the constitution that he wrote for us."

Lizzie glanced around them nervously. "But, Mr. Andronikos, should you not be careful what you say? After all, you have just said that the government here does not want anything happening that threatens the stability in this part of the world."

He smiled at her. "Do not worry for me, dear lady. There is always danger for men who wish to change the way of the world, but soon I will be gone from here."

"Gone? Where are you going? May I know?"

"Assuredly you may know. I need to learn more about being a soldier, so I am going to Paris to join the French army. There can be no finer training ground for me."

"But you are not a royalist!" she protested. "Will it not distress you to serve a king?"

"Ah, but for how long will there be a king, Miss Lancaster? That is what we must ask ourselves."

Lizzie had no desire to question him any more closely upon that point while they were in such a public place, but she did venture one more comment. "But the French army was defeated, Mr. Andronikos, and although other countries helped us, it was our English army that brought that defeat. Does that not make our army superior to the French?"

He smiled at her and shook his head. "That army is gone, dear lady—disbanded once the war was over. Some were sent to America for the war in progress there, others simply went home. There is only a skeleton of the original left."

Lizzie had not ever considered the fact that Wellington's army no longer existed, and she discovered that it was not a comfortable thought. Particularly not when thinking of Mr. Andronikos' comments about the French.

She remembered, too, what Mr. Thoreau had said about Napoleon's promise to return with the violets. She did not wish to discuss that publicly, however, so she turned the conversation back to the gypsies and what had transpired between them and Mr. Andronikos.

Smiling, he held up a paper-wrapped bundle. "I have in here, Miss Lancaster, golden jewelry such as the dancer wore, and a bolt of bright cotton. I shall leave the bundle at the desk of your hotel. Also, as you wished, I have engaged the fiddlers for the night of the ball."

She smiled at him. "You have been wonderful to me, Mr. Andronikos. I shall never forget it—nor shall I ever forget you."

"What more could I ask, dear lady?" he asked, leaning over to kiss her hand.

Once they were safely back in the privacy of the carriage, she once more turned the conversation to her fears. "Do you believe what Napoleon said?" she demanded. "That he will return with the violets?"

"Who can know?" he shrugged. "One may only hope."

"Hope?" she said in disbelief. "He would bring war and chaos once more!"

"He would bring an opportunity," said Mr. Andronikos gently. "And for people who wish the world to change, that would be an opportunity to be seized."

Lizzie sank into silence. Much as she had looked forward to seeing the gypsies and acquiring what she needed for her costume, she could not work up any enthusiasm now for enjoying herself as a gypsy and striking back at Matthew. What Mr. Andronikos had told her had suddenly thrown her off balance and she felt as though she was teetering on the edge of an abyss. If Napoleon were to return, war was inevitable.

And she was far from home.

And if there were a war, Wellington would unquestionably lead the English. And so Matthew would also go once more to war.

Sixteen

That desolate feeling was still haunting her when she awoke the next morning, and Lady Thalia was still in bed recovering from influenza. Everything in life seemed as gray as the weather, and Lizzie could feel herself slipping into the slough of despair. She was haunted by thoughts of a war and felt more than a little homesick. She sat by the fire and drank a cup of chocolate, thinking fondly of the Lodge and her family—even of her laughing, careless brother who had caused the family such distress. Despite his thoughtless ways, he was a kindly person, never mean-spirited nor miserly when he was flush with funds. She had received a letter from him, telling her how ashamed he was that he had cost her the precious dowry and promising to make it up to her. She had not responded yet, not for lack of time, but because she hadn't been able to think of the best way to phrase her thoughts. She did not wish to let him see how bleak her future appeared to her. Alice, of course, was in no better state with regard to her dowry, although she doubtless knew nothing of the matter yet.

Finally, she gave herself a shake and determined to go right along with her plans. After all, how could it help anyone if she became as blue as megrim? It could not help her family, her concern meant nothing to Matthew, and she certainly could do nothing about a possible war. Since she could not help, she decided that she would enjoy herself and do what Mr. Thoreau had advised her to do—focus on the world outside herself.

She went down first to see the concierge and pick up her package from Mr. Andronikos. She decided that she would tell Lady Thalia about her costume idea because she was bored and sickly and she too needed something more cheerful to think about. She would not, of course, tell her about going with Mr. Andronikos to pick up the materials.

As she had hoped, her gypsy costume was just the medicine that Lady Thalia needed. She sat up in bed, demanded a cup of tea from the long-suffering Beavers, and commanded Lizzie to lay out on her bedcovers what she had acquired thus far.

"*Very* dashing!" she murmured, looking at the jewelry. "I shouldn't let you do this, of course, but then *I* am going as Cleopatra, so I can scarcely criticize."

She held up the golden anklet strung with bells and examined it with interest. "Lizzie! Are you wearing this just for the sound of the bells, or are you planning on showing your ankles in public?"

"If I dance as I enter the ballroom, even for a moment, my ankles shall undoubtedly be seen," Lizzie pointed out practically.

"*Dance?*" Lady Thalia regarded her with mesmerized horror. "Do you mean that you plan to dance like a *gypsy?*"

Lizzie nodded, then did her best to imitate a few of the gypsy girl's movements. "Well, you can see what I mean, at any rate. I shall only do a couple of quick turns to make my skirts twirl as I enter the ballroom, and of course having the gypsy fiddlers playing will help with the effect."

Lady Thalia's expression had not changed. "Gypsy fiddlers?" she demanded, waiting for more information.

Again Lizzie nodded with satisfaction. "Mr. Andronikos has arranged for a pair of them to be there with me. He will manage our entrance."

"*Will* he indeed?" said Lady Thalia, collapsing back against the pillows. "Why, this sounds for all the world like a *stage* performance, Lizzie! Beavers, are you attending to what she is saying?"

Beavers, who was opening the draperies and putting the room to rights, nodded comfortably.

"I suppose that a stage performance is really what we are planning," Lizzie agreed. "I want to have an effective entrance, and I should like very much to be noticed for at least the first few minutes I am there."

"Oh, I have not the *least* doubt that you will be!" Lady Thalia assured her. Her horror had faded and had quickly become fascination. "But why, Lizzie, *why?* For whom are you performing?"

"For Matthew," she replied simply. "And, at least in part, for myself."

"I suppose that you wish to set Matthew's back up once again," said Lady Thalia, "and I am *certain* that I understand why you wish to do so. But in what way is this for *yourself*, my dear?"

"The gypsies make me think of everything that I am not—wild and free and careless of what anybody thinks of them. I should like to be that way for just one evening, I think."

She paused a moment before she went on. "When we go back to England, I shall more than likely have to marry someone who will accept a dowerless girl or, if I think that I cannot face that, I mean to be a governess.

I thought perhaps you might be able to help me find a position, ma'am."

Lady Thalia, who had been unaware of how serious the family's financial straits were, sat silent for a moment before answering. Lizzie suddenly looked, she thought, quite desolate, and she made up her mind to think of some means to help her without injuring her pride.

"But of *course* I will help you, Lizzie, if that should be what you decide to do—but we need not think of that until later. Now we have *much* to do if we are to have our costumes ready."

"But you are still not well, Lady Thalia—and the doctor told you to rest. You may not be able to attend the ball."

"I *am* resting! As for not attending, that is a nonsensical notion! Of *course* I shall attend! And I feel *immeasurably* better now that we have your costume to prepare! You were absolutely correct that it is good to focus on something cheerful."

Lizzie started to protest, but Lady Thalia wagged a warning finger at her. "I shall *not* get out of bed, Lizzie— I promise. I will simply send for the dressmaker and tell her what your plan is for your costume. I have been an *extraordinarily* good customer and I am certain she will come to us."

She eyed the red cotton lying on the bedcover as she called for Beavers to bring her travel desk so that she could write a note to the dressmaker. "A *wonderful* color, naturally, but the cloth is far too coarse. I shall send a sample of it to Fräulein Schlosser, and she can bring some material that she thinks will serve. After all, a gypsy's skirts *must* move gracefully."

Lizzie started to observe that the gypsy girl's skirts moved like silk, even though they were made of cotton, but she caught herself in time. She could not let slip that she had gone to see the gypsies in the company of Mr. Andronikos. She wanted to do nothing to overset the present happy mood, for Lady Thalia appeared to be reviving quickly now that she had a new project to think about. By the time Fräulein Schlosser appeared, Beavers had dressed her hair and given her a fresh cap and dressing jacket. She was still pale, but she was once again animated.

Fräulein Schlosser, always appreciative of an excellent customer, entered into the spirit of the thing immediately, and Lizzie's costume was soon planned—a peacock glory of red, gold, and green. After the dressmaker had left, they both heaved a sigh of relief, but Lady Thalia was still studying her speculatively.

"And, after you arrive at the Riding School, do you plan to take off your slippers and go barefoot?" she asked. "No matter how cold it is?"

"Well, it would rather spoil the effect to be wearing slippers, don't you think? And I'm certain that I can whirl about more safely on my bare feet than in satin slippers with smooth leather soles. I should kill myself outright."

"Very possibly," Lady Thalia conceded. "However, if you take to the dance floor in your bare feet, you shall very probably be killed in a slower, more painful manner."

"That is true," agreed Lizzie. "We shall think about it. At least we don't have to bother with masks. I should certainly fall while turning if I couldn't see."

"Yes, and Matthew would not know at a glance that it was you in the gypsy costume. My Cleopatra would be ruined as well. Too often the effect of fancy dress is quite destroyed by the addition of a mask."

The night of the fancy dress ball was clear but cold, and Lizzie was deeply grateful that she was at least wearing slippers in the coach instead of going barefoot. Her costume had arrived, looking as wildly exotic as Fräulein

Schlosser could manage to make it, and Lizzie had arrayed herself in it happily. She had brushed her dark hair until it shone and then floated loose over her shoulders, and arranged all of the gold jewelry, so much showier than anything she would ordinarily wear. She was even wearing a little rouge, and Lady Thalia, who was most definitely wearing paint, had outlined her eyes in black, as she had her own, using a brush and a dark paste that she had had Beavers concoct for her. Being Cleopatra, she had outlined her own eyes very heavily, and she wore a long wig, as brilliantly black as a raven's wing. Her white gown was narrow and thin to the point of indecency and she wore a handsome three-strand necklace made in the Egyptian fashion. On her feet were trim white sandals.

She and Lady Thalia both wore opera cloaks over their costumes and planned to cast them off at the last possible moment so that their outfits would have the strongest theatrical effect possible. They had agreed that when they came to the head of the wide staircase that descended to the ballroom floor, Lady Thalia would be announced first, and she would proceed halfway down before Lizzie was announced.

"After all, my dear, you can't expect me to try to enter after you give *your* performance," she had told Lizzie earlier.

"I would suggest that I wait until you are all the way to the bottom of the stairs. Then, should I fall, at least I shall not take you with me."

Lady Thalia looked thoughtful. "A very prudent suggestion," she agreed. "I have *no* wish to have a broken leg."

With this encouraging remark, Lizzie grew even more nervous. Mr. Andronikos was waiting for them, and he took Lady Thalia's cloak first and they watched as she was announced. Most of the names could not be heard over the music and conversation, of course, but people frequently turned to see who was entering and to inspect their costumes. When Lady Thalia made her way languorously down the staircase, fanning herself with a large palm leaf and looking regally over the people as though they were indeed her subjects, a brief hush fell over them and then there was a buzz of conversation and a brief splattering of applause. Lady Thalia acknowledged it with the very slightest inclination of her head.

Swallowing hard, Lizzie handed Mr. Andronikos her cloak—and her slippers—and stepped to the head of the stairway to listen for her name. The two gypsy fiddlers stood close behind her.

"Please don't let me trip and fall," she was thinking wildly, looking down at the sea of faces below. Unfortunately, Lady Thalia's impressive entrance had attracted their attention and Lizzie was already being scrutinized.

"You look beautiful, Miss Lancaster," said Mr. Andronikos softly—but she could scarcely hear his words.

"Focus, Miss Lancaster, focus!"

She looked up sharply at the sound of Mr. Thoreau's reassuringly crisp voice. He was smiling at her. "Focus outward and you'll be quite all right. Don't think about yourself. Think about the music."

Just then her name was announced and the gypsy fiddlers began to play, making their way gracefully down the steps behind her. Anyone who had not been paying attention at that point immediately turned around to see where the music was coming from. Even some of the members of the orchestra seated at the end of the gallery stopped playing to listen and watch.

Fortunately, however, Lizzie saw none of this. As the music began, she did what Mr. Thoreau had told her to do—she lost herself in it. She had always thought gypsy music the most beguiling she had ever heard, and tonight—just for one night—she was a part of it. Remembering the movements of the gypsy girl, she had been practicing faithfully, and now she whirled down the steps, bending and turning in time to the music, a single rose in her hand. When she reached the foot of the stairway, she was greeted with a burst of applause, and someone called, "Throw the rose! Throw the rose!" And so she tossed it lightly into the crowd, and a handsome young man caught it with a crow of delight.

The gypsy fiddlers melted from the scene before she had even had the chance to realize that they were gone, and Lizzie found herself surrounded by admirers. She could not see Mr. Thoreau or Mr. Andronikos, but when the young man with her rose requested the next dance, she laughed and told him that she had best find her slippers first. Heeding Lady Thalia's warning, she had decided that barefoot dancing in the ballroom was both too cold and too dangerous among so many feet shod in leather. He escorted her to the top of the stairs once more, and there they located her cloak and slippers, still safely held by her friend. The young man retired to a discreet distance so that Lizzie could speak to the holder of the cloak and slippers privately.

"Thank you so much! You are the dearest of men!" she told Mr. Andonikos as he returned her slippers. Without thinking twice about it, she stood on tiptoe and kissed him on the cheek, and he smiled at her, his eyes glowing.

"For that, dear lady, I would swim oceans!"

"You will dance with me tonight, will you not?" she pleaded. "Promise that you will dance with me before you leave tonight—George." After his friendship and the success of the evening, it seemed inadequate to call him

Mr. Andronikos—besides, she thought, tonight she was a gypsy.

He suddenly grew serious and took her hand, raising it to his lips. "I promise that I will dance with you before I leave," he promised gravely. "Nothing could keep me from it, dear Lizzie."

"Well, this is quite delightful, Lizzie!" said Matthew, his tone indicating that it was anything but delightful. "First you make a spectacle of yourself, and then you come up here and fling yourself at this—this—" He paused, searching for words.

"Thank you, Matthew," she replied with composure. "I am glad that you enjoyed my entrance. I was a little fearful of falling on the steps, but Mr. Thoreau's advice got me through it, and—" Here she paused to glance at Mr. Andronikos and smile. "And George helped to see me through it all."

"That is exactly what I hear! Mr. Andronikos appears to have been very busy indeed!" retorted Matthew, giving his full attention to that gentleman. "I have heard from reliable sources, Andronikos, that you took Miss Lancaster away from the ball last night, and that you took her to a tavern unsuitable for ladies—or indeed for any person of reputation. In fact, you took her to a place where she could have found herself in a great deal of trouble!"

Mr. Andronikos shrugged. "You are making too much of a small matter, Mr. Webster. It was a necessary trip."

"Yes, indeed it was, Matthew," said Lizzie. "George was helping me because I begged him to do so, so pray don't be cross with him when you know that I am the one who has made you angry."

"Lizzie, would you please stop calling him by his Christian name as though he were your brother or—"

"Or my former fiancé?" she asked innocently. "George

has become my good friend, Matthew, so you may as well stop behaving in such an odiously toplofty manner. It really does not suit you."

She took George's arm and smiled at the young man waiting for her, who hurried over and took her other arm. Together they escorted her down to the dance floor, leaving Matthew to stew alone. In a moment she could see him pacing back and forth along the gallery, trying to walk off his anger.

Lizzie and the young man with the rose were midway through their dance when she saw a latecomer making an entrance. At first glance, she thought it was a young officer in the Hussars, apparently a member of Matthew's former regiment, when she suddenly had a clearer view. It was a lady—dressed impeccably in the Hussar jacket, cape, and breeches, her boots shining in the candlelight. She had removed her hat, and her fair curls fell loose. It was Miss Blackwell.

Lizzie glanced about quickly to see if she could see Matthew—and she did. He was standing frozen in the gallery, watching his fiancée descend the stairs, nattily attired in uniform. Dressing in breeches was a behavior confined to actresses, one considered far too fast for a lady. He looked stunned as he watched her, and for a moment Lizzie could almost feel sorry for him. But then she remembered his sharp criticism of her own behavior, and the unfavorable manner in which he had compared her to Miss Blackwell, and she hardened her heart. This was a lesson that Matthew very well deserved.

There was a light smattering of applause that died almost at birth, followed by a low murmur of comment, but Miss Blackwell continued her descent, unperturbed. Lizzie could see that Matthew was hurrying down to join her. That, she thought happily, would be a most interesting conversation to overhear. With that thought in mind, she excused herself from her partner, promising that she would be back in just a moment, and strolled in the direction of what was clearly an animated discussion. They were so entirely absorbed in each other—or at least Matthew was so entirely absorbed in what he was saying to Miss Blackwell—that she was able to come quite close before either of them noticed her. Matthew's face was flushed, and Miss Blackwell's rose-petal complexion was a little paler than usual.

"Well, if it isn't little Miss Lancaster, just passing us by chance!" she exclaimed as Lizzie neared. "Have you come to hear my scolding?"

Ignoring Matthew, she pulled the St. George medal from beneath her jacket so that it gleamed in the candlelight. "You see that my costume as a soldier is quite complete, ma'am. I even have my own talisman against danger." She left the medal dangling outside the jacket.

"That was unnecessary, Teresa," Matthew said in a low voice, then turned to Lizzie with misery in his eyes. "I am so very sorry, Lizzie. I intended to tell you about the medal, but I couldn't bring myself to do it."

"And why should it matter to me, Matthew?" Lizzie asked evenly. "I gave it to you for protection, and if you choose to give it to someone else, then that is your own affair."

Miss Blackwell smiled at her knowingly. "And I understand that you gave it to Matthew because you fancied yourself engaged to him, Miss Lancaster. Matthew told me all about it. What a pity you were so naïve."

"Stop that immediately, Teresa!" said Matthew furiously, and then turned to Lizzie. "That is not the way it was, so don't listen to her for a moment. I am so very sorry, Lizzie—if you would just let me explain."

"I believe that I understand well enough, Matthew—and again, I wish you happy. As I told you earlier, I think that you and Miss Blackwell will suit very well."

As she turned to walk away, Mr. Thoreau stood there waiting. Without a word, she took his arm and they left the dance floor, abandoning Lizzie's partner to his fate.

"What a fool I have been to think for a moment that he would return to being the Matthew I knew simply because I came here to find him! I have always fancied myself intelligent, but I see now that I lack all common sense and judgment! Miss Blackwell was quite correct when she said that I am naïve!"

"Most of us like to think that what we want is possible," replied Mr. Thoreau calmly. "But you have seen now, Miss Lancaster, what you have known all along—that we all change and that there is no going back. Even if he left Miss Blackwell, he would not be the same Matthew that you loved, any more than you would be the same Lizzie. It cannot be."

Lizzie realized with horror that great tears were sliding down her cheeks, and obediently followed Mr. Thoreau as he led her over to the privacy of a small grouping of orange trees and palms. He pulled out his handkerchief and patted her cheeks softly.

"Oh, pray don't do that, Mr. Thoreau. You will ruin your handkerchief! I am wearing paint, as you see, and it will make a tremendous mess." She caught herself mid-sob. "And I must look frightful with all of the paint running!"

"You could never look frightful to me, Miss Lancaster," he said, still patting her face dry. "I do have one criticism of you, however."

"What is it?" she demanded, hiccupping this time as she tried to hold back another sob.

"It does not seem quite fair to me that Andronikos, whom you have known for a much shorter period of time, now has the right to call you Lizzie, while I, whom you have known for ever so much longer—"

"Three weeks longer," she inserted.

"May only call you Miss Lancaster," he finished, ignoring her interruption.

"Please do call me Lizzie," she said, smiling in spite of herself. "And I shall call you Daniel."

"Agreed," he said, bowing. "And now, Lizzie, what would you like to do? Do you care to dance? To walk about for a little? To sit and talk?"

She managed a smile. "I should like to dance, of course. After all, Daniel, for tonight at least, I am a gypsy! I will not care a fig what anyone thinks of me!"

"Then dance we shall," he agreed, and they proceeded to do exactly that. Although it was not considered proper for a young lady to dance more than twice with the same partner, she and Mr. Thoreau broke that rule to the tune of several dances. Even when many others wished to dance with Lizzie, the pair smiled brightly at the interlopers and declared the next dance taken. Even Matthew—or perhaps, most especially Matthew—who appeared at last, was blithely refused.

"Please don't make a further spectacle of yourself because you are angry with me," he said to her in a low voice, ignoring Mr. Thoreau.

"Tonight, Matthew, I am—as you can clearly see—a gypsy! So I shall do just as I please!"

And Mr. Thoreau swept her away into the next waltz, leaving him standing forlornly beside a potted palm. Across the dance floor, they could see Miss Blackwell dancing with Mr. Mansfield. She too appeared to have danced the whole evening, but not at all with her fiancé.

They could see that Lady Thalia, at the moment, was happily engrossed in conversation with Talleyrand and his niece.

"I believe that you are universally admired, Lizzie," observed Mr. Thoreau, for she was the focus of many admiring—and some envious—glances.

"Not universal," she corrected him. Before her spirits began to sink at the thought of Matthew, however, and to show that she was able to focus outward as he had taught her, she smiled and added, "But very close to it, I believe. It must be immensely gratifying to possess a gypsy spirit all of the year."

Mr. Thoreau did not reply immediately because another gentleman arrived to request the pleasure of her company. At a glance from her, however, he once again declined to yield his place, and the newcomer, defeated, bowed and retired to seek another partner.

Indeed, Mr. Thoreau did not yield his place to another gentleman until Mr. Andronikos appeared beside them. "I have come to claim my dance, dear Lizzie," he said, bowing deeply. "That is, if Daniel will allow me to do so."

Lizzie made a deep curtsey and smiled at him. "I am glad that you remembered to see me before you leave, George," she said lightly. "I should not wish to be forgotten."

He exchanged a grave glance with Thoreau, before taking her hand and saying, still with an unaccustomed touch of gravity, "I shall never forget you, Miss Lizzie Lancaster."

Once the music began, he seemed much more himself, light in movement and manner. "Your evening has been a great success, Lizzie," he observed. "If you were to dance with all the men who wish to be your partner, you would still be dancing a sennight from now—and like the princesses in the old fairy tale, you would wear out countless pairs of slippers."

Lizzie laughed, thinking yet again what a pleasure it was to be with a man who enjoyed life so intensely. Daniel Thoreau took pleasure in life, too, but it was a steady, sensible pleasure. For him there were no peaks of joy or valleys of despair. For George Andronikos it was otherwise, although the peaks of joy appeared to predominate.

"You exaggerate again, but I thank you for the pretty sentiment. And I must thank you again, dear George, for helping me have this delightful evening. I should never have managed without you."

"But of course you would have managed, Lizzie—you will always manage. I merely happened to be the one at hand who could become a part of your plan." He smiled down into her eyes and lifted the hand he was holding to his lips. "Doing so has given me great joy."

"My brother is named George," she said suddenly. "I had not thought of it before, but in some ways you remind me of him."

"I am desolated, of course, to be compared to your brother—for how may I be your sweetheart if that is so?" he responded. "But I am honored as well, for you feel deep affection for him, do you not?"

"I do indeed," she answered, knowing that it was true, no matter how upset she had become with him for some of the things he had done. "He is always charming and always kind."

Mr. Andronikos inclined his head in a brief nod. "And I must be grateful, Lizzie, if you believe that I possess such qualities."

"You do, of course," she answered, "for you make it

always a pleasure to be with you and you have shown me great kindness. Unfortunately, however, George lacks something very important that you and Daniel both possess."

"And what might that be?" he inquired with interest.

"Focus," she said. "You serve a greater good than your own needs, and Daniel turns his attention outward to the world about him, as he has tried to teach me to do—but neither of you places your own personal interests before everything else."

"And your brother George, he does this?" asked Mr. Andronikos gravely. "He thinks first of himself?"

"Always," she sighed. "Or almost always, it seems. And I do not know how to help him change that. Indeed, I don't think he wishes to change!"

"Possibly not," he answered seriously, "but it may be that life will teach him otherwise."

Lizzie shook her head. "Perhaps it may happen, George, but I have little hope of it. When I have looked about me here in Vienna, I have observed that many people are just like my brother."

Mr. Andronikos nodded. "All too often that is true. But do you know what is amazing, dear Lizzie?"

She looked at him inquiringly, waiting for him to answer his own question.

"That sometimes, most surprisingly, they are not! Is it not amazing that there are indeed also many who place something or someone above their own personal good? We must find that encouraging, Lizzie."

She sighed. "Yes, I know that you are correct, but I confess that it is lowering when I reflect that I am not one of them. I certainly have no business criticizing my brother. After all, what have I been thinking of save my own pleasure?"

He shrugged lightly. "That is not necessarily such a bad thing. After all, it does no one any good to sit in sackcloth and ashes and moan of the end of the world. Even if you do no more than take pleasure in the day—and share that pleasure with others—is that not a gift to them?"

She thought about it a moment. "Well, I suppose that is true—if, that is, you do indeed *share* that pleasure with others. I'm not at all certain that I do so."

"But you do, Lizzie. You have shared it with me and with Daniel and Lady Thalia—and undoubtedly with others that you are not even aware of."

She looked doubtful, so he continued. "Think of it in this way, Lizzie. Have you not stopped to buy hot chestnuts and gotten a cheerful greeting from the man who handed them to you? Or passed a stranger on the street who smiled at you?"

"Well, naturally, I have but—"

"Then you have seen people who were sharing their pleasure in the day with others—just as you do without even realizing it. If the vendor had spoken to you rudely or if the stranger had frowned at you or looked weighed down with the troubles of the world, your response would not have been the same."

"No," she conceded, "but it seems a very small thing, nonetheless."

"Lizzie, life is composed of all those small things! It is not the momentous things that compose our lives—it is all the little ones!"

She was not completely convinced, but she smiled at him as the dance ended and they made their way back toward Mr. Thoreau. "You are always a pleasure, Mr. Andronikos—George, I mean. I always look forward to seeing you."

"And I to seeing you, dear lady," he said, kissing her hand once more, "but I fear that I shall not see you again, perhaps for a very long time."

"Why not?" she demanded, alarmed at his sudden return to gravity. "Are you leaving?"

He nodded, but before he could speak again, she said in a low voice, "Paris! You are going to Paris, are you not?"

Again he nodded. "But I shall always think of you, dear Lizzie, and thinking of you shall give me the greatest pleasure. Most of all, I shall think of you dancing down the steps tonight, with a gypsy in your soul."

She shook her head, suddenly completely deflated. "There is no gypsy, George. Just plain Lizzie Lancaster."

"Never plain!" he insisted. "If you cannot wear the colors of the gypsy every day, you can wear them in your soul. You have too much to give to allow yourself to become bleak in spirit."

"I shall remember," she said, trying to smile. "And I know that thinking of you shall always bring me joy."

"Dear Lizzie," he said softly, and bent and kissed her tenderly on the lips, ignoring the people around them. And then he turned and left, weaving his way through the crowd.

Mr. Thoreau took her arm and looked down at her.

"No more dancing, Daniel," she said. "Not tonight."

Seventeen

It was odd, Lady Thalia thought, that the absence of one flirtatious young man, no matter how charming, should have left such a void. Lizzie had seemed very low in the days following the departure of Mr. Andronikos for Paris. She said that he had business there—more of the business that he and Mr. Thoreau were involved in, no doubt. Some sort of import-export affairs, she suspected. Mr. Thoreau seemed to feel his loss as well. Of course, they had been friends since childhood, but she would have thought Mr. Thoreau would have been grateful to have an entire room to himself now instead of being obliged to share it with Mr. Andronikos. She sighed. Her health was much better now, but her own spirits were a little low as well. Soon she would be in no better a state than Lizzie.

Suddenly remembering what she had planned to do about Lizzie, she rang for Beavers to bring her traveling desk. A careful and tactful questioning of Lizzie had elicited more information about the Lancasters' situation—and about young George's gaming problem. She had pondered it all for a while, wondering just what she could do without appearing to help them, and she had finally struck upon a plan, one that she thought proudly that no one else would have been likely to think of. At first she could not see just how she could bring it about, but then she had thought of Timothy Holywell. He spent much of his time in London, he was clever and sophisticated and discreet—and he owed her a favor after not forewarning her of the travel conditions between Paris and Vienna.

She wrote a very long and carefully detailed letter to Timothy Holywell and sent it off immediately. If this did not work, she would think of something else.

Lizzie had been thinking about what Mr. Andronikos had said to her on their last evening together—and trying very hard not to think of his joining the French army and preparing seriously for battle. She had been doing her best to assume a cheerful façade, but she knew, both from the way Lady Thalia and Beavers watched her so carefully and from the greater frequency of Mr. Thoreau's calls, that she had convinced no one. She was indeed trying, but she could not feel her usual self. Everything, including herself, seemed dull.

Mr. Thoreau was present when a letter arrived, accompanied by an oversize bouquet of red and white roses, tied in broad blue ribbon.

He grinned at her. "Have you any doubt, Lizzie, just who has sent those to you?"

Lady Thalia had grown accustomed to the two calling one another by their Christian names, but she had begged them to be discreet and, when in public, to be more formal. As soon as she had once again recovered from hearing Mr. Thoreau say "Lizzie" so casually, she focused on what he had been saying and upon the bouquet itself.

"Why, Lizzie! That is *precisely* like the one you received

in Paris!" she exclaimed. "How lovely they are! Beavers, do put them in water immediately!"

Beavers bore them away, and Mr. Thoreau watched Lizzie with amusement. She was staring at the letter in her lap as though it might snap at her.

"What is it, Lizzie?" he inquired. "Are you afraid of what your captain of the Dragoons might have to say?"

"No. No, of course not," she replied, giving herself a little shake and taking the letter in her hand. She broke the blue seal and read swiftly.

"He is here, of course. We knew that must be so from the roses—but he says that he hopes that we will be attending the Carrousel tonight. He will be riding in it."

Thoreau gave a low whistle. "It seems that your captain must be quite an important fellow, Lizzie."

"He must indeed!" exclaimed Lady Thalia. "Why, there are only twenty-four riders in the entire Carrousel!"

"And they all must be from noble families and must have proven their courage in battle," added Thoreau.

Preparations for the Carrousel had been going on for weeks, and it was to be presented in the best medieval tournament fashion possible. It was to be held in the Hofburg's Spanish Riding School, and the event was the focus of great anticipation.

"And what else does your captain say, Lizzie?" Mr. Thoreau inquired.

"He writes that he has come to take the place of his cousin, who broke his leg during a hunt and so is unable to participate. And he also writes that each of the 'knights' who rides in the Carrousel has his own chosen lady among the audience, and that he would like for me to be his."

Mr. Thoreau raised his eyebrows and even Lady Thalia

looked taken aback. "This is more serious than we had thought, Lizzie. What will you say to him?"

To their surprise, Lizzie laughed and shook her head. "He tells me that I am not to feel that I have committed myself in any way should I choose to accept, and he reminds me that he knows no other lady here so, if I refuse, he will have none."

"I think that is *not* the case, Lizzie, no matter what he says. I *personally* know of dozens of women who would kill to be chosen," said Lady Thalia. "I myself would not mind it at all."

"I don't imagine it could do any harm, and it would seem ungracious to refuse," said Lizzie slowly.

"I would say that he has made it impossible for you to refuse without feeling that way," observed Mr. Thoreau a little dryly, and Lizzie looked at him in surprise. "Just consider, Lizzie. How did he find where you are staying? He went to great lengths to find you."

"And just in time, too," added Lady Thalia approvingly. "It's very clever of him to have discovered your direction."

"And so what answer will you send him?" asked Mr. Thoreau, watching her face.

"I believe I shall accept," she said. "It seems so unkind not to do so. He writes that his man is waiting for my answer, and that if I accept, he would like for me to send a scarf so that he may wear it tonight."

She rose and walked toward the door. "If you will excuse me, I must go and write him an answer immediately—and find a scarf that I may send."

Lady Thalia and Mr. Thoreau looked at one another for a moment.

"Well, it is all very flattering," she said.

"Yes, Captain LaSalle was most attentive to her in Paris."

"But you do not see any real harm in it, do you, Mr. Thoreau?"

He shrugged. "I daresay there is no danger of her losing her heart to him in the course of the evening."

Lady Thalia laughed. "Of course there is not! Are *you* planning to attend?"

He shook his head and grinned. "There is not a ticket available in Vienna, so I shall stay at home and think long thoughts."

"Nonsense! You *must* come with us. Lord Danvers now has the influenza that plagued me, and we would be delighted if you would take his place tonight. You simply must *not* miss what they are saying will be the spectacle of the century. And afterward there is to be a supper and a grand ball."

To her pleasure, he accepted and arrived to escort them that evening with his usual promptness. As they entered and took their places, he glanced at Lady Thalia and nodded. "You were correct, ma'am. Before the Carrousel even begins, it is already the spectacle of the century."

And so it was. All of the members of royalty—the emperors, kings, queens, princes, princesses, grand dukes, and grand duchesses—were seated on a raised dais, and their collective splendor alone would have set the evening off from all others. The diplomats were seated on one side of the galleries and the nobility on the other. The white elegance of the Riding School itself, with its forty-six Corinthian columns and magnificent coffered ceiling, made a memorable backdrop for the pageantry of the proceedings.

Lizzie watched it all, concentrating intently because she had felt herself growing more and more distant from everything that was taking place. She had written to Captain LaSalle and sent him a green scarf, she had eaten dinner and dressed carefully for the Carrousel and the subsequent ball, but she had done everything in what seemed to her a dreamlike state. So now she attempted to force herself to focus.

After the paladins entered the arena, attired in costumes from the fifteen hundreds, their horses handsomely caparisoned, they arranged themselves for the first exercise. For this, they tilted their lances at rings hung from ropes around the arena, attempting of course to put the lance through each of the rings. It all looked like something from a painting or a storybook, and many had been consulted as the Carrousel was planned.

As she watched the riders move through the sets of exercises—charging wooden heads mounted on posts and cutting them off with a single blow, slashing apples in half with their sabers, charging one another in an attempt to unseat the opponent—everything seemed to blur into one vivid whirlpool of movement. She could hear the military music playing, but it seemed to her that it grew more and more distant.

As the Carrousel drew to a close, she heard Mr. Thoreau say, "Lizzie, are you quite all right?"

"Of course I am," she had replied. "Just overcome by all of this."

He and Lady Thalia had contented themselves with her answer. Together, they had risen and walked down a corridor decked with flowers and orange trees to the hall where supper was to be served. As she walked, it seemed to Lizzie that the velvet gown that she was wearing had grown heavier and heavier. To her relief, they were finally seated, and minstrels moved among them, playing ballads from the days of knights and ladies.

"Lizzie, I saw you at the Carrousel, but I did not have the opportunity to come and talk to you. I have wanted to see you for days, but I didn't have the courage to face you."

She heard her name and looked up to see Matthew standing there—or at least wavering there. How suitable, she thought to herself, that the minstrel nearest them should begin the strains of "Greensleeves."

"Lizzie? Did you hear me? I should like very much to talk with you if you would just come and walk with me for minute or two."

"Yes, I heard you, Matthew," she said slowly. "I was just listening to the song."

"To the song?" he said blankly, and then he listened for a moment and flushed. "Yes, I hear it, too. Come walk with me and we will talk after the song finishes."

At that moment, there was a new arrival, and the impressive figure of Captain LaSalle bore down upon them.

"Mademoiselle Lancaster," he said reverently, going down on one knee beside her chair and taking her hand, "I am eternally grateful for your kindness in sending me your scarf to wear. It brought me good fortune." He kissed her hand and then held it to his heart. "You have honored me greatly, mademoiselle."

"Not at all, captain," she returned gently. "I am the one who is honored." It was curious, she thought. She could hear herself speaking, but she seemed quite far away from it all. And it felt as though she was speaking very slowly, but everyone appeared to understand her.

She turned toward Matthew. "Captain LaSalle, I should like to present Mr. Matthew Webster. Matthew, this is Captain François LaSalle."

LaSalle rose and the two men bowed stiffly to one another. Then LaSalle turned back to her and bowed. "Miss Lancaster, I cannot stay just now, but I wished to request the first dance with you—and, if you will allow it, the rest of the dances as well."

Lizzie smiled. She knew that because she felt her cheeks lift slightly. "Of course, Captain." She had meant to add that they would see about the other dances after the first was over, but she could see that she had not, because he kissed her hand, said something to her that she did not quite take in, bowed to the others, turned, and walked away.

"Lizzie!" she heard Matthew gasp in protest. "Please don't do this again!"

"Oh, Matthew!" she said slowly, as though she had quite forgotten him. "Your walk."

She rose from her chair and took a step toward him but, as she did so, it seemed to her that he—and the rest of the world around her—suddenly receded from her at a shocking rate, and she felt herself falling.

Eighteen

Over the next weeks, Lizzie lay, as they say, "at death's door," and even after the doctor had determined to his own satisfaction that the worst was behind her, he shook his head when Lady Thalia demanded absolute assurance that there would be no relapse. Influenza had brought death to more than one in Vienna during these winter months. Helpless, Lady Thalia and Beavers took turns at her bedside, and Mr. Thoreau and Matthew called daily to ask about her progress, as did Captain LaSalle until his leave was over and his presence required once more in Paris.

"I pray for her good health, madame. Please tell her so when she is herself again."

"I will indeed, sir," Lady Thalia assured him. He had been a faithful caller, begging her to give him something to do that might help Lizzie. There was, of course, very little that anyone could do except pray, as Captain LaSalle had said. He also continued to deliver fresh roses each time the last bouquet had begun to fade. Upon taking his leave of Lady Thalia, he had assured her that they would still be delivered regularly, even in his absence.

As for Lizzie, she lived for weeks in a strange sort of half-world, inhabited by real people and dreams, merging together in fantasies that were sometimes pleasing, sometimes frightening—but always fantastic. In one, she married Captain LaSalle, and at their wedding, everyone threw violets at them as they left the church. As he helped her into their carriage to leave, she looked back at the crowd and into the unsmiling eyes of Napoleon Bonaparte, a violet in his lapel. In another, she was home at the Lodge, watching out the window for Matthew. Suddenly she noticed her hand, which looked odd. Looking in the glass at her dressing table, she saw that her dark hair was grey and her face lined with wrinkles. In still another, she married Daniel Thoreau and traveled around the world with him, giving money to groups that were planning revolutions. As the kaleidoscope shifted, she was a gypsy, dancing in the streets, and Teresa Blackwell, her hand securely on Matthew's arm, tossed her a coin. Then she was at the Carrousel once more, and instead of the wooden head on a post, George Andronikos stood there in the middle of the arena, and the paladin was bearing down upon him with a sword.

She had opened her eyes many times during her illness, but those caring for her had been able to tell that she was not herself, for the people she saw and spoke to were not present in the room with them. There were periods when she appeared to be resting normally, and they would grow hopeful, but then the troubled times would return. So it was a very happy moment when she finally opened her eyes late one January afteroon, saw Lady Thalia sitting there with her book, and said quite distinctly, "May I have a cup of tea, please?"

Lady Thalia looked at her, shut her book, leaned closer to her, and said, "Lizzie? Is that truly *you?*"

Lizzie looked at her helplessly. Lady Thalia was looking at her so intently that she feared something was wrong. "Yes," she said, wondering who else she might be. "Are you quite well, Lady Thalia?"

To her shock, she saw that tears were running down her friend's cheeks, but she was smiling.

"Yes, I am doing *wonderfully* well now that you have come back to us, Lizzie!" Losing all semblance of dignity, she ignored the bell cord and ran to the door calling, "Beavers! Henry! *Someone*! Lizzie has requested some tea!"

When Beavers hurried in with a tray for her, they helped Lizzie to sit up in bed. It was surprising, she thought, that she could not do that herself. Then Beavers brushed her hair and sponged her face and neck before setting the tray on her lap.

She discovered that she needed help even to lift the cup to her lips, and she looked at Lady Thalia in puzzlement. "I must have been sick," she said. "I thought that I had just had a nightmare."

"And so you did," replied Lady Thalia. "A *very* long one. But we are delighted that it is over, Lizzie dear."

"So it *was* a nightmare?" asked Lizzie. "How long did I sleep?"

"It was a nightmare caused by sickness, Lizzie. You have been sick for a very long time."

Lizzie's eyes had alighted on the vase of roses near her bed, and she smiled. "Not really so very long then. The roses are still fresh."

Lady Thalia and Beavers looked at one another. "That isn't the *same* bouquet of roses, dear."

"Captain LaSalle brought another? That was very kind of him." She thought for a minute, trying to remember. "I was going to dance with him."

Lady Thalia leaned toward her encouragingly. "Yes, yes, you were, but you got sick before you could do so."

Lizzie's brow creased as she tried to bring back that evening. "I remember bits of the Carrousel," she said. "And how very heavy my gown was, and how far away everyone seemed." She paused a moment, thinking. "Matthew! I was going to talk with Matthew!"

Lady Thalia nodded. "That is when you collapsed, Lizzie. Matthew carried you to the carriage, and he helped me to get you home while Mr. Thoreau went for a doctor."

Lizzie lay back on the pillows, turning her head from side to side as she tried to remember more. Beside Lady Thalia was a small table with a pitcher of water, a glass, Lizzie's medicine—and her gold music box.

"Why is my music box there?" she asked. She usually kept it on her dressing table. Even with all the heartache over Matthew, she had not been able to make herself put it away.

"Because that was the *one* thing that seemed to calm you, my dear, when you were at your worst. Beavers or I would open it and you would grow still and listen to it."

Lizzie felt a tear rolling down her cheek. "'Greensleeves,'" she said. "The minstrel was playing it and Matthew was going to listen to it with me before we talked."

Lady Thalia nodded.

Lizzie lay quiet for a few minutes, still puzzling things out. Suddenly she asked, "Have you been with me all the time I have been sick?"

Lady Thalia nodded again. "Beavers and I have taken turns. One of us slept while the other watched."

"But how dreadful I feel for what I have done to you, Lady Thalia! You came to Vienna to see everything that was happening and I have made you miss some of the events you were so looking forward to and live in a sickroom instead!"

Lady Thalia shooed away the comment with a wave of her hand. "Nonsense! This was *much* more important than any party or ball could be—and, of course, Catholic homes do not have dances during Advent, so things grew much tamer then."

Lizzie stared at her. "Is it already Advent?" she asked. "That was several days away when I took ill."

Lady Thalia looked slightly uncomfortable, but then she leaned close to Lizzie and took her hand. "You have been sick quite a *long* time, my dear. Advent is over."

"Advent is over?" she asked, astonished. "And Christmas?"

"Over," replied Lady Thalia. "As is New Year's." She smiled. "Twelfth Night has only just gone, though."

Lizzie went to sleep almost immediately, but they were relieved to see that it was now a peaceful sleep. Henry had hurried around for the doctor when she had first awakened, and he arrived after she had fallen asleep. He examined her quickly, then turned to Lady Thalia with a look of satisfaction.

"She has no temperature, her pulse is steady, and she appears to be breathing easily. If what you say about her rational behavior is true, then I believe we may safely say that Miss Lancaster is on the road to recovery."

He went on to caution them that it would be a long recovery, and that she should by no means rush it. Lady Thalia, looking down at her, could only agree. Lizzie was still deathly pale, and she was so thin that she looked as if she could be broken like a twig. Together with Beavers, she planned a nourishing diet for the invalid, one that would help her to build her strength. They agreed to abandon barley water for a nourishing tea caudle, and Beavers, who had strong Scottish ties, firmly advocated the introduction of porridge onto the menu. Now, too, they would be able to gradually abandon the broths they had been spooning into her mouth each day, and work her gently toward more substantial fare.

For the next fortnight, Lizzie did little but sleep, but it was a restful, healing sleep. During the brief periods when she was awake, she ate and asked an occasional question, often drifting off to sleep in the middle of both. Once she awoke to see Daniel Thoreau seated beside her, but she decided that must have been a dream, for when she looked again, he had gone.

"*Was* Daniel here to see me?" she asked the next day. "I rather thought he was, but then I thought I might have been dreaming."

"He was *most* definitely here, my dear. Of course, he has been here to call *every* day since you took ill—and he has been *wonderful* about getting the doctor and the medicines and being here as moral support. Yesterday he asked to see for himself how you are doing."

"You must thank him for me, Lady Thalia."

"You will be able to thank him yourself this afternoon if you feel well enough for a real caller."

Lizzie shook her head. "Perhaps tomorrow," she said. "I must have a bath and wash my hair—although I know I shall probably drown if Beavers doesn't help me. Doing just that will take all my energy. Tomorrow I shall feel more like receiving a caller."

Lady Thalia smiled. "Now I know that you *are* truly getting better, Lizzie. Worrying about your appearance is a *very* good sign, indeed."

"Have I had any other callers while I was ill?" Lizzie asked hesitantly.

"More than I could *possibly* count," Lady Thalia assured her. "*Droves* of young men that you have danced with at the balls have come, most of them with nosegays.

If you walk into the drawing room, you will see that we look like a greenhouse. The doctor said not to put them in here, but I *insisted* that the captain's roses be where you could see them. He has sent them every week."

"How lovely of him," murmured Lizzie, but without noticeable enthusiasm.

"And you have had *letters*, of course. Beavers has put them all away for you to read when you feel like doing so." Lady Thalia hesitated a moment, then continued. "And, Lizzie, I did *not* tell your family how serious your illness was when I wrote to them. I had to let them know that you were ill, of course, because they would be expecting your letters. But if I had told them how *very* ill you were, they would have attempted that dreadful trip, worrying about you all the way, and probably have become ill themselves."

Lizzie did not reply, and she finally said anxiously, "I *do* hope that you think I did the proper thing, Lizzie."

Lizzie seemed to come back to life with that, and she patted Lady Thalia's hand. "Naturally I think you did the proper thing. You have taken excellent care of me, for which I am *most* grateful, and I can only be sorry that I have created such a problem for you."

Lady Thalia again protested that she had been no problem, but after they had both been silent for several minutes, Lizzie said, "Did anyone else come?"

Lady Thalia nodded. "Matthew came every day. He waited to see me each time so that he could hear the latest report, and he begged me to let him come in to see you."

"And did you allow it?"

"No. I did not think he had that right—and he is, of course, still engaged to Miss Blackwell."

"I understand, Lady Thalia," she said softly. "Indeed,

you do not have to worry about me. I shall be quite all right without Matthew."

"Of *course* you will!" she responded encouragingly. "And you have Mr. Thoreau coming to call. *That* will give you something pleasant to look forward to."

Lizzie smiled. "You seem to have become quite fond of that gentleman while I was ill."

"You have *no* notion what a support he has been, Lizzie," she replied earnestly. "I *gladly* take back every criticism I ever made of him. He has been a *rock*!"

Amazed by Lady Thalia's glowing opinion of Mr. Thoreau, she confided it to that gentleman when he came to call the next day. "You have made quite an impression," she concluded with amusement.

"Lady Thalia has been beside herself ever since you collapsed, Lizzie," he replied. "Not only was she worried about you as a friend, but she felt the entire responsibility for your well-being. She was terrified that she would have to go home and tell your parents that you had been lost while in her care."

All sign of amusement disappeared from Lizzie's face. "The poor lady. I knew it had been difficult—and very taxing physically, of course—but I had not thought about that aspect of it."

"Well, happily for all concerned, she will not have to face that particular horror," he said cheerfully. "We must be grateful for that."

"Well, *I* most certainly am," she responded. She held up a letter, one from a stack on her bedcovers. "This is from George," she said.

"Your brother?" he asked.

She shook her head. "George Andronikos. He wanted to wish me well. He had heard—from you—about my collapsing."

Mr. Thoreau nodded. "I wrote to him immediately. I knew that he would be most concerned about your welfare."

"Do you know what he is doing?" she asked.

"Naturally. He is becoming a Hussar, like your captain."

"He is not *my* captain, as you very well know, sir! Stay with the subject, please. Do you know of any of George's *other* activities?"

Mr. Thoreau shrugged. "He doubtless attends the theater and has an extremely active social life." He grinned at her. "I do hope that you didn't think of settling down with George. It would never answer, you know. He is too much a will-o'-the-wisp."

Lizzie smiled in spite of herself at the thought of anyone settling down for long with George Andronikos. She opened the letter and showed him the paper upon which it had been written.

"Look at it, Daniel. The whole of the sheet is edged with a wreath of violets."

"I see that it is," he replied, scarcely glancing at it.

"And so he is working for Napoleon?" she asked.

Again he shrugged. "I do not answer for George," he said. "His affairs are his own."

"Very well. Do *you* support Napoleon, Daniel?"

"You already know my thoughts about him, Lizzie," he responded. "I believe that you can answer that for yourself."

"But I have heard that when the British burned Washington, there was a great outcry of support from the French. I thought perhaps you might have changed your mind."

"No, Lizzie. I still favor democracy and a constitution—which is precisely the reason that I would never support Napoleon."

They sat in silence for a moment, and then he said, "You were still ill when I had my good news, Lizzie."

"Indeed? What news would that be, sir?"

"Our countries are no longer at war. Arrangements for a peace were finally agreed upon at Ghent just before Christmas."

"At Ghent?" she said, looking at him closely. "Does that possibly explain your journeys there?"

"You have far too suspicious a nature, Lizzie Lancaster. It is not becoming," he chided her gently. "You should be celebrating the peace with me, not prying into my affairs."

She smiled, knowing that he was completely unruffled. "I am very glad to hear of it, Daniel. Will you be going home soon?"

"Are you trying to rush me away?" he inquired, his brows raised.

"No, of course not. We should be delighted to have you stay—particularly now that you have become Lady Thalia's great favorite."

"You manners are sometimes quite appalling, Lizzie. I believe that I must speak to Lady Thalia about them," he observed, smiling. "There is other news, too. Castlereagh is returning to England and Wellington is coming here very soon to take his place."

"Is he indeed? It is comforting to know that the Iron Duke will be so close, although I felt far more secure before George informed me that there is not any longer much of an army for him to command."

"Well, if we are fortunate, he will have no need of it," replied Mr. Thoreau. "He will be keeping your friend Matthew very busy, I am sure."

At the mention of Matthew, Lizzie sank back among her pillows, and he watched her, troubled. "Is there something wrong, Lizzie?"

"It is Matthew. Lady Thalia said that he came every day to see me, just as you did while I was ill. He wants to talk to me."

"And do you want to talk to him?"

"No. Not I don't really wish to see him at all—but I feel as though I should, as though *he* needs to talk to me."

"Then you must do whatever you think would be best."

She nodded. "I suppose I shall see him tomorrow. Will you come and see me afterward?"

"Naturally I will. Let me know what time I should arrive and assuredly I shall be here."

She put out her hand to him. "What a great comfort you are, Daniel. I don't know what Lady Thalia or I would have done without you."

"You would have managed very nicely," he replied, smiling. "Both of you are more than capable of taking care of any difficult situation in which you find yourselves."

She heard the echo of George's words to her in what he said, and she wondered if what they said was true. She was quite certain that Lady Thalia could manage anything, but far less certain about herself.

She looked at him and smiled. "But we are both very glad that we have had you to rely upon, Daniel."

When she met with Matthew the next day, she felt as awkward as she might when meeting with someone she scarcely knew. Conversation was stilted, and he kept casting sidelong glances at her, as though to assess the damage the illness had done.

"I am mending, Matthew!" she said impatiently. "And I do not plan to turn up my toes, so you needn't keep watching me as though you fear it will happen at any moment."

"Don't be angry with me, Lizzie. I am only concerned about your welfare."

"And you have inquired into my welfare, and I have answered you. I am grateful for your concern. What else do we have to say to each other?"

Matthew cleared his throat. "I need to tell you about the St. George medal, Lizzie."

She shook her head violently. "You do *not*! I have told you that I had no desire to know the details of the story."

"I didn't just *give* it to Teresa, Lizzie. I wore it every day and she thought it was a pretty thing, so she took it—just as a child would—without realizing what it means to me."

"Miss Blackwell appeared to be quite well informed about me and about how you came to have the medal, Matthew. Are you sure she took it in all innocence?" Lizzie knew the answer to this herself, but she was quite certain that Matthew was too besotted to admit the truth to himself.

He shook his head eagerly. "Of course I am. She is not vindictive, even if she is at times—a little unthinking. She did not intend to hurt your feelings when she told you that you had been naïve."

"Well, that is good to know, Matthew, for otherwise I might have misinterpreted her motive. I might have believed her to have a streak of malice in her nature."

"Malice?" he said, trying to sound affronted. He stared at her a moment, then shook his head. "It's no good, Lizzie. Everything you're saying is true, but I'm quite trapped. I proposed to Teresa, she accepted, and I cannot break our engagement. I shall have to see it through."

Lizzie could see the misery in his eyes.

"Lizzie?" he said in a voice so low she could scarcely hear him. "If I were no longer engaged to Teresa, would you consider marrying me?"

She stared at him coldly. "No, Matthew. I'm afraid that you've shown me that you're not to be depended upon. I would not marry such a man as that."

He stood, bowed to her, and went silently from the room. She should have felt wonderful, having humbled him and heard from his own lips that he regretted his decision and would marry her if he could. She had planned to make him a very uncomfortable young man, and she had succeeded beyond her wildest dreams.

Strangely, however, all that she could feel was a great sadness that seemed to engulf her. Not even Daniel's visit immediately afterward could cheer her. She told him precisely what had happened, reproaching Matthew for his infidelity and herself for her cruelty in telling him the truth.

"And so, Lizzie, you would not wish to marry him, even if he were free?" asked Mr. Thoreau, watching her expression carefully.

She moved restlessly on the pillows. "How could I, Daniel? He betrayed my trust. There is no gaining that back again."

"No, that is true, of course. But remember what we talked about once before. You can never go back again to what has been. He will never be the same Matthew nor you the same Lizzie. Your decision would have to be made upon who you both are now."

"Well, there is no point in even thinking about it since he is still engaged and he will not betray *that* trust, at any rate! I suppose that I should have had a formal engagement and a ring to bind him before he left for the Peninsula. Then things might be otherwise now."

She gave a brief, unamused chuckle. "Miss Blackwell was quite in the right of it, however much I may dislike her. She said that I was naïve, and I most certainly was!"

"It is true that you will never be so innocent again," he agreed. "But would you wish to be so?"

Startled, she looked at him for a moment, then sighed and shook her head. "I don't know, Daniel. Just now I truly don't know."

Nineteen

The arrival in Vienna of the Duke of Wellington created a new wave of receptions and balls and breakfasts, but that all meant little enough to Lizzie, who was still too weak to participate in any of them. She insisted, however, that Lady Thalia go out once more, for Beavers and Henry were always there to care for her needs.

"I shall feel less guilty if you are out and enjoying yourself once more," she told Lady Thalia firmly. "And that will undoubtedly speed my recovery."

Thus encouraged, Lady Thalia once more plunged into the social whirl of Vienna, bringing home delectable tidbits of gossip and news with which to regale the invalid. Daniel Thoreau, still a daily caller—the only one she allowed at this point—brought her more solid political observations, to which she listened attentively.

"The Duke is an interesting man," he told Lizzie. "I believe he encourages the social activity to keep the meddlers busy. Vienna abounds in troublemakers, gossips, and spies, so anything that will keep them busy is desirable." The Congress, an unheard of experiment among the countries involved, had moved slowly and weightily and had, Metternich told Wellington upon his arrival, accomplished nothing.

"While you were still ill, Lizzie, a secret treaty was

signed between England, Austria, and France in order to secure themselves against the perceived threats of Prussia and Tsar Alexander's Russia. Since it was secret, it took a full twenty-four hours before it was known all over Vienna, rather than becoming immediate food for conversation and speculation the moment it was signed."

"Does Wellington agree with it?" she asked. "After all these years of war, it seems odd to be in an alliance *with* France instead of against her."

"That is the work of Talleyrand, of course, who could convince anyone that a raven and a nightingale are precisely the same bird. But Wellington does apparently agree. He is not a slippery customer like Talleyrand and Metternich, but he does appear to have the same sort of cosmopolitan view of things."

"What do you mean?" Lizzie asked.

"He believes that there must be a balance of power so that we may have a stable Europe, so they must be certain that legitimate sovereigns rule within all the countries concerned, and that no one power—or group of powers—gains too much control. Wellington is like Castlereagh—he sees that England has an interest in keeping the Continent stable and out of war. Too many of your countrymen, including those in Parliament, do not see the importance of concerning themselves abroad when they have pressing problems at home. Mine, of course, are no better," he added.

Lizzie thought about what he had said. "And if they are seeking stability at all costs, Daniel, that means that George—and others like him—will be crushed if they try to upset matters."

He nodded gravely. "Yes. For the sake of peace, such uprisings would be quelled as quickly and ruthlessly as possible."

Lizzie rose and walked to the window, looking down at the snow-covered streets. "I dreamed of him when I was ill. I saw a soldier bearing down upon him to kill him."

"In a war, that of course can happen, Lizzie. I cannot tell you that it would not. However," he said, deliberately lightening his tone, "you must remember George. If anyone can survive, he is the one. And who among us can be certain of just how things will develop?"

That night, Lady Thalia decided to stay at home and recruit her strength, for she had been out each day and evening during the past fortnight.

"I am *exhausted*, Lizzie, and I have neglected you *most* shamefully! I know you must be bored to distraction, sitting at home all day."

Lizzie laughed. "No, I have not been bored, ma'am, nor do I wish you to feel that you must sit at home with me. I have read and thought about any number of things, I have discussed the world with Daniel, and both he and Lord Danvers have very kindly kept me supplied with newspapers and books."

She did not add that she had found a curious contentment in the past two weeks. Nothing was expected of her, for she was to be resting, and there was none of the busyness of a household that there would have been at home at the Lodge. She missed all that—and she knew that homesickness could fall upon her at any moment—but her days were reassuringly quiet and regular, insulated from all the bustle of the outside world. She found that she had much to think about, but at times her mind would simply drift and she would think of nothing at all. It was all very peaceful.

"You seem to have grown quite serious once more, Lizzie—rather like you were when you were a very young girl." Lady Thalia had been thinking of the change in her, wondering if it was the lingering effects of the illness, or something deeper.

"Yes, I have thought about that, too," Lizzie confessed. "I think perhaps I was far wiser then—although very naïve about the ways of the world, of course."

She thought again of Miss Blackwell and frowned. "I was not meant to have a gypsy spirit. I knew that, of course, but it seemed that trying on a few personalities that were different from my own should do no harm."

"Nor *has* it," said Lady Thalia firmly. "You needed go get away from home and experience a little of the world. Then you may come closer to choosing what is right for you."

Lizzie nodded. "I think you are correct, Lady Thalia—and I shall be eternally in your debt for giving me the opportunity to do so. It is just that it has been harder than I had expected it to be."

Lady Thalia patted her hand. "Many things will be difficult, my dear—*but*, on the other hand, some will be surprisingly simple and joyful. You must simply accept them as they come and make the most of them."

"Like the oyster making a pearl of the bit of sand that is irritating it?" ventured Lizzie, smiling.

"*Exactly* so!" exclaimed Lady Thalia, relieved to have elicited at last a positive remark from her charge. "Oh, and I very nearly *forgot*, Lizzie. Henry brought up the mail and there is something here for you!"

She hurried back to the tray beside the entrance to the drawing room and picked up a letter addressed to Lizzie in an unmistakably masculine hand.

Lizzie opened it curiously, and glanced at the signature. "Why, it is from George!" she exclaimed.

"It docs not look like his handwriting, though," said Lady Thalia, watching her.

"No no, not George Andronikos—my brother George!"

"Indeed!" she replied, and waited while the letter was read.

At last Lizzie dropped the letter into her lap, and stared at Lady Thalia. "He has restored my dowry!" she said in disbelief.

"But how *wonderful*, Lizzie! Is he *certain* of it? Does he tell you anything more?"

"He says that our father will be writing to me about it, but that he wanted to be the first to tell me since he knew that losing it was his fault."

"That was good of him," said Lady Thalia, still watching her closely.

Lizzie nodded. "But the most extraordinary thing about it is that he *won* the money!"

"Do you mean by *gambling*? I thought that was how he had gotten himself into trouble in the first place."

"Yes, of course it was! But he says he was determined to do something about the problems he had caused, so he used the diamond stickpin that our grandfather gave him, and managed to win back everything that he had lost during the past months! Is that not the most *extraordinary* news?"

"Most extraordinary," agreed Lady Thalia. "Does he say anything more?"

"But that is the most wonderful thing of all! He says that the gentleman who lost to him told him a terrible story about a young man he knew in his youth who had gambled away his family fortune, and had driven his father to taking his own life rather than facing ruin!"

"What a perfectly *dreadful* story!"

"Yes, of course it is—but it apparently made George see things in a different light. He hadn't thought about the possibility of such dire consequences for his own actions, and he swore to that gentleman and to our father that he would never gamble again. This time he has gone back to the Lodge of his own accord, and he is determined to learn how to take care of the property."

Lady Thalia leaned back in her chair and silently blessed Timothy Holywell. He had managed the affair even better than she had hoped. She had simply laid out the problem for him, and asked that he try to address it, using his own clever means.

"*Well*, my dear! This means that there will be *no* more talk of your becoming a governess nor of marrying the first gentleman who asks you! This is *splendid* news!"

"Yes, yes, it is," said Lizzie thoughtfully. It meant, too, that the family had no pressing need of the settlement that Matthew's father had arranged for once they were married. She had no immediate demands upon her now, and she need not feel that she had plunged the family into even more dire straits by failing to marry Matthew.

There was, she found, a great deal to think about.

Her recovery, as the doctor had predicted, was a long and very slow one. By the beginning of March, she was able to go for a short carriage ride on a fine day, and she had begun to gain back a little of the lost weight.

"You simply must *force* yourself to eat more, Lizzie!" Lady Thalia had insisted, viewing her with a critical eye as they were about to go out for a drive. Lizzie was wearing one of the gowns made by Fräulein Schlosser, but it looked as though it had been made for someone else. Although its line was simple and capable of covering a multitude of shortcomings, even the fitted bust and sleeves hung loose.

Lady Thalia turned to Beavers. "Order the most delectable things you can think of for dinner, Beavers—perhaps a thick soup and venison cutlets with cream sauce. And by all means, order dessert."

"*Apfelstrudel?*" inquired Lizzie, smiling.

"Most certainly *not!*" retorted Lady Thalia. "I am gaining all of the weight that you have lost, Lizzie. Very soon I shall have to go back to Fräulein Schlosser for larger gowns!"

Then she smiled. "Did I tell you, Lizzie, that Mr. Thoreau brought me an *apfelstrudel* while you were so ill?"

"I knew that he had done something to win you over, but I did not know that was how he managed it," conceded Lizzie, enjoying the dreamy expression on her friend's face. "He is a very resourceful man."

"Well, quite enough of *that*," responded Lady Thalia, resuming her customary briskness. "Beavers, perhaps a torte—with as much whipped cream on it as possible."

Lizzie remained cocooned in her snug little world for a few more days, but when the change came, it arrived with a vengeance.

Lady Thalia had gone to a breakfast, but she came rushing back to the hotel almost immediately.

"Lizzie! Lizzie, you *cannot* imagine what has happened! Bonaparte has escaped from Elba!"

Lizzie stared at her, and Lady Thalia, her bonnet askew, nodded violently. "That was *precisely* my own reaction! I could not *believe* that such a thing could be true! But it is, Lizzie, it *is*! It will be war once more!"

Lizzie walked to the window and looked out. Although it could not be told from here, on her last rides to the Prater she had seen that early spring was upon them once more. It was time for the violets.

That day they waited impatiently for the arrival of Mr.

Thoreau so that they could catch up on the latest news. Lord Danvers was out, as was his wont, and undoubtedly would not return until late. When Henry announced Mr. Thoreau, the ladies pounced upon him at once.

"Do tell us, Mr. Thoreau, just what you have heard!" begged Lady Thalia, taking his arm and guiding him to a chair.

"Yes, Daniel! We are going wild here with only our own imaginations to fill in the spaces."

"It appears that Wellington and Metternich both received the news early this morning," he told them, speaking as calmly as he always did. "Wellington was supposed to hunt in the park at Schönbrunn this morning at seven, but when they brought his horse around for him, he sent it back. He had already heard. Metternich received the news while he was still in bed, and he bolted over to tell Talleyrand as soon as he was dressed."

"But where is Napoleon now?" Lizzie demanded.

Thoreau shrugged. "No one appears to know—although they all seem to agree that he would not go first to France. Some think he will land in Italy, where his brother-in-law is still King of Naples. He could find immediate support there."

"So no one really knows anything," remarked Lady Thalia unhappily. It seemed to her that knowing nothing was a great deal worse than knowing the truth of the matter, even if the truth was unpleasant.

Thoreau shook his head. "It will take time," he replied.

"There is one thing that we do know," said Lizzie, and the other two looked at her inquiringly. "We know that everything will change."

* * *

That, of course, was true, and the focus of everyone at the Congress of Vienna was now upon the renewed threat of Napoleon. Their quarrels were set aside so that they could organize themselves. Very soon, the members of the Congress drafted and signed a statement that declared that Napoleon was an outlaw, and would be treated as such.

News sifted into Vienna all the month of March. Contrary to what had been expected, Napoleon had indeed landed on the coast of Provence, accompanied, it was said, by a thousand men, forty horses, and two cannon. However, as he marched toward Paris, he was joined by deserting members of the French army and bands of peasants who cheered him on. Paris fell to him without a shot, the king, his court, the whole of the government and most of its supporters, having already fled. According to some of the stories, Napoleon was carried into the Tuileries on the shoulders of the crowd.

"He is most certainly back," said Mr. Thoreau to Lizzie one afternoon late in March, "but I believe he made a serious tactical error by not waiting until the Congress was over."

She looked at him, waiting.

"It would have taken far longer for those who oppose him to organize themselves and come to an agreement about how the problem should be addressed. As it is, they will be ready to face him very soon."

Lizzie discovered just how rapidly things were moving when Matthew came to call upon her. It was the first time that she had seen him since their discussion of the St. George medal, and she was troubled to see that he looked tired and strained.

"It is good to see you looking so much better, Lizzie," he said warmly.

"There is no need to tell me what is not true," she replied. "I have a glass and I know that I still look like a walking skeleton, Matthew."

He shook his head. "You look quite wonderful. I was frightened by your appearance when I saw you last."

"Scarcely a gallant thing to say, Matthew," she pointed out. "I believe I like it better when you are flattering me."

"Please let us not cross swords today, Lizzie," he said, sitting down and drawing his chair close to her. "I have come to say good-bye."

Lizzie found that it was difficult to swallow. "Good-bye? I take it that the Duke is leaving."

He nodded. "We will go to Belgium. Do you know if you plan to stay in Vienna?"

She shook her head. "I don't know what Lady Thalia's plans are," she answered. "But the doctor has said that I must not travel for another month, and Lady Thalia has said that when we do leave, we shall have to make the journey in easy stages. I'm afraid that I've become a dreadful burden to her."

"I don't think she regards you as a burden, Lizzie. She thinks very highly of you—as do all those who know you."

She turned her face away, not wishing to remember that time so long ago when he had said good-bye before going off to war.

He took her chin and turned her face gently back toward him. "Are you thinking of our good-bye in the garden, Lizzie?" he asked. She saw, with some astonishment, that his eyes were filled with a tenderness that she had not seen there in a very long time.

She nodded, afraid to speak and betray herself.

"So was I. We were little more than children then, you and I. When I think of it, it seems like another life."

"It was," she said briefly, looking away.

Once more he turned her face back toward him. "I came to thank you, Lizzie—not just to say good-bye."

She looked at him in surprise, and he nodded. "I wanted to thank you for loving me as you did—even though I didn't know the worth of it then." He patted his the front of his jacket. "I am wearing your St. George medal, Lizzie. I shall wear it until the day I die."

Not wanting to focus on his last words, particularly the mention of the day of his death, she said as lightly as she could manage, "And Miss Blackwell was willing to give it up?"

The creases around his mouth and eyes—creases that she had only just noticed—deepened and his eyes grew brighter. "She was not—shall we say—completely understanding about the matter, but I was able to convince her."

"I am glad you have it once more," she said. "It was meant for you."

"And it will protect me, as you had intended. I will, as I told you so long ago, put my faith in St. George—and in you."

He leaned toward her and kissed her long and tenderly, pulling her close to him. It seemed to her a very long time until he released her. "I shall always love you, Lizzie."

She looked up at him and patted his cheek gently. She knew that he was waiting for her to tell him that she loved him, too, but she could not bring herself to do so. After all, there was still Miss Blackwell.

Instead she said, "I wish that Mrs. Clary were here."

He nodded his head and forced a smile. "Yes indeed, and that Alice and Tussie were here to wave a great white sheet in farewell."

Kissing her once more, he rose and walked silently to the door, closing it gently behind him.

Lizzie was still sitting in the same position when Lady Thalia arrived two hours later.

"Are you ill, Lizzie?" she asked. "You look very pale and still."

Lizzie shook her head. "No, I am merely thinking of St. George and of steak and kidney pies—and of war."

Lady Thalia looked at her in genuine concern now. "I shall ring for a cup of tea, my dear. That will set you to rights."

Lizzie shook her head once more. "I do not think that can be done, Lady Thalia—not, at least, for a very long time."

That night when she went to bed, she set the music box beside her bed and listened again to its haunting melody. The world was shifting under her very feet, and she could not think of any place where she could go for refuge. As things stood at the moment, not even home seemed to offer what she needed. At home, there would be no Daniel Thoreau—and no Matthew.

And, after the war was over, there was no promise that Matthew would be one of those who was able to return home.

She listened to "Greensleeves" one more time, then closed the box firmly and tried to sleep. Her uneasy dreams shifted back and forth between the Christmas ball where Matthew had fallen in love with her, the garden where he had said good-bye, and the Carrousel with a paladin charging down upon a human figure rather than a wooden head—only this time it was Matthew rather than George Andronikos.

Twenty

By the end of May, Lady Thalia and Lizzie had arrived in Brussels. Lady Thalia would not allow them to leave until the doctor pronounced her charge unquestionably well enough to travel, and even then they went—as Lizzie had told Matthew they would—by very easy stages. Beavers and Henry accompanied them, of course, as did Lord Danvers. Once Mr. Thoreau was certain that Lord Danvers would be making the trip with them, he announced that he would go on ahead of them and make arrangements for their housing in Brussels.

"That is *more* than kind of you, Daniel," Lady Thalia informed him, for by then she too had come to use his Christian name.

"Are you going to Brussels to look after us or to be close to where all the activity is?" inquired Lizzie. Wellington was headquartered there, and Brussels was bustling with visitors and with the military.

He grinned at her. "Both, Lizzie. I could not possibly go home now—not until Boney is defeated once more."

"You seem very certain of that," she replied.

"One has only to read that Wellington is certain of it to have immediate confidence," he informed her, still grinning.

Lizzie looked more doubtful. "From the things Matthew

has told me about him, the world could be crumbling under his feet in the greatest earthquake of all time and he would calmly tell those about him that all would be well—it was only a tremor."

"Exactly," agreed Thoreau. "But the amazing thing about Wellington is that he keeps his word. Even though he is commanding this patchwork army of foreign troops and inexperienced British ones, I have every confidence that he will make it work."

When they finally arrived in Brussels and took up residence in the house that Thoreau had acquired for them, Lizzie felt that she had fallen into the midst of yet another social whirl. Although soldiers were everywhere to be seen, they were indeed *everywhere*. One saw them dancing, picnicking, going for long rides in the country, and generally enjoying themselves.

"*I* find it comforting," Lady Thalia announced when she mentioned it. "It makes me feel quite protected. And if worse *should* come to worst, we can take ship to England fairly quickly."

"Yes, we and a few thousand others with a similar desire to escape," said Lizzie dryly, conjuring a mental picture of what such a stampede would be like.

"You worry *far* too much, Lizzie," Lady Thalia informed her. "I had thought at first that you were *losing* some of that propensity while we were first in Vienna, but now I see that it is back again in full force."

"I believe it is called practicality," said Lizzie, but she softened her words with a smile. It was impossible ever to be truly cross with Lady Thalia.

"We are going to Lady Fulbright's ball tonight, my dear. Do you feel that you are up to attending? I shouldn't wish for you to exhaust yourself when you have not been accustomed to staying out late and dancing."

"I am looking forward to it," Lizzie assured her. "It will be very pleasant to see people dancing again, and I shall come home the instant that I feel tired."

The evening was, as she had hoped, a very pleasant one. Seeing the young girls in their summer gowns and the young officers in their finery made her feel nostalgic— quite as though she were fifty-nine rather than nineteen. She did not fill her dance card completely, leaving time to sit and rest. She was feeling worlds better than she had, but she had no intention of suffering a setback at this point.

Daniel Thoreau had joined her during one of these periods, and together they were enjoying the sight of a long-limbed member of the Foot Guard, looking rather like a particularly animated grasshopper, dancing with a very short, very round young lady. No words had passed between them. They merely watched and enjoyed— knowing that the other was thinking much the same thing.

"Well, how very cozy you two are!" exclaimed a voice sweet as syrup. "I have been hoping that I would en-counter you again, Mr. Thoreau."

Miss Blackwell was standing next to him, looking, Lizzie thought, quite ravishing in yet another of her di-aphanous gowns. She was suddenly aware that she herself was still quite thin.

"*Do* dance with me, Mr. Thoreau. You promised me in Paris that you would tell me about America—and possi-bly counsel me about my duties," she added coyly, giving him one of the sidelong glances that now irritated Lizzie almost more than anything she could ever have imag-ined. The omnipresent fan came into play, too, as she tapped Mr. Thoreau on the arm and leaned ever closer to him.

"I cannot imagine for a moment, Miss Blackwell, that your dance card is not full," he replied, smiling at her.

"Of course it is, Mr. Thoreau—but I would not let that stop me for a moment if you will but dance with me now." She held out her hand to him with an appealing little smile.

To Lizzie's dismay, he took her hand and stood up, turning back to grin at Lizzie. "I will return to you very soon, Miss Lancaster."

Miss Blackwell also looked at Lizzie—and smiled. Lizzie had not realized that so small a mouth could hold so many teeth.

She watched them dance for a while, then turned her attention to other couples, finding that the sight of Daniel dancing with Teresa Blackwell was most unpalatable. She glanced around the room to see if Matthew was also present, but she did not see him. Miss Blackwell was clearly on the loose. She discovered that she was suddenly exceedingly angry with Daniel Thoreau. She had thought him a sensible man, impervious to the obvious wiles of one such as Miss Blackwell. Watching him look down into her face and smile at her indicated otherwise, however.

Mr. Mansfield danced with Miss Blackwell next, and Thoreau rejoined Lizzie. "Well, I have come safely home, Lizzie," he announced cheerfully, "with only assorted small dents from the fan."

Heartened by his light dismissal of Miss Blackwell's tactics, Lizzie managed to smile at him. "I am glad to hear that you survived it, Daniel. I confess that I was surprised when you allowed her to coax you into dancing with her."

He shrugged. "It was not so very dreadful." He glanced over at her. "I see that *you* are not carrying a fan tonight, Lizzie."

"I have renounced them," she replied.

"A very good idea," he said, patting her hand. "Fans are not meant for everyone—and definitely not for you."

"I have no idea whether that is a compliment or an insult, Daniel."

"Ah, Lizzie—if you do not, I shall leave you to consider it carefully."

They were joined at that point by Lady Thalia and Lord Danvers, and the conversation became more general. Lizzie enjoyed the rest of the evening—until the very last moment when Miss Blackwell appeared once more, fan in hand.

"I shall look forward to our drive tomorrow, Mr. Thoreau," she said, smiling at him as though there was no one else present. "It was so gallant of you to offer to show me some of the sights of Brussels. Having arrived so recently, this is all quite new to me."

"I didn't know that you knew any of the sights of Brussels," said Lizzie grimly after Miss Blackwell had departed, trailing triumph in her wake.

"I shall find them," replied Mr. Thoreau blandly.

The next two weeks were a horror for Lizzie, for Daniel Thoreau was seen everywhere with Miss Blackwell. Matthew was away for most of that time, carrying messages for Lord Wellington, and he had no time to serve as her escort. Daniel Thoreau appeared to fit into that role very handily. Lady Thalia tried to calm Lizzie, but she was not to be comforted.

"It is quite hard enough that she snapped up Matthew,"

she exclaimed to her friend, who was listening sympathetically, "but I can almost understand that because he had the excuse of his youth and inexperience. He had never fallen into the hands of someone like Miss Blackwell. But for Daniel to do so! I had thought better of him."

Lady Thalia, who was equally mystified, did her best to comfort her. "A man, when all is said and done, Lizzie, is *only* a man," she said. "One simply cannot expect of a man what one can expect of a woman. No doubt Daniel cannot help himself and is suffering from an infatuation. It will pass."

"I hope that it does for his sake," Lizzie responded bitterly, "but it does not matter to me. I do not feel that we can ever be friends again in the same manner that we were."

Sighing, Lady Thalia did her best to keep their schedule busy so that Lizzie would have less time to fret over Daniel Thoreau. Whenever possible, she tried to avoid places where she might expect to see them, but that was difficult. They were seen everywhere together, and the gossip had begun. She could find it in her heart to pity Matthew, who was being served very poorly by his fiancée. She wondered if he already knew of the problem, or if one of his friends should tell him.

Lady Thalia was not forced to wonder for very long. Matthew, who had not come to call upon them since their arrival in Brussels, appeared at her door very early one morning. She was up and dressed only because she had expected to go riding with Lord Danvers, and she looked at him with astonishment when Henry showed him in.

"Matthew! Is there something wrong that you have called so early? Is there news about Bonaparte? Should we pack to leave?"

He smiled at her, looking happier she thought, than he had since he was a boy at home. "I am not here about Bonaparte, Lady Thalia. I am here to see Lizzie, if you please."

"Well, I daresay she *might* have awakened by now, but I'm not certain, Matthew. This is very early."

"Which chamber is hers?" he demanded.

"The first one at the top of the stairs," she replied. "Why do you ask?"

She was, however, speaking to an empty room. Matthew had sprung out the door and was at the top of the stairs before Lady Thalia could take in the fact that he was gone.

He stopped at the door, opened it a crack, and peeked in. Lizzie was sitting at her dressing table, brushing her hair. He walked silently over to her and bent so that he could look at her in the mirror.

Lizzie, having heard nothing, almost fell off the bench, and then she rapped his hand with her brush when he tried to catch her.

"Matthew! What do you think you're doing? You have no business to be here!"

"I know that, Lizzie. Come dance with me!" he exclaimed, opening the music box so that the melody would begin.

"Dance with you? Have you quite lost your mind?" she demanded.

"No! I have found it!" he answered, sweeping her up from the bench and into the dance. "I have loved you all my life, Lizzie Lancaster—though I didn't know it until I thought it was too late to ever be able to do anything about it."

"And what do you think you're going to do about it now?" she demanded, clutching her dressing gown as they danced.

"I am going to marry you and take you home," he replied, folding her into his arms and kissing her firmly.

By this time, Lady Thalia had made it to the top of the stairs, and she stood in the doorway watching with unabashed interest.

"But what about Miss Blackwell?" she asked, once she could speak again.

"She has cried off, Lizzie—and I am a free man once again—free to ask you to marry me. Tell me that you will!"

"But what of the war, Matthew? What of Bonaparte?"

"When that is over, Lizzie, we will go home—to stay. I have seen quite enough of the world. It will last me the rest of my days, so long as you are there with me."

It suddenly occurred to him that she had not yet answered him. He held her at arm's length and looked down at her gravely. "But I know that you have had a good many love affairs in this past year, Lizzie. Perhaps you have decided that one of them suits you better. I could not blame you if you had."

She looked at him for a very long moment, then walked back into his arms. "I have had only one love affair in my life, Matthew Webster. It has taken you long enough to come back to me."

Another interested spectator joined Lady Thalia in the doorway.

"Why, Daniel!" she exclaimed. "It is the most *delightful* thing imaginable! Lizzie and Matthew are to be *married*!

"Yes," he responded calmly, "I thought that they would be. I was rather hoping that they would marry soon, so that I am able to attend."

"Are you leaving, Daniel?" asked Lizzie, who had heard the last part of the conversation.

He nodded. "Very soon." He turned to Matthew. "I see that I am to wish you very happy—and I do, sir."

Matthew shook his hand vigorously. "And I must thank you again, Thoreau, for setting me free. I did not think it would ever happen."

Thoreau bowed. "It was my pleasure. Having realized by now, however, that I am not going to propose marriage—hence my unseemly haste to leave Brussels—I believe that Miss Blackwell has fixed her sights upon the hapless Mansfield. I believe the odds are against him."

Lizzie looked from one to the other. "Do you mean that you managed this between you?" she demanded.

Thoreau grinned and nodded. "It was obvious that you were both going to pine away, and that someone had to take a hand. I have always enjoyed a calculated risk."

Lizzie smiled and kissed his cheek. "You are a most amazing man, Daniel Thoreau! If I were not marrying Matthew, I would most certainly marry you!"

"I am overcome," he replied, bowing low. "Come with me, Lady Thalia," he said, turning to that lady. "We have wedding arrangements to make."

Lizzie looked up at Matthew as he pulled her close to him once more. "I am glad to be home again," she said quietly—and knew that it was true.

Epilogue

Lizzie and Matthew were married on the eve of the Battle of Waterloo, with only their closest friends at hand. Before the evening was over, news of Napoleon's approach sent the troops scrambling to their positions. During the days of the battle, those left behind waited for news, taking to the streets to give water and food and aid to soldiers who made their way back into Brussels.

The news finally came of the victory of the Allies, but Matthew had not returned. Uncertain where he might find him, for Matthew had ridden with messages from Wellington to his commanders across all the battle lines, Daniel Thoreau acquired a carriage and set out to look. Lizzie waited nervously, hoping for the best, and finally he pulled up in front of Lady Thalia's house, dust-covered and weary—but triumphant. In the carriage he had not one but two wounded men—Matthew and George Andronikos.

With the help of Lord Danvers, they got both of them inside and into beds with clean linen sheets. Carefully, the blood and grime and gunpowder were cleaned away, as they waited for a doctor to come.

"Thank you, Daniel," she said, gripping his hand tightly. "If you had not found him, he might have died before someone could help him."

"But he has not, Lizzie," he said. "He and George will be well and whole again in only a few weeks." He paused a moment, trying to decide whether or not to tell her, but he decided that the truth was best.

"I saw your captain, too, Lizzie."

"Captain LaSalle? Was he injured, too?"

He nodded. "I'm afraid that there was nothing that could be done for him, however. He was all but gone when I saw him."

Tears slipped down her cheeks. "But how dreadful, Daniel! How terrible a thing war is!"

"He recognized me when I bent over him—and he asked about you, Lizzie—the lovely Mademoiselle Lancaster."

The tears would not stop now, and it was long before they would. By morning, however, when Matthew was awake, she had done with them and managed to show him a smiling face.

"It is over, Matthew," she said, bending over him to kiss him and smooth his hair. "And we are going home."

"You said it best, Lizzie," he replied smiling up at her and putting his good arm around her. "We are already home. We are together."

ABOUT THE AUTHOR

Mona Gedney lives with her family in Indiana and is the author of thirteen Zebra Regency romances and is working on her next, to be published in August 2004. Mona loves to hear from readers and you may write to her c/o Zebra Books. Please include a self-addressed stamped envelope if you wish a response.

Historical Romance from
Jo Ann Ferguson

Available Wherever Books Are Sold!

Visit our website at **www.kensingtonbooks.com**.

More Regency Romance
From Zebra

BOOK YOUR PLACE ON OUR WEBSITE AND MAKE THE READING CONNECTION!

We've created a customized website just for our very special readers, where you can get the inside scoop on everything that's going on with Zebra, Pinnacle and Kensington books.

When you come online, you'll have the exciting opportunity to:

- View covers of upcoming books
- Read sample chapters
- Learn about our future publishing schedule (listed by publication month *and author*)
- Find out when your favorite authors will be visiting a city near you
- Search for and order backlist books from our online catalog
- Check out author bios and background information
- Send e-mail to your favorite authors
- Meet the Kensington staff online
- Join us in weekly chats with authors, readers and other guests
- Get writing guidelines
- AND MUCH MORE!

Visit our website at
http://www.kensingtonbooks.com